PRAISE FOR

RED ULTIMATUM

"An American cabinet member kidnapped in Panama, a North Korean sub lurking ever-closer to American waters, a brazen assassination of an ex-president—it's three-dimensional chess played on a global board with no rules. *RED ULTIMATUM* is a must-read warning of just how far a power-hungry dictator will go to upset the balance of power and ignite a new Cold War. Another, even more compelling narrative that captures the complex geo-strategic challenges of today."

WILLIAM GRIMSLEY
MAJOR GENERAL, US ARMY (RETIRED)
SECRETARY OF SOUTH CAROLINA
DEPARTMENT OF VETERAN AFFAIRS

"In *RED ULTIMATUM*," Grossman and Fuller have delivered both a thrilling read and a terrifying warning that today's geopolitical fiction could very well become tomorrow's headlines!"

LARRY MONDRAGON
EXECUTIVE PRODUCER
THE WHEEL OF TIME
SONY/AMAZON TV SERIES

"I've spent my career traveling to global hot spots, but nothing prepared me for the adrenalin rush I would get reading *RED ULTIMATUM*! Fuller and Grossman have driven the needle straight up in their latest book in the *RED HOTEL* series that will transport you around the world. Be sure to set aside plenty of time when you begin because you won't be able to set *RED UILTIMATUM* down! With Grossman at his side, this book doesn't just come from Fuller's imagination—it's directly from his experience. Absolutely captivating!"

ALAN ORLOB
INTERNATIONAL SECURITY CONSULTANT
FOUNDER & CEO, ORLOB GROUP

"*RED ULTIMATUM* takes all the action in *RED HOTEL, RED DECEPTION,* and *RED CHAOS,* and turns up the heat well past the boiling point. The scenarios are all too real to ignore and with a very real wake-up call for how one rogue player can bring the entire world to the brink of disaster. In today's world, this is more of an issue for all of us than ever before. A big wow to Fuller and Grossman for keeping me on the edge of my seat!"

DOUGLAS F. MULDOON
CHIEF OF POLICE (RET)
CITY OF PALM BAY, FLORIDA
FORMER FBI NATIONAL ACADEMY ASSOCIATES PRESIDENT

"Fasten your safety belts, *RED ULTIMATUM* will take you on a thrill ride through geo-politic perils that need attention today. Written with insider experience and the vision we hope is within the highest levels of our security apparatus, this latest nail-biter from Fuller and Grossman will have you thinking. No, make that worrying whether we're out-thinking our enemies enough. Tops on my list!"

ROGER DOW

FORMER PRESIDENT & CEO, U.S. TRAVEL ASSOCIATION

"Reading *RED ULTIMATUM*, I discovered that I appear as a character; a U.S. Navy captain of a nuclear-powered submarine—something in real life I am definitely not qualified for! Yet, in this wonderfully dramatic, fast-paced novel, I find my counterpart-self on patrol in the Northern Pacific, thrust into a 21st-century Cuban Missile Crisis tracking a North Korean sub enroute to the U.S. West Coast. That's just part of a complex, integrated international plot designed to bring down the United States and NATO. And with all that and more, buckle up and get ready for one hell of a fun read in Grossman and Fuller's thriller delivered with white-knuckle high-speed twists at every turn!"

DWIGHT JON ZIMMERMAN

AWARD-WINNING #1 *NEW YORK TIMES* BESTSELLING AUTHOR

PRAISE FOR

THE RED HOTEL SERIES

"Feverishly paced with surprising twists and turns, *RED HOTEL* starts with a bang and the action gets faster and tenser from there. Get ready for one late night when you dive into this gem of a read!"

DANIEL PALMER
BEST-SELLING AUTHOR

"Welcome to my world. *RED HOTEL* is a thriller that dramatically covers a very real global threat that could redraw nation boundaries and lead the superpowers to the brink of war. Fuller and Grossman echo the warning, 'If you see something, say something.' They're saying it loud and clear in *RED HOTEL.*"

STEVE TIDWELL
FORMER FBI EXECUTIVE ASSISTANT DIRECTOR, CRIMINAL, CYBER,
RESPONSE AND SERVICES BRANCH

"Gary Grossman and Ed Fuller have done it again in *RED DECEPTION*. Plot, characters, and details are gripping and captivating. A page-turner by authors who might as well sit on the National Security Council. A fantastic read!"

"Laced with drama culled from recent events, *RED HOTEL* places the reader directly into the role of intelligence analyst and operative as well as business and political strategist. Read *RED HOTEL* and it's doubtful you'll ever travel again without conjuring up possible intrigue from observations that used to seem like normal occurrences."

"Grossman and Fuller deliver gritty insider detail in their thriller *RED HOTEL*, bringing fact and fiction together in an explosive mix. *RED HOTEL* is a must-read for international travelers and anyone seeking to understand the new Russia."

"*RED DECEPTION* provides an in-depth and realistic ground level view of the type of asymmetric Nation-state sponsored threats faced by the Agencies tasked with protecting the United States both domestically and abroad. Thoroughly researched with thrilling pacing, it follows a worst-case scenario with the resulting fallout and a complex investigation that unfolds all over the globe."

EDWARD BRADSTREET
SPECIAL AGENT- DEPARTMENT OF HOMELAND SECURITY
HOMELAND SECURITY INVESTIGATIONS (HSI)

"Forget 'ripped from the headlines,' because *RED DECEPTION* threatens to write its own! Everything a great thriller is supposed to be! High stakes, incredible action scenes, a deadly plot, and a dynamic hero in Dan Reilly. Gary Grossman and Ed Fuller have crafted a relentlessly riveting tale that hones in on our greatest fears and takes us right to the brink in breathless fashion."

JON LAND
USA TODAY BEST-SELLING AUTHOR

"*RED HOTEL*, a terrific, fast-paced, stylish, eye-opening spy thriller, with a knowing, insider's look at the intersects of terrorism, the CIA, and world politics. *RED HOTEL* will forever change the way you look at hotels, and use the phrase 'Road Warrior.'"

BRUCE FEIRSTEIN
JAMES BOND SCREENWRITER, *VANITY FAIR* CONTRIBUTING EDITOR
BEST-SELLING AUTHOR

"*RED DECEPTION* is a Thriller with a capital 'T'! Not for the faint of heart. "The doomsday scenarios depicted in this fast-paced, can't-put-down nail-biter are real-world accurate and truly scary. Dan Reilly is a terrific new hero for today's troubled times!"

RAYMOND BENSON

BEST-SELLING AUTHOR, JAMES BOND NOVELS AND

BLUES IN THE DARK AND *THE BLACK STILETTO*

"As the former Director of Intelligence (J2) for the U.S. Pacific Command in Hawaii and Joint Chiefs of Staff in the Pentagon, I know these dangerous scenarios are plausible, which makes *RED DECEPTION* all the more thrilling. Infrastructure attacks, Russian aggression, bumbling national leaders, North Korea malign activity, Venezuelan dangers—Fuller and Grossman's exciting story mirrors reality!"

REAR ADMIRAL PAUL BECKER, USN (RET)

FORMER DIRECTOR OF INTELLIGENCE, U.S. PACIFIC COMMAND

"*RED DECEPTION* is an adrenalin-laden thriller and as true to life as it gets. As a former intelligence operative (linguist/analyst—Soviet/Warsaw Pact) with assignments to Field Station Augsburg, Germany, and the Defense Intelligence Agency at the Pentagon, I know that all of the explosive events, all of the alliances, and all of the deceit detailed in this book are realistic. This book just can't be put down. Outstanding!"

G. MICHAEL MARA, JR

FORMER MEMBER OF THE U.S. ARMY INTELLIGENCE

& SECURITY COMMAND (INSCOM)

"Plans are nothing; planning is everything."

GENERAL DWIGHT D. EISENHOWER
SUPREME ALLIED COMMANDER EUROPE
34TH UNITED STATES PRESIDENT

RED ULTIMATUM

ED FULLER

GARY GROSSMAN

BEAUFORT
BOOKS

Hardcover ISBN: 978-0-8253-1044-7
Paperback ISBN: 978-0-8253-1045-4
Ebook ISBN: 978-0-8253-0919-9

For inquiries about volume orders, please contact:
Beaufort Books, 27 West 20th Street, Suite 1103, New York, NY 10011
sales@beaufortbooks.com

Published in the United States by Beaufort Books
www.beaufortbooks.com

Distributed by Midpoint Trade Books
a division of Independent Publisher Group
www.ipgbook.com

Cover designed by Christine Sullivan

Printed in the United States of America

PRINCIPAL CHARACTERS

WASHINGTON, DC
DAN REILLY
President, International
Kensington Royal Hotel
Corporation

ALEXANDER CROWE
former U.S. President

SEAN ALLPHIN
President of the United
States

DR. HAMZA ALI
National Security Advisor

ELIZABETH
MATTHEWS
U.S. Secretary of State

MIKAYLA
COLONNELLO
U.S. Senator
Chair Senate Intelligence
Committee

BOB HEATH
CIA Case Officer

TOM HUNTER
Diplomatic Security Service
Agent
U.S. State Department

YIBING CHENG
U.S. State Department
Consultant

REESE McCAFFERTY
FBI Director

GERALD WATTS
CIA Director

ADMIRAL RHETT
GRIMM
Chair, Joint Chiefs of Staff

ADMIRAL NICK
MIRAGE
Chief of Naval Operations,
Joint Chiefs of Staff

GENERAL ZARIF ABDO
Vice Chair, Joint Chiefs
of Staff

DOREEN GLUCKIN
White House Press
Secretary

MEGAN TRANK
"Meet the Press" anchor

MICKY RUCIRETA
U.S. Under Secretary of
State

KATIE KOEHLER
FBI analyst

BILLY PEYTON
U.S. Senator
Senate Minority Leader

SETH SULLIVAN
Chief of Staff for Senator
Peyton

**PYONGYANG, NORTH
KOREA**
MARSHAL PAK PONG
JU
An aide

GENERAL LIV ZAITSEV
A Russian emissary

RO TU-CHOL
Supreme Leader

BEIJING, CHINA
YICHÉN YÁO
President, People's Republic
of China

EY WING LI (AKA
"SAMMY")
Chinese envoy

CAIRO, EGYPT
SHAKIR AFFIR
A driver

ALI ABDUL AZIZ
Minister of Interior

CHICAGO, IL
EDWARD JEFFERSON
SHAW
President/Founder
Kensington Royal Hotel
Corporation

BRENDA SHELTON
Dan Reilly's Executive
Assistant

ALAN CANNON
VP, Global Safety and
Security

RUSSIA
NICOLAI GORSHKOV
President, Russian
Federation

GENERAL VALERY
ROTENBERG
Director, Foreign
Intelligence Service

SERGEI BORTNIK
General, Russian Federation

ALINA OSTROVSKY
A spy

MIAMI, FLORIDA
CARLOS SANTIAGO
State Department
Diplomatic Security Service
Agent

PARISA DHAFARI
An unknown woman

PUERTO RICO
RYAN BATTAGLIO
Former President of the
United States

SHIRLEY & ERICKSON
Secret Service Agents

JILLIAN ROBBINS
Freelance biographer

PACIFIC OCEAN
ANDREW POLICANO
Captain, USS *Cape St.
George*

JANG SONG-TAEK
Captain, *Wonsan Yong-
Ganhan*

DWIGHT ZIMMERMAN
Captain, USS *Annapolis*

PANAMA CITY, PANAMA
NASARIO HERRERA
A terrorist

COLOMBIA
KEVIN KIMBALL
Commander, U.S. Navy
SEALs

SCOPE, KING, POKER,
KNIFE, WOODY, DOC
U.S. Navy SEALs

ROBERT WELLER
U.S. Air Force F-18 pilot

STEVE HIRSEN
U.S. Navy SEALs
Lt. Commander

PROLOGUE

ATHENS, GREECE

"I saw you die!"

"You saw me fall off the building."

"Yes, and you died! I saw it happen. The explosion from below. The fireball that swept up. Your last look. I've relived that moment every day since. Oh my God, Marnie, I was there. I saw it all."

"And I'm here with you, Dan."

"You're not. You can't be."

"I am and we can be together again."

She reached out to him. Dan Reilly stepped back and stared. She was wearing the same dress, green blouse, and leather jacket she had worn that day in Stockholm, the day Marnie Babbitt returned to his hotel room seemingly regretful; wishing things were different, wanting to make them so.

"You loved me, Dan," the brunette said softly. "You can love me again. Tonight. Here in Athens."

Dan Reilly stopped retreating. Yes, he thought. Here. Athens.

He looked at the surroundings. Nighttime traffic was flowing along Adrianou Street. Horns honked. Couples walked arm-in-arm. Tourists window-shopped. Everything was normal until the woman he had desperately loved, the woman who had betrayed him stepped out of the shadows in front of him and into the light of a street lamp.

Dan Reilly had just concluded a successful business meeting at Kuzina, one of Athen's most celebrated restaurants that boasted a magnificent view of the Temple of Hephaestus, the Agora, and the Acropolis. He had come to discuss the final terms for his company's acquisition of a luxury hotel property currently owned by a Greek billionaire. It would take lawyers months to solidify the terms, but atop the restaurant's tarátsa, with the golden glow of the Acropolis backlighting them, Reilly and the seller toasted to their relationship with a final glass of ouzo.

It had been a good night for the International President of Kensington Royal Hotel Corporation. As he had walked along the cobblestones on Adrianou Street, Marnie Babbitt was not on his mind, but suddenly she was there alive and vibrant as ever. Her beauty took his breath away. Her voice was as soft and lilting as the last whispers in his ear.

Or the last lies, he thought.

"No lies, Dan," she said as if reading his mind. "This time it will be different."

At first, Reilly had felt immobile. Then he was drawn to her.

She reached out to him and stroked his cheek. Her touch was as present as ever. The light gave her an almost ethereal glow. She looked longingly into his eyes and proved she was alive with a lingering, deep kiss. Then she said, "Is that the kiss of a dead woman?"

Her tongue, her scent, and her breath were just as he remembered. Just as he missed. So was the quickening of his heartbeat.

He withdrew and looked into her brown eyes. They were so bright and inviting.

"You missed me. I know you did." She smiled and took a step back into the shadows. "Come with, Dan."

The sounds of the city faded away. Gone were the car horns and sirens, people talking, dogs barking, car doors slamming, and footsteps on the sidewalk. Everything around him blurred. There was just Marnie and him. He felt his desire for her grow. Then he thought of Yibing Cheng, the woman now in his life.

"But—"

"It's all right my darling. I know that there's someone else. But I'm back. You want me."

More thoughts from his head. How did she know?

"You want us to be together again."

"Marnie, I saw…"

"You saw what we wanted you to see."

She leaned forward and kissed him again. She felt him. He responded.

"Now I'm here. To be with you."

He withdrew.

"Don't you want that, Dan? Don't you want me?"

"Marnie…"

"Yes."

"Marnie," he said again.

"Yes, my love."

"But you're—"

She suddenly laughed. Her brown eyes went black.

Maybe it was the ouzo, but all he initially felt was a prick in his stomach. Then he looked down. There was the hand that he had loved caressing. But now it held the black handle of a Russian Kizlyar Spetsnaz Special Forces knife.

He brought his eyes up to hers. She smiled cruelly, waited a moment, and then twisted the 6.5-inch blade and sliced upwards.

Reilly tried to speak. He couldn't. He felt his legs crumble, but Marnie Babbitt's grip on the knife kept him on his feet. She twisted again.

"Why?" Reilly silently gurgled.

"Because this is the way it should have ended."

Marnie's words confused him. He grabbed her hand with his. Blood soaked them both.

Should have ended?

Reilly tried to pull out the knife, but she was stronger. Life began to leave him.

With a sickly sweet laugh, she repeated, "This is the way it should have ended. You, not me."

Should…have…ended. The words were familiar. He'd heard them before. Many times before.

"No!" Reilly shouted in full-throated defiance. "This is not how it should end! And…you…are… dead!"

"What?"

"You're dead," he shouted. "You're dead!"

"No, Dan. No! It's all right."

He was shaking violently.

"Dan!"

Dan Reilly bolted upright. He automatically grabbed his stomach. It was wet, but from sweat, not blood. And the woman whose concerned voice was cutting through his dream belonged to Yibing Cheng.

"Dan, Dan, it's okay. You're here with me. Yibing."

Reilly slowly collected his thoughts. Yibing turned on a night light and faced the man she'd been seeing for just a few months. They were in Athens, but he was not on the street bleeding. But he had had nights like this—in Paris, Washington, and where Reilly and Yibing had first met, Beijing.

"Your dream again?" she asked.

He gathered his thoughts.

"Yes, except this time it was here. Outside our restaurant last night. The street—"

"I'm so sorry," Yibing said pulling him close to her naked body. What did she do?"

"At least she didn't throw me into a wood chipper this time," Reilly replied lightly. "No plastic bag over my head. No fall from a cliff." He rubbed his gut. "But she was pretty good with a knife, even for a dream."

Reilly knew what was going on. Shrinks might call it PTSD. He saw it more as a combination of guilt over the fact that he failed to recognize Marnie Babbitt was a Russian plant and guilt that he couldn't save her the moment he realized she wanted out. It was all manifesting itself in very vivid revenge dreams. But it was not paranoia.

There was more that wasn't in his dream world. Dan Reilly had seen drones out his window after he and Yibing had returned from Beijing. He'd spotted people following them. And they were not his people. Not Yibing's either.

For now, he viewed the tails and eavesdropping as intimidation. Russian or possibly Chinese. But it could get worse. It likely would get worse and not strictly because he was an international hotel executive. It was his moonlighting. Dan Reilly had deep ties with officers at the CIA and even deeper ties with the United States Secretary of State.

PART ONE

"Fortune favors the bold."
LATIN PROVERB

1

Carlos Santiago handed over his American Express card to the young woman at Oceana Boats, a popular harbor rental facility. Cate Callaway, wearing a bright yellow Oceana t-shirt over a two-piece blue bathing suit, processed the paperwork, asking a series of questions about her customer's boating experience to which he answered, "Yes" to all.

Santiago signed the rental agreement and picked up a container of Banana Boat Ultra Sport Sunscreen with SPF 30 protection. It wasn't the highest rating. After all, he wanted to show off some tan back in the office.

"You're good for five hours, Mr. Santiago. Happy fishing."

A day of leisurely sailing and a line in the water was exactly what Santiago wanted. More than wanted—needed. He was on a week's vacation with nothing but sun and quiet time ahead. Seven days away from never-ending unknowns that had to be known, long threads that had to be unraveled, and possibilities he fought from becoming inevitabilities.

Five hours today. Maybe five hours every day of his vacation. No challenges unless a blue marlin fought back. No conversations unless the fish pleaded for leniency. Even then he would probably give in.

"Thanks, Cate," Santiago said taking the keys.

"She's out there to the left, Mr. Santiago. All gassed up and raring to go."

Carlos Santiago stepped aboard the rental Glacier Bay 2664 Canyon Runner catamaran with all he needed: fishing gear, sandwiches, water, beer, and a good cigar. Not a Cuban. He'd hate to explain even such a small infraction to the Coast Guard if he was pulled over. His boss wouldn't like it either. And then there'd be the ribbing at work from his team. He cared about things like that.

Santiago stowed his rod and reel before casting off. It didn't really matter to him if he caught anything. He was out to clear his mind. No tie and jacket. No gun tucked in a holster. Just shorts, a t-shirt, a baseball cap without a work logo, and checkered Vans on his feet without socks.

He was ready to go. Two steps up to the helm, a key to start his craft. His left hand gripped the stainless three-spoke steering wheel; his right was on the throttle.

He moved out of the marina, hardly taxing the twin 150 hp engines that he'd soon throttle up. The white 26-foot-long boat cruised along. Santiago, 38, with short-cropped hair and a body far more trim and fit than during his high school and college football years, smiled. Vacations didn't get much better than this.

* * *

Two hours in and no marlin. But that wasn't because the fish hadn't bit. Santiago was floating lazily in the waters six miles off Miami without a line in the water. This was all he needed.

One sandwich gone. One bottle of water. It was still too early to crack open a beer. The cigar was another thing. It was half-smoked when he saw a small somebody adrift some 300 yards away. He strained his eyes. A person, he thought a woman, was waving frantically on a drifting Jet Ski. It looked like she was calling out, but he was too far away to hear. Duty kicked in. Santiago engaged the engine, brought the cat around, and pushed ahead at 12 knots.

He was right. The person in distress was absolutely a woman, an olive-skinned beauty in a bikini. Indian, he first thought, maybe

Brazilian or Middle Eastern. Nothing unusual for such an international city as Miami.

"My engine died," she said apologetically with no noticeable accent. "Thank God you were out here."

"You got that right," Santiago said nudging up alongside her. He slowed and tossed the woman a line which she attached to her Jet Ski. "How'd you get out this far in that?"

"I guess I calculated distance badly. Then I ran out of gas."

The woman definitely needed help. He was used to being around to help.

"No problem. I can tow you back in."

As he extended his hand to her, he considered, there were worse things in the world.

She smiled as she came aboard.

"You're damned lucky."

"I sure know that now. Thank you. I lost sight of the shore and didn't remember east from west."

"Well, you went way east."

"But ending up in able hands," she replied.

It sounded suggestive, enticing, almost unbelievable. Bells should have gone off in Santiago's mind. Training should have kicked in. Instead, he offered the woman a sandwich and a beer.

"I suppose names would be good since we'll have a few hours together."

"Of course, I'm Parisa. Parisa Dhafari."

"Iranian," he said noting the name and placing the accent.

"Very good, Mister—"

"Santiago. Carlos will do."

The name Dhafari sounded familiar. He couldn't place it. And it didn't seem important. It was.

After another hour with the waves kicking up and Dhafari's Jet Ski bouncing on the tow line, he said they should head back. Santiago offered to secure her craft better.

"I'll do it," she said. "You ready your boat."

She hopped back over, doubled the line, and returned with her backpack that had been tied to the Jet Ski.

Santiago started his engine, checked the map, got his bearings, turned the catamaran toward the shore, and reacted to what felt like a bug bite on his neck.

He automatically reached up and scratched. He sensed a certain numbness. Numbness? No, worse. He turned with more effort than seemed necessary. The woman stood aft, near the outboards. She was now covered up with a sweater and looking anything but sexy.

His brain sent words to his mouth—her name, but he couldn't talk. Her name? He knew it was familiar. Then the thought was gone.

Santiago's heavy eyes drifted down. She was holding something. Pointing it toward him. He struggled to identify it. Somewhere through his fog, he recognized the item: A gun. A Glock 17. Police and military. U.S. Army Special Forces and—and who? A recollection formed.

He desperately tried to speak. He mouthed her name, but nothing came out. His legs began to buckle. Carlos Santiago wobbled forward. Report…in. But that notion faded. And again he reached for the woman's name. Syllables formed. Da-far-e, Yes, yes. He knew it. He'd read it—on a report—from work—a woman who had been killed planting a bomb on the exterior of a hotel—flights up. But…

Then came a swirl of overlapping, fleeting images. Blue Marlin on the end of a fishing line. Someone named Elizabeth. A badge. A huge airplane with a red, white, and blue flag. And, a little boy saluting a man in a uniform leaving his house. Daddy.

Carlos Santiago collapsed onto the deck. He wasn't dead yet, but he was paralyzed. Parisa Dhafari now moved fast before his bladder released and she would have to clean up the mess. The catamaran needed to be spotless when she left.

She put her pistol down. Fortunately, it hadn't been needed. She dragged Santiago starboard, lifted him, and leaned his torso overboard. He didn't resist. He couldn't resist. Next, she reached into her backpack, produced a switchblade, opened it, and sliced his arm that was draped over the side. She tossed the knife into the water and then, with one hefty push, flung the Director of the Secretary of State's Diplomatic Security Service, the DSS, overboard wondering if the sharks that feasted on him would also be affected by the poison still working its way through his body. She didn't wait to see.

After wiping the rental boat clean of her fingerprints, she returned to her Jet Ski, released the line, and drifted away from the unmanned rental with ample fuel and a half-smoked cigar.

One problem solved, mused the assassin, sister of Dominique Dhafari, who had been killed in a Washington, DC hotel bombing. Easier than most. This was the first of three assignments. The next would be harder, yet more thrilling. The third, pure revenge.

"This is unacceptable. We were scheduled to meet."

"The Supreme Leader sends his regrets but asks that you not take his absence as any measure of disrespect."

The two men sat across one another at a massive conference table for 40. Facing the window, Liv Zaitsev, a decorated major general, a veteran of Russia's brutality in Georgia, Crimea, and more recently Ukraine. Opposite him, Marshal Pak Pong Ju, an aging functionary with colorful insignia representing bravery for wars he never fought. Beside him was his translator, a young uniformed woman.

General Zaitsev tapped his fingers on a leather briefcase squarely in front of him.

"Disrespect no. Surprise, discontent, disapproval—yes."

If Pong Ju believed he was in control, the retort instantly worried the North Korean.

Zaitsev scanned the walls. He found them interesting on two counts: what was on them and what wasn't.

On one wall, photographs of the latest military hardware. On the other, nothing except for the telltale holes where photos had hung, undoubtedly photos of the former Supreme Leader.

Just a month earlier, an unexpected accident, which was still being investigated, had suddenly thrust a new young leader forward. Ro Tu-Chol, a distant cousin of the previous North Korean Supreme Leader, was only 27, but he was quickly making his presence known.

Zaitsev laughed to himself. Tu-Chol likely didn't know that his photograph was not yet prominently displayed in the conference room for all to see, particularly the emissary of Russian President Nicolai Gorshkov, whom he was presently snubbing. In Gorshkov's Kremlin, such a faux pas would be execution-worthy.

"Marshal Pong Ju, President Nicolai Gorshkov was assured, that I, as his emissary, would have an audience with the Supreme Leader Ro Tu-Chol specifically at this appointed hour."

"Ah, I must apologize. However, circumstances have required the Supreme Leader's immediate attention. He is overseeing most necessary changes in the Korean People's Army today."

Zaitsev recognized the meaning and almost smiled. Tu-Chol was eliminating generals who were against his ascension. The established manner, a carryover from his cousin, was a bit messy, but highly effective. Those judged to be insubordinate, or even family members who might likely stand in his way, were facing anti-aircraft guns not aiming at any aircraft. And while Tu-Chol was proving himself inexperienced in the art of diplomacy by not being present for the scheduled meeting, the advance word reaching Russia was that he was more than excelling in the art of tyranny.

"Duty calls," Zaitsev stated.

"I'm pleased you understand. We can surely reschedule—"

Now the Russian smiled as if he agreed. Then in a flash, his entire demeanor changed. He lowered his thick, bushy eyebrows and stared coldly at the North Korean officer.

"I do not understand. Apparently, neither does your Supreme Leader."

The translator blanched, afraid to communicate the precise words; an affront to the Supreme Leader that could earn her a place in front of the cannon, too. She looked at General Zaitsev. Pak Pong Ju waited.

Zaitsev straightened and forcefully said, "Tell Marshal Pong Ju that it is imperative that I meet with Supreme Leader Tu-Chol today as scheduled. Personally."

The translator, more comfortable with this statement, translated. The two North Koreans traded a few words. Then:

"Marshal Pong Ju sends his regrets," the translator said, "but—"

Zaitsev stood suddenly and balled his hands into tight fists. The translator jumped. Pong Ju had been told to meet and greet the Russian, tour him through the new semiconductor factory, and, at the end of the day, put him back on his military plane with appropriate gifts. A simple diplomatic mission. The possibility of Zaitsev having an actual meeting with the Supreme Leader, though acknowledged, was never meant to be real.

"It will happen!" Zaitsev demanded. "As agreed."

Marshal Pong Ju appeared to shrivel in front of the Russian general. "I'm certain we can make your stay comfortable while we find another time," he meekly offered.

"Perhaps the magnitude of my visit was not made clear," Zaitsev stated. "I have an important proposition to convey to the Supreme Leader."

"Oh?"

General Zaitsev took in a deep breath and sat down.

"Yes," he added calmly.

The two opposites, and definitely not equals, exchanged glances. Zaitsev patted his briefcase.

"A most important proposition," the Russian emphasized. "Today, not tomorrow."

He spun the lock's digits on his briefcase to 815, the month and day Gorshkov had become president of the Russian Federation in an uncontested election. He flipped two latches sideways and removed a folder, which he placed face down on the desk. Marshal Pak Pong Ju stared at it with immense curiosity and looked up at the Russian.

"Yes. As part of a trade, we are prepared to upgrade the missile complement of your submarine fleet."

Zaitsev did not enumerate the details. The new Supreme Leader, despite his inexperience, would find those details profound. Russia would modernize three Gorae-class submarines delivered the previous year to handle Russia's newest generation of RSM-56 Bulava Submarine Launched Ballistic Missiles. SLBMs.

Pak Pong Ju tipped his head, confused and uninformed. As an army officer, he was not familiar with the submarine fleet. Zaitsev explained.

"That is to say, our submarine-launched ballistic missiles will bring your fleet to full fighting capacity with long-range influence."

The word "influence" had a strategic meaning. It would extend North Korea's ability to target the United States.

The Korean major ventured a smile. He began to reach for the file. Zaitsev crossed his hands over it.

"But there is more. President Gorshkov requests your government's assistance in furthering certain interests of ours."

The North Korean thought deeply. There was only one answer now.

"It will be my duty to pass along your," he nearly choked on the word, "request." He should have thought more about the phrase "certain interests."

"Of course, you will," Zaitsev said assuredly as if he had a gun to the marshal's head. "And you will do so at this moment, while I am here. While you still have a job with the Supreme Leader."

The translator gasped. Zaitsev turned to the woman and said in Russian, "Please tell Marshal Pong Ju precisely what I said."

The woman swallowed hard and translated word for word. Pak Pong Ju sat stunned. He thought about his wife and his daughter. How they had ample food and government benefits because of his position. They had status. They had relative freedom of movement. This brute was all but threatening him. And now he saw his status diminishing. After all, he had created the problem, advising the Supreme Leader to dodge the meeting as evidence of his dominant authority in his own country.

Suddenly he regretted his decision as the agenda became abundantly more urgent than anticipated.

"General, I will convey your," he substituted a different word for request, "wishes."

"Thank you."

"Please excuse me." The North Korean stood and bowed. "I will return shortly."

"I'll be here," Zaitsev said knowing he had played the North Korean perfectly.

THE KREMLIN
MOSCOW

Nicolai Gorshkov walked between the raindrops. None of his machinations had come back to dislodge him as President of the Russian Federation whether by ballot or bullet. He defeated, imprisoned, or eliminated every foe in the time-honored dictatorial way. He felt no guilt. He survived because he had to. He kept friends on a short leash, a choker. The same for his allies. They were his tools or worse, his puppets.

Gorshkov, now into his 70s, looked fit enough to last to 100. That meant more people would die following his dictates, more victims would be slaughtered in his assaults, more votes would be compromised in foreign elections, and to his greater dream, more nations would become aligned with, or part of, the new Russia.

It was time for the Supreme Leader of North Korea to fall under his spell. He would get missiles and upgrades to his beloved navy without knowing Gorshkov's real goal.

But it didn't stop with the Democratic People's Republic of Korea. Gorshkov knew how to lure susceptible leaders, promising that they'd get a piece of his part of the world, when, in reality, what he sought was theirs.

He was moving neighboring nations to turn against NATO, pushing Iran to be even more aggressive toward U.S. ships in the Arabian Sea sending more rockets to Hezbollah and Hamas forces, and actively planting Russian flags deeper in South American soil with heavy arms to Venezuela and money to prop up Brazil's new regime.

They were all his puppets that he strung along with money, promises, arms, and lies. So far, nothing had gotten in the way. Yes, there were delays. There were setbacks. There was the untidy business of getting rid of suspected opponents or those who might one day turn against him. There were all the Russian soldiers who fought in Ukraine to bury and the propaganda to spout to their families that they were heroes to the Motherland.

Yes, Nicolai Gorshkov had mastered the art of walking between the raindrops. So far, he hadn't gotten wet.

PYONGYANG, DEMOCRATIC PEOPLE'S REPUBLIC OF KOREA

"Tell the Russian general I will be there in due course," the young Supreme Leader said to his lesser. "First, I have a few more farewells to dispense."

With that, the video phone link went dead.

Pak Pong Ju bowed, though Ro Tu-Chol did not see him.

Ninety minutes later, Tu-Chol drew in a deep breath as he approached the conference room door with Gorshkov's envoy on the other side. He had thought through the scenario. He would get something; they would want something. That's how negotiating went. Something for something. In this case, he'd get the Russian's latest SLBMs that would fire with pinpoint accuracy. They'd provide enhancements to his submarines that he couldn't turn down. In return Pong Ju had indicated that Zaitsev wanted certain favors that would benefit President Gorshkov. That seemed appropriate, though unknown.

Ro Tu-Chol steeled himself as he walked in to meet the Russian. He immediately became infuriated. *The walls are bare! Where are photographs of me?*

Angry, the Supreme Leader now wished he had moved the meeting to his office, where he would have been surrounded by all the symbols that defined his authority. He still had much to learn including who to trust on his senior staff.

"My dear Major General Zaitsev, thank you for your patience."

No apologies. No showing lower status.

"Supreme Ruler Tu-Chol, thank you for the audience today. I offer you warm wishes from President Nicolai Gorshkov and the people of the Russian Federation. The President looks forward to a time soon for you to visit. Our two nations are destined to forge a new era of friendship."

"Thank you, General. I understand you have a proposal that can lead us there."

Zaitsev smiled. He asked a question that afforded Tu-Chol respect. "May we sit and talk as comrades?"

North Korea was staunchly Communist in name. Russia was not, and yet, under Gorshkov's rule, it was still every bit the Soviet Union.

Tu-Chol felt he had the upper hand. In fact, he had no hand.

The Russian general reviewed the first part of the deal. The missiles.

"We will rearm your Navy. We will train your forces and test the weaponry with you. This will take 24 months. Then you will be able to demonstrate to the world that you are a world-class force to be reckoned with. Not only in nearby waters but closer to America's. You will show them your resolve, your authority."

Zaitsev continued strictly for the sake of stroking Tu-Chol's ego, "and will stand eye-to-eye with our enemies. No one will fail to notice."

Ro Tu-Chol felt imbued with power, thrilled with the arrangement that would catapult him onto the global stage. In that same moment, he decided what to do about his aide who had advised him not to meet directly with the Russian and had not properly seen to the walls. A serious error in judgment. An embarrassment. He would take care of that problem as he had others earlier in the day, and there'd be an opening left by the departure of Marshal Pak Pong Ju.

"You look pleased," Zaitsev observed.

"I am," the North Korean leader declared. "But I have a condition for you to convey to President Gorshkov."

"Oh?"

"For every missile we openly fire to test the Americans, you will give us five more."

"Five?"

"Yes, five."

Colonel Zaitsev smiled. He had expected ten and in, fact, he had much more in mind than a test.

Zaitsev looked down, feigned concern, and then offered, "I will bring that to President Gorshkov with my recommendation."

"Thank you. But how will we reach beyond our present sailing capabilities?" the Korean dictator asked. "Our fuel will only take us—"

Zaitsev raised a finger. "Ah, you are quite right. We will solve that problem for you. We have submerged oil reserves. Your submarine fleet will have access to them on missions that are of interest to the Russian Federation."

There it was. Russia's quid pro quo. Russia's interest.

"Now, allow me to show you how you will strike fear into America's leadership and how you will help change the world."

General Zaitsev opened the file. Tu-Chol marveled at the photographs of the refitted submarines, the missiles they'd carry, and a map with an area circled in red. The new Supreme Leader felt utterly supreme, thinking that soon he'd be seen as an equal in the realm of political public opinion, when in fact he was unwittingly about to become another Gorshkov pawn.

3

THE OVAL OFFICE, WHITE HOUSE
WASHINGTON, DC
PRESENT DAY

"It's only Tuesday. I can't imagine what'll be on my desk by Friday."

President Sean Allphin, new to his job since the surprising resignation of President Ryan Battaglio, settled into his chair behind the Resolute Desk. He held a tablet containing the PDB, the President's Daily Brief, prepared by the Office of the Director of National Intelligence and the CIA. Today's report echoed yesterday's and built on the assessments and the threats he had read every day last week and all the weeks since he first took office.

The world, he thought, was a mess.

The others present today included the Chairman of the Joint Chiefs Admiral Rhett Grimm, CIA Director Gerald Watts, Allphin's Chief of Staff Lou Simon, and Secretary of State Elizabeth Matthews, who waited for the president to digest the report.

The 72-year-old president ran his fingers through his thick mane of gray hair. He had ascended to the presidency without wanting the job. Surprisingly and with no warning or thorough explanation, Ryan Battaglio had stepped down after a short term as president. Battaglio had replaced President Alexander Crowe after Crowe was wounded during an assassination attempt. Without a vice president confirmed to serve under Battaglio, Sean Allphin, Speaker of the House of Representatives, moved up. No political thriller could have written such history in so short a time.

Allphin had been a powerful Speaker. Powerful, but not power hungry. He was satisfied advancing legislation on behalf of his party and the country. He'd built a reputation whipping votes and whipping up voters. Thirty-four years in Congress had earned him cross-aisle respect and name recognition, and just when he was considering retiring, his Speakership and reality catapulted him into the Oval Office.

News commentators speculated why Battaglio had abruptly left office. The internet blew up with rumors of his sudden exit. None that were reported were even close to the truth, and no one with any actual knowledge was talking. Ryan Battaglio promised to shape the narrative himself in a memoir. This worried people in the U.S. and elsewhere.

"One day at a time," offered Matthews. "Maybe, minute-by-minute, Mr. President."

The comment drew laughter. Gallows humor. Indeed, every day brought more challenges, more critical decisions to make, and the potential for more mistakes.

It had been like that since Allphin affirmed he would, to the best of his ability, "preserve, protect and defend the Constitution of the United States."

He feared the best was going to take more than he had.

At home gas prices had hit new highs, a reaction to what had happened to oil flow on a grand scale.

Terrorists had hit, disabled, and sunk ships in the Suez and Panama Canals. An attack in the narrows of the Strait of Hormuz delayed passage there. To America's intelligence community, it was a coordinated effort requiring sophisticated planning, money, and talent. Less obvious was who was responsible. The CIA had its theories. Members of Congress had their own, typically party-dependent. TV pundits and radio talk show hosts went in every direction. The public increasingly moved toward conspiracy theories.

Iran, North Korea, China, and Russia were all mentioned. Lone wolves and rogue groups were bandied about but viewed as less likely.

The National Security Council reasoned that whoever was behind the first, was behind all the terrorist attacks. Fingers continued to point to North Korea, though Secretary of State Matthews personally believed Nicolai Gorshkov had his fingerprints all over the plot.

The easiest to reopen, the Strait of Hormuz, where nearly 90% of the oil exports from the Persian Gulf transit each day, amounting to upwards of 20% of the daily worldwide oil demand.

The Strait was strategically significant to the world because of what sailed through the 90-mile-long, 21-to-52-mile-wide passage: principally cargo ships and Middle East oil. It linked the Persian Gulf to the west with the Arabian Sea and the Gulf of Oman to the southeast.

It took less than a month with the muscle of the U.S. Fifth Fleet that anyone who got in the way would be dealt with immediately. That included small suicide boats, anti-ship cruise missiles, and anyone planting new mines. Even Iran, the most belligerent nation along the Persian Gulf, initially offered assistance. But in recent months they were tightening the screws.

Meanwhile, the 120-mile-long Suez Canal remained impassable. Prior to the attack, every year 17,000 vessels passed from the Gulf of Suez to the South and the Mediterranean Sea to the North.

With two ships sunk by shoulder-fired missiles, estimates put clean-up anywhere from nine months to a year. Sitting idle and currently going nowhere were ships from the world's leading carriers including Maersk Line, Hapag-Lloyd, COSCO, and CMA CGM.

The impact on Egypt wasn't just to the operation of the channel; it led to unrest in Cairo, with local insurgents seizing on the instability. It had led to attacks against government infrastructure, against Egypt's elected officials, and in the past 48 hours, against the private sector, primarily American concerns.

The closure added an estimated 2,700 extra miles of transit from Saudi oil ports to the United States, around the Cape of Good Hope.

The result: higher oil prices in the U.S., even with increased domestic production.

And then a third attack, this one in the Panama Canal, further escalated the global problem at the gas tank, home oil furnaces, and every product that was made of plastic. In geopolitical terms, it was a terrorist's dream come true, a perfectly executed attack on the 900-foot cargo ship *Adagio*. In less than 12 minutes, terrorists boarded the ship and overpowered and killed the bridge crew. Then they rammed the vessel into a fully loaded tanker ship. The collision with *Harmony Gold* fractured the hull plates below the tanker's waterline. *Harmony Gold's* cargo of liquefied natural gas leaked out from its aluminum refrigerated compartments, hit the air that was hundreds of degrees warmer, and ignited in a firestorm. One of Panama's two canals was immediately impassable in both directions.

The inferno spread from *Harmony Gold* to Margarita Island Port, a facility managed by the Chinese, which added political fuel to an already inflamed situation.

It was a disaster long feared by the American military. Retired General Gordon Sumner, a former U.S. Ambassador-at-Large to Latin America, had warned, "If you wanted to get at the United States, you don't go attack the lion in the cage, you go down to Panama and attack Bambi."

Right now, Bambi was bleeding badly.

As in Egypt, extremist guerilla groups were rearing their ugly heads in Panama. Homegrown groups operated in the jungles inspired by fanatical fringe groups. They had graduated from knocking off small craft for cash to bigger stakes like yacht hijackings and kidnappings.

It was all in the president's daily briefing.

"Sir," Admiral Grimm said, "So long as there was peaceful passage, our policy remained hands-off. The canal would be open to all. But that has changed. We have the authority to move in. The Panama Canal Treaties

Act guarantees the United States the right to intervene militarily should any aggressor, nation or terrorist groups, threaten the canal's operations."

"Troops back into Panama?" President Allphin asked.

"Yes, sir. The first time since the 1989 invasion. The first since we took down General Manuel Antonio Noriega."

"Everyone in agreement?" Allphin scanned the Oval Office for confirmation. He saw the blank stares. "Let me ask it another way. Any disagreement?"

The room remained quiet.

"All right, what are we hearing from the advance team?" asked Chief of Staff Lou Simon.

Admiral Grimm, wearing the expression that went with his name, continued. "We sent Major General Mark T. Holmes from USSOUTHCOM to evaluate. Holmes arrived with the team from the Army Corps of Engineers and has been coordinating with the Agency and DoD. His recommendation, like mine: mobilize, contain, and control without delay."

"What does it mean in terms of manpower," Allphin asked.

"Years ago we maintained 70,000 troops to deter aggression. It worked. In 1979 with the final phase of the Panama Canal Treaties, we withdrew, shuttering 93,000 acres of bases and 5,000 buildings that had provided round-the-clock protection for the Canal. We sent some 26,000 back ten years later. Now? Not knowing exactly what we're facing, we should act as if they're in a worst-case scenario."

"In real numbers, general."

"Twenty-five thousand."

"I don't know," Allphin said. "It puts President Cortez in a real bind with China. They're not going to like U.S. forces running around their Canal ports. President Yáo will go apeshit."

"Fewer troops then. Cut the number to 15,000. It's still a sizable show of force," Grimm offered.

"Ten, fifteen, twenty-five thousand.. No one's going to be happy with whatever number," President Allphin replied. "And where the hell do we put them?"

"We reopen our base south of Panama City. Sixty-five hundred troops go in immediately. The rest to follow." Admiral Grimm paused. "Mr. President, Panama's defense team has as much admitted they're worried that local terrorist groups will use the attack on the Canal to make their bold statements. Even one guy carrying a suitcase packed with dynamite could close down a lock. With a coordinated effort, including shoulder-fired, armor-piercing anti-tank missiles, they could sink ships in multiple locations and bring the entire passage to a complete standstill. Every one of the steel gates in the locks, which hold back the 52 million gallons of water used by each ship, could be blown with little more than a few pounds of plastic explosives."

"Do we have intel on any credible threats?"

"No, sir. Not yet," CIA Director Watts stated. "But—"

Allphin raised his hands, a signal to put the debate on pause. A half-minute later the president began again.

"Here's the problem. I'm trying to make our initiative count with the Chinese. I believe sending troops to Panama could, make that would set those talks back."

Now Allphin stood and crossed to the front of the Oval Office. He picked up one putter from a modest brown G/Fore leather golf bag that was leaning up against an end table. He took aim at an imaginary ball and prepared to swing. He stopped midway back and looked around.

"Too many things to break," he laughed. Allphin rested the club against the wall. "And not the vases and photographs. I'm talking about progress with China."

Allphin turned to Elizabeth Matthews. "You have a trip planned to Panama."

It wasn't a question. It had been on the calendar for three weeks.

"Yes, sir. Due to leave Tuesday."

"Okay. Here's what I want you to do. Tell President Cortez we're only sending enough forces to watch the backs of engineers. Ours, theirs, and the Chinese. No boots on the ground for show. No political statement. If he agrees, we'll inform President Yáo, taking the pressure off

Cortez. Hell, it might even help our relationships."

The plan earned nods.

"But," Allphin continued, now addressing his CIA director, "if you pick up any chatter from the bad guys, that's when we will mobilize." And to Admiral Grimm, he asked, "How much time would you need?"

"If they're already staged and ready to go, 12 hours. If not, 48."

"Spread them around. Nothing that sets off alarms in Yáo's satellites."

"Got it," Grimm said.

"Considering you've spiked my blood pressure, you might as well give me the rest of the picture," President Allphin said. "Anyone have any good news this morning?"

The short answer was no. Newly appointed National Security Advisor Dr. Hamza Ali rattled off more crises: Another oil pipeline blown up between Russia and Germany. Moscow blamed NATO. NATO blamed Moscow. China turned down participating in the upcoming Pan Pacific Climate Change summit but committed to bringing more business to three African nations. "And," Ali added, "the British prime minister is a day away from resigning."

"What no bombs?" Allphin joked. "Only bombast?"

"Oh, we've got that too," CIA Director Gerald Watts said jumping in. "Overnight Turkey fired missiles into northern Kurdish encampments defying a United Nations ban. President Tiryaki is playing with fire."

"Goddamn him."

Allphin wrote the Turkish president's name on his call list. "What else?"

"An Iranian patrol boat blinded a Greek cargo ship with high-intensity beams claiming it was crossing into its territorial waters. When it didn't heave to, they fired some rounds."

The president shook his head. "Casualties?"

"Two."

Allphin turned to Secretary Matthews. "Elizabeth, what can we do?"

She shrugged her shoulders and tossed to Admiral Grimm to respond.

"Nothing. The captain claimed it was a bad GPS."

"Two dead and he blames the GPS. What about a fucking sextant?"
Secretary of Defense Vincent Collingsworth spoke next.

"The USS *Thomas Hudner* will be on-site in two hours to guide the
Greeks out. Of course, Tehran is demanding an apology."

"I'm sure they are," the president said sarcastically.

"And every incident further delays the progress of reopening shipping
through the Strait of Hormuz," Dr. Hamza Ali added.

Sean Allphin knew the dangers and the ongoing impact on the
economy. He'd brought together the G7 nations, the U.K., Canada,
France, Germany, Italy, Japan, and the United States, to discuss freezing
oil and natural gas prices. There was no agreement among the members,
nor with OPEC, and definitely not with Russia. But that point was
obvious. Russia was now a major oil supplier. Considering their tankers
primarily traversed the open Northern Sea Route, the NSR, thanks to
the warming Arctic water, they vetoed the agreement. Even before the
closures in the Middle East, the NSR offered the shortest and safest
route between Russia and the Asian markets, cutting shipping time in
half from the Suez route.

"God almighty. I really need a vice president," Allphin said rubbing
his forehead and winking at Elizabeth Matthews. Then he looked at
his simple Timex watch. It was now the top of the hour. He stood to
end the meeting. That's when the CIA Director's phone beeped, then
Admiral Grimm's, and National Security Director Ali's. Each had a text
alert with relatively the same message.

"What is it?" Allphin asked.

"Sir, give us a minute," Ali said.

"What's going on, Vincent?" Allphin asked his Secretary of Defense.

Before Vincent Collingsworth could answer, his phone rang.

Two minutes later the meeting resumed.

"We have a problem," Grimm began.

"I can fucking see that," Allphin said.

Allphin sat. "Don't tell me you saved the best for last?"

"JICPAC, Pacific Command, the Joint Intelligence Center—"

"I goddamned know what JICPAC is. Get to it."

"The USS *Annapolis* is tracking a North Korean Gorae-class submarine. A former Russian Kilo."

"We do that all the time."

"Yes, sir. Off the coast of Asia, down into the Sea of Japan. Not midway across the Pacific. Until now, the Gorae-class sub's fuel range has been limited to 1,500 miles. That's going and coming. Seven hundred fifty miles out of port and back. That risks South Korean and Japanese targets, but their capability hasn't included mainland U.S. targets."

"Speak plainly. What are you saying, Admiral?"

"They've sailed some 3,400 kilometers."

"In miles."

"Over 2,100. Almost halfway to the U.S. mainland."

"And how the hell did their range increase by more than three?" Allphin demanded.

"Much more than three if they intend to get back home."

"And how the hell did they pull this off? Refueling ships?"

"Mr. President. Can we put a pin in that for a few minutes? I'd like to bring in General Abdo to brief you."

"Oh God! That bad?"

"Possibly."

With little more than a nod, the man who never wanted to be president grasped that an even greater threat might be coming his way.

4

Nicolai Gorshkov didn't know what to do with all the rooms in his palatial dacha. Actually, dacha wouldn't begin to describe the ornate palace. It was completed a year earlier and cost—well, the cost didn't matter. Gorshkov was the richest man by far in Russia. Rumors were that the country spent more than 150 billion rubles, a billion-and-a-half in U.S. dollars, to make him happy.

The two-story Italian complex covered more than 200,000 square feet and had a view to die for. Four workers lost their lives during the six years it took to complete the mansion. Gorshkov assuaged the families. In three cases with money. The wife of the fourth threatened to go to the press and quite surprisingly had an accident that started on the roof of her apartment building and tragically ended on the street below.

In Gorshkov's Russia, that's how accidents often happen.

The president named his Kremlin getaway Юпитер for the biggest celestial body in the solar system aside from the sun—Jupiter. It included all the usual trappings of a royal palace and those of a citadel: a ground-to-air missile installation, a helipad, and long and deep secret tunnels leading to multiple escape routes. Inside, spas and saunas,

Turkish baths—plural baths, a hookah bar, a casino, a wine cellar, a cinema, and more. He'd fucked in half of the 34 bedrooms. Never twice in the same room and never the same woman, or girls, barely women. He'd played pool only once and not yet bowled, gone swimming, or played tennis. But he'd also screwed women there.

Gorshkov visited it at least once every few months, and rarely with advance notice. However, it wasn't hard for American spy satellites to detect when he was there. But knowing where he was, wasn't the same as knowing what he was talking about within the walls of Юпитер. The current discussion would have been particularly interesting.

"Checkmate," Gorshkov declared knocking down his opponent's king.

General Bortnik had seen the chessboard move in question, but winning was not an option for his long-term prospects.

"My dear friend," Gorshkov offered, "Chess is life. To the skilled competitor, his pieces are the armies to protect him, to advance his goals, to take kings and queens down, and to win. Strategy is rewarded. Mistakes become folly. The West had a name for it. Manifest Destiny. For me," Gorshkov cleared his throat, "for us, it is Mother Russia's providence. In another sense, it's about one's willingness to sacrifice. Do you ever consider what you are willing to sacrifice?"

Of course, Bortnik had. Dignity, any sense of fairness. Honesty and individuality. It wasn't like in the old Soviet days when the state owned everything. But it wasn't that much different since Nicolai Gorshkov owned him.

The general sipped his Jewel of Russia Ultra Limited vodka and nodded. Gorshkov had moved onto a far bigger playing board—world-building. Russian Federation rebuilding. Ukraine, and in time, the Baltic States, and all of the Arctic. But to General Bortnik, a co-conspirator, a partner, a pawn, he would hear more. Gorshkov was in a talking mood.

"It is time for our missiles to return to the Western Hemisphere, to America's doorstep. To undo a wrong. To exert our right. To demonstrate our strength. To reveal Washington's weakness. And this time it will be our demands that Washington's feckless leader caves to rather than the other way around. Except it's not we. We will remain on the outside, concerned world citizens. We will have no direct attachment with the North Korean mission or others. But we will be the beneficiaries."

Bortnik listened. Gorshkov was bordering on giddy.

"What do Americans value the most, Sergei?"

The general raised his glass encouraging Gorshkov to tell him.

"They claim it's their freedom. Fuck freedom. Too many decisions to make about things they do not know of. Places that are far away. Countries they'll never visit. Capitals they can't pronounce. Their freedom buys them nothing. Americans are ultimately like everyone else. What they really want is to be free…of decisions. The majority of their people, and people around the world, don't need to be governed. They need to be ruled. And they want to be ruled with strength. Under the right circumstances, they will choose a strong leader. One of our making."

Gorshkov walked across the room to a cedar humidor on a bookcase shelf and removed two Cuban Montecristo N°4s. He offered one to the general, who accepted. After lighting and taking long draws, Gorshkov continued.

"It's all coming together, my friend. Disillusion and disunity. America will bend to our will. Ours, Sergei. And we will control who leads them."

Gorshkov examined the lit end of his Montecristo. It burned hot. He pressed the butt end onto Bortnik's fallen king in the last chess match.

"Like that," he said as the paint burned away. "Just like that."

Gorshkov handed Bortnik the burned king. "You know you lost the game the moment I seized your first rook."

"I didn't see the move."

Gorshkov laughed, so Bortnik laughed. "Of course you didn't. I had you looking at four other lesser threats, not the most critical moves. Even though you struggle here, you have proven yourself expert on the greater battlefield."

Indeed, Bortnik had led Nicolai Gorshkov's forces to some decisive victories before he moved into the Kremlin. Now, as one of Gorshkov's most trusted confidants, he was privy to the extraordinary plans that had taken seed. Soon all the seeds of discontent that had been sown would bear fruit. A very deadly fruit.

As General Bortnik learned through the evening's matches, Gorshkov was well into three calculated and dangerous moves on the global chessboard. They were bold. Bortnik considered them highly risky, a point he also purposely did not share with his president.

The more Bortnik thought about what he heard, the more he realized that everything was chess to Gorshkov. Strategy, feints, and daring moves, with an element of cheating.

Already Russian jets buzzed American pilots just shy of Alaska's borders. In European capitals, drones controlled by dug-in spies crashed into government buildings. The change in Turkey's leadership had begun the process of that country withdrawing from NATO.

And there were other dramatic gambits. Russia was limiting international transit through the Northern Sea Route. Its icebreakers were keeping the route clear, but Russia was not allowing ships through from countries it deemed unfavorable to its best interests. That meant any nation sailing under flags that contributed to Ukraine's defense. And he continued to pump money, supplies, and terror into Ukraine, waiting for the time when the war would end and he would have all of Crimea for all time.

Russia was also playing a game of chicken with Finland's air defenses. Nightly border incursions frayed nerves. Frayed nerves put NATO on alert, but not yet taking action.

Of course, when confronted about his intentions, Nicolai Gorshkov lied. He couldn't remember the last time he had told the truth in public. He did, however, remember the last time someone in his inner circle accused him of lying. That was just two days ago. He cleanly eliminated the problem, another fall from grace.

To Bortnik, Gorshkov was an open book. He made promises that served his goals and broke those that didn't. He never acted without purpose. And those things that may have appeared impulsive were worked out in detail. Gorshkov existed to win, to return Russia to its former glory, and to be his country's most enduring leader. Beyond Lenin and Stalin. Beyond Khrushchev and Brezhnev. Enduring, all-powerful, and great. For now and for all time.

To achieve everything meant he had to control everything. The fact that the nation's press, the internet, and the media belonged to him gave him ultimate control over public opinion. That control included his age. He was getting younger than older. A few years ago he was 67. Today, 64. Maybe the same next year. He professed to have a happy marriage. The goings on in his bedrooms at Юпитер and a Moscow pied-à-terre could tell a different story. But that story wouldn't be told.

Since the fall of the Berlin Wall, when Gorshkov was a young KGB agent, he vowed to restore the boundaries of the Soviet Union, given up by the cowardly Gorbachev whom he termed a traitor to Communism. And though Gorshkov's new Russia was no longer a Communist state, he ran it with an iron fist.

"Yes, dear Sergei, there will be sacrifices as in chess," Gorshkov said as they set up the pieces again, "but most of all, we will win back the Russia that traitors had lost."

Game on.

THE OVAL OFFICE, WASHINGTON, DC

After a break, the meeting resumed in the Oval Office with the promised additional participants.

"Mr. President, General Zarif Abdo can pick up where we left off."

The four-star was Vice Chair of the Joint Chiefs and possibly the bluntest of all. He was a strategist with a reputation for questioning everything and not accepting bullshit answers. In years past, Abdo had commanded America's NATO forces abroad, headed National Guard troops at home, and served in South Korea. During this most recent period, he became an acknowledged expert in North Korea's military capabilities. Above and beyond his other experience, that earned him a seat at the table today.

"All right. What do we know now that we didn't," Allphin looked at his watch, "like 31 minutes ago?"

"I'll start with how they got as far as they have," General Abdo said. "Submerged refueling stations."

"Go on."

"Tanks anchored along ocean shelves. Likely dropped by Russians from trans-Pacific cargo ships. We've explored the possibility ourselves, but floating islands to refuel drones."

"Russian?" Allphin asked. "Why don't we have them?"

"Our nuclear fleet doesn't need them and our diesels are all supported by tankers in the fleet. That gives us expansive global capability. But a foreign diesel with the intent to go beyond its range? This is exactly what they need. Places to fill up."

"Okay, so they've got Shell stations they can tap to sail further."

"More like Gazprom, Lukoil or Surgutneftegas," General Abdo said. "Part of a trade deal between Pyongyang and Moscow. Gas for arms."

"Not China?"

"Not in this case. North Korea has turned to Russia as it's accelerated its nuclear and missile development. Beijing has say, but not all the sway they used to."

Allphin said, "What's that mean?"

"Tab 4.1, Mr. President." This was from CIA Director Watts.

Allphin reopened his briefing. He shook his head.

"Right. This has been here for two weeks. Your asset in North Korea reported that Pyongyang's subs have been retrofitted with Russian Submarine Launched Ballistic Missiles. But the range—"

"…Was not an issue until now," Abdo stated.

"Go ahead, General."

"If the Gorae-class sub stays on course and speed, they'll be in the bubble in less than a week. At that point, their ICBMs could take out San Diego, Los Angeles, San Francisco, and Seattle or anywhere up and down the coast within 15 minutes."

"They wouldn't," Lou Simon blurted.

General Abdo replied with a stone-cold expression. "It would be a mistake to assume that."

"Oh, Christ. I think this is where you give the president his options," Allphin said referring to himself in the third person.

"Depending on reports from *Annapolis*," Grimm said, "you issue the order to take out the sub."

"And at what point do I do that?"

"The second it is in range."

Allphin walked behind the Resolute Desk, where so many decisions had been made by previous presidents. He pulled the curtains aside and looked out into the Rose Garden. Without turning back around he asked, "Who's captain of the *Annapolis?*"

Admiral Grimm replied, "Dwight Zimmerman, sir. Twenty-eight years in the service. Six on *Annapolis.*"

"If we order him to kill?"

"He'll act without hesitating."

"And from there?"

"Pyongyang may never know what happened," Abdo noted. "Their sub will just disappear. Worse case, we launch a strike on Sinpo. Thirty-two subs are presently there. In two minutes we could destroy much of their naval infrastructure and set back their operation a decade or more."

"And start a war, General Abdo?"

"Not a war, an operation, sir. A strategic stealth strike by our special forces. As we've seen in Panama, the Arabian Sea, and the Suez, it doesn't take much to accomplish a great deal."

Allphin paused to think. Everyone held on his next words. They came after a minute's thought.

"Twice daily updates," the president demanded.

"Yes, sir," Abdo said.

"Yes, sir," Admiral Grimm and CIA Director Watts seconded.

"If there's any change during the night, someone better be knocking at my bedroom door."

He heard another chorus of "Yes, sir."

"Now please tell me that's it," President Allphin said, "so I can hit the bathroom."

"Almost," the CIA Director replied. "Egypt. Tab 8. Cairo's still a mess. And," he nodded to General Abdo, "we have more on Iran's hand in the disarray."

"No surprises there."

"Well, as a matter of fact, there are, Mr. President," Abdo said. "Money, arms, and advisors to support rebel factions in Egypt. The whole area remains a tinder box, potentially more dangerous than ever.

Puts oil tankers, cargo ships, and the USS *Eisenhower* Carrier Strike Group, patrolling the Red Sea, in the crosshairs. It sure keeps me awake."

Elizabeth Matthews shivered. She had a friend in Cairo. More than a friend, a resource. Eyes and ears. A man who, right now, was on his way into the thick of it.

CAIRO, EGYPT

Dan Reilly's iPhone rang in his sports coat breast pocket. He ignored the call as the Ford van he was riding in tore around Tahrir Square looking for a safe route out. Shakir Affir, Reilly's young, terrified Egyptian driver circled again. The centrifugal force thrust Reilly's body against the safety belt strap across his chest. His head nearly hit his passenger side window.

The phone continued to ring. This was not the trip he had intended. When he scheduled it, he felt things would be relatively calm for visits to his company's hotels in Cairo, Alexandria, and Luxor. That was when it was first on his calendar. Before the Suez Canal was bombed. Before political opportunists took to the streets. Before police barricades went up. Before tanks rolled. Before the disruption of normal life. The situation had gotten far worse, especially in the last 24 hours.

"That way!" yelled Reilly. He pointed to a garbage truck pulling over. "There's room around him."

That was debatable, but Affir floored the gas and steered sharply around the truck and debris field.

The phone rang a fourth time. Reilly fumbled with it, answered, and pressed speaker.

"Yes!"

"Hello!"

It was a woman's voice; authoritative and as clear as if she was calling local.

"Dan, it's—"

He knew the voice: America's Secretary of State, Elizabeth Matthews. "Can't talk now. I'm a little busy."

At that moment a wiry teen wearing a shemagh scarf and gas mask ran up to the van with a smoking canister. He was about to hurl it when a blast from a water cannon knocked him down.

"It's clear, keep going!" Reilly yelled.

Reilly was wrong. The canister exploded in the road ahead of them. Affir swerved but clipped the mirror on the passenger side as the van scraped an upturned SUV. Now Reilly's head slammed against the window.

"Sorry. You okay, Mr. Reilly?" Affir asked.

"Yay, just get us out of here."

Here was downtown Cairo. Here was the middle of the latest violent clash between unaffiliated rebels and the barely standing government. Here was where they needed to get through.

Dan Reilly had landed in Egypt two hours earlier and was scheduled to have dinner with the Egyptian Minister of Interior that evening. The agenda called for Reilly to pitch the Minister on information sharing between Kensington Royal and Egypt's police and intelligence agencies. It was the type of meeting that Dan Reilly was having around the globe, wherever Kensington had properties and wherever there was likely to be political unrest.

The next day Reilly planned to visit his company's properties in Alexandria and Luxor. A private plane would be waiting for him, but the question was, could he even get back to the airport safely under the circumstances?

The circumstances: The Minister, Ali Abdul Aziz was someone who, under normal circumstances, could help. The Ministry is part of the Egyptian Cabinet and under normal times it's responsible for law enforcement. Right now it looked like there was little law and no enforcement.

The phone was still in Reilly's hand. Over the screeching tires and explosions, he heard Secretary Matthews ask, "What's going on?"

"Just trying to stay alive. I could use a little help."

"You've got better eyes on things right now than I do."

"What—?"

At that moment, a group of five teenage rioters with clubs and bricks rushed from the sidewalk. Affir maneuvered around them but not before a brick crashed through the driver's side window hitting him. He slumped forward. The van hit the curb and came to a sudden stop. Reilly quickly unbuckled Affir, pulled him across the seat, climbed over, and took the wheel. The rioters began banging on the van. Reilly gunned the engine, and cut up onto the sidewalk clipping one of the rioters. Reilly had no time to look back. There was only going forward.

Reilly was the senior executive for the international hotel chain he'd helped grow from a moderate size to a global leader. At the same time, and not on his resume, he unofficially consulted for the U.S. State Department. It was a relationship that didn't quite qualify him as a spy, but certainly put him close to the line and earned him phone calls from the woman who was still on the line—America's Secretary of State, Elizabeth Matthews.

His boss, the founder and CEO of Kensington Royal Hotels, knew that line all too well. Edward Jefferson Shaw, better known as EJ, had given Reilly a year to figure out his future—who he really wanted to answer to. He had six months left to decide.

Reilly still hadn't decided whether he would stay with Kensington or sign back on with his long-time government confidant and contact, Secretary Matthews. And then there were his CIA relationships, most notably with a former Army buddy, Robert Heath.

On the advice of friends within the Department of Army, Elizabeth Matthews recruited Reilly when she was an Under Secretary of State. She saw him as a candidate capable of working his way up in State. However, after three years, the private sector called. A high-priced head-hunting company identified Reilly based on the needs outlined by Kensington Royal. He had international experience. He was a critical thinker and a team player. His Harvard business pedigree, military training, and demonstrated willingness to jump into the fray checked all the right boxes.

Though he disguised his knowledge in his negotiations, Dan Reilly was proficient in Arabic, Russian, and Mandarin. And so, EJ Shaw had made him an offer. With very little negotiation and terms the government couldn't match, Daniel J. Reilly joined the firm as an Associate Vice President. He was given a company credit card and soon an unlimited spending limit. Within two years he advanced to Marketing VP, and finally, President of Kensington International.

However, his work for Kensington never became routine. In one sense, he was informed. In another, he was an informant. Intelligence flowed both ways. To and from Matthews at the State Department. To and from Heath at the CIA. To and from Reilly to other international intelligence agencies. To put it another way, he got and he gave, and in the course of his work, he saved lives.

Reilly would soon turn forty-four, a birthday he'd probably celebrate either alone or somewhere in the air at 35,000 feet between hotel meetings and managing hotel crises. He had a new woman in his life. He hoped he'd live to see another day and spend another night with her. She was Yibing Cheng, a State Department analyst recently assigned to him in Beijing by Secretary Matthews. They were early in their courtship. But Reilly saw promise. Maybe more if he could get off the road.

Reilly made sure he ate right despite all his travels. He was just over six feet, stayed a trim size 40 long, and so far no gray had crept into his wavy black mane. He valued information, associates, and honesty. His avowed management philosophy was "You can't lead with your feet on your desk," which is why he was rarely seen at his offices in Chicago and DC.

Dan Reilly prided himself in learning about, understanding, and respecting local culture and making key administration hires that would be well-received on the ground. It had helped in both exotic resort locations and danger zones around the world.

Reilly circled the globe multiple times every year, meeting with company executives and government leaders, evaluating acquisitions, advising on sales, and keeping a keen eye on political shifts that would have an impact on operations and lives.

He reported hotel matters to Chicago headquarters and passed along intelligence he gathered to contacts within the Beltway. That put him not so comfortably on the razor's edge, a place he'd lived ever since his Army service.

In the past two years, assignments had sent him rushing to the capitals of Europe, Asia, South America, and the Middle East. To a hotel bombing in Tokyo and a murder in Beijing. He marched into a Mexican cartel stronghold to broker a deal for the safety of hotel guests and after a plane crash, convinced Venezuelan militia that he wasn't a person of interest when he actually was. He faced an assassin in Brussels, chased down a killer on Stockholm's streets, and was stalked by a beautiful Russian sleeper spy. Not the typical work of a business executive. But then again, Dan Reilly was nowhere near typical.

Pockets of angry men roamed around Tahrir Square, now an urban battleground cordoned off by barriers that weren't holding anyone back. Some protestors held anti-regime posters. Others, guns. Cars honked. People ran for their lives. Some lying on the ground hadn't made it.

A man—no, a kid, ran toward him yelling in Arabic. He lit a bottle, an improvised Molotov cocktail. Reilly braked again. The kid flicked a lighter. He was ready to launch the explosive, but inexperienced, he waited too long. It went off mid-throw. The boy was consumed in flames.

"Dan!" Matthews shouted.

"Later!"

Reilly looked over to Affir. He was bleeding but getting his wits back. "Can you buckle up?" Reilly asked.

"I think—" Suddenly the Egyptian, lifting his head, screamed, "Stop!"

Reilly jammed the brakes as a new group assembled some 50 feet ahead. Reilly threw the van into reverse, craning his neck to see behind.

The last time Dan Reilly drove like this was in Afghanistan and under similar conditions.

The small group became larger. No room for a three-point turn.

"Faster!" Affir said. "Another guy's lighting a Molotov cocktail."

Reilly pressed the pedal to the floor, dodging vendor carts cluttering the street.

The crowd came on quicker than Reilly's backing up. A bad situation getting worse.

"Right turn up ahead!" Affir said looking behind.

"Right?" Reilly had to think. Right was left looking backward. "Which way?"

"Left. Sorry. At the bus stop." A moment later the Egyptian yelled, "Now!"

Dan Reilly swung the vehicle and turned onto a sidewalk just as another makeshift bomb exploded where the van had been moments before. Still, the impact lifted the van. Stable again, Reilly plowed through a trash can and steered through the cloud of smoke. Once clear, he returned to the street, but they were not out of harm's way. Protesters hurled more homemade explosives. One started a fire on the van's hood. They could feel the heat inside.

Reilly spotted a broken fire hydrant spurting water upwards and out onto the pavement. He drove toward it. The water did its job dousing the flames.

One block after another they dodged dangers. Accelerating. Decelerating. Stopping short. Making sharp turns and nearly hitting a man who refused to get out of the way.

"Five more blocks. Then we try a right on Fahmy!" Affir said pressing his jacket up against his head wound.

It was actually six blocks, but an Egyptian Army tank blocked the turn.

"Next one. Nobart. From there we can work our way to the American Embassy. Might take—"

"No!" Reilly demanded. "The hotel."

The hotel would have been a straight shot as an Egyptian House Sparrow flies, the most abundant bird in the country. But Reilly had to navigate around roaming gangs to get across the Nile to Gezira, the island west of downtown Cairo.

Four bridges connected to Gezira. Affir, increasingly weaker, directed Reilly toward 6th October Bridge which would get them to the hotel and closer to his meeting with the Egyptian Interior Minister at his villa in the northern section of Zamalek.

That all depended on surviving the ride.

Splinter political groups and disgruntled civilians were armed with simple homemade explosives like Molotov cocktails and heavy armaments. They had the sitting government in their sights. Americans, too. The police and army were doing their best to suppress the insurrection. Reilly feared it wasn't anywhere near enough.

Only months earlier, terrorists had attacked and disabled ships in the Suez Canal. The resulting impact on the world's economy was hitting the area hard. Hard on the government. Hard on everyday Egyptians who were losing jobs. Hard on their hungry children.

Prices spiked. Durable goods were running out. Looters took what they wanted off store shelves. People hoarded everything they could not knowing what the next day would bring.

Blame turned inward to President Nigel Bin Aba. Unable to control the growing crisis, Bin Aba suspended the Constitution. Now after two weeks, he dreaded he would never make it through the last year of his six-year term. He probably wouldn't even make his next birthday.

Coup d'état appeared all too inevitable. But calm was unlikely to follow immediately. Competing factors competed. Each driven by bloodlust. For now, the Army remained loyal to the president. But that loyalty would only go so far. If and when Bin Aba left, there were any number of generals ready to fill the void.

"Left, left, left!" Reilly's wounded and bleeding passenger pointed. Then a sudden change in direction. "No! Go straight!"

Reilly saw why. An MRAP was rolling into the intersection of Marouf and Champollion. The Mine-Resistant, Ambush Protected vehicle was bigger and heavier than their van, and depending upon the army's political leaning at the moment, they might view the fast-moving hotel vehicle as a threat.

The MRAP did not give the van the right of way. The armored vehicle was moving in to block the way. Reilly sped up, swung wide, and clipped the right curb on Marouf, narrowly missing a light pole.

They were clear, but they still had to get to Nile Corniche, the thoroughfare that hugged the river. From there, up to the October 6th Bridge. Based on the way the day was going, there was no guarantee they'd make it.

A window in a Gucci store blew out, rocking Reilly's van. Gunshots ricocheted off the pavement.

"We're not going to make it!" Shakir Affir screamed.

"We'll make it!" Reilly said.

Positivity mattered. Faith mattered. Driving skills mattered.

Stay focused, Reilly told himself.

So far, an estimated 1,500 rioters had been cut down by forces that remained loyal to President Bin Aba. More than 100 officials were taken hostage. Many were quickly tried before a makeshift tribunal and hanged. Those members of the Shura Council, the Egyptian Senate, and the House of Representatives who could flee, did.

And Dan Reilly drove faster toward his hotel.

* * *

The Kensington Royal Star of the Nile had risen from the sand, replacing hotels that had come before it and the huts that had preceded those centuries before. It was constructed around a former historical Royal Palace built by Napoleon for his Egyptian mistress in 1799, the year Napoleon's explorer Pierre-François Bouchard discovered the Rosetta Stone. The Egyptian beauty only stayed one night.

Over the years, the hotel had hosted heads of state and movie stars, religious leaders, and gangsters. It had views of old and new Egypt. From the east side, visitors could take in the Egyptian Museum with artifacts that tell the 5,000-year history from the earliest human settlements to the dynasties that emerged and disappeared.

In good times, no more than a few months ago, the hotel catered to tourists from around the globe. They strolled admiringly through the luxuriant lobby decorated in gold, walked down the long halls on golden Oriental carpets, ate off inlaid gold plates in the 11 restaurants, and used their gold credit cards in bars and lounges.

Tourists swam in the Olympic-sized pool and were pampered in the lavish spa when they weren't off on excursions. Businessmen and -women, and politicians came from around the world for conferences and events in the numerous meeting rooms and ornate ballrooms.

In fact, that night a Greek shipping magnate's daughter was supposed to be married at the hotel. The service and party were canceled because the shipping company was now looking at bankruptcy and the daughter's fiancé had realized he wasn't marrying into the kind of money he previously expected.

That was just one example of how the chaos on the streets of Cairo was making its way into the opulent Kensington Star of the Nile. There would be more.

* * *

Reilly and Affir passed ambulances and fire trucks, police vehicles, and abandoned cars. Protesters carried flags and waved signs. Some waved shoes in the air, bottom-up, a gesture that conveyed disgust at their president. They hurled curses in Egyptian and English. Helmeted riot police, shields, batons, and weapons in hand did what was expected. They pushed, they shoved, and they fired.

TV cameras and cell phones piped footage back to cable news channels and the internet. From there they reached the world. Reilly did not doubt that Elizabeth Matthews was watching live coverage in her DC office, possibly still listening on the phone. He couldn't check.

The bridge was ahead. Burned-out cars made the passage difficult, but not impossible. Affir continued to give directions, but his speech was slurred. Reilly was certain he was fading.

"Stay with me, Shakir. A little further."

"I'm good, Mr. Reilly."

He wasn't. Reilly sped up.

Getting near the resort was one thing. Getting into it was another. Cement bollards were up 25 feet from the building to prevent any vehicles crashing through the glass at the main entrance.

The resort had 180 cameras recording the comings and goings on the property. They'd provide a record of any assault, but who could prevent it?

No American flag flew over the hotel. All signage relating to the United States had also been removed. The changes, two of many, were implemented according to standards created by Dan Reilly and his senior staff and military, law enforcement, legal, and intelligence experts who served as the Kensington Royal Crisis Team.

Reilly turned onto a service road leading to the rear of the building. He drove the 100 yards at a faster-than-safe clip and hoped the security posted at the gate would recognize the van and raise the bar in time. If not, there was going to be splintered wood and car parts to clean up.

Reilly braced and honked. He spelled out S-O-S in Morse code in short horn beeps. The bar flew up.

The van lurched to a full stop. Reilly slowly withdrew his hands from the ten and two positions on the steering wheel. He looked over to Affir. The young man was breathing, but unconscious. Reilly said a prayer for the brave Egyptian, not convinced anyone's god was taking political positions right now.

7

WASHINGTON, DC

Power is the most sought-after commodity in politics. It's what everyone in government needs. With power comes influence. With influence comes money. With money, the circle closes. More power.

It works pretty much the same in the city council as it does on Capitol Hill, in a democracy as well as a dictatorship. What can I do for you? What can you do for me?

It's not always a simple equation, however. And it's rarely equal. Some of the time what you can do for me comes with a higher price than money. It comes with whispers and threats, with blackmail photos and videos, with no way out.

The best practitioners are well-schooled and well-heeled. Career politicians with the ability to buy and sell people. One of Washington's most adept was the minority leader of the Senate who, when he closed his eyes or spoke in public, saw himself in the White House—and not as a guest.

This man was Billy Peyton. Always Billy. Never Bill.

Peyton, a good old boy from Comanche County, Oklahoma, site of the state's biggest oil fields, excoriated his opposition with the popular refrain that they were socialists, no matter their party. He branded the press with the familiar "enemy of the people" claim. He fought special interest groups that were in no way special, but especially when they were unhelpful to him. And now, with his eyes on a run for the White House, he had a war chest growing as big as his ego and one list of people who owed him favors and another list of those whom he virtually owned.

The senator, 52 and rich with his own oil money and the money of equally rich if not richer donors, despised the new president and the one before him. He despised the whole leftover administration from President Crowe and all who had joined since. And most of all he hated Secretary of State Elizabeth Matthews, who according to most pundits and Las Vegas odds makers, stood between him and his political aspirations.

"He's going to pick her," Peyton complained to his Chief of Staff, Seth Sullivan.

"Of course, he will," said Sullivan, Billy's right brain function for the past five years. Next, he half expected Peyton to shout, "Fuck her!"

He did.

If and when Allphin choose her, Peyton would be ready with opposition research, real or invented. It didn't matter anymore. Sullivan would feed his boss everything he needed. First, to dampen the glow around Matthews, and when the Senate confirmation hearings began, whatever he was given by the people on the outside ready to influence the inner Beltway and the whole nation.

"Timing?"

"I'll hear soon," Sullivan said, "maybe in a few days. But there's talk of a trip. So probably after rather than before."

"Not much time," Peyton complained.

"Don't worry. I'm told it's good shit."

"That she can talk herself out of?"

"She can talk all she wants. But pictures say a thousand words."

"Real?" Billy Peyton asked.

"What's real? In the meantime, hit her hard tomorrow at your committee meeting."

"Fuck yes."

8

PACIFIC OCEAN

350 MILES NORTH NORTHWEST OF HAWAIIAN ISLANDS

"Turning again," the USS *Annapolis*'s STS operator called out.

Okim Katema was one of the team of sonar technicians working in shifts aboard the submarine. This was his second day tracking the North Korean sub which was sailing way out of its lane.

The ballistic missile sub had varied its route with various short jogs north and south but eventually returned to a general easterly heading. Now it seemed to be on a straight shot.

"Back on niner-one, seven-two, Captain," Katema said.

"Exactly?" Captain Dwight Zimmerman, commander of the *Annapolis*, asked what he had been asking hourly.

"Exactly. Bearing niner-one, seven-two, sir."

"Picking up screws at six knots. Losing it five."

"Any awareness of us?"

"No, sir."

"Okay, Mr. Katema. Stay on her." To the helmsman, Zimmerman said, "Steady as she goes."

"Roger that."

Annapolis lurked 15 kilometers behind, silently matching the North Korean's depth and speed. Zimmerman kept the U.S. Seventh

Fleet command appraised via brief VHF transmissions. In turn, the Pentagon followed the pursuit with great interest. That interest was communicated by the Joint Chiefs to the Commander in Chief. It was particularly noteworthy because it fit right into the intelligence that had been reported by a deep undercover CIA operative at the Sinpo Submarine Base in the Democratic People's Republic of Korea.

* * *

Jang Song-Taek, the captain of *Wonsan Yong-Ganhan*, checked with his sonar technician.

"Nothing, Captain. We are alone except for the whales and that last cruise ship."

Song-Taek wasn't so naïve as to believe an American Los Angeles-class submarine wasn't stalking them.

Normally the Gorae-class *Wonsan Yong-Ganhan*, with a range of 1,500 miles, remained closer to Asia, close enough to do harm in Japan if so ordered. But the orders were different on this voyage. The submarine crew had been told they were testing operational capabilities far beyond their home waters. It was honorable duty for the sailors whose ship had been named for a North Korean city attacked in 1950 by American forces under the command of General Douglas MacArthur. Added to the name, Yong-Ganhan, which in English meant brave.

"Son, we are not alone. Put your ears to it. You find him, and let me know the moment you do."

"Yes, sir," Sonar said.

"Do you completely understand?"

"Yes, sir."

"Like your life depends on it."

9

WASHINGTON, DC

SENATE HEARING ROOM S-116

THE NEXT MORNING

As U.S. Senate hearing rooms go, S-116 appears austere, but not regal. The real focal point is the obround-shaped table where each senator at the committee hearing sits at an assigned seat identified by a personalized engraved nameplate. But for everyday people entering, the eye naturally wanders around to the two 1872 marble mantels that support Rococo Revival mirrors decorated with an ornamental scroll, stylized leaves, and flowers. On the ceiling, there's a decorative painted banding dating back to the early 1900s. A bronze bust of Cordell Hull, America's longest-serving Secretary of State, looks over the Foreign Relations Committee from a central window well. It was hoped his wisdom of 11 years in Franklin Roosevelt's administration might somehow carry over to the proceedings.

The Senate Committee on Foreign Relations has a storied history dating back to 1816. It was one of the eleven original permanent standing committees in the Senate. It's been at the forefront of debate to develop and influence foreign policy. It considers and negotiates significant treaties and related legislation. It's helped shape America's foreign policy and made historic decisions in war and peace.

The Chair, a friendly face to the woman in the hot seat, gaveled the meeting to order. Senator Frasier R. Curtis's voice cut through the lingering chatter setting the tone for the hearings. Serious. He was like that. His term as a CFO of a major auto company and board member of several Fortune Five corporations provided Curtis with the experience to dig down into the details and sum up complex problems. But it was his years as a Boston University law professor that earned him the reputation as one of the great legal minds on Capitol Hill.

The Michigan Senator noted he had a quorum and continued. "In the interest of time and with respect to the Secretary of State's schedule, I'll reserve my right for comments for now and yield the microphone to the senator from Maine so we can get started. If there are no objections—"

Senate Minority Leader Billy Peyton wasted no time throwing a wrench into the proceedings. "I object, Mr. Chairman, and I will not yield my opening statement."

"Really, Mr. Peyton? In consideration of Paragraph 5(a) of Senate Rule XXVI, the two-hour meeting rule, and concerning the Secretary of State's time, I ask you to hold your thoughts until your time with the witness."

Peyton objected. Senator Curtis repeated his request, certain that the minority leader was just trying to rattle Matthews early. After another minute of sparring, the meeting moved forward with the chairman calling on Senator Melissa Bellanca to begin.

"Thank you, Mr. Chairman." The co-chair of the committee was a Navy veteran pilot with missions she couldn't talk about. If her colleagues assumed they were just routine flights because she was a woman, they'd be wrong. Very wrong. She served with 16 other pilots aboard the USS *Enterprise* and was *the* top gun among other top guns.

Cool and collected then as now, she was ever ready to "support and defend the Constitution of the United States against all enemies, foreign and domestic." Though she wasn't willing to consider the man sitting on the other side of Chairman Curtis as a domestic enemy, he certainly was a political one. She viewed the honorable Senator Billy Peyton less than honorable. He was already proving that true today.

Bellanca turned her attention to the witness. For her appearance, Secretary Matthews wore a conservative gray suit, and white silk blouse, set off by black freshwater pearls. On her jacket, a yellow and pink flower brooch. Like always, her pins gave something away. Sometimes her mood, sometimes the state of politics. Sometimes a coded message. Today it was an angel's trumpet, hanging upside down. The flower was originally native to South America but is now found around the world. Finding one doesn't mean it should be touched. It's extremely poisonous with deadly results.

No one in the room recognized the meaning of Matthews's pin. Someone watching on TV would undoubtedly figure it out with a little research. Then, within the hour, it would surely go viral. Matthews's watchers lived for it.

Behind the Secretary of State were her two advisors in international affairs: Under Secretary of State Micky Rucireta and Yibing Cheng.

Rucireta, 41, with a Ph.D. from Stanford in Russian history, was an encyclopedia of Russian leaders from the tsars up to Nicolai Gorshkov. Her hazel eyes never revealed what she was thinking or for that matter, telegraphed any foreign policy. She left that to Matthews unless they wanted to play any situation otherwise. She wore her sandy brown hair shoulder length, which perfectly framed her oval face that rarely cracked a smile in public, though friends knew she had a warm sense of humor. She favored warm tones in her Ann Taylor clothes and usually coordinated with Secretary Matthews when they stepped out together for the cameras.

Yibing Cheng was the China expert on Matthews's staff. She was steeped in oil and energy matters and fluent in Mandarin and Cantonese. That made her a particularly valuable State Department asset. Matthews had recently sent Cheng to Beijing where she aided Dan Reilly during an ill-fated oil conference at a Kensington Hotel. She also became Reilly's lover during the trip. No surprise. He took to her immediately. She was a natural beauty, Chinese-born, America-raised when she and her mother emigrated. The best of both worlds.

Before the hearing, Chairman Curtis told the Secretary that the first round would go smoothly. "Then gloves off. Peyton will drill down on you. I'll do my best to control him."

"Don't worry," Matthews had said. "He doesn't scare me."

"Maybe he doesn't. But beware of the people he empowers. They're even more dangerous than he is."

"Secretary Matthews, I'll begin with a question that gets to the heart of your appearance today," Senator Bellanca stated. "China has not hidden its intentions for expanding its influence in Central and South America, and the Caribbean. What is the State Department doing to monitor President Yichén Yáo? And what is his and China's goal?"

"Thank you, Chairman Curtis, Ranking Member Peyton, and all the members of the committee here today."

As the Secretary of State spoke, she glanced at each of the committee members. She wanted to look into everyone's eyes, to study them, to evaluate them. Those in the majority were focused on her. Some in the minority were pretending badly to read a document. Another senator was on her phone texting; others were giving her hard cold looks. Billy Peyton was turned around, whispering to his aide Seth Sullivan.

Got it, she thought. *I'll be preaching to the choir.*

"To the point of your question, China is using investments and aid to further its influence in all the areas you cited."

She addressed the committee without the benefit of notes, though she had documents at the ready.

"This poses a grave challenge to our diplomatic relations and our national defense. Taiwan's sovereignty and our support of Taiwan directly ties into that, which I'll address. But the bare facts are Central American countries—Panama, Nicaragua, and El Salvador—have switched diplomatic recognition from Taiwan to China. The same for the Dominican Republic in the Caribbean. They're swayed by China's money. They're willing because we have not stepped up to the plate."

Senator Peyton interrupted, making his ire abundantly clear. "Mr. Chairman!"

Curtis had been waiting for Peyton to disrupt the proceedings again. "Point of order. Opinion from the witness."

"Senator Peyton," Chairman Curtis calmly stated, "I think you'll have ample time to take that up with Secretary Matthews. Let's allow her to make her presentation."

Peyton sulked. Better acting than his colleagues pretending to read.

Matthews continued. "China's presence has grown since management of the Panama Canal transferred in 1999 from the joint U.S.–Panama Canal Commission to the Republic of Panama. Soon after, the Panamanian government signed with a Hong Kong–based company to operate ports on both the Atlantic and Pacific sides. Following that, Chinese companies have been heavily involved in Panama's electrical and manufacturing infrastructure. Now, China has more than 20 projects going including railways, power stations, and bridges.

"And there's more. Belize, Guatemala, and Honduras are now business partners with China."

Matthews cast her eyes on Peyton.

"Previously these countries turned to the United States. Previously we were there with support, critical support in vital areas. We put troops in those countries to protect our interests even when local governments resisted. Our interest was Caribbean and Central American exports, historically from the 1920s when the United States knew the nations as banana republics. That age lasted well into the 1960s and 1970s.

"Today, instead of us, it's the Chinese. And instead of just bananas, it's money and personnel to support infrastructure. Tomorrow it could be troops.

"The countries needed help, real help. When we stopped being that help, those countries believed they had no other choice than to talk to China. China was most willing. China is most willing, in the Western Hemisphere, just as they are throughout Africa.

"The list goes on. El Salvador signed up with China's global infrastructure plan called the Belt and Road Initiative, the BRI for short, to build overland and maritime shipping lanes.

"Costa Rica joined China's BRI. Then Jamaica. And for all of the deals they struck, they switched alliances from Taiwan to China. And of course, Panama, where Chinese corporations have ports on both the east and west coast of the canal. When I say corporations, make no mistake I'm talking about the Chinese government.

"But there's another nation in the playbook," Matthews said. "Cuba. When our own diplomatic and business relations were halted midstream during a thawing a few years back, China immediately came in to fill the void. Cuba inked a deal with the Belt and Road Initiative. More infrastructure dollars. More new roads. More equipment and supplies. More handshakes. And with handshakes came a Chinese intelligence collection center that targets the U.S."

She paused, but not long enough to prompt a new question.

"I'll restate that," Matthews said. "China has a fully functional spy facility 100 miles from Florida where we have key military command centers. They have the keys to Cuba. God only knows what's next."

This had been known for some time, but Matthews's delivery sent a chill down at least some of the members' spines. Those paying attention.

"To put it in perspective, Soviet Russia had a listening post in Lourdes, Cuba, for nearly five decades. So with the Russians out, it was only natural for China to step in since we walked away."

"Mr. Chairman!" Peyton shouted.

"Senator Peyton, the Secretary is citing the record. Check Google if you've forgotten."

Billy Peyton shook his head.

"And," Matthews said in an almost scolding elementary school-teacher's voice, "We could have prevented it."

She now had everyone's attention.

"Of course, this is only part of China's global plan. The rest includes Africa, Asia, and the Middle East. Maybe one day, Europe. Possibly Australia. China seeks to own the digital high ground. Cuba, the Central

American nations, they're all part of it. President Yáo intends to complete a global digital 5G grid including satellite, undersea cables, and the whole shebang to gain military and economic advantage…"

She paused and then stared directly at the unblinking C-SPAN camera.

"…over us."

Matthews took a sip of water from a metal blue, gold, and white State Department–branded water container. She kept the emblem facing out.

"For decades Central America suffered from slow to no economic growth. Hurricanes and tropical storms bore down and did their damage."

Matthews purposely didn't relate the disasters to the term "climate change." That would have certainly drawn a political outburst from one or more of the senators.

"The result of all the factors, the countries had greater need for investment help. To put a time stamp on this, it was during the COVID-19 pandemic, and Western investors had little interest in risking exposure in developing countries. But China was."

"How would you characterize China's expansion?" Senator Bellanca asked.

"Simply said, their aim is to defend and expand their interests, whether economic, diplomatic, or military."

"And their surveillance activities?"

"To hack into our top secret intelligence agencies," Matthews sharply replied. "To steal intellectual property secrets. To support the overall goals of the Chinese Communist Party."

"How does their aim and their surveillance come together?"

"I'm not sure I understand the question, senator."

"I'll rephrase. What do they want?"

"On one hand, the theft of intellectual property, exploiting America's open sources, and reaching through firewalls to discover what they can discover." She paused, adjusted her glasses, and continued. "As I said, to defend and expand their interests, whether economic, diplomatic, or military."

"And in your opinion, what can we do?"

"If you're asking if there is a catch-all fix, someone to press a key on the computer to counter the Chinese espionage efforts? That's a question for intelligence experts. But I'd say we must shore up private and government cyber networks as well as the FBI's efforts to uncover ongoing espionage operations. That, of course, relies on providing the FBI with needed resources, rather than cutting them off."

Matthews expected Billy Peyton's next disruption with her statement. The senator didn't disappoint. Predictably, Curtis's gavel came down once more, but Senator Bellanca's time was up, so it was a moot issue.

"Now the gentleman from Oklahoma can proceed," he said. "Let's keep decorum in mind."

"Thank you, Mr. Chairman. Always," Billy Peyton said, meaning rarely. "Madame Secretary," he continued sickly sweetly. "Thank you for your testimony today."

Peyton's insincerity was not lost on Matthews.

"Can you enlighten us? Does the Chinese government have listening devices in Washington at their embassy just blocks from here?"

"That's a question for the CIA Director."

"The question is to you and that it's not our fault they moved into Cuba."

"That would be your opinion, Senator" she declared.

Peyton, annoyed by her response, looked over his shoulder to Sullivan. Sullivan whispered in his ear. Peyton nodded and returned to the microphone.

"Please explain how the State Department sees Taiwan playing into this."

"Into China's data collection? What are you asking?"

"For god's sake. What's Taiwan got to do with this?"

"Senator Peyton, the nations I've cited have established diplomatic relationships with the People's Republic of China and ended ties with the

Republic of China. That weakens the overall global support of Taiwan."

Peyton chuckled. "I'm sorry I'm just a simple country lawyer. Would you mind explaining which China is which for me and anyone watching who needs a reminder?"

"The People's Republic of China is the Beijing government, Senator. The PRC. Communist China. Taiwan is The Republic of China. The countries I cited have switched allegiances from Taiwan to the People's Republic of China."

"To Communist China," Peyton repeated.

"Yes."

"And you're blaming our business?"

"I'm noting American foreign policy which impacts business decisions."

"I'm confused. As Secretary of State, aren't you in charge of all that?"

"Senator, if your desire is to find a scapegoat, I'm not it. A series of policy decisions by previous administrations, along with political pressure and a global pandemic contributed to the situation we are now in. Plus another factor: the economy.

"For example, thousands of people across Cuba, furious with the lack of food, basic sustainables, and vaccines to combat COVID-19, went to the streets in the biggest protests since Fidel Castro took over. Their anger went viral to the world over social media. What did Cuba do in a move to quash the protests? The government turned off the phones and internet services. And who built much of their current telecommunications infrastructure? China. All because—"

Peyton cut in. Matthews was controlling the moment that he wanted as his own. Sullivan tapped him on the shoulder, but Peyton waved him off. He needed to change the dynamic.

"Secretary Matthews, did you..." He shuffled through a few notes. "...no, can you confirm that you wrote the committee on April 30th of this year that we should do everything possible to conduct meaningful discussions with China on multiple subjects because—"

"Yes, I did."

"What kinds of meaningful discussions?" Peyton asked.

"Yet to be determined. We have special relationships building, and in my estimation, we have an opportunity to renew positive relations with the PRC, make meaningful new trade agreements, including some that give us renewed political leverage with our neighbors."

"And how do we suddenly have this opportunity, Madame Secretary? Why does luck and fortune shine upon *you* now?"

"There's no luck, Senator. It's hard work. We call it negotiation. We want something, they give a little. They want something, we give a little in return. Considering all their holdings in the U.S., China wants to see their investments pay off. We do a great deal of manufacturing in China. They don't want that to go away."

"You're forgetting about Russia, Madame Secretary."

"I'm not. But we have much more to talk with China about, and it's all related to money."

Peyton leaned into the microphone. "For what purpose?"

Matthews took a beat. She'd been waiting for this question.

"To tamp down dangers in the South China Sea. To buy time for Taiwan. To demonstrate that we understand and respect Chinese culture. To show President Yáo that he needs another friend other than Russia. To avoid war, senator."

Peyton hadn't expected such a sharp response. It was time to backpedal.

"And those special relationships as you noted in your memo?"

"Yes," Matthews said.

"Who are they?"

"I'm not at liberty to discuss names."

It was just one name: Dan Reilly.

"May I remind you that you are under oath?"

"Senator, I am not under oath. And as I believe you well know, most briefings, which this was intended as, do not require swearing-in. It would take a vote of the committee to change that."

Peyton fumbled his papers and broke eye contact, and Matthews chose her next words very carefully.

"But, Senator Peyton, I also believe you understand the importance of not publicly identifying back channel sources in open hearings. To do so could risk the very objectives we seek especially when they're at the intermediary level prior to formal talks."

"Who?" Peyton demanded.

"As I stated, I'm not at liberty to discuss that."

The decorum Chairman Curtis sought was gone. No amount of his gavel hammering stopped Peyton.

"So these are secret meetings."

"With all due respect, Senator Peyton, I will read my memo to the committee just as you did." She opened a folder that she'd slid to the top during Peyton's rant.

"The same words, so as not to mince them. Quote: 'We have the opportunity to conduct meaningful discussions with China on multiple subjects because of special relationships that we're developing.' The key word, senator, is 'developing.' If there are factors to be addressed by this committee, rest assured I will bring them forward."

"Madame Secretary," he continued without a fully formed question in mind.

"Yes."

Control...control...control, he calculated. *A speech would be better. Shut her up.* But Matthews beat him to it.

"Senator, I'll explain it this way. The United States tends to take the short-term view. Europe does the same. But China looks at politics not in terms of administrations, but centuries or millennia. The PRC wants Taiwan back, and they're willing to wait as long as it takes to get it. However, if we can kick that plan down the road, we actually might find another solution to maintain peace in the region and peace in the world. That's my priority. China is my priority, but that doesn't mean we aren't watching Russia carefully."

Unseen by the C-SPAN camera facing Matthews, Micky Rucireta lightly tapped her boss's shoulder, an atta girl. Yibing Cheng smiled.

They had briefed the Secretary, and she covered all of the talking points.

Peyton hadn't listened for anything other than the chance to jump back in before his time was up.

"Madame Secretary, I'll be completely honest."

He rarely was.

"I don't trust you talking to the Chinese. I don't trust your so-called unnamed secret relationships that you refuse to disclose. The time you're putting into making nice with China, Madame Secretary, is time you would be better served protecting the United States. Clearly you don't want to answer my questions. Clearly there is more you can share with this committee. And I get it. You're not going to do it. But I tell you here and now, you and the administration are looking in the wrong direction. You can send the right message, but you aren't. You're doing nothing but appeasing them and allowing now, not five years ago, not ten years ago, the Communists to take advantage of us."

Billy Peyton paused to take a breath. Matthews jumped in.

"Do you have a question, senator?"

"You bet I do!" he declared.

But he didn't. Just more ranting.

"This is what's going on. As my daddy used to say when I spun yarns like yours as a kid, 'That fits her like a sock on a rooster.' The president is ultimately going to give Taiwan to China. For what? Who knows? The administration is planning on selling out an ally to get a more favorable trade deal that will only embarrass us to the rest of the world; to weaken us in the eyes of our allies. All when you should be in Moscow tonight, tomorrow, the next day until you can work things out with President Gorshkov. That's where you should be, Madame Secretary."

He was winding up to his payoff.

"But no, you will sell us out in the hopes of your own spoils. And is that becoming Vice President of the United States?"

"Is that your question? You covered a good deal."

"Yes, it's my damned question!"

"No."

Peyton suddenly shot up from his seat.

"No, what?"

"No, I am not now, or ever will I ever sell out the interests of the United States."

Chairman Curtis's gavel came down.

Peyton ignored the chairman. Still standing and glaring at Matthews he demanded, "Madame Secretary, I insist you change your agenda and make Nicolai Gorshkov your priority over President Yáo. Focus on Russia, not the PRC. Let's keep in mind they are Communist China. Come back to this committee with those results."

"With all due respect, Senator—"

Peyton interrupted. "Oh, and when you do return, will it be your intention to answer the committee's questions as Secretary of State or Allphin's choice as Vice President?"

"If you're asking if I'm seeking another job?"

"I am."

"I'm not seeking another job."

"Is the president seeking it for you?"

The chairman hit the sound block so hard with his gavel, the gavel handle cracked. Before she answered, Curtis firmly stated, "The gentleman from Oklahoma's time is up."

Elizabeth Matthews took another sip of her water. She had 45 minutes to go. Most of the remaining back-and-forth she could manage and dodge. She felt the worst was over.

* * *

An hour later, outside the hearing room, the press gathered, waiting for Matthews. The Secretary of State wasn't in the mood for more grilling, but CNN's Paulette Lombardi's voice made her stop and turn.

"Secretary Matthews, based on your direct testimony, is it accurate to conclude that the United States is developing a new China strategy, stepping away from decisions made by the last two administrations while we still have serious problems in Russia?"

"Paulette, I can walk and chew gum at the same time. But the size, the strength, the economics, and China's ever-expanding global influence require us to make them our friend, not our enemy. Comparing the urgency of China and Russia, China is an international economic player in every sector and every continent. Russia is a regional gas station that has customers but not the influence." She added for impact, "Our enemy. Walking and chewing gum at the same time? This administration can do both."

10

THE WHITE HOUSE

"Walk and chew gum, Elizabeth? Really?" President Allphin joked the moment she walked into the Oval Office.

"Seemed like something easily understood."

The president's Chief of Staff Lou Simon laughed. "Very easily, but I suggest you don't go online for a while. The memes have already started. Pretty funny in fact."

"Hey, instead of campaign pins, maybe sticks of gum," Allphin joked.

"Like I said, the memes have started. Your face is already photo-shopped to a Wriggles wrapper."

"Wrigley's," she corrected.

"No, it was mocked up as Wriggles. Like in twisting and turning in a quick moment. Pretty clever, actually."

"Oh, Jesus," Matthews offered contritely. "Sorry, Mr. President."

"No worries. Have you seen what they've done with me?"

Matthews smiled. "As a matter of fact, I have. They never seem to capture the real you or—"

"I think we've spent enough time on memes for today."

"Yes, sir," Elizabeth Matthews said stifling a real laugh. She'd seen what was up on the internet. The caricatures of the president often emphasized Allphin's least attractive features including his ever-expanding waistline and penchant for colorful tie patterns rather than the standard solid red or blue ones in every president's rack.

"So, to the issues at hand." Allphin addressed his Chief of Staff.

Lou Simon had the agenda. He was a carryover from President Crowe's administration and a survivor of Ryan Battaglio's short term. He promised to serve out Allphin's remaining time. After that, it was off to a cable news channel, maybe to host, since he had come out of radio decades earlier.

"Number one, Battaglio," Simon stated. "He's ready to publish. He's got some people worried."

Battaglio, Ryan Battaglio, was the reason Sean Allphin was president. The American public, the world for that matter, was told Battaglio resigned because of ill health. Those who knew differently were Allphin, Matthews, and Simon, the president of China and his aide, and Dan Reilly, who was currently in Cairo.

Ryan Battaglio had been unceremoniously removed. He claimed that the police photographs and video evidence that brought him down had been faked. They hadn't been. They showed him with a young girl; a teenager, drugged, raped, and strangled in a seedy Macau hotel room.

Battaglio had sealed his fate in that hotel room. It just took 12 years for it to catch up with him.

"I thought we had more time," Matthews stated.

"So did I. We don't. No one knows what's in it. But I'm sure it's going to hurt us. You, me, our relationship with President Yáo. God knows who else."

"His lies, we have the truth."

"And how well are people doing these days with the truth on their side?"

Matthews thought back to the internet and its memes. She took a seat dead center on the couch. Allphin sat opposite her in a red barrel chair he had brought over from his Speaker of the House office.

"So he's finished his book?" Matthews asked.

"According to his Secret Service detail, it's about to be delivered."

"No advance word?"

"None."

"Can't the Secret Service get a copy out?"

"Private property, Elizabeth."

"Right—"

She kept the *but* to herself.

"Besides, Secret Service said he's kept the lid on it. Battaglio has it on one computer with no Wi-Fi. He and his ghostwriter work alone. She's been sequestered there the whole time and not able to take anything out. She's checked for thumb drives every night."

"Printed copies?" Matthews asked.

"No. He's going to deliver a drive to his publisher himself."

"Where?" Matthews asked.

"England."

"What about his ghostwriter when she leaves?"

"Battaglio has her tied up with a non-disclosure agreement."

"That Justice can't untie?"

"Elizabeth," the president said, "*they* don't do that."

He stopped and looked at Matthews. Sean Allphin was sending a message to the woman he wanted to nominate as his vice president. He had said *they*, rather than *we*, a calculated choice of words. He was giving her permission to talk to Battaglio's wordsmith.

"And there's another consideration," Simon added. "Justice."

In this case, Justice meant the Department of Justice. It was investigating a possible charge of collusion between Ryan Battaglio and Russia during the president's private meetings in Stockholm with President Nicolai Gorshkov. The investigation was completely under wraps beyond the people in the Oval Office, Attorney General Randy Kenton, his key assistant, and White House lawyer Gregory Payne.

Elizabeth Matthews had already given her deposition. It was damning, but should she become vice president, and then run for president, it could blow up in her face since she was on the same trip to Stockholm.

"Elizabeth," President Allphin said, "Young will be making a decision soon about assigning a special prosecutor. I'd like to get you through the Senate before then and by my side."

She took a deep breath. Besides walking and chewing gum, she might be dodging slings and arrows.

VIEQUES ISLAND, PUERTO RICO

Ryan Battaglio said goodnight and goodbye with a $58,333 check in his gloved hand, the third and final payment for Jillian Robbins. She had just finished ghostwriting, final editing, and proofing the former president's quickly written explosive memoir.

She combined her interviews with Battaglio, government documents she was permitted to review, and her research to construct a scenario that bore some resemblance to the truth and told a great many lies. To a degree, she was aware *what was what*, but she left her journalistic standards on the mainland and at her old desk at the *New York Times*. This was a work for hire. Her name wasn't on the cover. It had very little likelihood of making the best-selling list. At least in the nonfiction category.

The pay was good. One hundred seventy five thousand. Divided into three months of intense work, it amounted to $1,944.44 per day with no days off. Her best freelance assignment yet. Based on the NDA, she couldn't tell anyone about the job, but of course, there were always rumors surrounding the possible identity of political ghostwriters. Her agent might see to that, and that could lead to more work.

"Thank you, Mr. President," she said trying not to grab the envelope too quickly. "It's been an honor working with you." Jillian Robbins figured if the president lied, so could she.

"You do understand the terms of our agreement."

"Completely," she said.

"You know what will happen if you violate those terms."

"I do."

He held a sinister stare hoping never to see her again.

Robbins had been a Capitol Hill reporter for six years. Before that, she had covered Albany and the New York State Assembly, Senate, and two governors, one whose peccadillos cut his term short and the second who was serving the last year of sentence in Otisville, a minimum security prison that had housed athletes, models, lawyers, and billionaires, and now one governor. Given what she'd just gone through she wondered whether the former New Yorker's story might be worth writing. Then she dismissed the idea. No more scum.

"We will never meet again. We will never have another conversation," Battaglio said.

"Yes, Mr. President."

Wearing gloves, he passed the check to Robbins taking in her slender form one more time. He was divorced and hungered for the reporter. Robbins had read the signals and made certain she gave none back.

She was thirty-seven. Battaglio was sixty-two. She was desirable, and he was loathsome. Robbins had heard stories about him—from women aides on the Hill when he was a congressman and senator. Drunken binges. Foreign sex parties. If the talk was even half true, there'd be a real book to write.

Sadly this wasn't the one.

"Like the others, it's a third-party check. My fingerprints aren't even on it."

"You can trust me," the brunette said.

He ignored her comment. Instead, he added, "I've written a good book."

"Yes, you have, Mr. President."

"And we'll stay on that page."

"Yes, we will."

"Then it's been good working with you."

"Likewise, Mr. President."

She felt this was going on far too long. She was ready to leave.

"So where to next?" he asked.

"A few days on the beach at the Condado with an open bar tab," she said with a lilt in her voice.

Battaglio pictured her in a bikini. So did a man listening to the conversation through a wireless voice-actuated microphone hidden in Battaglio's door frame. It was one of ten, strategically placed around the ex-president's Caribbean retreat, and every spoken word between the former president and his ghostwriter had been recorded. Every story that was going into his book. Every invention that could make Ryan Battaglio look good at the expense of others... very significant others.

11

THE KREMLIN

MOSCOW, RUSSIAN FEDERATION

Nicolai Gorshkov monitored the incoming reports. He was not one to show emotion, but Sergei Bortnik was certain he read amusement on the president's face. Gorshkov's operations were moving forward better than he expected.

A North Korean submarine with a ballistic missile onboard was sailing further than ever before. A private airplane was about to embark on an uncharted course. A kidnapping was taking shape. In time, internet bots would flood social media with rants and rumors that would drive the American stock market down. Depressed prices would spike oil prices. And there'd be a shakeup in the next U.S. presidential campaign.

Discontent, disarray, disunity. Nicolai Gorshkov thought it was better than sex.

"Mr. President, you've brilliantly stretched the West to the limit."

General Sergei Bortnik had mastered the art of giving the president precisely what he wanted to hear. He'd learned that from the mistakes of his predecessors.

"America's military structure can't manage multiple threats. They're slow to evaluate and coordinate in rising crises. Their command structure is hapless under this new administration. It takes weeks to months to mobilize across the globe. They are a paper tiger. A mere kitten with no teeth."

This wasn't exactly what Bortnik believed, but it kept him close to Gorshkov for when the time was right to move against him.

The general was one of Gorshkov's smiling acolytes who secretly conspired against the president and waited. They waited to see if he possibly suffered from early-stage Parkinson's, if he was slowly dying of cancer, and if any rumored diagnosis were true. None were. Bortnik believed that Gorshkov himself spread the rumors to flush out rivals.

No, Bortnik reasoned. Poor health wasn't going to bring Gorshkov down. Remaining on the inside, remaining alive, and waiting for opportunity was the only way. And now he wanted to hear more details of Gorshkov's grand scheme.

"Mr. President, there's the issue of the former American president, Battaglio." He pronounced it Batt-gilio. "His book."

Gorshkov raised a bushy eyebrow. "I wouldn't worry about him."

The answer shut the door on any follow-up. But it also told General Bortnik that something was in the works.

"Of course," he said cautiously. "However, if there's anything I can do—"

"Thank you, but no. You're handling enough as it is. Thank you."

The *thank you* was for the most immediate information. A plane was in Puerto Rico ready to transport a VIP. The *enough* was because Bortnik was Gorshkov's go-between with a number of oligarchs including one who was a silent partner in a Canadian private jet leasing company.

Gorshkov continued, "Just stay focused, my friend, and everything will be under control."

Control in Nicolai Gorshkov's world included a basic rule of physics: gravity, the force that attracts a body in motion downward toward the center of the earth.

Gravity in Russia today had more immediate meaning: the force that tended to deliver someone unpopular to the regime from a high open window to the ground. And whether it was a dissident journalist who hadn't taken a first hint, an oil oligarch outwardly critical of the president, a government official breaking with the party line, or even a military general who knows too much, Nicolai Gorshkov would nudge gravity along.

Often people would get sick and be rushed to a hospital to recover. But in the Russian Federation, illnesses had a habit of taking a bad turn right toward a window. Accidents. The state news agencies routinely reported, "He died from injuries sustained from a suicidal act...She had a heart condition and was apparently on antidepressants...He slipped and fell....His death came as a shock."

General Bortnik understood the real shock to be the sudden stop. Amazingly, CCTV cameras always seemed to be off-line and under repair on the floors where the last 20 "accidents" had occurred.

Bortnik didn't especially like heights. As an Army general, he was all about ground forces. He would have to take great care not to meet the ground in a way others had.

"Good to hear," he said, vowing to do more to reinforce his loyalty. That was the way to remain trusted. The way to stay alive.

SAN JUAN, PUERTO RICO

Jillian Robbins was relieved to be done with the former president. She had come to the job as his ghostwriter full of enthusiasm for a great opportunity; an inside job that would open important doors for her. Instead, she signed an NDA and listened to Ryan Battaglio spin story after story that she viewed from her research as invention: Meetings he trumpeted where the record was in opposition. Political figures he belittled whom Robbins admired. Legislative achievements he took credit for that weren't his. His assertion that a close relationship with Nicolai Gorshkov had avoided war when all he did was help the Russian president attempt to redraw the map of Europe.

Robbins was a journalist, but now she felt like a hack. She had read letters and papers before going to Puerto Rico that told a different story. The more interesting story. The truth. But that didn't make the pages she had written for the ex-president. Maybe someday she could leak what she discovered surreptitiously to friends at the *Times* or better yet, *Reuters*. Less likely to point back to her.

The more she thought about it, she'd have cover. Battaglio would surely look elsewhere. He'd blame and deny. Blame the White House, his political enemies, and the Justice Department. Deny the claims that countered his version of the record. He might get away with it, but he'd kill his book sales. That alone would help cleanse Robbins from the swamp she had plodded through and the uncomfortable advances she dodged from the ex-president.

But now it was the warm Atlantic that was going to wash away her forced smiles, the praise she heaped upon Ryan Battaglio and the fiction she wrote.

Jillian Robbins had checked into the San Juan Marriott Resort the night before. She rose early, showered, threw on a one-piece bathing suit, and readied herself to lay a towel on the sand and run headlong into the 87-degree water. It was time to feel refreshed, rejuvenated, and restored.

She was just about out her door when she doubled back to write two texts. One to her agent.

FINI, DONE, SEE YOU IN 2 DAYS

The second to a friend in DC.

WE SHOULD TALK. JESSIE

Nothing special. Nothing revealing. And definitely nothing long. Jillian Robbins had a date with the Caribbean that she was intent on keeping.

She was a good swimmer. A smart swimmer. She ventured out to what she estimated to be 100 yards, and swam parallel to the shore; first 200 yards west, then she reversed direction, passing her hotel and going toward Numero Uno Beach. Robbins alternated strokes. The Australian crawl, the side stroke, and backstroke, never over-exerting herself and always making sure she was clear of surfers.

It was a perfect morning in San Juan. Ryan Battaglio seemed much further away than the 50 miles that separated Puerto Rico's Condado from Vieques Island. She swam without a care in the world, leaving Battaglio and all her anxieties behind.

After a thoroughly exhilarating 40 minutes, Robbins turned back toward the hotel. She had the Marriott in sight when she felt a slight tickle on her left foot. She laughed to herself thinking she had attracted a butterfly fish or a queen angelfish that were typical in the local waters.

Another brush at her ankles, then another on her thigh. Robbins stopped, tread water, and looked down expecting to see a cluster of green, yellow, or striped fish.

Nothing in front or to the sides. But behind, something sharp dug into her calf. Her eyes bulged. She gasped and cried out.

* * *

Young honeymooners strolling hand-in-hand at the water's edge heard a scream. They looked seaward just as a swimmer, with hands shooting straight up, dipped below the surface.

Three seconds. Four, five. Then the swimmer popped back up, flailing, yelling for help, and at what looked like double speed, dragged through the water. First one direction, then another.

The man pointed and instinctively yelled, "Shark!" His companion did the same. But no one else was on the beach to hear.

"Go to the hotel!" he ordered. "Get help!"

The woman ran right across an abandoned towel on the beach while the man looked for a boat to launch. None were around and diving in was out of the question.

He watched in horror as the swimmer was pulled down. She emerged three more times until she didn't.

THE KREMLIN

Sergei Bortnik was ready to leave. Nicolai Gorshkov was not ready to dismiss him. While Gorshkov finished a phone call, the general wished he had taken any of the dozens of opportunities in the past few years to leave Russia. Not to lead a coup, not to officially defect, just to pull his off-shore savings together and retire to some palatial estate on a remote island. Instead, he remained, adding to his accumulated wealth, and biding his time.

If ever suspected as a traitor, Bortnik feared he wouldn't be able to endure torture. He'd give up the names of everyone in his circle who worked in the military, government, and business. Even if he was never suspected, someday, someone else might name him.

Maybe Gorshkov would make him watch as his men did unspeakable things to his wife. Maybe he'd kidnap their daughter out of Oxford and bring her back.

Sergei Bortnik straightened his uniform, stood tall, and waited to be dismissed.

"Sergei, you're always in a rush to leave. Stay. Valery's on his way. We can have a drink and toast to great years ahead."

Years. Bortnik wondered if he'd last years.

"My dear general," Gorshkov said as he poured two glasses of domestic vodka, "no one understands how lonely this job is. I've spent my whole life working for the state. First, as a young KGB recruit serving in Germany, betrayed by the Kremlin which gave up on the Soviet dream. A dream that for decades, good men and women had given their lives for. Their dream, the dream you and I share that Russia would become the greatest power the world had ever known."

Bortnik had heard this speech, this rant, dozens of times. But he dutifully listened as if it was the first time.

"Unfortunately, feckless leaders betrayed us. I fought my way to the top of the Russian Federation to restore the promise of all that had been lost. And now, whether we rebuild through the domination of Ukraine, our plans for the Baltic States, and beyond, we *will* take what is rightfully ours. And now we have Chinese money to fund us. Soon we will have Europe's breadbasket feeding us."

"Of course," Bortnik said as he wondered whether Gorshkov really might be sick, or at the least, losing his grip on reality. *Does he know how often he repeats himself?*

"The West is weak, Sergei. We shall see the collapse of the American democracy and its European collaborators. Not all at once, but they will crumble from the inside out. All that you've done for Mother Russia has gotten us closer."

"Thank you, Mr. President."

"Now I have one other thing for today."

Bortnik said, "Of course," hoping he showed the proper degree of enthusiasm.

"I'm looking for your opinion. Is there anyone you consider unfaithful to our cause? To me?"

The question shook Bortnik. An answer *no* might show a lack of concern for the president's well-being. His failure to notice on his part. A lack of awareness to spot a threat. A *yes* would require identifying conspirators or making some up.

Instead, he took a middle ground. "Yes, businessmen who showed their disloyalty by running away with their cash. Spineless capitalists."

"I know, but specific people?"

"I'm always watching," Bortnik replied.

Gorshkov nodded, then asked a very pointed question. "What about Valery Rotenberg? Tell me what you think of him."

"I'm not sure I know what you mean."

"Just what I asked. What is your opinion of our illustrious spy chief?" Gorshkov kept his eyes on Bortnik. "Is he loyal to me?"

"Mr. President——." The general spoke carefully, measuring his words. Gorshkov was notorious for pitting one party against another. There were never any winners in this game other than the president himself.

"I have no reason to question his loyalty to the Russian Federation."

"That wasn't my question. Is he loyal to me?"

Bortnik declared, "Sir, I believe Director Rotenberg is loyal beyond reproach."

Gorshkov held his gaze for ten long seconds and then smiled.

"Well, thank you, Sergei. That's all."

Sergei Bortnik left wondering whether Gorshkov would ask

Rotenberg the same thing about him. He worried if Rotenberg suspected or knew anything? And even if he didn't, would the FSB head make him a scapegoat to further his own gain? And, on his exit, Bortnik asked himself if his wife had discovered his peccadillos and reported them to Gorshkov.

No, that wouldn't matter to Gorshkov. The president led by example. Everyone at the top had their mistresses.

What the decorated Russian general didn't know was that his mistress did have someone to report to. She'd been doing it for the past 14 months. The information she had been gathering from whispers in her bedroom resounded in the ears of her superiors far away—expedient for developing strategy, and so valuable for bargaining.

SAN JUAN, PUERTO RICO

Jillian Robbins was dead, but she hadn't been bitten by any shark. Not yet.

Before she died she may have seen what had actually occurred. A swimmer in a wet suit and scuba outfit had clamped onto her. At first, she only felt slight tickling, then more. Fight or flight instincts kicked in, but after a long swim, Robbins had little energy for either. With too much water in her lungs and not enough energy to break away, she went down, looking every bit like a shark victim.

Now ten feet below the surface, Robbins was carried out with sharp kicks into deeper water. There, her killer took a blade and sliced her leg and her abdomen. Sharks as far away as a quarter mile would smell her blood and converge. Maybe rescue boats would find her remains. There'd be a sad story to report about a former *New York Times* reporter who had been the victim of a rare shark attack off the northern coast of San Juan, Puerto Rico. People would say the woman had tragically ventured out too far, a warning to others to take care. Surfers and water sports enthusiasts would avoid going in for days.

Twenty minutes later, after jettisoning the wet suit and breathing apparatus, a blonde beauty in a bikini that left nothing to the imagination, emerged from the water onto the beach at the Caribe Hilton Hotel. She casually took a seat at a table adjacent to the pool and ordered a piña colada, reputedly created at the hotel in 1954 by bartender "Monchito" Marrero. Parisa Dhafari didn't know that fact, but when the drink came she knew she'd never had one better.

12

THE SAME TIME

The Kensington Royal Star of the Nile was officially at RED HOTEL status. That meant it was a hardened target, hopefully less attractive to insurgents because it would be that much harder to take. A bomb-laden truck couldn't get past the bollards. Suspicious deliveries were turned away. But fortified didn't mean the hotel was impregnable, and with both organized and disorganized factions laying claim to territory, armed with heavy weapons, Reilly was justifiably worried. Worried more by the hour.

Two years earlier, Reilly had developed a four-color system for the entire Kensington International Hotel chain. He remembered the stunned face of his boss and upper management when he pitched his proposal. He argued that hotels were soft targets; perhaps among the softest, and they immediately needed to do something about it.

* * *

"Our properties are meant to be welcoming and friendly," Reilly had explained. "That's nice for anyone coming to our web pages. But it's also an open invitation to bad guys looking for easy access," Reilly had told the company CEO and senior management. "We're like other open places where people assemble—airports, trains, restaurants, and night-clubs. All soft targets unless made otherwise. And the truth, more often than not, is that terrorists identify targets where satellite news coverage can quickly pump out live video to heighten impact. They want control of the news cycle. They want to cash in on the exposure. As we know, hotels in major tourist locations provide just that. American hotels in particular. Our hotels. We're in the hospitality business. But we're also in the anti-terrorism business.

"As international and domestic hoteliers we have to understand the steps terrorists take when selecting a target. The smart ones plan stra-tegically. They train and stage off-sight, they infiltrate, and they attack. The stupid ones just attack. We have to be prepared for both.

"For both groups, selecting an objective comes with a shared goal. Will it cause maximum physical damage and loss of life? Will it get the attention they seek? Will they determine it a success?

"Another key part to their preparation," Reilly had continued to explain, "at least the smart terrorist, is surveillance. They'll check out a location inside and out. They'll take photos, identify where closed-circuit cameras are, and calculate their field of view. They'll scope out hotels to see if there are retractable bollards or cement barriers, metal detectors, or dogs. They'll create a target folder based on their field intelligence and select a primary target out of alternatives. Our job, even though we're not law enforcement, is to disrupt and deny. Make our property, their target, unattractive."

At the meeting, Reilly laid out four tiered color-coded systems. BLUE to YELLOW, then ORANGE, and finally RED. RED triggered the most tightened on-site security. It included all of the preliminary protections, staff posted in all public areas, American flags removed, bollards at the entrance; metal detectors at the entrance with bomb-sniffing dogs on rotation; proof of residency required for admittance into elevators; removal of waste receptacles; public access denied to the roof, engineering, the heating plant, and all nonpublic floors; hourly inspection of the public restrooms; and thorough check of delivery trucks and packages. And whenever there was a threat, the Crisis Committee would assemble at Kensington Royal headquarters in Chicago.

* * *

Thinking back on that day Reilly remembered the most important question that came from his presentation. It was voiced by the Founder and CEO, EJ Shaw. "Are you positive all of this will be necessary?"

Dan Reilly answered without hesitating. "Yes."

Current events in Cairo were proving him right again.

13

Friday finally came and the intelligence reports reaching the White House sounded worse than the day before, and the day before that. It had been that way since President Allphin raised his right hand and repeated the Oath of Office, and Allphin knew that global threats never took a weekend off.

The accounts were vivid and disturbing, jumping out at him like action scenes in a Tom Cruise movie. However, these didn't have any promise of being neatly wrapped up after two hours and five minutes.

First in Egypt.

"Infrastructure is collapsing," National Security Advisor Ali offered. "It's safe to predict a total government collapse in a matter of days, maybe sooner."

"What about our people?"

"Clearing out. All but essential members of the embassy have been evacuated. But the ambassador is holding forth."

"I want him out."

"So do we. But the ambassador says he wants to be the guy who locks the door behind him."

"We've got Marines for that," Allphin countered. "God love him, but you named the stubborn bugger to the job."

They laughed.

"I want hourly reports," Allphin said

"Yes, Mr. President."

"All right, next?"

Next was disturbing, a Russian provocation in the Bering Strait. As the president read, he mouthed a very familiar four-letter expletive. It was a word the National Security Council members had already used when they prepared the account.

Twenty-two miles off the coast of Dutch Harbor, Alaska—America's top fishing port by volume—the Russian nuclear submarine *Omsk* had surfaced a mere 30 yards away from a fishing trawler. The wash from the rising sub nearly swamped the boat. The sub and trawler were both in international waters, though the Russian sub captain was pushing the point so close to the Aleutian Island port.

The account noted that Captain Ted Romberg of the *Go Big and Go Large* ran to the cabin to radio for help. He tuned his transceiver to VHF channel 16, 156.8 MHz, the emergency frequency monitored by the United States Coast Guard. That's when his boat nearly capsized with the fury created by missiles screaming out of nowhere just off the deck. Seconds later he heard huge explosions. It wasn't until he used binoculars that he saw what was left of a group of barges some three miles away.

"Sir, we've reached out to Moscow. The Kremlin explained they had conducted military exercises in international waters."

"Sure it was," Allphin replied sarcastically. "Right off our shore. A test of the ship captain's nerves."

He read further. Two fishermen were blown overboard. Fortunately, they were rescued before they went under in 50-degree water.

"Goddamned lucky they survived to tell the story."

"It was intentional, Mr. President," the National Security Advisor concluded. "The Russians wanted eyewitnesses. It was timed. The sub breaching, the missiles, the maneuvers. You know, like a tree falling in the woods. They wanted you to know."

This time, Allphin said it aloud and loudly. "Fuck!"

He hit the next tab, a report from the Black Sea where there had been Russian flyovers earlier in the week. There, the USS *Arleigh Burke* was cruising at 22 knots through the Black Sea after routine passage through the Bosphorus when a pair of Russian SU-24 fighter jets buzzed the destroyer's deck. Over the next 15 minutes, the planes made eight more passes, each increasingly lower. The last, clipping the ship's antenna array. A ninth pass would have earned retaliation from Captain Mike Brown, with approval by 6th Fleet command.

"Is Gorshkov crazy?" the president shouted.

The question didn't require an answer. But there was more.

A USAF Boeing P-8A Poseidon aircraft was on surveillance patrol between Malta and Libya when it was intercepted by a pair of Russian SU-35 fighter jets. The Russians crossed directly in the flight path of the Poseidon. In a quickly executed countermove the Poseidon nosed down, throwing two crew members into their consoles. One died instantly from head trauma.

And more occurred overnight.

Seven vessels from Russia's Northern and Baltic Fleets converged in the waters off Finland, Gorshkov's reminder for NATO to think twice about the risks of engagement.

Eighteen miles offshore were the RFS *Olenegorskiy Gornyak*, RFS *Georgiy Pobedonosets,* the landing ship RFS *Pyotr Morgunov*, and landing ship tanks RFS *Minsk*, RFS *Kaliningrad*, and RFS *Korolev.*

NATO nation ships from the France, Belgium, Denmark, and the Netherlands monitored their passage. Beneath them, America's Los Angeles–class nuclear submarine, USS *Chicago.*

Allphin put the tablet down on his desk. "Anyone have a theory?"

"It's a lot even for Gorshkov."

Secretary of State Elizabeth Matthews spoke first.

"Rising stakes. Intimidation. He wants to see *how* you'll respond. *If* you'll respond."

* * *

The distance between Finland and Russia is the size of a thumb on a global map. Across the Baltic, a straight shot between Helsinki and St. Petersburg is merely 188 miles. Further north, the two countries share a land border spanning 832 miles. The nearest Russian Air Force base is less than an hour's flying time to Finland.

Since the attack on Ukraine, Russian press had whipped up concern at home that the enemy was just a breath away. Lies to gin up fear.

Gorshkov had turned fear and hate into an art form. For the present, Gorshkov's latest moves and maneuvers were used to unify his support at home and divide his enemies. In his long game, he hit the West in their pocketbooks. Their countermoves and maneuvers cost money and political capital. And heated debate in the halls of the U.S. Congress, echoed in America's polarized news world, empowered Gorshkov to take more chances. But these were minor flea bites compared to the bigger stings to follow.

* * *

"Let's get Gorshkov on the phone," President Allphin said. "Time to talk. Depending on what happens, Secretary Matthews can use her *Meet the Press* appearance to tickle the tiger. Make that the bear."

14

THE OVAL OFFICE

Sean Allphin had met Nicolai Gorshkov twice before; both times as Speaker of the House with no administration agenda. Today would be different, his phone call would be as president of the United States.

Gorshkov had complete command of English, and National Security Advisor Dr. Ali, through his channels, had been told that the Russian president would not require a translator. "He undoubtedly wants to be able to rebut your arguments quickly and in real time. No waiting."

"Lucky me," Allphin said as they waited for the connection.

A minute later, the two presidents and their staffs were introducing one another.

In the Oval Office, Ali, Secretary of State Matthews, Chairman of the Joint Chiefs Admiral Rhett Grimm, and Chief of Staff Lou Simon.

Surrounding Gorshkov at his conference were his chief aides and advisors including FSB Director General Valery Rotenberg, General Sergei Bortnik, Moscow Mayor Boris Rykov, and two generals and three admirals who had coordinated the provocations in the world's oceans. They remained unintroduced and silent.

Allphin began tepidly. "Mr. President, thank you for joining me on a call today..." He ignored the warm and fuzzy preliminaries with the traditional good wishes for family, health, and happiness. Better to get right to the point. "…and conducting our conversation in English, though I will understand if your advisors need time to consult with you."

"Mr. President. What is the point of this call?" Gorshkov said dismissively. This was the Russian's attempt to put Allphin off balance. "It is late here, and it has been a busy day."

"Mr. President, the point is," Allphin said without hesitating, "your aggressive actions against the United States, in the Pacific Ocean, the Aleutian, Mediterranean, and Baltic Seas. One American serviceman has died because of the reckless actions of Russian Federation fliers. Two fishermen were nearly lost at sea when one of your subs suddenly surfaced. It was all coordinated, undoubtedly planned to test our resolve."

Gorshkov said nothing. Allphin continued.

"Rest assured, if you think we are unwilling to respond to your blatant actions, you are mistaken. Moreover, if you think so little of NATO's unity, think again. That is the point of my call, Mr. President."

THE WHITE HOUSE PRESS ROOM

THE SAME TIME

Hands shot up. Doreen Gluckin, the White House's newly named press secretary, scanned the assembled reporters and called on Reuters's reporter, Deborah Noy.

Noy stood with her iPhone in hand to record the answer. The pool cameras also focused on her as she asked, "Doreen, does the president have any plans to visit Finland in light of the Russian exercises on the border and his not-so-veiled threats today against, well, much of the world?"

Gluckin gave a slight nod. She'd expected the question and didn't have to consult her briefing notebook. She also knew the Reuters reporter. Fifteen years ago they had been roommates at Yale, debating partners, and in each other's wedding parties. Now they were on opposite sides of a historic boundary, a member of the press facing the White House spokesperson, live on television where friendship didn't count, but definitive answers, often in short supply, did.

Gluckin stood ready. Her long black shoulder-length hair, parted in the middle, framed her face. She spoke with deliberation.

"The president has no current travel plans to the region, Deborah. But the White House is monitoring the situation. As for the rest of President Gorshkov's actions," the word was deliberate and approved by Allphin, "we are addressing every element with the Joint Chiefs, our allies, and representatives of Finland."

The press secretary was prepared to move on. Noy wasn't.

"Excuse me, Doreen, but we've heard that Finland's President Vanhanen has requested a renewed aid package from the United States. She was very specific in her press conference. Munitions, missiles, and intelligence. Finland shares a long border with Russia, and Gorshkov doesn't seem deterred by the fact that he would have more than a Finland problem if someone makes even an unintended move. It would be a NATO problem. That makes it a United States problem."

"Is there a question in there about NATO, Deborah?" Press Secretary Gluckin asked.

"Yes, there is. What would it take to invoke NATO Article Five?"

"I thought that might be it."

The press corps laughed.

"Of course, we're talking with our NATO allies, and we are deep in discussions with Finland's President Vanhanen. As for Article Five, it speaks for itself. I don't need to comment."

Article Five states that any attack on one NATO member country will be viewed as an attack on all NATO nations. That would directly put the United States in a war with Russia, which was not the case with Russia's invasion of Ukraine, a non-NATO member.

"Are we close to that tipping point?" Noy asked.

"Countries play war games all the time. Sometimes they get out of hand. We're watching Russia's moves just as they watch ours. But the moment we think it's not a game, the rules will change."

Hands shot up.

THE OVAL OFFICE

"What I think, Mr. President, is that the United States has no regard for the Russian Federation's territorial integrity," Gorshkov countered. "NATO is encroaching on our borders. You think you own the land? Why are we to believe you also don't think you own the seas? The Russian Federation is shipping oil to the four corners of the earth. Your actions in Europe, your sanctions against us, are the threat."

National Security Advisor Ali quickly scribbled a note for President Allphin. He read it and nodded.

"Mr. Gorshkov, we have both gotten our accusations out like old Cold Warriors. Where is your interest in maintaining peace? If you don't want sanctions, then withdraw from Ukraine. Stop meddling in Latvia, Lithuania, and Estonia. Your attempts for regime change in Turkey that will lead to their departure from NATO won't be successful."

Allphin was new to the job, but not new to political discourse. He intentionally tossed a grenade into the conversation.

"A bit of advice, Mr. President. Do not underestimate the resolve of the American people. Do not read political division in the press as a lack of American unity when it comes to our defense. And on a personal level, do not underestimate me."

WHITE HOUSE PRESS ROOM

Now NPR's Stan Deutsch shot up and spoke over the crowd.

"Doreen, is the administration expecting any surprise revelations from President Battaglio's forthcoming book? He was, after all, involved in controversial conversations with President Gorshkov over Ukraine and Latvia. Any comment from the Oval Office?"

Press Secretary Gluckin knew an answer to this question would take some careful wording. She had it.

"Stan, we have no knowledge of the contents, and President Allphin has not spoken to the former president about his autobiography or anything since his departure. Like you, we have heard it's been in the works. Beyond that, I can't help you."

"Yes," Deutsch continued, "but President Battaglio has been posting on his social media accounts that he is not through with politics and he has more to tell about his presidency. He described them as revelations. Does the White House have any indication what he means?"

"I have no idea, Stan."

"I meant the greater White House," he countered. "President Allphin?"

Gluckin took one step toward the podium. Forward signaled control. A step backward could have telegraphed hesitation.

"President Battaglio is as free to write his own narrative as you and I," Gluckin said. "We, I'll emphasize *we*, do not know what that is. But," she offered lightly, "be sure to let us know if he sends you an extra advance copy. I don't think we'll be getting one here."

THE OVAL OFFICE

"Mr. President," Gorshkov replied, "the one thing I will promise you is that the Russian people will not be steamrolled by the United States or any country. We are a global power. Threaten us in one region, you threaten us in all. You might say we've learned from your NATO policy. We have done nothing wrong. You, on the other hand, have made the good people of Russia suspect of your intentions. We will not be bullied by you or your political partners over borders or business. We know our fundamental rights. We will protect them at all costs. If you want to invoke the Cold War, then so be it. I, for one, admired Russia's strength in those days. Don't make the mistake that we are anything less today. We are not. We are more."

The response was typical Gorshkov bluster. Omit, mislead, deny, obfuscate, attack, and deflect. Allphin knew Gorshkov had a hundred ways to lie and no path to the truth. So what was the purpose of the call? To make the Russian president question whether the lack of America's response from his coordinated war games suggested the U.S. would do nothing. Tough talk was just talk. But Sean Allphin's call also demonstrated that he definitely was not Ryan Battaglio.

President Allphin waited a moment before speaking. He wanted his last comment, certain to end the conversation, to be unmistakably clear.

"Mr. President, I understand growing up you enjoyed old American westerns. John Wayne, Randolph Scott, Gary Cooper."

"Yes, I did. Clint Eastwood as well."

"Then I'm sure you'll understand the reference. Don't overplay your hand. Don't think you're the fastest draw in town. And make no mistake, there's a new sheriff in town."

THE WHITE HOUSE PRESS ROOM

"Next question?"

Dozens of hands shot up. Even more called out. Gluckin heard a cacophony of questions, reporters calling out names and places: Finland, NATO, Secretary of State Matthews, Taiwan, and Panama. She picked NBC's new White House correspondent, Norm Strassner.

"Doreen, we can all agree there's no end to the challenges President Allphin is facing. There's one area we haven't yet talked about today."

"I imagine you're going to raise it," Gluckin replied.

"As a matter of fact, yes. Egypt."

15

CAIRO, EGYPT

Options. Reilly needed options.

Reilly and the Kensington Royal Star of the Nile general manager Abdul Bashari searched through the bowels of the building for possible hiding places. No place seemed to offer protection, though one area in particular made him think. He'd have to talk to the company's head of security, Alan Cannon, about the possibility. With time they could test it. But time was not on his side. They needed help now.

Reilly phoned a private cell phone number. It belonged to Ali Abdul Aziz, the Minister of Interior, the man he was supposed to have dinner with this evening at the Gezira Sporting Club, Egypt's largest multi-sport facility, now a makeshift hospital.

Reilly began respectfully, as is the custom in Middle East greetings. "Mr. Minister, *As-salaam 'alaykum*. I trust your family is well."

"For now, yes. But times are difficult. *Wa-Alaikum-Salaam*. And yours?"

"I'll need time off to start one," Reilly joked. Then he thought Yibing Cheng might just be the right person to make that happen. But she was miles away, and marriage and family might only come in another lifetime.

"I wish you great happiness when you can find it," Aziz stated still keeping the banter light. Then he lowered his voice. "But you'd do better to seek it in your own country."

At that moment Reilly heard a tremendous explosion over the phone line. Aziz swore loudly in Arabic. The explosion occurred near Aziz's compound. Reilly wondered if Aziz's state police authority was making him a target.

Two seconds later the sound wave from the explosion traveled the 2 km to the Kensington.

"Ali, circumstances dictate that we reschedule."

"I had the same request, my friend. Another time."

"Absolutely, but we need help. They're coming closer."

Aziz said nothing. Reilly continued.

"I have 135 guests and more than 50 employees here, along with American TV news crews shooting reports from the roof. Our security is unarmed. I need to get our guests to the airport, and we can't make it there without escorts. I was lucky I made it in."

"For now, the airport is impossible, my friend."

"Then are you able to divert any forces here? Our bollards can stop a vehicle rushing the building, but not an undisciplined mob that hates Americans."

"I'll see what I can do. But we're limited. You saw that yourself. Maybe I can release a gunboat and meet you at the docks."

"Not me. My people!"

"I'm sorry—"

Suddenly the phone line went dead. Two seconds later, Reilly heard why. The Minister's compound had been hit or the cell tower near it. Whatever happened, Dan Reilly, and everyone in his charge, were on their own.

More gunshots. Another explosion. Fifteen minutes later Reilly assembled everyone in the lobby. He hopped atop a table and invited people to close in tight. Bashari joined him, he'd translate in Arabic and French.

Reilly looked around the room ready to speak when a nearby blast, from a few blocks away, nearly knocked the two men off the table. The chandeliers rattled, paintings and tapestries fell off the walls. People screamed and ducked.

Reilly climbed back up. "It's all right. Not a direct hit, but close."

An understatement.

Shakir Affir, bandaged and back on his feet, went to a window on the north side of the ballroom. He pushed the heavy gold curtains apart. What had been a neighboring 16-story classic hotel was reduced to three smoldering floors.

Affir screamed. "The Queen Nefertiti!" He glanced back at the group. "It's gone."

Suddenly, automatic gunshots filled the air. Affir described what he saw: Two dozen armed insurgents running toward the rubble. Then a leader pointing toward—

"They're coming here!"

Reilly shouted, "Listen everyone!" The GM immediately translated. "Everyone down to the loading dock and out the back! Get clear of the property fast!"

People started to move, then there was a rumble. Not from explosions, but from the crowd. Some stopped. Word was going from person to person.

Reilly, still on the tabletop, blared, "Now!" He leaped off, and ran out toward the lobby while yelling to the general manager, "Get them out, Abdul!"

23 YEARS EARLIER

BOSTON, MA

"This way!"

That was what Dan Reilly, Dan Reilly a Pinkerton Security Officer, exclaimed when the fire alarm sounded in the Boston Prudential Tower.

He was a student at Boston University then, earning part-time money on weekends, never with a real threat on his mind. He was trained to chase away students who ran up the down escalators from Boylston Street. From the Top of the Hub restaurant, he helped paramedics transport heart attack victims down with stops every ten floors to lessen the effect of the speed on their descent. For some, an unsettling fast elevator ride up in Boston's tallest building, followed by a 16-ounce steak, made for a last meal. There were also weekend nights when drunken revelers got sick in the revolving restaurant. Getting them to stable ground wasn't pretty.

His worst, yet life-changing night came one March.

It was eleven on a Saturday night. Few workers were at their desks in the 52-story Pru. But the restaurant and bar were open until 1 a.m. in those days, and this day in particular—St. Patrick's Day—was extremely busy. Three hundred patrons were allowable by law. The restaurant had more than that.

Reilly was checking floors 40 on up when an alarm blared, and safety lights shot on. It wasn't the first time for him, but each occurrence had to be considered real. Twenty seconds later his walkie-talkie squawked.

"Reilly, where are you? Over?"

It was another part-timer, tonight working in the security office.

"Forty-six. All clear? Over."

"No!"

No shook his body. He had not heard *no* before.

"Get up to 52. There's a fire in the restaurant!"

Dan Reilly ran to the nearest stairway, flew open the door, and raced up the cement steps. On 50, he was met by the people charging down. Their faces answered any question he would have had if he stopped to ask.

Reilly pulled to the right and pushed on. Reaching the Top of the Hub, he saw everyone who remained, desperately trying to push their way onto the elevators. He saw a man collapsed in a corner. A woman hunched over him.

"Can you help us," she cried. "Please!"

"Yes, I will, but wait!"

Now he shouted above the screams. "Calm down. Take the stairs. There are more stairways down." He directed them to other doors.

"This way!" Reilly instructed. "Don't run. Everything will be all right. Just stay calm."

Studies varied on the time it took for sober men and women to descend 52 flights, from 7.8 to 15.5 minutes. There were no statistics when people were panicked and inebriated. The elevator made the trip faster: 739 feet in a half-a-minute fast. But in a possible fire, the elevators were not supposed to be used.

Reilly ran inside, into the kitchen which was filled with smoke. Cooks were fighting back with CO_2 extinguishers. The grease fire was still going, but they were getting it under control.

"Is everyone okay?" he asked.

"Yes."

Reilly triggered his walkie-talkie and reported in. "Situation is contained. I repeat, situation on 52 is contained. Need paramedics up here. One down. Possible heart attack." He described the scene. Ten minutes later he reported that the fire was completely out.

Other Pinkertons joined him: three out of breath from climbing the stairs, two from a rising elevator. Reilly directed them to the man who needed immediate help. He was conscious but struggling. The guards could assist until the first responders arrived, which was only five minutes later. Their hook and ladders stretched up the building as far as they could from the street. Not all the way. However since their hook and ladders couldn't reach any higher than the 7th, maybe the 8th floor, they had to hoof it up.

Fortunately, aside from rattled nerves, a broken leg, dozens of bruises, 18 people requiring oxygen, including the man on the floor whose condition would be checked in the hospital, everyone was alive.

Reilly's shift ended at 7 a.m. He took the Green Line to his apartment in Brighton, but sleep was not on his mind. Understanding what he did not know was:

Safety procedures and protocols in high-rise buildings. Maximum extension heights for metropolitan hook and ladder trucks. The psychology of crowds in a crisis. Projecting leadership authority.

These were all things he hadn't had in college and he didn't get on the job. But after the night he'd been through, Dan Reilly resolved to learn everything he could.

Now some 20 years later, Reilly knew a great deal more. People were alive today because of what he had garnered on his own and from training—in the Army and the civilian quarter. He took that experience right through the door of the Kensington Royal Star of the Nile hoping he could at least buy his staff and guests some time.

CAIRO

PRESENT DAY

As Abdul Bashari led the guests out to uncertain safety at the rear of the resort, Reilly rushed to the main entrance. The first thing he was aware of was pure fury. It was in the air and in his lungs. Bellowing smoke from across the city. Gunpowder from close by. Then, through the haze, came the mob, marching, but not like an army. They were an unregulated swarm.

It looked like 30 or 35. But then more. Fifty more. They carried clubs and guns. Improvised explosives and weapons seized from government troops. They were enraged. If, at first, they had come out seeking excitement, they were now whipped up into a frenzy. They wanted blood. They wanted a prize. They wanted the hotel, a symbol of Western entitlement. They wanted the Kensington Royal Star of the Nile.

Dan Reilly stood in their way.

Stop them? Reilly had no weapon. *Negotiate?* With what?

Reilly wondered what he had been thinking. Then he remembered. *Buy time. Seconds wouldn't be enough. It takes minutes to quiet them down. To reason with the unreasonable. To give Aziz's rescue boats time to come, if that was even still a possibility.*

He faced the hoard. Teens with Molotov cocktails, men with guns, women with rocks. They all pressed forward. Not a battalion, a loosely formed group of fighters caught up in the moment and driven to a fever pitch. A leader, likely self-anointed and probably only temporary, held up his hand. For now, he had the authority to stop the rioters.

They obeyed.

He stepped toward Reilly and shouted, "Out of the way, American! Out of the way or die."

The man, who looked to be mid-twenties and definitely not military, swept an Uzi overhead. He fired a dozen rounds in the air.

"We take this building in the name of the Egyptian people."

More shots.

Reilly stood his ground.

"You do not understand your own language, American?"

Ten seconds passed. Twenty. Reilly needed more time for the people under his charge to get to safety. He straightened and pulled in a deep breath. "There are innocent people inside."

"No infidel is innocent in the eyes of Allah."

The young man aimed his weapon at Reilly. His followers took it as a sign to do the same.

"Do you want me to count to ten? Like in one of your movies?"

Engage him.

"Who do you represent?" Reilly asked.

The man laughed. "The future of Egypt."

Short answer. Not long enough.

"I understand, but—"

"The people who fight against your unholy influence, your exploitation of our culture, and our history. First, it was the Macedonians and Romans. Then the French and British. You, American, are the latest in a long line of plunderers."

A longer answer. More educated, Reilly thought. *And he's talking. That's good.*

"And what kind of authority do you have to threaten us? Do you speak for a new government?" Reilly asked still stalling for time.

This stymied the leader of the moment. He paused. But pausing for too long would mean someone else might step up. So he did what would end the conversation. He again raised his gun, aimed, and fired at the metal hotel sign in gleaming gold paint, directly above the American.

So much for talk.

The sign shattered. Pieces fell to the ground making Reilly move quickly. But not backward, forward toward the rioters. A sign of defiance.

Another volley to Reilly's sides, shattering the large floor-to-ceiling glass windows.

The leader of the moment leveled his weapon and smiled. "You want to die today, American?"

"I want you to leave," Reilly said calmly.

"Enough!" The revolutionary turned to face his minions, behind, right, and left. Then forward, he fired another well-aimed shot. This one was near Reilly's feet.

"Last warning. We will go around or over you. But we will go in."

Five seconds. Ten. Fifteen. The man took a first step forward. With him, his followers, guns out, clubs raised, hatred burning in their eyes.

Thirty-five feet separated Reilly from the horde. They shouted in Arabic. Reilly knew the chants. *God is good! Death to the Americans!*

They pressed forward. More taunts. Angrier than before. More threatening.

Twenty-five feet. Twenty.

Reilly heard the hotel doors open behind him. Then footsteps. Someone was joining him. Reilly glanced over. Abdul Bashari nervously walked up beside him.

"Police?" Reilly asked.

"Not here." But he nodded over his shoulder.

Suddenly Reilly was aware of two things. First, the oncoming crowd stopped at 15 feet. Second, he heard noise behind them. Crunching. Like people walking on cereal or rocks. *No, broken glass. From the shot-out window!* And rising above the crunching, an intonation. Notes of a song. *Damn,* he thought, *they're singing.*

Reilly turned around and was astonished by what he saw. Most of all, utter bravery. The entire hotel staff that was supposed to leave, was singing.

He recognized the tune, sung in Arabic by an ever-growing chorus emerging from the hotel. "*Bilady, Bilady, Bilady*," the Egyptian National Anthem. "My Country, My Country, My Country."

Reilly looked back at the mob. They were focused on the most unbelievable sight. Men and women carrying shovels, brooms, mops, plates, and candlesticks. Metal tops from trash cans, kitchen knives, and their own Molotov cocktails ready to light and toss. If something could be used as a handheld weapon, they had it.

The housekeepers, the waiters, the desk clerks, and the kitchen staff all formed a line flaring out from Dan Reilly. The general manager to his left, and his driver Shakir Affir to his right. They might die on the spot, but they valiantly stood their ground and sang:

My homeland, my homeland, my homeland
You have my love and my heart.

Egypt! O mother of all countries,
You are my hope and my ambition,
And above all people,
Your Nile has countless graces!

My homeland, my homeland, my homeland,
My love and my heart are for thee.
My homeland, my homeland, my homeland,
My love and my heart are for thee.

Egypt! Most precious gem,
A blaze on the brow of eternity!
O my homeland, be forever free,
Safe from every enemy!

Egypt, noble are your children.
Loyal, and guardians of the reins.
Be we at war or peace
We will sacrifice ourselves for you, my homeland.

My homeland, my homeland, my homeland,
My love and my heart are for thee.
My homeland, my homeland, my homeland,
My love and my heart are for thee.

When they finished the final chorus, the taunts had stopped. The leader held his automatic weapon at chest level. He took in the hotel employees one by one; some he appeared to know. Thirty tense-filled seconds ticked off. He brought his glance to the center of the line. To the American businessman. He nodded his head slightly. Reilly nodded back. Then he smirked, began whistling the same tune, turned, and with his weapon high again, led his group out.

Reilly and the ragtag hotel troops finally relaxed. No one would be advancing toward the hotel today. The Star of the Nile was Switzerland.

Back inside, celebrations, backslapping, and praise for Allah. Reilly hugged everyone, but it was his driver, Shakir Affir, whom Reilly wanted to talk to.

"How? Why? I've never seen anything like it, Shakir."

"We decided as one, Mr. Reilly. This is where we work and provide for our families. We have better lives because of our jobs. So today, we wanted to make sure we had jobs to come back to when this is over. You will tell your people that we care. I know you will honor us in return."

Dan Reilly vowed he would. But first, he had more work to do in Luxor and Alexandria, assuming he could make it out and it was safer there.

16

MOSCOW

Alina Ostrovsky's ₽128,152.51 per month apartment, equivalent to $2,100 USD, offered her privacy. Privacy was important to her. Not for her day job as an economist at Gazoil, a new mega-company born from a recent merger between two already huge petroleum corporations, but for her night work, which took place in her bedroom on *Leninskiy prospekt*.

Ostrovsky had been rising in the Russian business world as a smart, savvy mid-level executive able to cover her basic needs: rent, food, dinner, and bar tabs. Her other expenses, particularly when it came to expensive jewelry and sexy undergarments, were presents from men she kept close for a variety of reasons. For the past 12 years, Alina Ostrovsky, a Russian beauty, drew powerful men to her bed. Most of them eager for *her* gifts. None of them aware who she was.

Years ago, a young university student named Alina Ostrovsky traveled to Beijing, China, for studies at *Guanghua School of Management,* the business school at Peking University. Six months in, she became sick and was quarantined at a small hospital near the school. While there, her mother, her only living relative, was struck and killed by a hit-and-run driver back home in St. Petersburg. The driver was never found.

Alina's recovery was slow. An actual recovery never happened. Alina

Ostrovsky died in her Chinese hospital. Another young woman, a virtual look-alike, then spent four months infirmed before being released. This woman, a trained agent of China's intelligence division, the Ministry of State Security, withdrew from Guanghua and enrolled in Beijing Technology and Business University, where no one knew her. Three years later she graduated, and then spent two more years in China's capital, working for Kaplinksy Labs, a giant Russian tech firm.

Moving back to Moscow, the new Alina Ostrovsky began doing what she had been trained for, *sexpionage*—the age-old confluence of sex and espionage.

Her doorbell rang. It was a rainy night. Her gentleman caller would be wet. She laughed to herself. *Wet, but not a gentleman, though he was generous.* For what she gave him, she thought he should be. Then again, she got the better half of the deal. *Intelligence.*

By now General Sergei Bortnik felt comfortable complaining to his mistress. Particularly after sex. And Bortnik was no different than the other Russian executives and officers she had been assigned to lure into her honey trap. Sex-blinded reasoning.

It usually began quite naturally; an *accidental* meeting that was completely planned.

A man suspected of knowing secrets bumps into a beautiful woman at a convention or a hotel bar. They strike up a conversation. One thing leads to another, the *another* being a bed. A relationship develops. The sex is great, better, and more exciting than at home. Egos are stroked, among other things. No money. Nothing's asked for. It's fun…until…

Businessmen, scientists, politicos, and military officers with security clearances—in foreign capitals and even in their own countries—were perfect subjects for compromising. Women could be turned, too. Women-by-women and men-by-men. The honey trap didn't discriminate.

Blackmail was usually the game. "Get me *this or that* and I'll keep the photographs, the video, and the audio. Your wife, your superiors, your committee chair won't ever need to know. Think about what you could lose: your livelihood and your family. It's an easy decision. And maybe I'll still fuck you."

That wasn't the way this version of Alina Ostrovsky worked. She never turned to blackmail. She never revealed herself or her true intentions. She just did what she did and got what she wanted from Russian, British, French, and American lovers. She played with their emotions well, allowing each, under the sheets, to fall under her spell.

The Russians in particular were warned about being caught in a honey trap. So she took extra care not to raise suspicion, especially with the general now at the door. He had already shown that he had a great deal of knowledge and he was always willing to talk after he caught his breath.

First bed, and then Alina would complain about how work had changed at the oil company since the merger. General Bortnik would sympathize, console her, then, unprompted, he'd start saying the quiet part out loud about his conversations with the president. The information would eventually work its way to her commanders in Beijing who would give weight to the intelligence and then do whatever they did with it.

The recent pillow talk was well worth the death of the first Alina Ostrovsky.

17

THE NEXT DAY

"We're ready, Madame Secretary."

The *Meet the Press* producer led Elizabeth Matthews from the show greenroom into the Washington studio. Two armed Diplomatic Security Services agents flanked her. Others were posted at the entrance to the NBC Washington headquarters.

The Secretary of State took a seat across from the host, the network's new White House correspondent, Megan Trank. "Good to see you again," Trank said.

"Nice to be here, Megan."

"We'll be out of our break-in—"

She looked to the stage manager, Russ Grant, who said, "Thirty seconds."

Trank acknowledged the time cue. The rest would come quickly. She leaned forward across the glass desk, brushed her short brown hair to the side, and said, "Madame Secretary, we have a great deal to talk about today. The ongoing insurrection in Egypt and the status of the Panama Canal, but I want to start with Finland."

"I can tell you where it is," Matthews joked.

"Well, maybe a little more than that," Trank replied.

Matthews nodded and thought to herself that would be her last joke. From here on she'd be completely serious.

"In ten," the stage manager announced. "Stand by."

Megan Trank addressed the camera and teleprompter. Secretary Matthews adjusted her blue blazer and moved into the zone. *Think before you speak. Be ready to pivot. Don't smile when answering seriously. Address Trank, not the camera. Be authoritative. And Elizabeth, if you put your goddamned foot in your mouth, get it out fast!*

"Coming out to you in five, four—" The stage manager counted down the remaining three seconds with his fingers and cued Trank.

"Joining us now, United States Secretary of State Elizabeth Matthews. Secretary Matthews is a career diplomat. She's spent 17 years with the State Department, the last 12 months, through rather tumultuous times, in the administration of President Alexander Crowe, the attempted assassination against him, his resignation, the short term of Ryan Battaglio, and recently, the ascension of Speaker of the House Sean Allphin to the presidency."

The anchor turned to Matthews. "Welcome, Madame Secretary. Quite a ride."

Matthews's first thought, *That's why I keep my safety belt on tight.* Instead, she more professionally replied, "Goes with the job, Megan."

"I bet. We have a great deal to cover today. Let's begin with developments in the Baltic. Finland and Russia in particular. Dueling press conferences between Presidents Kaarina Vanhanen and Nicolai Gorshkov. Military buildup under the name of exercises. Is it your opinion that Gorshkov is crossing a line? And what are we willing to do?"

Elizabeth Matthews handled the points one by one; strategically and in plain English. She did pivot where she had to avoid making any pronouncement that should come from the White House, but she gave the host and social media posts to follow good soundbites. Most of all, she wanted to be *on the news*, not *become the news*. So she took her time and avoided getting her foot anywhere near her mouth.

* * *

Tom Hunter stood off-set, beyond the cameras, watching Matthews. As Number Two in the Secretary of State's Diplomatic Service detail, and in the absence of his direct boss, the missing Carlos Santiago, Hunter now had responsibility for all planning and members of the Secretary of State's security team.

He attentively watched her and kept a constant eye on the TV crew. When it was time to move, he would move with her. If it was necessary to take down a threat, he wouldn't hesitate. Hunter had been with the State Department for six years. He'd earned both Matthews's and Santiago's respect and served with distinction.

His cell phone vibrated with an incoming text. He looked at it. It was a simple code to call in the DSS communications center. He thought it could wait until a second text hit his screen:

URGENT

* * *

"Megan, nations don't have friends," Matthews said in response to Trank's question about America's overall global position. "They have interests. Some of them are shared. When they are, countries establish relationships on different planes: economic, political, and social. They're often based on geographic proximity, national identity, commonality of languages, and current needs. It also comes down to the chemistry between the leaders and working through inherent cultural differences. For example, China is primarily an optimistic society with a long 50-to-100-year view.

"Chinese leadership believes in its ability to succeed over time. Its people share that positive nature. China sees its strength through economic growth, boasting both export gains and investments in the West and Third World countries. On the other hand, Russia defines its character through military might. It has a shorter worldview. The Kremlin needs to score immediate results in major ways. However, as we've witnessed, Russia's military is poorly organized and, by twenty-first-century fighting standards, anything but professional. But as we've also seen in Ukraine, their ruthlessness cannot be ignored."

Matthews continued, "I'll put it another way. China grows. Russia struggles. China has an empty gas tank. Russia has a full one. As Senator John McCain said, 'Russia is a gas station masquerading as a country.' Selling its reserves to China guarantees them the hard currency they need, but there's a psychological principle at play. That's to say, the party with the lesser investment in the relationship has the most power. The winner using that equation is China."

So far, so good, she thought.

"And how does that affect America's strategy?" the moderator asked.

Elizabeth Matthews now assumed her most serious look. She was ready for this one. "We *encourage* Mr. Gorshkov to seriously recognize how united the West is. His actions have brought the United States and its allies closer together."

* * *

Agent Hunter missed hearing most of the Secretary of State's answer. He was on the phone. The news was indeed urgent, and it was bad.

"Sir," the communications officer explained haltingly, "the Coast Guard picked up a pilotless boat adrift some 35 miles south of Miami. The registration showed that it belonged to a rental company in Key Biscayne. Twenty-four hours earlier the same company had reported one of their crafts missing. The boat was rented by Agent Santiago." His voice cracked. "The Guard presumes he's dead."

"Oh God, no!" Hunter exclaimed. "Mechanical issues, bad weather, evidence of malfeasance?"

"None reported, sir. I'm relaying everything I've been told. But I think we can conclude that Agent Santiago went overboard. The boat was on a five-hour rental. That was two days ago. Chances of surviving—" He left it unsaid.

* * *

"And yet, Secretary Matthews," Trank continued, "Russia's actions have only intensified fears that China *will* move into Taiwan."

The *Meet the Press* anchor waited for a response. It came after Matthews took a beat.

"China claims Taiwan is theirs since the island split off from the mainland in 1949. And in the years since they have vowed to resolve the 'Taiwan question.' To make matters more complicated, the United Nations views Beijing as a rightful landowner. This means Taiwan's people live an uncertain existence."

"Then, Secretary Matthews," Trank cut in, "how important is it to the Allphin administration that Taiwan *not* be assimilated into mainland China?"

This time, Matthews allowed herself two beats.

"It's of utmost importance to the United States, I'll include Republicans, Democrats, and Independents, and people who use any electronic devices that the island's economy and security are essential to the West's interests. But there's no doubt that Taiwan's location presents strategic challenges to its 23 million citizens. Taiwan lies off the coast of China, just across the Taiwan Strait, which is part of the South China Sea. At its narrowest part, just 80 miles separates the two opposing governments. That's closer than the U.S. is to Cuba.

"If the Beijing government moves against Taiwan, China would immediately become the Pacific's superpower, with the ability to choke off oil shipments to South Korea and Japan. It would take over the manufacturing of the globe's most cutting-edge technologies, and such a move would interfere with America's influence in Asia. So, yes, Taiwan is definitely in Beijing's world view *and ours*."

"Is the United States prepared to go to war with China over Taiwan?" the NBC anchor directly asked.

Matthews knew she had to take great care with this answer.

"Peaceful resolution comes with negotiating and successfully doing business with China. To do that most effectively, we have to understand

Chinese values. We are a country, China is a culture rooted in thousands of years of history. The native nation of China is comprised of the Han Chinese, the most ethnocentric people in the world and the globe's largest ethnic group, amounting to more than 1.4 billion people.

"Ninety-two percent of the total population of the People's Republic of China is Han. But 97% of the population in the Republic of China, Taiwan, are also Han. Culturally, Beijing maintains that Taiwan is, and always has been, theirs. While Taiwan's political ties are to the West, culture trumps politics every time, everywhere."

Trank was excited. She thought she might get a great quote with her follow-up. "That would make them highly suspicious of us in the long term."

"Long term, short term," Matthews answered. "Yes, China wants Taiwan. In the mind of Beijing's leaders, in their historical and cultural consciousness, it is their inevitability. Our challenge is to help them see that Taiwan's existence as a free and independent nation does not deny their cultural bond. At the same time, the lessening of tensions increases global economic stability. China needs that as much as we do."

Good, but Trank wanted more.

"So, Madame Secretary, wouldn't a summit between President Allphin and President Yáo be helpful?"

"We can hope."

"Has one been scheduled?"

"Not at present."

"All right, the president isn't going now. Are *you* planning a trip?" Trank made sure she placed enough emphasis on *you*.

"In time. For now, the president wants me elsewhere."

Trank suddenly felt she might have that breaking news soundbite she wanted.

"Where?"

"Panama. To discuss Panama's security and the renewal of safe passage through the Panama Canal."

Matthews stopped short. This should come out a little at a time.

"Isn't China a major strategic player in the operation of the Panama Canal?"

"Yes. It's a good place for us to show how we can come together. We both have stakes in Panama. More directly, we both have an interest in maintaining the successful operation of the Panama Canal. Yes, China's holdings include operations on either side. At the ports of Balboa and Cristobal along with Margarita Island, Panama's largest Atlantic port. That makes China a significant player that we must play with like adults, not children."

"Madame Secretary, will your visit include discussions with the Chinese about deploying American forces to Panama and—"

Elizabeth Matthews gracefully interrupted Trank.

"We're sending enough men and women to speed up repairs. Engineers and advisors. We will confer with the Panamanian government on what it wants and advise Beijing accordingly."

Matthews felt she had successfully talked herself through a potential political thicket.

"Just one more question, Secretary Matthews, and probably not unexpected. Will you be taking that trip to Panama as Secretary of State or, as has been rumored, the next Vice President of the United States?"

Elizabeth Matthews smiled. "I've got a job, Megan. No one's ordered any new business cards for me."

The *Meet the Press* host laughed. "Do people still use business cards when we share contacts on our phones?"

"Old-school, but I have them."

The interview concluded with polite thanks and the host's toss to the commercial break. As an audio technician removed Matthews's microphone, Tom Hunter dashed across the set to whisper in her ear, "Madame Secretary, we need to leave *now*."

There was something in the agent's voice and his emphasis on *now* that meant unexpected complications and trouble.

"Oh?"

"Outside."

They picked up the rest of her DSS detail. One agent radioed for their car to be ready. The other flanked her. Matthews called out to the NBC show producer who was hoping for a photograph.

"Sorry, they've got me on a tight leash today. Next time."

The agents made a corridor for Matthews to walk through, right to her limo parked in front of the NBC Studios at 4001 Nebraska Avenue, NW.

Once in the car, Matthews slid closer to Hunter. "What's going on, Tom?"

"We don't have all the details. We're talking with the Coast Guard. The FBI is into it."

"Into what, Tom? Get to the point."

"Madame Secretary," he choked on the words, "Agent Santiago is missing. He'd taken a Miami fishing boat out for a day. That was days ago. The rental outfit where he picked up the craft called the Coast Guard. They found the boat earlier today. Looks like he was swept over—"

"Bullshit! Navy vet. Lifetime fisherman. Not possible!"

"Madame Secretary, accidents happen."

"Not to Carlos!"

"The FBI has impounded the boat. They'll be examining it stem to stern. We'll send a team down. I want to head it."

"No." She lowered her eyes and said softly, "I need you here with me, Tom."

18

President Allphin ushered the Secretary of State to a couch in the Oval Office. He sat across from her. For some reason, this woman, normally forged from steel, seemed to lack her typical metal. He figured he'd draw her out during their conversation.

"You handled yourself well today, Elizabeth."

"Thank you, Mr. President. However, I have to think a bit more before answering. Less is best."

"Yes, it is. The press, even those supporting us, constantly put us on the defensive. It was far easier for me, too, in Congress. I could be the attack dog. Now there's not enough pepper spray to keep them at bay."

The comment called for a laugh, but she couldn't. Not now. Instead, she merely replied, "Yes, Mr. President."

Sean Allphin had never wanted to become president. He never campaigned for it, never spent a dollar running. He was elevated from Speaker of the House under the 25th Amendment to the United States Constitution. Now he was determined to serve with distinction.

"Ah, Mr. President. You know, I'm still having a hard time responding to the title, Elizabeth. When I started teaching high school I was Mr. Allphin. That was hard enough. I kept looking to see if my dad had walked into the room. When students called me Professor

Allphin at Harvard, it was even harder. Then Councilman, Governor, Mr. Speaker, and today, Mr. President. Now more than forty years later, I wonder where Sean went. Nobody dares call me by my first name anymore."

Elizabeth Matthews understood and expected she was going to have a period of adjustment soon, too.

"Sir, I'm honored to talk with Sean Allphin, the president of the United States."

"Unelected."

"Qualified," she argued.

"Hell, what did writer Gore Vidal say?" Allphin asked. "Half of the American people never read a newspaper. Half never voted for president. One hopes it's the same half."

"Sir, the nation needs you. You're already making a difference."

"Thank you, Elizabeth," he said appreciatively. "And so will you as vice president. Trank would have loved it if you'd broken the news live on the air."

Matthews smiled. "It's your announcement to make, Mr. President, but the timing will be better after Panama."

Allphin thought about her response. "Actually, I'm not so sure. Your visit could carry more weight as the designee. You won't have had your day on Capitol Hill before you go, but you will be viewed as having more authority as my vice presidential nominee."

"With all due respect, we should stay on point. You saw where Trank wanted to take it during the interview. Besides, if things don't work out as planned, my trip could work against you."

Allphin nodded. She was right. A political advantage today could be tomorrow's political liability.

"All right, but I'm going to get things ready. The White House speech writers will work up a short acceptance, which you can retool, then the staff will run you through your prep for your Senate confirmation. Lots of homework, Elizabeth. Lots of practicing."

"All for when I return."

"Yes," the president reaffirmed. "None of it will be a walk in the park. No balloons and cotton candy. Be ready to take some shots from the disloyal opposition. Rest assured Billy Peyton and his minions will be in the room. Knives out."

The president was referring to the Senate Minority Whip, the enemy within.

"He's a little man with a big grudge."

"And a fool, Mr. President."

"Take care. He wants the job, and he will do everything he can to trap you, to make *you* out to be the fool."

"Yes, sir."

"Elizabeth, my daddy used to tell me there were two kinds of fools. One kind of fool parades naked in front of your house. The other invites him into the house. Don't be the one that invites him in. Keep Peyton as far away as possible. And make everyone else see that he's the intended emperor with no clothes."

She looked beyond Sean Allphin to a bust of Lincoln on the mantelpiece. Her master's thesis was on Lincoln. She recalled a quotation from the very last speech President Lincoln gave. It was on April 11, 1865, three days before he was assassinated.

"We shall sooner have the fowl by hatching the egg than by smashing it."

Matthews wasn't so sure Lincoln's advice applied to the politics of today. If Congressman Billy Peyton had every intention of publicly smashing her, she would have to do the same, but sooner.

Allphin continued. "But be prepared, be very prepared for how the less-than-Honorable Billy Peyton will come after you. And he will, with all he's got and all he can make up. You better want this job, Elizabeth. And the one beyond this."

"I do, Mr. President."

"He can't touch your testimony directly, but that won't prevent him from hitting hard on what you know about Battaglio's resignation and what he, and by implication, you gave away to Gorshkov in Stockholm."

"Battaglio sent me home. I wasn't there for the deal he made."

"Then you say just that when asked and stick to it."

"And the resignation?"

"Exactly what Battaglio agreed to," Allphin said. "He resigned for health reasons."

"And if he comes up with a different story in his book?"

"Stick to his written letter of resignation."

Even if it wasn't the end of this particular discussion, the comment earned another, "Yes, sir." This one with a prolonged sigh.

Allphin picked up on her reaction. "Are you worried about the publication?"

"It's not that."

"Then what's wrong, Elizabeth?"

She told him what she knew about Carlos Santiago's disappearance.

"He was fishing off the coast of Florida. They say it was a boating accident. The last person in the world I'd expect to have a boating accident would be Carlos Santiago."

19

NEW YORK, NEW YORK

People had been calling, emailing, and texting New York literary agent Benson Bruckheimer for days. Everyone was shocked by the news of Jillian Robbins's death. He said he felt responsible. After all, he had put the deal together that took her to Puerto Rico. He cried in his wife's arms. He walked aimlessly across Manhattan. Now his calls went unanswered.

Four months earlier he was contacted quite surreptitiously while he was alone reading a manuscript in the historic Algonquin Hotel bar. A man stopped by his table and simply said, "Call me." He handed over a sheet of Algonquin stationery that read: "I have a top-shelf job for a writer of yours. A woman." He named Jillian Robbins. "You'll want to hear what I have to say." There was a phone number at the bottom with the DC area code, 202.

The man left. This certainly wasn't the way writing assignments for his clients typically came his way in the past. He considered throwing the paper away, then he figured, *what the hell*!

Bruckheimer had worked for big agencies. Now he was on his own. He cultivated young writers who had no credits, veterans who had lost their gas but not their creativity, and repped established newspaper journalists ready for freelance assignments. Jillian Robbins was in that third category.

Back in his office, he dialed the number. "Hello, this is Benson Bruckheimer. I was given this number to call."

"Yes. We'll talk, but not this way. Meet me in Central Park." The voice on the phone gave him a specific location, a specific park bench, and a specific time.

Jesus, he thought, *it was the damndest thing I've ever heard.* But it was intriguing.

At the appointed time and place Bruckheimer met the stranger, a lawyer for the former president of the United States, Ryan Battaglio.

"President Battaglio wants Jillian Robbins as his biographer. He has a short timeline. The money is at the top of the scale for ghostwriters." He told him the quote. "She'll need to sign an NDA."

Bruckheimer didn't say anything immediately.

"If you're interested enough to talk to Robbins, tell me. If she's interested, I'll need to know by 6 p.m. today."

The agent looked at his watch. It was already four. "8 p.m.," Bruckheimer replied.

"There are other writers I can go to. But I will accept eight. If she says yes, we'll fly her to Puerto Rico where she will stay until the book is finished. Robbins will work directly with the president. It is a work for hire."

"I understand."

"No credit."

"Yes."

"Never to be discussed."

"I understand."

Bruckheimer stood. As he walked away he thought it was the damnedest deal he'd ever heard. He reached Robbins at 6:30. They had two conversations before she agreed. The agent called the lawyer just before eight. He took the chance to get the offer from $150,000 to $175,000. The former president's attorney agreed and a week later

Jillian Robbins was flying first class to Puerto Rico to ghost President Ryan Battaglio's autobiography.

Now, Benson Bruckheimer was consumed with utter despair. Friends were worried about him. He had hardly eaten since he'd gotten the news of Jillian's death. His wife pleaded with him to stay home and let time do its thing. Bruckheimer couldn't.

He should have listened to his wife. Two days later he was found five floors below his office on Park Avenue South. Police investigated Benson Bruckheimer's death. His wife and others explained he had been depressed and inconsolable over a writer client's tragic death. It was determined he had committed suicide. However, the man who casually left the building minutes after Bruckheimer's fall knew differently. He had experience in such matters. He'd been flown in from Russia to personally handle the assignment.

20

THE U.S STATE DEPARTMENT

OFFICE OF THE SECRETARY OF STATE

Elizabeth Matthews never felt she ever had enough waking hours to deal with everything on the nation's plate. Now it only intensified. She had a high-level, controversial diplomatic trip coming up, and she was without the benefit of her trusted head of security.

"You look absolutely haggard," Mikayla Colonnello noted.

Most people the Secretary of State encountered would not be so bold as to make such an observation. They'd keep it to themselves or gossip about her later. Senator Mikayla Colonnello was not one of those. She spoke openly, with real concern.

"Any sleep last night?"

"A good two hours."

"Elizabeth!" Colonnello chided.

"I said it was a *good* two hours. Better than a bad two."

Matthews and Colonnello were friends and had been for years. Colonnello, a California native like Matthews, was born and bred in Santa Barbara. She'd earned her master's degree in international business at UCLA, risen from CFO to CEO ranks at a startup Santa Monica Silicon Beach tech firm, oversaw its sale to Amazon, and used her earnings to bankroll a run for the U.S. Senate. Now midway through her second term, she'd distinguished herself as fiercely independent, yet a loyal colleague. It was Senator Colonnello's committee work, first on Homeland Security and Governmental Affairs and now as the new chair of Intelligence, that brought her closer than ever to Matthews.

Though a little more than a decade in age separated them, Matthews never treated Colonnello as a junior. They regularly met for lunches and dinners, spoke in the halls, and confided behind closed doors.

"Promise me you'll get some sleep."

"Absolutely. On the plane."

"Right," Colonnello said mockingly. "You'll be reading reports, making notes, preparing for your meetings."

Matthews smiled.

"And walking into your sessions dead tired."

"Then when I get back," Matthews said trying to get a laugh.

It didn't work.

"Do you have any idea how dangerous it is—" Colonnello stopped short. Of course, she knew. They both read the same intelligence briefs. "Wait a few weeks."

"Can't. Too many moving parts. But it'll be a fast in and out."

Matthews now leaned in. "We've got to shore up the defenses and get the Canal operating again at full capacity. If we don't, China will protect its own assets. And if they do, it will set up more of a challenge over control. They already have destroyers on the west end, and they are heading up the coast of South America to the Canal's east. We have to exert our influence. You know, use it or lose it."

Senator Colonnello nodded. "Allphin?"

It was a one-word question that asked whether the new president had the balls to send American troops into Panama and how much he was willing to stand up to China's growing presence elsewhere in the world.

"All in."

Colonnello weighed the ramifications of pulling one thread attached to Panama and risking the chance that it was attached to another. Pull too hard and the U.S. could give China license to finally launch an invasion in Taiwan.

And then there were other troubling factors out of the control of both the U.S. and China that could accelerate changes in the decision map—critical scenarios played out and presented to the president from the intelligence community, the Pentagon, think tanks, and consultants. If the U.S. does "A," then China may do "B," "C," or "D." Multiple variables in play at the same time.

One of those variables was Venezuela. Another North Korea. But in ways they couldn't even imagine.

* * *

Matthews's briefing papers detailed the history of the Panama Canal. It would be important for her to have the facts down to effectively state America's position, which meant redeploying more American troops.

The history began in 1881 when the French broke ground for a canal. President Theodore Roosevelt schemed to buy the property, which was then a province of Colombia. Roosevelt planted riflemen in Colombia to start a revolution. He dispatched the U.S. Navy to blockade the Colombian Navy from entering Panama's waters. Soon Panama became an independent republic and U.S. Secretary of State John Hay negotiated a lease to a ten-mile carve-out. Construction resumed under the American flag on May 4, 1904. Not so surprisingly, residents of the new republic had no say on the agreement.

Ten years later, the full 50-mile passage was completed. Ships sailed in either direction cutting shipping time from twenty-two days around South America's Cape Horn to eight-to-ten hours. It was an engineering marvel and a boon to business. But in the 1950s, and for the next twenty years, Panama sought more access to their own country, literally cut in two, with no way across the canal except by ferry.

In 1963, the United States Army Corps of Engineers constructed a bridge. It linked the two sides, but it did not unite the country's disparate factions.

A year later, Communist-instigated riots broke out and American soldiers took to the streets. Relationships between Panama and the U.S. worsened. The geopolitical impact reached all the way to Russia, which led the Soviets to stake ground and make new alliances in Latin America. Chief among Premier Nikita Khrushchev's goals was gaining a foothold in Panama. He negotiated with Panama's dictator Omar Torrijos to build a new canal, which, if completed, would make the existing Panama Canal obsolete.

In a countermove, President Richard Nixon began talks to revisit the terms of America's permanent Canal Zone lease. The negotiations continued through the Ford and Carter administrations. In 1977 the deal was concluded.

The Panamanians got their canal, but the U.S. did not leave empty-handed. Washington booted the Soviets out of the game, guaranteeing international neutrality of the Canal Zone and first right of refusal over any other nation's interest in expanding the current canal or digging a new one. Moreover, the new relationship granted America the exclusive rights to defend the Panama Canal.

This last clause in the treaty gave the United States the authority to invade Panama in 1989 to capture and remove Dictator General Manuel Antonio Noriega Moreno, who was threatening the stability of the region. Noriega was convicted of drug trafficking, money laundering, and racketeering and sentenced to forty years in prison.

Ten years later, on New Year's Eve, 1999, final control of the zone fully reverted to Panama. The nation built a second series of locks which allowed heavier, larger cargo, container, and cruise ships to pass through.

While the United States has remained the canal's number one customer, China planted an economic flag on the ground and through the Panamanian waters. In a strategic geopolitical sense this has given China a deep-water port for mega-ships in the southern shadow of the United States.

China has also invested heavily in other infrastructure initiatives including energy facilities along the Canal's expanse and water-management systems to combat drought conditions. When the Canal's eastern port was recently attacked by terrorists and the route was shut down, China took it as an opportunity to increase its visibility and protect its interests, especially in light of growing unrest.

* * *

"The thing that we're united on, or at least I think we are," Elizabeth Matthews continued, "is that the Chinese view the attack in Panama just as much a danger to their interests as we do. What they do could have profound impact on the Canal."

"Chinese troops?" Senator Colonnello asked. "To even things out between us and our presence in Taiwan."

"An escalation that we couldn't accept," Matthews replied.

"But could we prevent it?" Colonnello asked.

Matthews hoped America's intelligence was ahead of what instantly flashed through her mind. *Escalation until a compromise. China backs out of Panama if the U.S. does the same in Taiwan. The canal becomes their greatest bargaining chip.*

"You said no troops in your interview," the Senator said. "Is that really the best course?"

"What?" Matthews asked still lost in thought.

"A U.S. show of force. It's worth bringing up to Allphin before Peyton makes it his battle cry."

"Do you have any reason to think he would?"

"If I came up with it, he certainly could."

"I'll talk to Allphin, but I know what he's going to say."

In addition to talking to the president, Matthews was going to ask the NSA to game it out, if they already hadn't.

Jesus, she thought. Then *fuck*.

21

CAIRO, EGYPT

TWO DAYS LATER

With the Star of the Nile secure and a surprise ceasefire negotiated overnight, the airport reopened for limited travel. Reilly had been able to fly non-commercially to his other two properties where all was safe. Then a return flight to Cairo and a nonstop to Dulles. He arrived exhausted from his four-day whirlwind trip at 3 p.m. local time. All he could think about was a bath and bed with Yibing Cheng in both.

The moment the plane landed, Reilly called Brenda Sheldon, his assistant in Chicago, to catch up on what he had missed while he was in the air. *Too much:* Russia making more noise over Finland, but the company's hotels were fine. China's renewed exercises in the South China Sea, but no threat to properties in Taiwan. Not yet.

Problems to consider. Meetings to schedule. Decisions to make. Dan Reilly had seriously wondered on the flight back to the States whether enough was enough. Enough running around, enough international politics, enough serving multiple masters.

And he thought about Yibing Cheng and what life would be like if he was willing to give their relationship a real chance. He wanted to try. It would take immense power of persuasion to convince others, let alone himself.

Reilly sighed. First, he would call Elizabeth Matthews and tell her he had a change of heart. He couldn't continue freelancing for her. Of course, she would ask him to reconsider and give him reasons why she believed the relationship would work out. He would listen politely, then explain he had made up his mind. He didn't want to switch jobs. *Thank you, but no thank you.* Next, he would call EJ Shaw in Chicago and tell him he was committed to the company, but it was time to get off the road.

Reilly stopped at a Bar Symon in Concourse D, ordered a scotch, and braced himself for the hard conversations ahead. That's just when his phone rang.

"Daniel."

It was Elizabeth Matthews. She sounded upset.

"Where are you?"

"Just landed. Why, what's the matter?"

"I need you."

Ninety minutes later, Matthews and Reilly were walking along the Washington Mall with Tom Hunter off to her side. A team of DSS agents accompanied them while searching front, back, and sides for any threats.

Hunter knew nothing about Reilly other than he was a friend of Matthews. He wasn't certain why she had even called him, but Matthews made it apparent that Dan Reilly should be viewed as a member of the family.

Matthews and Reilly strolled at a brisk pace set by Matthews. This was not the afternoon and evening Reilly had been looking forward to.

She did the talking.

"Daniel, the head of my security detail is missing. People like Carlos Santiago don't just go missing."

She explained what Santiago had been doing in Florida and why she didn't buy any of the answers she was getting. She told him that the FBI had been all over the recovered boat, that they found Santiago's prints and no others, except those belonging to the rental staff.

"Does a forever sailor, a career Navy officer, a man trained to handle himself in any situation just wash overboard in calm seas?"

"Maybe fighting a 1900-pound blue marlin," Reilly replied.

"Santiago? Not even Moby Dick. And his line was still out."

Matthews stopped walking and faced Reilly.

"Dan, I want you to go to Miami and find him. Or find out what happened."

"Elizabeth you've got the wrong man this time."

He pointed to Hunter, who was hanging a few steps back.

"Send him. He looks like he's made for the part."

"I can't. Hunter is working on details for a trip I have coming up. He's running my security now."

"Jesus, Elizabeth." All that he had considered talking to her about evaporated. "I just came back from Egypt, isn't there—"

"No!" she said, revealing her state of mind.

Tom Hunter overheard her distress. He caught up with them.

"Anything wrong, Madame Secretary?"

"We're fine, Tom. Just a recruiting drive with my friend."

Hunter raised an eyebrow, uncertain what she meant.

"Trying to talk Mr. Reilly into helping on the Santiago investigation."

"Excuse me?" Hunter asked. "With all due respect, I don't think that's a good idea."

He gave Reilly a cold stare. Matthews casually waved her hand.

"Tom, give me a few more moments."

"Yes, ma'am," the DSS officer replied. He drifted back and signaled for his team to spread out and keep their eyes open. Unseen, but also observing them, were drones high over the nation's capital.

"Daniel, please. I can't believe this was an accident."

"Elizabeth, the FBI—"

"The FBI was examining an accident scene, not looking at it as murder on the high seas. You'll ask questions no one else would ask. You'll dig deeper. And if you're completely convinced it was an accident, then convince me."

"One call and you can have the whole Justice Department and the complete intelligence apparatus working for you," Reilly argued.

"Daniel, you're not listening. I want you. It's important to me."

Reilly said nothing for a long beat. Then: "Elizabeth, just before you called I was steeling myself with a drink at Dulles. I was about to phone you…to say I was through. That I'd had it. I can't keep serving two masters. Shaw and you."

She nodded. "Well, you can retire later. I've got a job for you right now."

Reilly sighed deeply and nodded his reluctant acceptance. "My God, how do you do that?"

"Do what?"

"Talk me into walking a tightrope."

She smiled. "I guess I just know how to press the right buttons."

Dan Reilly laughed. Tom Hunter peered over but couldn't gather what was suddenly funny.

Elizabeth Matthews gently touched Reilly's arm.

"Thank you, Daniel."

"You're welcome."

"I have to know."

With that, she handed Reilly a sheet of paper with details reported to her, then called Tom Hunter and waved her right index finger in a circle. Wheels up. Time to go. Hunter radioed for their hardened car to come across the Mall and pick them up.

* * *

Reilly wasn't really surprised that he caved. He even laughed as he played back the conversation. Elizabeth Matthews had a special hold on him, not unlike EJ Shaw's. And since his job as a part-time security guard in college, through his military service, and his former State Department duties, he placed service to others above himself.

It had cost him a marriage. It nearly cost him his life in Stockholm. And tonight it was going to cost him his bed, bath, and beyond with Yibing.

"Hello," he said to his assistant Brenda Sheldon. "Me again."

"I thought you were through for the day."

"Not even close. Heading to Miami."

"Oh?"

The *Oh* meant it wasn't on his calendar the last time they talked, which was after his plane landed.

"Another change of plans."

She gave him another, "Oh." Brenda Sheldon was used to changes. She had been with him for nearly nine years, and she'd be surprised if anything in Dan Reilly's life would ever go as scheduled.

"What's up?" she asked.

"A fishing expedition," Reilly said.

"Well, now that's a surprise. I didn't think you fished."

"I don't."

The answer caught her off guard.

"Can you get me on a flight out of National this evening and a hotel along Biscayne Bay? As close as possible to a launch called Oceana Boats? Doesn't have to be fancy. Definitely not one of ours. I don't want to draw any attention. Oh, and use my personal card, not the company's. It's off our books."

The last line threw her. Reilly always opted for Kensington Hotels.

"Are you sure, Dan?"

"Yes."

"Do you want me to tell Mr. Shaw?"

"I'll spare you that pleasure. I'll do it."

Brenda Sheldon said she'd have his flight in short order. Reilly thanked her. They hung up, and Reilly was ready for his next call.

"It's Reilly. Is he in?" he asked Shaw's secretary, Nancy Barney.

"Just a moment, Mr. Reilly. I'll see if I can wrest him from a meeting that I'm sure he'll be happy to leave."

"Ah, Mr. Collins and his legal team, I assume."

"Bingo."

During the five minutes he waited for EJ Shaw to pick up, Brenda

Sheldon texted Reilly his flight and hotel booking—a small, serviceable chain.

"All right, I have Mr. Shaw for you, Mr. Reilly." Barney connected him.

"Dan, so glad to hear you're safe!" Shaw bellowed. "Quite a demonstration the staff put on in Egypt."

"I've never seen anything like it."

"Neither have I," Shaw said. "Nice work, Dan."

"It was all them."

"Because of you."

Reilly said nothing. Shaw was talking about his leadership.

"So now, take a few days for yourself."

"Well, I was going to, but—"

"But someone has asked you to do something?" EJ Shaw asked.

"Yes."

"A certain friend in high places."

"You've got that right."

Reilly explained. Shaw listened, but it was Reilly's concluding remark that surprised him.

"Boss, when I'm back, I think I need to come in from the cold."

22

SOUTH PACIFIC OCEAN

"At periscope depth now, sir, and holding. Sixty feet." Aboard the USS *Annapolis*, Okim Katema had been plotting the North Korean's sub on its passive sonar for ten days. "Raising its snorkel and antenna."

The snorkel mast is a hollow tube with a float valve on top to prevent taking in seawater. Through it, fresh air is drawn in while exhaust is pushed out. The maneuver serves to recharge the diesel-electric engine batteries and give the crew fresh air. The antenna pulls down the latest transmissions from the home port admiralty and direct orders from the Supreme Leader.

"Confirming on radar," offered technician Jonas Johnson. "Periscope rising."

Captain Dwight Zimmerman expected the *Wonsan Yong-Ganhan* was curious to see if the sub's course would change with new orders. So far it had zig-zagged on a generally east heading. East-northeast, east, east-southeast. The common denominator being east.

Equally concerning were the refueling stops that the sub had been able to schedule in open waters. There was nothing illegal about taking on more fuel. No one owned the Pacific but topping off allowed the sub to sail further. And one of the places further was the U.S. mainland.

Thirty minutes later, "She's going down," Katema announced from his sonar station.

"Heading, Mr. Katema?"

"Stand by, I'll have it for you."

Zimmerman stood by his map ready with his pencil and ruler. The seconds clicked, then the minutes.

"Returning to niner-one, seven-two, Captain."

"Repeat, Mr. Katema."

"Bearing niner-one, seven-two," he said facing Zimmerman.

Zimmerman wrote down the bearing with a grease marker on his Pacific Ocean chart that laid flat before him. Then he plotted the course. His sonar operator did the same on his computer.

Niner-one, seven-two was a due east heading. From where they were, should *Wonsan Yong-Ganhan* stay on course, niner-one, seven-two was a straight shot to California's West Coast. Specifically, San Francisco Bay.

* * *

Aboard *Wonsan Yong-Ganhan*, Captain Jang Song-Taek brought his Executive Officer into his stateroom.

"Coffee?" Song-Taek offered.

"Thank you, Captain," Lt. Ha-Yoon Cho replied. "I could use another cup."

Song-Taek served the brew from a chipped white vase into a green mug with the sub's name printed crooked. He handed it to his XO and poured himself a cup.

"Long way from home, Lieutenant."

"Yes, sir. Good training for the crew."

Song-Taek took a sip and considered the comment. He then asked, "How are the men holding up?"

"Good, Captain."

"That sounded like the kind of answer you think a captain wants to hear. Very quick. I'll ask again. How are the men holding up?"

Lt. Cho put his mug down. "Apologies, Captain. They haven't been this far from home even though they've had long periods away. So they're worried. Sonar is tired. They've never had to watch their screens so intensely. And they're worried about invisible American submarines."

Song-Taek took it all in. He waited a full minute before responding. The new coded orders he received elevated his worry, too.

"XO, keep them at battle ready," Song-Taek said. "They know their duties. I expect the best from them and even more from you."

Cho straightened in his seat and snapped, "Yes, sir."

"The Supreme Leader has entrusted us with a long-range test, XO. And yes, it is good to assume that the Americans may be lurking close. But under 5 km per hour, we are equally, if not more invisible. It's only when we've snorkeled that they could have spotted us. Now we have no more stops. Still, turn your men's worry into vigilance."

"I understand, Captain. Perhaps if I knew more—"

"You will when the time is right." He glanced at his computer and a countdown clock flashing on the screen. There were days to go until all the zeroes lined up.

"Yes, sir," the XO replied.

"Good. Now until then, make sure your men are worthy of their ship's name: Brave."

23

THE NEXT MORNING

Reilly considered what to wear: casual Miami or business Washington? He went for the middle ground. Sports jacket, jeans, blue shirt, open collar, no tie. He approached the Oceana Boats rental desk clerk with a broad smile.

"Good morning, hope you can help me."

Cate Callaway sized him up. This wasn't a customer. He wasn't even a sailor. He was coming on like a cop.

"Yes?" she offered cautiously.

Reilly read the reaction. Maybe he should have gone more native.

"Hi, I'm Dan Reilly. I'm following up on the disappearance of the man who rented from you a few days ago."

"Carlos Santiago, yes. I'm so sorry. He was really nice. But I've spoken with the police already. And some other people."

"Of course. I'm not with any law enforcement." *Less is best,* he thought. "But I'd still like to go over a few things. It won't take long. May I ask your name?"

Callaway told him.

"Thanks, Ms. Callaway."

"Cate's okay."

Reilly smiled warmly. "Then Cate it is. I work with Mr. Santiago's boss. It gets complicated from there, but let's just say he was important and she's *very* important."

Callaway was intrigued. No one had indicated VIPs might be involved.

"Okay, but I'm not sure I have anything new to tell you. They were pretty thorough."

"Let's just start at the beginning, like I don't know anything."

That much was true.

In the course of their conversation, Callaway confirmed she had waited on Carlos Santiago. It had been a slow morning, and she was happy for the rental. He might be interested in taking the craft out for the entire week and would decide after the first day. She also confirmed that no other boats left the marina until late afternoon for the sunset cruises.

"When Mr. Santiago was 90 minutes overdue and hadn't responded to my radio calls, I contacted the Coast Guard. Just before closing two Coast Guard officers and a Miami Dade sheriff came in. I had dated one of the guard. I told him Mr. Santiago was really nice and indicated he was experienced. Well, I guess he wasn't as much as he thought."

Reilly said nothing.

"They recovered our boat two days later." She lowered her eyes. "No sign of Mr. Santiago."

Reilly wrote down all the relevant points: Hours, contacts, and the fact that the marina was quiet. That meant something.

"Of course, there are other launches nearby. I can give you names."

"That would be great."

As he was leaving, Callaway said, "I never really got where you're from and who this important person you both worked for is."

"No, you didn't. Thank you, though." Reilly smiled and left.

For the rest of the day, he checked out the other boat rental offices along Biscayne Bay. He was looking for leads on anyone who would have rented a boat that could have caught up with Santiago. Anyone out of the ordinary. Anyone particularly memorable.

All the boaters that day were either families on short runs or sport fishermen who came back with their hauls. He'd pass the information on so the FBI could check them all out if they hadn't already. But to his thinking, no one rose to the surface.

It was an image that he regretted.

He began the second morning at seven with a new set of questions. His own. *How would I do it? What would be the most unusual way to intercept Santiago? Would I be waiting ahead of time? And, if so, how would I know? Would I have been tipped off?*

On the wild side, he wondered if there were personal submarine rentals. He looked online. There weren't. *A parachute?* Possibly, but Santiago would be highly suspect of someone dropping from the sky in his vicinity. *Too complex and it would require another boat for an escape plan.*

He wondered if he should extend his search to launches further up the coast, but he figured that would take too much effort to coordinate an interception.

He put the *how* and the *what* aside and focused on his other questions.

Yes, I'd already be off-shore. I would have been tipped off and waiting.

Then came another line of reasoning. If someone was lying in wait, what would get Santiago to let them close, or onboard? For that, he needed to call Elizabeth Matthews.

Reilly quickly posed his questions: "How on alert would Santiago have been to any surprises? Would he automatically help somebody in trouble?"

"Without hesitation. That's his training. But it's also his nature."

"Alright. Now paint me a picture of Carlos Santiago. What was he like? Married? Single?"

"Daniel, what's that got to do with—."

"I'm trying to help, Elizabeth."

Carlos Santiago had worked with the Secretary of State for more than four years. She couldn't say she knew him so personally. She didn't open up to him, and he was all business with her. But she did have impressions.

"He was single. Athletic, of course. Solid. Very. Guarded, as he should be. Handsome. Very."

"Straight or gay?"

"Daniel, really?"

"Really."

"Carlos was available. A fact not lost on the young women in the building." She paused to think. "He noticed them as well. Especially the blondes. Why?"

"Was he unhappy? Can you think of any reason he'd commit suicide? A boat is a perfect place to do it."

"No!" Matthews said emphatically.

"Are you sure?"

"Yes!" she said equally as strongly.

"Any depression?"

"Absolutely not!" She thought for a moment. She really didn't know.

"You've seen his psych eval?"

"Stop it. Carlos Santiago was the most well-adjusted officer I've ever met. Happy, friendly, and dedicated beyond belief. He reminded me of you."

This made Reilly pause.

"I'm sorry, Elizabeth. I realize my questions are off-putting. I have to eliminate possibilities."

"It's all right. I'm just really upset." Then she stopped. "Daniel, do you think he was baited?"

"Well, he wasn't on his boat when the Coast Guard found it. I'm taking your word that he was a first-class sailor. The woman at the boat rental was certain he left the dock happy. So, I've got to think someone gained his confidence off the coast and out of view. Timed. Maybe someone appearing to be stranded. And if so, we have to ask ourselves, *Why?*"

"He'd certainly be on guard if anyone approached who looked like an assassin."

"And if someone didn't look like an assassin?" Reilly asked.

Matthews took in the thought. "Like a woman?"

"Yes," Reilly affirmed. "Like a beautiful blonde."

The possibility shook Matthews. "Which could have meant he left himself open," she theorized.

"Exactly. The problem is I've checked with likely harbor rentals in the immediate area. No one who took out a boat fits the bill. Man or woman."

"Then are we back to an accident?" Matthews sounded resigned.

"Give me another day. Let me see what I come up with."

24

"Hello, Dan."

It was Yibing Cheng, Reilly's girlfriend, and increasingly more.

Dr. Yibing Cheng was a friend of Secretary of State Matthews. It was through Matthews that Reilly met the Chinese American woman in Beijing a few months earlier. Reilly needed an oil expert to help him understand the complexities of global oil politics while also trying to prevent the death of an international oil minister attending a conference in China. He was only half successful.

They instantly hit it off. She had the information he needed and the credentials to boot. The 33-year-old academic was respected for her scholarly work on the impact of the ever-evolving geopolitical strategies linked to fossil fuels. She was a well-respected predictor of future energy trends and how the fate of the world is intrinsically tied to the flow of oil and gas. But as far as she could see into the future in her field, she was taken by complete surprise by the romance that quickly developed with Dan Reilly.

Even though they knew virtually nothing about each other, they both felt an immense sexual and intellectual connection to one another. Reilly was completely smitten. He was captivated by her knowledge and lured in by her long dark hair, her open face, lips that curled into an inviting smile, and a neckline that led to great mysteries to be discovered.

Reilly and Cheng waited until they couldn't. Now they got together whenever they could. He learned more about her each time they met and each time they talked on the phone. Because of their conflicting travel schedules, it was more on the phone than across a restaurant table or under the covers.

Reilly learned about how she came to America from Tianjin, China.

Reilly said he knew the city. It was the third-largest and fastest-growing metropolitan area in China. Kensington had considered opening a property there.

As for her family, it was just Yibing and her mother. When she was born, the rule had been one child per family. Besides, she explained, her father had died when she was seven. So far she hadn't explained what had happened. Reilly didn't push the point.

Through her childhood years, her mother taught economics at Tianjin University. At eleven they immigrated to California where Yibing's mother took a job at the University of California, Irvine. High school test scores propelled Yibing into an accelerated math program and that led to early enrollment at the UC and a PhD at MIT. From there, jobs at think tanks, and consulting assignments, and eventual recruitment by the Department of Energy and more recently, the State Department. She became an in-house economics geek, which earned her the attention of Secretary Elizabeth Matthews, which in turn led to her meeting Dan Reilly in Beijing.

They had spoken cautiously to one another in China. Hidden microphones and cameras were everywhere. Back in the United States, they didn't hold back. Or couldn't.

That was what ultimately worried Reilly.

Am I moving too fast again?

"Wish you could have stayed," she cooed over the phone.

"Believe me, me too. Another few days. Can you wait?"

"With open arms. And—"

"Hey," he said, "don't make me any more wild about you than I am."

"Is that even possible?" she asked.

Reilly smiled and stared at himself in his Miami motel room. He saw a very happy face reflected back. "I think there's room to grow."

"Well then—" She finished the thought with a very vivid proposition.

25

LATER THAT EVENING

The travel arrangements for Ryan Battaglio's flight from Puerto Rico's Luis Muñoz Marín International Airport to London Gatwick had been made by his London publisher Reggie Huntley through a private Canadian carrier, Xpeditious Air.

What Huntley didn't know was that his office phones were bugged and Xpeditious expeditiously became the best deal. Moreover, the private airline was going to have a plane in Puerto Rico a day before President Battaglio was due to fly. That cut the rate down. *Perfect,* thought Huntley, especially since Battaglio refused to fly commercially and the U.S. government wasn't about to put him back on Air Force One.

With the president's autobiography finished and the travel plans properly vetted, Battaglio's plans were cleared by the Secret Service in a five-word text back to Washington: FOX IS GOOD TO GO.

Ryan Battaglio liked his new Secret Service code name. During his short term in office, he was ZEUS. Upon his retirement, the White House gave him a different designation. FOX seemed perfect to him. Foxes were astute. They were hunters. Decisive; always planning. Cunning.

The Secret Service dubbed Battaglio FOX for a different reason: Foxes can't be domesticated. They live a predatory existence. That's how his handlers saw him during his short administration and through today.

Few members of the team liked Battaglio even a little. Most loathed him. But of course, they smiled, obediently performed their duties, and would take a bullet for him. They hoped that wouldn't happen before their transfers came in.

"Sir, we're ready," Agent Nate Shirley announced. "Vehicles out front, ready to roll."

"Got it," Battaglio said without addressing the agent personally. He rarely remembered the names of his constantly changing protection. They seemed to be coming and going all the time. He didn't understand why.

Since Battaglio's unceremonious departure, which he considered nothing short of a palace coup, he vowed to get back at the conspirators. At the top of his list was Elizabeth Matthews. Beyond Matthews and her cadre of conspirators were a CIA asshole and a hotel executive he initially viewed as nothing more than a nuisance. Now he saw each of them as enemies of the state, or at least his enemies. His book and subsequent press tour would expose them and other traitors on his list. Then he'd make good with Gorshkov and from there…. *From there* was still up in the air.

Secret Service agent Shirley nodded to fellow agent Wilson who rolled Battaglio's two suitcases. They led the former president out of the beach house, with the third agent following Battaglio and the fourth posted at the open car door.

Two minutes later they were on the road escorted by local police for the puddle jump from Vieques to their flight out of Muñoz Marín. Along the way, they learned the flight out of San Juan would be delayed for an hour and a half while a replacement flight attendant arrived from Miami. An impatient Battaglio made every one of those 90 minutes miserable for his fellow travelers.

Finally, they were ready to board. Battaglio and his agents were led to the plane. At the top of the stairs the captain, flanked by his crew, welcomed them.

"Good day, Mr. President, I'm Horst Mueller, your pilot. I'm honored to have you join us today." Flanking him were two others.

"This is Peter Lee, my copilot, and Shannon O'Connor will be in the cabin to serve you."

Battaglio gazed lasciviously at the beautiful, tall, redhead flight attendant. He had thoughts of finally earning membership in the Mile High Club.

"Flying time will be eight hours, forty-seven minutes," the pilot said interrupting Battaglio's reverie, "but I'll do my best to shave some time off."

Battaglio nodded but said nothing. He stepped into the plane still thinking of the leggy flight attendant.

Mueller smiled and addressed O'Connor. "Prepare the cabin. Let's make the president comfortable." To his copilot, he said, "Ready the plane."

As soon as the president settled in, the flight attendant presented him with a glass of champagne on a silver platter. "For you, sir," she said with a distinctive, sexy Irish accent. "We'll have appetizers soon after we level off. To start, caviar and deviled eggs. Dinner will be a choice between succulent Kobe beef, roasted broccoli, and julienne potatoes or branzino with basil, lime, and ginger. Or both; all to your liking. We have the same for your team. As for entertainment, there are video consoles with the latest blockbusters."

Battaglio listened through the entire pitch. The entertainment on his mind definitely was not a movie. But he replied, "Give me the caviar and eggs now."

"Of course, Mr. President."

Back at her station, O'Connor notified copilot Lee that she was going to start serving before takeoff.

"He can't wait 15 minutes?"

"He's not the waiting type," she replied.

"Go ahead. It's his funeral."

Shannon O'Connor laughed. Before plating the food she checked the mirror, adjusted her wig, and touched the fake mole she'd placed on her cheek. Everything was good.

Twenty feet behind, Battaglio leaned across the aisle to speak with Nate Shirley.

"God almighty. The pilot is German. Copilot is Korean." He eyed the flight attendant's ass.

"And the woman is Irish. Where'd they get the fucking crew? Epcot?"

The Secret Service agent said nothing. He wanted to be done with Battaglio.

The woman flying as Shannon O'Connor overheard the ex-president. Ryan Battaglio was living up to everything she'd heard. She'd do her best to serve him to the very end.

* * *

President Battaglio's young secretary was halfway out the door when her phone rang.

"Damn," she complained.

Monica Whitley doubled back and answered, "Hello."

"Hello. This is Ginny Gleason. I'm calling from the White House."

Whitley automatically straightened. Battaglio had not heard anything from the White House since he moved into a villa on the Puerto Rico island of Vieques.

"The White House?"

"Yes. President Allphin would like to speak with President Battaglio before he leaves for London. Will you please get him?"

Allphin, on his press secretary's advice, was finally, though reluctantly, making the call to his predecessor.

"I'm sorry, I can't."

"Excuse me? Is this Monica Whitley, President Battaglio's secretary?"

"Yes it is, but I really can't. He left earlier. I have no way to—"

Gleason began again. "Ms. Whitley, I expect you're rather new at this. I can appreciate that. But there's always a way." She said sternly.

"Yes, ma'am. But he's in the air now to London."

Gleason paused. This was not good news. She should have checked with the Secret Service first.

"Ms. Whitley, I understand. But you can save me a two-minute call if you give me the airline, the flight designation, and—"

"I'm sorry. President Battaglio didn't give it to me. I—"

Ginny Gleason quickly hung up and phoned Secret Service Director Karl Banks. In five minutes she had Battaglio's private jet flight itinerary. Next, she told the president, who asked her to immediately establish a link to talk to the agents onboard.

* * *

Three hours and ten minutes later, Battaglio's jet received a radio transmission. Captain Mueller responded. "This is Xpeditious Air, Gulf 435, over."

"Xpeditious Air, Gulf 435, this is Secret Service agent Karl Banks." Banks did not identify himself as the Director.

"Go ahead Mr. Banks. This is Captain Mueller."

"Thank you, Captain. I tried to check in with our team by cell phone about your crew change, but the call did not go through. Can you have Agent Shirley come on up for a quick conversation?"

Mueller, a former NATO fighter pilot from Germany, said, "Can do. Stand by."

Mueller reached for the plane's intercom and was about to buzz Shannon O'Connor's station, but thought better of it.

"Peter, watch things. I'll get the Secret Service agent myself."

"Sure thing," the copilot said. He'd been listening to the conversation on his headset and reached for something by his side.

An instant before Mueller de-pressed his buckle release, he felt a tickle in his throat. He looked down. What he saw didn't make sense until the tickle turned into horrifying pain and a stream of blood. Mueller tried to call out. He couldn't. He only had desperate gurgles. He grabbed his throat. A reflex, but a wasted move. The very last thing he saw was Peter Lee wiping a six-inch blade on his sleeve.

Lee removed duct tape from a side compartment. It was one of the go-to supplies for patching. Today it had a unique purpose. He quickly wrapped it around the dead man's neck to stop the blood flow. There was no need to move Mueller. Lee would have complete control of the Gulfstream from his seat.

The communication from the White House only sped up what had been already set in motion. Lee keyed his microphone.

"This is Xpeditious Air Gulf 435. Mr. Banks, are you still there? Over."

"Yes Xpeditious Air, Gulf 435."

"This is copilot Peter Lee. Captain Mueller left to get Agent Shirley. He's in the head. Can you wait for a moment—"

Lee suddenly began cutting his words short as if he were having transmission problems.

"When…come…he—"

"Xpeditious Air Gulf 435, I'm having difficulty hearing you. Please repeat."

"Radio…minutes…will—"

With that Lee turned off the radio and checked the time and his chart. Less than an hour to their rendezvous point.

Lee assumed the White House would soon be checking with Air Traffic Control along the route, likely Shanwick Oceanic, which covers a huge swath over the Atlantic between the U.S. and Europe. For now, with the plane's transponder still pinging their location, Lee kept the Gulfstream on the established flight plan. No need for the U.S. to scramble planes. Just a radio problem. Besides, based on the intelligence he was given, the nearest carrier, USS *Wasp,* was enroute to Panama in the opposite direction. Too far away to act.

He thought it was almost comical.

* * *

Shannon O'Connor sat comfortably reading a Raymond Benson mystery that was left on the plane. She heard a light beep and automatically looked up to a small blue blinking bulb on the partition between her seat and the passenger cabin. She checked her watch and nodded. She flashed the cockpit three fast blips.

She rose calmly, gracefully, removed a small rectangular box she'd stored in the galley, put it on a silver tray, and covered it with a napkin. A surprise for the president. She pulled the curtain back and smiled. O'Connor checked the four Secret Service agents and held a finger to her lips. They looked comfortably asleep in their seats, with their heads back on the headrest and their eyes shut.

Hell, Battaglio thought, *it was their job to remain awake.*

Shannon whispered. "It's okay, Mr. President. We won't disturb them. In fact—" She paused and smiled broadly, "We can't."

The former president shot an inquisitive look. "What?"

"It's too bad you had to bring all four with you," Parisa Dhafari said. "You couldn't have traveled with just two?"

Another odd comment.

"Pity. Handsome young men. Each with wedding rings. I can understand two, but four? This was all avoidable, Mr. President."

Battaglio, confused, reached across the aisle and shook Agent Erickson. He slumped sideways bumping Nate Shirley, who lurched forward. Battaglio looked behind him. The others were also immobile.

"They can't help you, Mr. President. Something they ate."

"But I—"

"Also had the meat. But it wouldn't have mattered. I was saving you for last."

O'Connor uncovered the box, opened it, and removed a syringe.

"It'll be quite painless. You'll simply fall asleep. It's a rather peaceful way to go. Not my choice. I prefer more drama. But it's dangerous in-flight."

At that moment, Peter Lee stepped out of the cockpit. Blade in hand. "Is everything okay?"

She didn't take her eyes off her target.

"Of course it is. What did you expect?"

Battaglio screamed, "Who are you people?"

"Merely messengers with bad news. But not for long." She only slightly turned her head to Lee. "You've taken care of Captain Mueller?"

"A little ahead of time, but quite easily. For some reason, the Secret Service was trying to reach Battaglio. It sounded like a warning. I moved the clock up a bit."

"How far to the descent?"

"Thirty-two minutes."

Ryan Battaglio abruptly stood. He lunged at O'Connor. He hadn't gone after anyone so fiercely since he was in a college bar brawl, or when drunk, he murdered a teenage girl in Macau.

She easily sidestepped Battaglio. As he passed her, she thrust the needle into his neck and depressed the plunger in one swift move.

Battaglio stumbled backward down the aisle. His eyes bulged. Fear consumed him.

"You should take a seat, Mr. President. Just close your eyes and go to your happy place. That's if you have one."

She waved behind her. "Get back into the cockpit. I'll take care of him."

Lee obeyed.

The former president continued to back up. He looked around, focused on the aft door, and smiled cruelly. The adrenaline pumping through his veins fought the effects of the poison. "Then we'll all die!" he shouted.

She ran toward him. He took more steps in retreat, steadying himself on the seat backs.

Two more rows and he'd be at the door. She caught one leg and inched up to his waist. He kicked her shoulder and she lost her grip. Battaglio fought like a rabid dog. Her red wig flew off. She inched up further. The ex-president bit her hand. She screamed but didn't stop coming on.

The former president shouldn't have had anything to show an experienced assassin; especially one on such a high after two kills—the first off the coast of Biscayne Bay, the second in the Puerto Rican waters. He was no match for Parisa Dhafari, or so she thought. And yet, he was still fighting.

Less than 20 seconds had lapsed since she'd stuck him. He crawled toward the door. She now held onto his sports jacket. Battaglio wriggled out and gained the extra feet he needed. His fingers were on the handle.

If he opened the door, even a crack, they'd be sucked out. If she pulled the gun strapped to her thigh and shot the ex-president, the bullet would go through Battaglio and likely produce the same result, blasting a hole in the plane. Instant pressure change. A failed mission. Her death.

She realized her mistake. She had toyed with Battaglio. She should have simply drugged him like she did the Secret Service agents or slit his throat.

She knew better. *A mistake?* Yes, but she was not going to die here. Not today. Not now. Not some six miles over the Atlantic Ocean.

Images of growing up flashed in Dhafari's mind: Thoughts of her younger sister, Dominique. She flashed on them growing up Iraq. Their lives. Their family's struggles. The day they were spotted in gymnastics class by a government recruit and taken to a special facility to train.

The Dhafari sisters were from the holy city of Najaf, Iraq, the daughters of a café owner. Though only a few years apart, they studied together in Syria at Damascus University, where their high grades and extraordinary athletic abilities garnered attention from the Military Intelligence Directorate. They continued to the Military College of Administrative Affairs in Masyaf.

From Masyaf, Parisa and Dominique received additional training in Russia at the revived Andropov Institute, where they learned and excelled in spy craft. After finishing, they returned to Syria and took positions in counterintelligence before being called back to Moscow and service under President Nicolai Gorshkov.

It was Gorshkov who told Parisa that Dominique had died in Washington; a hero's death on a mission for the Russian Federation. Parisa stood stoically at attention through the president's recital. He didn't tell Parisa that her sister was sacrificed. His order. Instead, he lied. He blamed the Americans. Now she did, too.

Dhafari, the gymnast, stood, leaped onto one seat arm, catapulted up and over, and stuck her landing, planting herself between Battaglio and the door. As he was rising, she delivered a gut punch with her right fist that landed on his head just above her knee. She brought it up and caught him under the chin. He staggered back, even closer to the door, but he was weakening. Dhafari pulled Battaglio into a tight choke hold.

"Why?" he managed.

"I don't know," Parisa Dhafari said.

With one quick motion, she jerked his head sharply, severing his spinal cord. The legs which hadn't collapsed under the poison, gave way now.

Ryan Battaglio, America's disgraced, short-term president, crumpled to the floor of the private jet.

The assassin had one other job to accomplish.

She entered the cockpit. Lee was in the copilot's seat. "It's done," she said.

"You cut it close, Major," Lee said employing Dhafari's official rank.

"The bastard wanted to take us all down like some sort of American hero."

"…Which no one will ever know."

Dhafari snickered. "No one."

"Get the parachutes out," Lee said. "I'm going to start the descent. We'll be over the target zone in twenty-five."

She removed the two parachutes stowed in the cockpit locker. She put one on the lap of the dead pilot. Lee was annoyed.

"Dhafari, I don't want his blood on my chute. Get it off."

She picked up the chute and placed it near the door.

"I'll suit up and be back soon," she said.

Twenty minutes later she returned to the cockpit with the parachute strapped on and a floatation device around her waist ready to be deployed.

"Leveling off at 6,500 feet. Two minutes. Go aft. Wait for my signal to open the door. We'll jump ten seconds apart. We might have a few minutes in the water, but the tanker ship will be waiting. Shouldn't be too bad."

Dhafari said nothing.

Lee looked over his shoulder. "I said get back there." He engaged the automatic pilot.

"Change in plans," Dhafari said.

Without another word, she pulled a second syringe that was hidden in the storage container and stuck it in Peter Lee's neck. But this time, for good measure, she reached around and also thrust a knife into his heart.

"And change of location and way out."

Parisa Dhafari watched the Korean die. It was messy, but it didn't take long. She lifted him out of his seat and dragged him into the cabin joining the other five dead men. Then she returned, got comfortable in the copilot's seat, took the controls, and set a new course for where a Russian submarine was waiting. The tanker was never the plan, but she was the only one onboard who knew that.

She dropped to 6,000 feet. Thirty-five minutes later, she pitched the plane down at a gradual angle. Dhafari walked to the door that Battaglio had struggled to reach, opened it, and jumped. About the same time that Parisa Dhafari was hoisted onboard the Russian typhoon class sub *Dmitri Donskoy,* the Gulfstream crashed into the Atlantic, sinking five miles to the ocean floor.

26

"Mr. President, we have a problem."

Six words the president of the United States does not relish hearing, but words that inevitably find their way to the Oval Office. Today they were on the lips of Chief of Staff Lou Simon. He started before he crossed the threshold of the Oval Office. The president looked up from his desk and asked, "Yes?"

"Relayed from the Pentagon, sir, but only after the Secret Service's call," Simon began. The sixty-seven-year-old former CIA Director was a holdover from both the Crowe and Battaglio administrations. He always went right to the point. No shading. No sugarcoating. No holding back. He was a Joe Friday-just-the-facts-guy, a description he had stopped using since probably no one under thirty knew what it meant.

Simon was flanked by Secret Service Director Karl Banks. Both men looked deadly serious, expressions that usually accompanied the six words: *Mr. President, we have a problem.*

"It's complicated," Simon started.

"When isn't it?"

"Never, but this time even more. President Battaglio."

Allphin sighed. "Oh, God! Let's have it."

Banks, a career cop-turned-head of the president's protection team, took over.

"At 1340, President Battaglio's plane, a Gulfstream charter, flying from Puerto Rico to London, disappeared. First, the radio cut out. Then the plane lost altitude. Thirty minutes later, its transponder stopped. We can presume the plane went down."

"Where?"

"Into the Atlantic, sir."

"Jesus! Do we have anything in the vicinity? The 2nd Fleet—"

"The Pentagon is on with COMUSFLTFORCOM. The immediate answer is 'no.' We only have a general location and quite honestly that covers some 24,000 square miles."

"Was this trip cleared with you, Karl?" the president asked.

"Yes. We vetted the carrier and the crew, though there was one last-minute change."

"What kind of change?"

"The flight attendant booked had a stomach bug and couldn't travel. Another was called in at the last minute."

"And?"

"Last minute, sir. Not much time to check. I was trying to reach our team onboard when the radio transmission went bad."

"Why was he going to London?"

"To meet with his publisher. He had his manuscript on a drive."

"God almighty! Battaglio never heard of the internet?" the president complained.

Simon noted, "You know how he never emailed anything and wouldn't trust people with computers."

"Lou's right," Banks said. "According to my guys, it was the only copy."

"Aside from social media posts on his phone, he didn't have much of a digital footprint."

"You do realize what kind of conspiracy theories we're going to be hearing before the day is through," Allphin said. "Mysterious death of

President Battaglio. Did the CIA kill him to stop his book or me, for Chrissakes? Why couldn't Battaglio just die peacefully in his sleep?"

Allphin sighed deeply and gazed at the portraits and busts around the Oval Office. Lincoln, FDR, JFK, and Reagan stared outward. There'd be no art of Ryan Battaglio going up. He pressed a buzzer on his phone.

"Yes, Mr. President," Lillian Westerman promptly said.

"Get me Secretary of State Matthews. Oh, and I'll probably need you into the night, Lillian. We have a...," he reached for the right words, "...situation developing."

President Allphin returned to Simon and Banks. "Why do I suddenly think this is more than it seems?"

"Because it could be," Banks replied.

* * *

Within sixty minutes the phone tree had spread out from the Oval Office in every direction. First, those who needed to know and investigate the crash, then those who would have to manage the message.

President Allphin insisted that the White House get out in front of the news before the Gulfstream's owners issued their report. That meant minutes, not hours.

Seventy-two minutes following Simon's entrance, Press Secretary Doreen Gluckin addressed members of the White House press corps.

"I have an announcement to make," she began gravely.

The reporters who could assemble quickly enough took seats and quieted. Unscheduled press conferences were not unusual. But Gluckin's tone indicated this was serious.

The decision was made that the White House would frame it as an incident under investigation by the FAA, the Pentagon, and the FBI with details to come. The CIA and NSA were not mentioned, but they were on Allphin's list.

"You'll certainly have questions," she began. "I'll answer them to the best of my ability, but at present, there's very little to share beyond my prepared remarks. A private jet charter carrying former President Ryan Battaglio has gone down in the mid-Atlantic Ocean."

MSNBC, CNN, and Fox News broke into their telecasts. The broadcast networks remained with their original programming.

Gluckin kept to the script, a single paragraph crafted by Allphin's speech writers and checked by the White House lawyers.

She concluded the statement by stating, "The United States 2nd Fleet has launched a search and rescue mission." The press secretary paused and looked up. "That's all I have."

That didn't stop the barrage of questions.

"A private carrier?"

"How far away is the fleet?"

"Where's the last known location?"

"Do you suspect any foul play?"

Gluckin raised both hands. "One at a time." And for each of the first three questions, she said in one form or another, "We're looking into that."

When NPR's Stan Deutsch re-asked his question, "Do you suspect any foul play?" Gluckin replied, "We have no reason to go there, Stan."

What she actually thought was, *Yet.*

27

MIAMI, FLORIDA

Reilly turned on CNN while he dressed. Even though little surprised him these days, this did. He wasn't going to miss Ryan Battaglio; however, he had a sinking feeling that there was more to the accident, and sometime during the day he was going to hear about it. For now, he just watched.

The morning anchor hosted a roundtable, or rather, boxes of talking heads, including a presidential historian, a *Washington Post* reporter, a syndicated columnist, and an aviation expert. They all appeared with the anchor via Zoom or other online portals. No one had any real information, but that didn't prevent them from speculating.

"Lightning?"

"I've looked into that," the columnist reported. "No storms in the area."

"That's right," the aviation expert added. "Besides, planes get hit by lightning without much problem, and Gulfstreams have an impeccable safety record. They don't just fall out of the sky."

"A fire caused by a lithium battery?" the anchor asked.

Shrugs. If it were possible, it certainly wasn't interesting.

Soon the conversation devolved into the conspiracies that had been swirling all night: Battaglio was murdered by the deep state or a foreign

155

government. Then, if so, who and why? And what was he going to reveal in his book?

"A bomb? A missile?"

They debated that for three minutes. The presidential historian finally put a period on it. "Like the Kennedy assassination, we may never know."

Reilly had heard enough. Enough of nothing. He clicked off the TV.

He thought about calling Elizabeth. He decided not to. One thing at a time. Right now he had more locations to visit. He was going to start with boat rentals that dotted the coastline south of Biscayne Bay.

His conversations led nowhere until his eighth stop and an intriguing response from a young brunette clerk in a tight pink Miami t-shirt and navy blue shorts at Open Seas Cruises.

Reilly began with some light banter. He learned her name was Chelsea Traynor and she'd be working the desk for two months. After a few minutes chatting lightly, he got to his questions.

"No boat rentals in the past few days. School's back, so business is a little slower. But I had a Jet Ski rental," Traynor said.

Reilly raised an eyebrow. "A Jet Ski? What kind of range can you get on them?"

"Fully loaded, heck, sixty, seventy miles. Maybe more. People scoot around them for hours, but no one should ever go out far."

"And how fast do they go?"

"Oh my God, seventy miles per hour if you know what you're doing. Safest is under fifty. Why? Are you interested?"

"Not me, but can you tell me about the rental you had?"

"I'm not sure I can talk about stuff. Who do you work for?"

"In a minute, but what do you remember?"

She opened her rental iPad and called up a document and smiled. "Is she your daughter?"

"Definitely not," Reilly laughed, but he had two bits of potential information: Jet Ski and a woman. "Can you describe her?"

Traynor examined the electronic receipt.

"Well, she was about my age. Seemed really cool."

Now if she were blonde, Reilly thought. Matthews had told him Santiago was partial to blondes.

"Anything else?"

"Tall, taller than me. Long blonde hair. Pretty."

Another box checked.

"Anything else you remember?"

She stammered. "I don't know if I should be talking to you. Did she do something wrong? Are you a detective or something? I'll need to see some identification."

"No, I'm not a policeman."

"Then who are you? Am I in trouble for renting to her?"

"No, Chelsea you're fine. But I do work with people in law enforcement and some pretty high-up people in Washington. If you need, I can get someone on the phone to explain. Most people don't get to talk to her."

Chelsea Traynor was getting nervous. That wasn't good.

"Like who?"

"Someone who is very close to the president."

"The president of what?"

Reilly smiled, and not judgmentally. "The United States. The president of the United States. You'd be a great service to the nation. We might be able to get you into the White House to meet him."

"I don't know. My boss will be in after two and—."

"Every minute counts, Chelsea. Please, may I see the agreement?"

"She was really nice."

"I'm sure she was, but this is very important, and you'd be a big help with my," he now used the word, "investigation. May I *please* see the rental agreement?"

"You never said why."

"A man, an important man died sailing the other day. The police are certain it was an accident. I need to check on anyone who may have been in the area and could have seen anything."

"Like," she looked at the iPad, "Tracy Alaro?"

A name.

"Yes, that's right. Tracy Alaro."

"You sure we can't wait for my boss? He's on a plane and will be here in just a few hours."

"I'm sure."

"Well, I guess—"

She turned the device around for Reilly to see. It covered the terms and had a scribble for a signature and a credit card number. Then Reilly pointed to a camera that covered the register and the front desk.

"Is that hooked up?"

"Yes. To a computer in the office."

"Can you go check to see if it's working?"

Traynor shrugged and turned to the door into an inner office. While she was away, Reilly quickly snapped a series of photos of the agreement on his cell phone.

She returned less than a minute later. "It's on. Since I've been here we've never had to look at it. We haven't been robbed. You know, basically, there's no cash, and everything's on credit card. No one can take anything out without keys, which are locked up."

"I'd like to see the video of Tracy."

She hesitated.

"Please, Chelsea. It's really important."

"Ah, I don't know. I'm not supposed to. I just check in and check out boats."

"I bet you do more. Don't you wonder about the people you rent to?"

"Well, yes."

"So let's look at the video. See what you think."

Traynor asked, "Do you have any identification? You know, so I can tell my boss."

Reilly had nothing other than his Kensington Royal International ID. It would have to do.

He pulled it out of his wallet and showed her.

"This doesn't say you work for the government."

"No, it doesn't. But I get called in to help. That's why I'm here."

"Are you a spy?"

Reilly smiled and decided to say nothing.

"I'm scared," she admitted.

"I understand. But you're not in any trouble. Now, please, Chelsea. I promise I'll talk with your boss when he comes in, but right now, every second counts."

The young woman gave in and led Reilly around the counter to the office. He'd won round one.

Five minutes later, she found the footage of the woman who had come in to rent the Jet Ski. Reilly watched once, then asked her play it again.

"What do you think?" he asked.

"I don't know. What do you mean?"

"What's her story?"

"Friendly. Athletic. Muscular. Yes, muscular. Really muscular."

"Like a body builder?"

"No," she paused. "Like a fighter. A boxer. Martial arts. Something."

"Okay," Reilly said. "Does that make her anything beyond friendly?"

"She was just friendly. But—"

"Yes?"

"She had something in a pouch with an antenna sticking out."

"Go on."

"I asked her what it was. She said it was just a radio."

"And what did you think?"

"That it was odd. I mean, who uses a radio with an antenna anymore. We've got phones and earbuds."

Reilly considered another option: *Portable radar.* Then he said, "Play it again."

While she did, Reilly shot video and some still frames of the sequence.

"One more thing, Chelsea."

"Sure."

"Has the Jet Ski gone out since the woman returned it?"

"No."

"Can you double-check?"

"Yes, but I know it hasn't."

"Why?"

"I'm the only one working shifts."

"Just check for me."

While Chelsea Traynor scanned the database back on the counter, Reilly walked to the front door and spotted the company's four Jet Skis moored to the dock.

"Nope," she said. "No rentals since."

"Do you know exactly which one she took out?"

"Of course." She joined him and pointed. "Number 1, far left."

"Alright, Chelsea. Now this is very important."

She was beginning to feel the gravity of the situation. "Yes, sir."

"Have you or anyone touched it or wiped it down?"

"No. No one. I haven't gotten to cleaning or refueling it."

Refueling was important. The amount of gas used could determine if the Jet Ski had traveled far enough out and back to be relevant.

"Good," Reilly said. "Don't. Next, do you have a tarp we can put over the Jet Ski without touching it?"

"Yes, but—"

"Put it on, Chelsea. And then I'm going to have a team come here and go over it."

"Like for fingerprints?"

"Yes and more. So while I make some calls, get your boss in."

Traynor swallowed hard. "Did I do anything wrong, Mr. Reilly?"

"No, Chelsea," Reilly said compassionately. "Just the opposite. You've helped me in more ways than you can ever imagine."

If his thinking and the inspection paid off, Chelsea Traynor would earn a special trip to Washington.

* * *

Outside Open Seas Cruises, Dan Reilly sat at a park bench. He dialed his phone. His friend Bob Heath answered. "It's Dan. Incoming pictures for you, Bob."

"Yearbook glossies? Can't wait."

"Not even close. Stills and video that I need the Company's eagle eyes on." By company he meant the Central Intelligence Agency where Heath was a senior case officer. Reilly didn't offer any further context. Heath had enough to put whatever Reilly was sending into the system for analysis or reach out to co-agencies. It would start with facial recognition.

"Is this a personal favor?" Heath asked.

"No."

That meant it wasn't for Kensington. Heath read it properly as government business.

"Priority?"

"I'd stay on the line if I thought you'd get it that fast."

"Where are you?"

"Miami."

Heath quickly put the pieces together. Miami was where Elizabeth Matthews's DSS agent had disappeared and Reilly was often called on by the Secretary of State for various assignments.

"And," Reilly continued.

"There's never not an *and* with you," Heath joked.

"This one's even bigger. Call your buddies at the Bureau ASAP. No, make that now. If I'm right, if this all pans out, they'll want the original video and paperwork. But they also need to inspect for prints and any DNA on a Jet Ski here." Reilly told him where here was. "I'll wait."

"I'm on it," Heath replied. "Good to be working with you again, buddy."

"Mission first, Bob," Reilly said invoking the army creed. "Mission first."

28

WASHINGTON, DC

THAT EVENING

Elizabeth Matthews's black Chevy Suburban rolled up to Annabelle, a Michelin-starred restaurant on Florida Avenue NW, at precisely the same time as Edward Jefferson Shaw's Lincoln Town Car arrived. It wasn't surprising considering the two extraordinary personalities both valued punctuality.

Matthews stepped out of her armored van, driven and guarded by her Diplomatic Service detail. The vehicle stayed in front while Shaw's driver dropped him off and found a space a half block away.

The restaurant was the Secretary of State's choice. They would dine privately in a room large enough for a party of 16. Security posted outside would guarantee that the only interruptions would be for service from vetted staff.

"Madame Secretary," Shaw began warmly.

"EJ, you know the rule. First names. We go too far back."

"Will that always be the case?" A veiled question to something certain to come up later: her rumored announcement as vice president and perhaps a run for the presidency.

"My, I have no idea what you're talking about," Matthews said slyly as she passed through the entrance. The companions said nothing else while the *maître d'* led them to their isolated candle-lit table in the back. They drew few eyes on the way. Washingtonians were generally nonplussed by dignitaries.

Matthews had budgeted 90 minutes. They each ordered vodka martinis with a lemon twist. For appetizers, Matthews opted for the fillet, beans and radicchio salad. Shaw ordered the chilled Athena melon soup. For their entrees, Matthews chose the grilled rainbow trout with sautéed Maryland crab and corn. Shaw preferred the Rhode Island skate prepared in a broth with sun gold cherry tomatoes, eggplant *courgette*, Bangs Island Mussels, and crostini with aioli.

The staff timed the meal allowing for twelve minutes of conversation over cocktails before the appetizers arrived.

In that time they quickly covered what everyone was talking about: Ryan Battaglio's disappearance.

Matthews added nothing substantive. Shaw wasn't surprised. Then they got onto the individual they had in common—Dan Reilly.

"I'm worried. I'm not sure how much longer Daniel can operate with split loyalties," Matthews said. "I have him out for me now, but he's torn."

"My thoughts exactly," the president of Kensington Royal International replied.

"But I need him, EJ."

"So do I. He'd make a good successor," Shaw offered. "But what do you have in mind?"

Matthews smiled coyly. "Help around the house."

"The White House, Elizabeth?"

"You're not going to get anything that easy, EJ. Let's just say Daniel knows the world. He speaks languages we normally need translators for, and he thinks like a—"

Shaw finished the thought. "An executive."

"A negotiator. A diplomat."

"I gave him a year to decide," Shaw continued.

"I know. Daniel told me." Matthews smiled. "The timing could work out perfectly."

"Back to my question, Elizabeth."

She removed a pen and a small sheet of paper from a compartment in her purse. She wrote a job name and showed the hotel executive.

"Impressive," he said.

"I thought so. Two, maybe four years and he comes back to you more ready than ever and undoubtedly more valuable to the company." She flashed a winning, political grin. "See, I'm only thinking of you, EJ."

With that, she put the paper to the candle flame and the flash paper did what it does when it meets 300 degrees Fahrenheit.

29

JUST AFTER NOON THE NEXT DAY, Reilly's plane touched down at Reagan National. As he came down the jet bridge into the terminal, he spotted a man in black. He wore a Secret Service pin. Reilly took him to be a member of the SPS, the Security Protective Services.

"Mr. Reilly?"

No question mark was needed. Reilly had a driver and someplace to go.

Thirty-five minutes later, they arrived at CIA headquarters in Langley, Virginia. Bob Heath was at the entrance to greet Reilly.

"Thanks for coming out," Heath said.

"Didn't seem like it was a choice," Reilly joked.

"Until we install a SCIF in your condo, there are things better discussed here."

"Got anything on our blonde?"

"Not yet, but I need to brainstorm with you about something. Inside."

They settled into Heath's Spartan office. Besides a few photos with presidents, not including Battaglio, there was little to suggest much about his life except for a go-bag in the corner, always ready to go.

Heath was a few years older than Reilly, but in many ways, they could have been brothers. Height, hair color, eyes. The most distinguishing difference, Heath walked with a slight limp. That was a present he never asked for from Afghanistan. The fact that he survived an ambush was completely thanks to Reilly.

"What's your reaction to Battaglio's plane going down," Heath began.

Reilly smirked. He thought, but didn't say, *Justice delayed is justice denied.* Instead he said, "Seems like a whole lot going wrong precisely on time. Planned and executed, with the emphasis on executed."

"Kind of my thinking, too, especially since we don't know what was in his book."

Reilly listened. It felt like Heath had a theory he wanted to test. They'd done this for each other ever since the Army.

"Apparently there's no way to find out now."

"That's good," Reilly replied. "Just as well that Battaglio didn't get another word in."

"Like I said, *now.*"

"Meaning?"

"I'll back up a bit. Battaglio had a ghostwriter who did all the work. She wrote on his laptop. No wired desktop. No Wi-Fi. Nothing was saved in the cloud. Battaglio was too paranoid. He stored the manuscript on a single USB thumb drive that he locked up every night. His Secret Service detail was not allowed to read anything. When Battaglio left for the airport he took his laptop, the drive, and a printed copy."

"Working drafts?"

"All shredded. He didn't trust anyone."

"So it's gone with him." Then some gallows humor hit Reilly. *Gravity finally brought Ryan Battaglio down.*

"Apparently so," Heath continued.

"What about the ghostwriter? She's probably free of any NDA."

"That's going to be a problem."

"Why?" Reilly asked.

"She's in different parts."

Reilly was confused.

"A shark attack while swimming in Puerto Rico. The day after she finished up with Battaglio."

"Christ!" Reilly exclaimed.

"Her body washed ashore. Well, some of it. Horrible accident."

"Awful," Reilly whispered.

"Quite awful. And today, while trying to track down her agent something else came up. Or more accurately went down. He took a giant leap out of his New York high-rise bedroom window. People said he was despondent."

"And you don't think so?"

"Three accidents, Dan. No way."

"Maybe four," Reilly replied.

"Oh?"

"Any news on what I sent you?"

The question prompted a call to Katie Koehler, Heath's goddaughter, and a rising star at the FBI's high-tech labs tucked away in rural West Virginia. He'd sent Reilly's video and still images to Koehler for her analysis on the bureau's Next Generation Identification (NGI) System, specifically the FACE Services Unit. More specifically, the world's most robust facial recognition software.

"Anything, Katie?"

"Nothing yet on the photo. Nothing at all on her name and ID. I had help running down the credit card. It's a temp, bought at a supermarket in Miami. On balance, that doesn't necessarily mean anything, but coupled with the fact that there's no record of a woman named Tracy Alaro that fits her description, I'd call that odd. Working on the handwriting, too. Feels like a righty using her left hand, but then again, signature scribbles on tablets are always crap."

"Stay on it," Heath said.

"Will do. You seem concerned," Koehler said.

"That's because I am."

Heath brought Reilly up to speed on the conversation. Baby steps that so far led nowhere. He was ready to leave.

"Couple of things," Reilly said.

"Go for it."

"One, can I hop a ride back in town? I have to fill in Elizabeth. Second, any video from the San Juan terminal where Battaglio departed?"

"I bet the bureau has it."

"Get it. I'm more than curious what shows up."

"You mean who."

Reilly nodded.

30

AS REILLY RODE INTO DC, he thought of that bath and bed again. Yibing was in town. This time they'd connect. But before that, he had to see the other woman in his life: Elizabeth Matthews.

The State Department building's footprint covers two city blocks bounded by C Street to the south, E and D Streets and Virginia Avenue to the north, 21st Street to the east, and 23rd Street to the west. Reilly entered on C and was met by Tom Hunter, which surprised him.

"Mr. Reilly."

"Agent Hunter. You didn't need to come down. I know the way."

"Thought I'd clear you myself and we'd get a chance to talk. As you know, Santiago and I were very close, and if there is anything, and I mean anything that suggests his death was not an accident, I want in."

"I understand," Reilly said stopping at the elevator and addressing Hunter. "But I hope you also understand that I report to the Secretary of State. What happens after that is totally up to her."

"Mr. Reilly," Hunter grasped Reilly's arm, "We lost a member of our family. I lost my mentor. So if you have any evidence—"

Reilly looked at the agent's hand on his arm. His intent was apparent. Hunter released his grip.

"I'll put it another way. I'm responsible for Secretary Matthews's safety. It's my job to know if there are threats and to prepare against them." He paused. "If I appear combative, it's because I am. I don't know you. Based on what I've learned, you have Secretary Matthews's ear. But I have her back. My responsibility is to vet any potential threats and to prepare against them. That was Carlos Santiago's duty. It's now mine no matter what your relationship is, or has been, with the Secretary."

Hunter kept his eyes on Reilly. The elevator door opened and closed. They missed the lift.

"With all due respect, Agent Hunter, and as I said, I report to the Secretary. I suggest you speak with her."

They stared at one another while another elevator door opened and closed down the line.

"Rest assured, Mr. Reilly, I will."

"Then I think we understand each other."

Then a third elevator door opened again to their right.

"After you, Agent Hunter."

"I insist, you first."

Reilly obliged. Three minutes later, Reilly was with Matthews in her cream-colored office, sitting opposite her across her long wooden desk. Tom Hunter remained outside the inner sanctum.

THE WHITE HOUSE

Now was also when FBI Director Reese McCafferty, CIA Director Gerald Watts, and Secret Service Director Karl Banks walked into the Oval Office together. President Allphin met them at the center of the blue carpet emblazoned with the Presidential Seal. He invited them to take seats wherever they'd like. McCafferty and Watts chose the couch, Banks, a high back chair to the left. The president sat in a Revolutionary-era Captain's Chair he'd turned around from the foot of the Resolute Desk.

"Karl, I'm sorry about your men. I'll call their families today."

"They'll appreciate that, sir. I have their names and numbers for you." He removed a folder from his briefcase and handed it to the president. "And the country has suffered a loss as well," he continued. "Have you thought about services for President Battaglio?"

Allphin hadn't gotten any further than ordering flags lowered to half-staff.

"Not yet," he said dispassionately. He genuinely wished Battaglio's memory would disappear with his body.

"All right. Down to business. Reese?"

"I don't have any tangible facts."

"All right, what do you believe?"

"You don't pay me to *believe*, Mr. President."

Allphin offered a half nod. "Then what do you suspect?"

"We have a lot to do before I can answer that. Agents are up in Canada talking to the jet leasing company. We're doing deeper background checks on the flight crew to see if anything was missed by Karl's people." He turned to the Secret Service Director. "No disrespect, Karl."

"None taken. There was a last-minute substitution, but the name and background came up clean. Of course, with more time—"

Allphin addressed his CIA Director next. "Gerald, any reason to think it wasn't anything but an accident? A missile from a sub or a ship in the vicinity? A bomb on board? You've heard what they're talking about on TV."

"I have, Mr. President. Nothing's shown up on the satellites. No plumes."

"Longer range?"

"Again, we haven't found any evidence of missiles in flight."

"Any chatter from the usual suspects?"

The list of usual suspects had expanded to North Korea's submarine fleet, which had been advancing beyond their home waters, though there was no evidence they were in the Atlantic. And Iran, which routinely sends its subs out into the Atlantic. Third on the list, Venezuela, but they had not proven themselves battle-ready under the new president. So the CIA Director answered, "No."

"Gentlemen, if it were up to me, this would end here. But we can't. Someone in Congress will begin to nose around. And we're left looking like…no, I'm left looking like I didn't have the balls to investigate the death of a former U.S. president."

The three men sat stone-cold silent.

"Now I didn't ask for this job. I was perfectly happy as Speaker of the House. But I'm sure as hell not going to let the death of that asshole ruin the short time I have in this office! So get me something definitive."

"And if we can put fingerprints on it?"

"Then we'll decide what to do. Even if I have to release Battaglio's full record."

"Excuse me," Karl Banks said. The Secret Service Director was the only one in the room who had not been briefed about what Ryan Battaglio had done as a Congressman one night in Macau, and why he was given the choice of resigning on his own or publicly in disgrace. Banks was about to find out.

THE STATE DEPARTMENT

Reilly took Matthews through his Florida inquiry, both facts and suppositions.

"The boat rental confirmed Santiago went out on his own. Traffic was light. The woman at the rental watched him launch. She was satisfied that he knew what he was doing. She also said no one followed him out of the harbor. Then somehow, somewhere, Carlos Santiago, a seasoned sailor on a calm day, falls overboard and disappears."

He stopped and shook his head. "You were right, it didn't seem plausible, so I checked further. Other marinas."

Elizabeth listened.

"And?" Matthews asked.

"And," Reilly continued, "14 other boats went out within the time frame. I ran all their names."

"How the hell did they give all that to you?"

"Must have been my good looks and winning nature."

"I doubt that."

"Okay, I lied," he paused again. "Just a little. But I started thinking about what would make a seasoned agent invite a stranger onboard who—"

"…Might need help!"

"Bingo," Reilly sharply replied.

"And who could that have been?"

"A woman in distress."

"Come on, Daniel, really."

"Like you said yourself. A blonde. A blonde in a bikini. But a blonde in a bikini adrift miles out. Of course, he'd help her."

"But he'd still be careful. He's trained to be cautious."

"A beautiful blonde all alone on the high seas?"

Matthews said nothing.

"So I asked myself how it would have played out: A boat taking on water or out of gas? Possibly a rental or someone's private craft. But they would have a radio and would have called in for help. Then something else came up. It wasn't a boat."

"What? A seaplane?"

"Another craft. A wave runner. A Jet Ski."

"Way out in the ocean? Aren't they only rated or at least recommended for lakes and rivers? The Intercoastal or near shore?"

"Yes and no."

"I get the yes. The no?"

"Depending on the make and model, weather, and sea conditions, they can have longer range, longer than I ever knew. And given that Santiago had an uneaten sandwich, two beers, and three bottles of water still in his cooler, I'd say whatever happened occurred between the time he ate one sandwich and planned on heading back. Figure he ate between 11 and one. That would likely place him no further out than 15 to 20 miles."

"How do you even figure he had lunch?"

"The Coast Guard recovered a single crumpled wrapper in the cooler, an empty water bottle and one beer can in the trash. Santiago, ever the good citizen, taking his discards back."

"You're leading up to something, Daniel."

"I am. Timing, Elizabeth. It's a big ocean, so assuming, and that's all I'm doing until we know more, what if someone on a Jet Ski had been offshore waiting and watching? Santiago would have been eyes forward as he sailed out and might have missed anyone tagging along in the distance. Especially someone in a low profile craft."

Matthews touched her pin. She needed to be wearing a question mark today, not an American eagle.

"I suppose so," she said.

"Well, lo and behold there was one. It went out before Santiago and returned five hours later. That's a long time on one of those things, but it's possible. That's what you asked me to consider, right? Possibilities."

"Yes."

"And you said that Carlos did have a thing for blondes."

Matthews said nothing.

"I copied the rental agreement along with video and screen grabs. The FBI can get a warrant for the real thing. I can tell you she was a real beauty. Maybe South American, Middle Eastern, Israeli, or Iranian. A blonde, at least for the sake of the mission."

"Wait? Mission?"

"An assassination, Elizabeth. In my estimation planned and, I'm sorry, executed effectively. The woman knew who Santiago was and where he would be. She appeared to be stranded. He helped her. She killed him, wiped all evidence of her work, dumped Santiago overboard, returned to her functional Jet Ski, and returned to port all smiles. According to the rental agent, our killer said she had an especially satisfying day."

Matthews stood and paced, processing what Reilly had reported.

"Then Carlos was stalked."

"Way more than stalked. Targeted."

"Why?"

"I can't answer."

"But how would she have known?"

"Elizabeth, that's the easiest question of all. Someone on the inside."

Matthews contemplated her answer for a good 30 seconds.

"I trust everyone on my staff. I know their families. Most have been with me for years."

"But people talk," Reilly replied. "Some people get paid to talk. Some get compromised. Others are sleepers."

Matthews covered her eyes with both hands and thought for a moment after which she said, "Send Agent Hunter in."

She buzzed her outer office and asked for the DSS agent, now the head of her team, to join them. Hunter entered and exchanged a cold look with Reilly. She instantly took the temperature between the two. Icy cold.

"Am I missing something?" Matthews asked.

Neither man said anything.

"Gentlemen?"

"May I speak freely, Madame Secretary?" Hunter asked.

"Of course."

"You know I wanted to go to Florida for you. Carlos was my friend," Hunter began. "Instead—" He glared at Reilly.

"Tom, I'll say this just once. I've put my trust in Dan Reilly for years." Then she turned to Reilly. "And Daniel, Tom has stepped up at a very difficult time. The more he learns about your trip, the better prepared he'll be. And the safer I will feel. That means no secrets between us."

"Yes, Madame Secretary," Hunter said while Reilly remained silent.

"Yes, ma'am," Reilly finally added.

Before peace was declared, Reilly's cell phone rang.

"Excuse me for a moment," he said noting the number. "I've got to take this."

Reilly stood and stepped out of Matthews's office. As he left, Hunter leaned in.

"Madame Secretary, I strongly urge you to leave this in our hands. Mr. Reilly doesn't have clearance to—"

"Tom, I should have explained that Daniel comes with top credentials in the intelligence services. He was fast-tracked into the Army's Officer Candidate School in Fort Benning, Georgia. From there he was assigned to Fort Huachuca, the U.S. Army Intelligence Center, and the U.S. Army Network Technology Command (NETCOM) in Arizona. He spent time with the Defense Language Institute at the Presidio in Monterey, California, where he studied Arabic and reported to Afghanistan. After that, he worked for me. I'm telling you this because most of his background isn't easily accessible on the internet or in his Kensington Royal bio. The bottom line, I trust him."

"Nonetheless, Madame Secretary, Mr. Reilly is now a civilian and not—"

She smiled broadly. "You don't have to worry about Daniel. He has my trust."

"People have made dangerous mistakes with unwarranted trust."

Her smile faded. "Tom, what are you really thinking?"

"Until such time that you're vice president under the protection of the Secret Service, your safety is in the hands of the Diplomatic Security Service. You are my responsibility. Carlos was not only my boss; he was like a brother. And if his death was anything other than an accident, then it's absolutely urgent that I tighten the net around you. And that includes keeping outsiders out."

Elizabeth Matthews nodded but only in acknowledgment of his concern, not in agreement.

"Tom, let me tell you a story about Dan Reilly. It's not public and it wasn't in defense of his country, but it speaks to his dedication."

She stood from her desk and began pacing.

"A little over a year ago, Reilly flew to Mazatlán to help secure his company's property ahead of a tropical storm that was threatening the area. That storm quickly intensified and turned into Hurricane Gracie; Cat 5 with 170-mile-per-hour winds. It was the worst to hit Mazatlán in forty years. Strongest winds on record there by far. Reilly had a resort full of guests, hundreds, and suddenly no way to get most to safety.

"He oversaw securing the place as best he could. But Gracie slammed the resort city. The leading edge was bad. After the eye passed, the back end was even worse. The hurricane slowed and pounded the region for three hours. Beachfront property took it the hardest. By the time the hurricane moved on, the place looked like a war zone. Flipped cars, downed trees and powerlines, knee-deep saltwater flooding everywhere. No electricity. No cell phones. Food quickly spoiled.

"Fortunately, Reilly had a satellite phone. He called for help from his company headquarters. No commercial flights could come in. No planes remained on the ground to leave. Reilly did two things. He chartered planes on his American Express Corporate Card. By the time he was through, it was more than 200 grand. He did it directly through the president of AMEX, and later asked permission from his boss."

Tom Hunter followed Matthews as she walked and talked. But he shrugged his shoulders. "He did his job. Good for him."

"That's not all. And this is above and beyond his job. Armed gangs, desperate to grab anything they could, rampaged the city working their way up to the hotel. Reilly got the hotel general manager to pull every bit of cash available from the safe. Then, with a driver, he did what no one else would consider. He went to people who held power in a lawless time. The cartel.

"It took him more than ninety minutes and a circuitous route to reach a huge compound guarded by men with semi-automatics. They'd been ordered not to let anyone through. Killing a trespasser might even earn them a bottle of tequila. Reilly explained why he was there and who he wanted to see. It was the head of the local cartel. The man inside that no strangers got to meet. The request was rewarded with the impact of a rifle butt across Reilly's back. He crumbled to the ground. Reilly slowly got up and stood face-to-face with his tormentor who laughed loudly. He was about to get another blow when a voice boomed over a speaker. The guard was ordered to bring Reilly forward.

"Inside he made a deal. I don't exactly know how. But Dan Reilly can be very persuasive when he needs to be. He left with a security force and no one bothered Reilly, the hotel, or the people in his charge. They all got out and not a word made the news. That's why I trust him.

"If he can survive a hurricane and a cartel leader, he can survive your concern. Give him a chance, Tom."

"Yes, ma'am," Hunter said. "I appreciate knowing."

He stopped in mid-sentence as Reilly returned. Hunter leaned back in his seat.

"Sorry," he said. "That was Heath."

Hunter cocked his head. "Heath?"

"A friend at Langley. I texted him photos."

"What photos?"

Reilly looked to Matthews for guidance. She nodded approval for him to explain.

"Start from the beginning, Daniel. Agent Hunter is feeling quite better, and he needs to know what you're thinking."

Reilly replayed what he'd told Matthews only minutes before. When he finished, Hunter had a question.

"Why Santiago?"

Reilly sat quietly. "I don't know. And I may be completely off, but my sense is—"

"And the call you just got?" Hunter interrupted.

This was the line that Reilly would not cross. Heath was doing him a favor, and as far as he was concerned he was not going to reveal anything to Hunter without first running it by Matthews. First meant alone.

"It was another matter."

"You certainly are a busy man," Hunter declared.

"Sometimes too busy," Reilly replied.

"Well, given the circumstances, we can *all*," Hunter looked at Matthews on *all*, "agree to share everything, no matter how small it may seem."

Reilly smiled. "Certainly."

With that Hunter stood and offered his hand. Reilly shook it.

"Mr. Reilly, understand it's my nature to be skeptical when people cross into my lane."

Reilly nodded.

"But if you're right then, of course, we must be extra vigilant."

Reilly tipped his head again.

"And of course, you'll be sure to put me in touch with your friend at the CIA if he has anything."

That was something he definitely wouldn't do. At least not immediately. Not when he thought there might be someone on the inside who couldn't be trusted.

31

THE NEXT DAY

General Valery Rotenberg strode into his president's Kremlin office with a report on an asset he was managing as director of the Foreign Intelligence Service of the Russian Federation, the FSB. The spy agency was the reconstituted KGB, charged with espionage and intelligence-gathering operations outside Russia's borders. It has more than 13,000 individuals devoted to the Motherland and duty. Some of them were bureaucrats, other clerks and functionaries, and still others, ambitious and talented killers and spies. President Gorshkov wanted to hear how one of the FSB's superstars in the final category was doing: Parisa Dhafari.

Dhafari, like her younger sister Dominique, was outstanding in her field. Her Middle Eastern looks and Iranian passport and multiple identities helped to hide her true allegiance.

Too bad, Gorshkov thought, *that her sister had to be sacrificed;* a fact that Parisa could never know. But her death in a Washington hotel explosion was part of a greater deception, bigger than her.

Rotenberg walked through Dhafari's successful mission off the Miami coast: The death of the State Department's Diplomatic Service Chief. "She left no evidence of her work and timed it when American satellites were not watching. A complete success."

"Very good, and her second objective?"

This was Battaglio's ghostwriter.

At the risk of joking, Rotenberg said, "That operation also went swimmingly. America's Coast Guard, people on the beach, and the press saw exactly what we wanted them to see. A terrible shark attack, which it ultimately was."

Rotenberg then regaled Gorshkov with the news about how the ghostwriter's agent, filled with grief, was encouraged to take a flying leap off his building in New York. That was the work of another operative. Someone proving his worth as a well-placed sleeper spy.

"Go on."

Still at attention, Rotenberg knew what Gorshkov was waiting for: how Dhafari had valiantly brought down the Gulfstream. "No survivors, sir. She's now on board our submarine heading to their rendezvous point."

"She's in good health?" Gorshkov asked.

"Yes, sir."

"And isolated?"

"Completely. The official word on board: a training exercise. No one knows who she is. Only a handful of men even saw her."

"A handful?"

"Captain Volkov, his first mate, two officers, and two enlisted men."

"Are they loyal?"

This was a trick question. Gorshkov's trickiest.

"I can only speak for the captain. I have known him for 25 years. As for the others?" He left his answer dangling.

"Make sure the same men assist with her transfer. No others. Then when they dock, let's be damned sure about their fidelity."

The director of the spy agency nodded. He had the means to find out and to dispense permanent corrective measures.

"And they're on schedule?" Gorshkov asked.

"Yes, according to the admiralty. As ordered."

32

THE WHITE HOUSE

"Thank you for seeing me, Mr. President."

"Perfect timing, Elizabeth. I want to go over your itinerary for Panama."

"And I've got something I want to discuss with you."

"Anytime day or night. After all, we're going to be a team, and the more access you have to me, the better. The more ready you'll be when it becomes your turn to take over."

"I'm afraid we're getting ahead of our skis, sir."

"Just being on them won't work for this job, Elizabeth. You have to be out ahead of them 24/7. As Oprah Winfrey once said, 'Skiing is the next best thing to having wings.'"

As Matthews laughed, the president picked up a file on his desk marked TOP SECRET and invited her to sit down on one of the cushioned chairs. He held onto the paperwork.

With the pleasantries over, Allphin got to the point. "We're moving your trip up."

"Oh?"

"The president's request. He wants time to manage the message and consider his political options."

"He does know that you've already committed some?" Matthews replied. "That troops will be arriving while there."

"He does, just on an earlier timetable."

"The good news is that it'll be a quicker in and out for you."

"When?"

Allphin told her. Matthews grimaced. When the meeting was over she'd have to tell her staff to pick up the pace, particularly Tom Hunter.

The president handed the file to Elizabeth Matthews. "This is what you'll be offering the president."

She read the terms.

The memo specified the American firepower that would be on the way as they met, including a rebuild of the abandoned U.S. Fort Sherman on the Caribbean Sea and supply stations at Panamá Pacífico International Airport, which was the decommissioned Howard AFB on the Pacific.

"A limited mobilization. Nothing too overt, but enough to show our commitment to get the Canal back up to full working order. The planes will land during your meeting. He'll hear the rumble from his office."

FIVE BLOCKS AWAY

Reilly quickly spotted the man's face reflected in the mirror at the Old Ebbitt Grill bar. He was six-three, military tough with short-cropped black hair, deep-set green eyes, and a square chin. He was sitting with an open seat next to him, swirling a glass with a dark drink. Reilly knew what he was drinking. Macallan Scotch. Probably 12 years old. One piece of ice. The man caught Reilly's eye contact. He raised his glass toward the mirror, an invitation to join him.

Reilly saddled up. They sat together facing forward.

"You've been busy freelancing again," the man said still looking straight ahead.

"A bit. I needed the extra frequent flier miles."

The man chuckled lightly. "Like that's ever a problem."

Reilly had flown so much on United over the past few years that the airline painted his name on one of their 747-300s.

"Through for now?" he asked.

At that moment, the bartender came by and interrupted. "What'll it be?"

"A Guinness will do nicely, and the menu." Reilly turned to his companion, "Hungry?"

"Starved. So, when do you get back to your actual job?"

"On it now. What do you have for me?"

Alan Cannon, Kensington International's Vice President of Global Safety and Security, and Dan Reilly's confidant, colleague and friend, removed a sheet of paper from his breast pocket. He slid the paper over. Reilly unfolded it. At the top, one word in 15-point Arial Black: Helsinki. Reilly read it once, then again, and said, "Trouble in River City."

It was a reference to the 1950s musical *The Music Man*, which had a recent revival. It also worked for Taiwan's capital.

"Security spotted what we're sure were surveillance teams on the property. I reviewed the video. I think they're right. I recommend we elevate the threat right to ORANGE. It may be enough to scare off any potential attack."

"Any sense of who?"

"No, not yet. I'm flying out tomorrow. You may want to follow. Anywhere else you need to be?"

"Not that I know of," Reilly replied. "But you know how fast that can change."

THE WHITE HOUSE

When the president finished briefing Matthews on the Panama trip he said, "Now your turn. You have something for me?"

"I do. You remember Dan Reilly?"

President Allphin raised his right eyebrow, his standard reaction to bracing himself for the unexpected. He said, "The Dan Reilly-hotel guy who took me from the frying pan into the fire? The Dan Reilly I have to thank for this thankless job? That Dan Reilly?"

"That Dan Reilly."

"What now?"

"He has a theory."

"And what's his success rate on theories?"

"In my estimation, 100%."

Sean Allphin laughed. "Then why the hell isn't he working full-time for us?"

"Give me time and the right offer and he will, sir."

"Okay, let's have it."

"Reilly believes the death of my chief of security, Carlos Santiago, was…," she searched for the right word; murder was not good enough, "…an assassination."

"Based on?"

She hesitated. "A gut feeling. But as I said, he has a pretty successful record listening to those."

"Help me with this. Reilly still works for the hotel chain."

"Yes, sir, but we, well I, also have an *informal relationship* with him. An understanding. His business provides us with information we might not ordinarily get. He's a go-between. In turn, we provide him with certain information relative to safety, as we do with other business executives working around the world. He just keeps his eyes more open for us than anyone else. And he did work in State before the private sector."

"Sounds like he's tightrope walking over the circus."

"That pretty much describes it."

"And I take it, you're his net."

"Haven't had to catch him yet," she said lightly. "For the sake of argument, let's just call him a source."

"We pay him for this?"

"No, but as I said, I'd like to bring him into the administration."

"Back to his theory," the president implored.

"Well, Reilly believes I've got a mole in my office; someone who fed information to the assassin about Santiago."

Allphin stood and filled his chest with doubly HEPA-filtered air. "And this is his gut feeling?"

"He gathered intel in Miami and he's passed it along to the CIA."

"What's the bureau think?"

"So far, they›re concluding it was a boating accident."

"Then?"

"Reilly doesn't agree. I'm inclined to believe him. And that would mean I have a security issue."

The president stood and crossed the Oval Office to an ornate silver coffee urn, a present from Queen Victoria to President William McKinley. "May I?"

"Yes, thank you."

She joined him at the sideboard. Allphin poured Matthews a cup, then one for himself. He handed her the coffee. He didn't need to ask if she wanted milk or cream. He knew her preference was black. They remained standing.

"What about the Coast Guard and the Miami police?"

"They were ready to close the case."

Allphin took a hearty sip of the brew. "You know, I'm not sure my brain has any room for another conspiracy."

Matthews understood. Most hours of most days were like that for her, too.

"Does this man spend any time at his day job?" the president asked only half-jokingly.

She laughed. "Yes, nearly all the time. He just came back from Egypt. He's always traveling."

The president thought carefully based on what Matthews had told him. Then he asked, "What does your new head of security believe?"

"Tom Hunter, Mr. President. He's looking into everyone's record on the staff, from secretaries, assistants, and interns, to the agent level."

"That doesn't tell me what he believes."

"He and Reilly didn't hit it off all that well. So he's not convinced. But if Reilly's theory bears out, he'll be all in."

Allphin took another of his deep breaths. "Why do I think there's another high heel shoe to drop, Elizabeth?"

"Because there may be."

PART TWO

"To know and not do is not to know"
CONFUCIUS PHILOSOPHY

33

WHITE HOUSE SITUATION ROOM

THREE DAYS LATER

The secure video conference started with updates on the investigation into President Battaglio's death. FBI Director Reese McCafferty went through his main points for the president, the secretary of state, CIA Director Watts, Admiral Grimm, and National Security Advisor Dr. Hamza Ali.

"An advance team from the FBI has gone through Battaglio's home in Vieques. We might have been able to extract data from Battaglio's computers, but they were smashed."

"By whom?" Allphin asked.

"We think Battaglio. But not sure. We also seized security video from the private jet terminal in San Juan and we're still looking into the flight crew."

Admiral Grimm was next. "Ships of the U.S. Second Fleet are just reaching the impact zone. AWACs are checking for signals. Nothing to report. But we're on it."

Watts said his team was interviewing Battaglio's London publisher.

"Accidents do happen," the president offered.

"Sure they do," Grimm replied. He lowered his already deep gravelly voice. "Airplanes crash. They develop on-board problems even with the most experienced pilots." He sounded moderately sarcastic. "The trouble is this just happened to be the first carrying a former president."

OFF THE COAST OF PORTUGAL

The Russian sub prepared to surface but for only a few minutes. Nine minutes, according to orders. Enough time for Captain Alexi Tuyrin of the recently commissioned Yassen-class *Andriyan Nikolayev* to off-load its special passenger, Parisa Dhafari. When it was time, Tuyrin simply knocked on her quarters, where she'd stayed secluded for the three days since coming aboard.

"*Gotov, tovarischch,*" Tuyrin said. Ready, comrade.

Dhafari was dressed in a leather jacket, wool turtleneck, jeans, and boots that had been brought on board for her. She arrived as a blonde and would leave as a short-haired brunette. Beautiful either way, Captain Tuyrin observed.

He wished his orders hadn't been so strict. The officers and crew were to have no contact with her. No questions. No conversations. That went for him, too. But now that she was about to leave, he thought it wouldn't be out of line to talk.

"I hope we attended to your needs satisfactorily."

"Yes, Captain. Your accommodations were fine."

"Good. The seas are calm. Your transfer will be easy."

She nodded.

"And where will you be off to next?"

Dhafari glared at him. Tuyrin instantly realized his mistake, a mistake that might be reported up the line. It was an unauthorized question in an unapproved conversation.

"I apologize," he quickly added.

"Like you. I go wherever they send me. And Captain, I was never here."

Alexi Tuyrin now hoped she would not relate his lapse. Such things could ruin his career or end his life. The woman was clearly more dangerous than he had suspected.

Precisely nine minutes after the sub returned to the depths, the assassin was safely aboard a fishing boat and alone in another cabin for the 12-hour voyage to Sagres, Portugal. From there she'd be driven some 86 km to the nearest airport in Faro. A short flight would get her to Lisbon. Then Parisa Dhafari would be onto her next assignment. Arrangements were already locked in, tied to the travel plans of another woman.

THE STATE DEPARTMENT

THE SAME TIME

Tom Hunter worked and reworked the secretary of state's itinerary based on the new schedule. He analyzed the variables: Was there proper security at the meeting locations? Were the travel routes between meetings safe? Where could surprises come from?

Hunter read folders on all the Panamanian officers assigned to him. He spread them across a conference room table. The team of twenty appeared well trained. They were his to command and Hunter would make sure that they were where they were supposed to be at all times.

Elizabeth Matthews entered. She saw Hunter poring over the files. In addition to the analysis from the locals, he'd marked street maps of Panama City with specific times, block by block. These covered their routes from the airport to the United States Embassy, the ride to Palacio de las Garzas for meetings with the president, the course to the helicopter port for the twelve-mile flight to Tyndall Air Force Base, and their return to the airport.

"You don't look happy," Matthews said.

"A lot of people are moving a lot faster to make everything work, Madame Secretary."

"And will they work, Tom?"

"Hey, I learned from the best."

"Yes, you have."

They were both talking about Carlos Santiago.

"Then make him proud."

Tom Hunter gave Matthews a smile that felt just a little off. She wondered if Hunter was up for the job. *He'd had to be.*

34

DAN REILLY DID WHAT HE RARELY ALLOWED HIMSELF TO DO. He relaxed. Yibing had taken days off as well. They visited the Rotunda for the Charters of Freedom at the National Archives to see the original Declaration of Independence on permanent display. They toured the Smithsonian Air & Space Museum, which he hadn't done since he was a kid, and Yibing had never gone to. They ate sandwiches and had cheap sweet wine sitting beside the fountain at Dupont Circle. Later they enjoyed an especially romantic dinner at Apéro, a small French restaurant tucked in amidst a row of Georgetown townhouses. The champagne and caviar starter put them in the mood for all that followed on the menu and everything they wanted to share back at Reilly's condo.

That was Day One. It cleared Reilly's mind of Egypt and Miami. Day Two took him further into the zone as they picnicked on the Mall, took in a showing of Costa-Gavras's classic political thriller *Z* at the 100-plus-year-old Avalon Theater, then dinner at the funky Mansion on O Street.

Day Three began with breakfast in bed. While Yibing showered, Reilly broke a promise and logged on to read his emails. Amazingly, the world was cooperating. No threats. No crises. No urgent trips. But that didn't mean he could rest easy. There were threats to think about, crises to prepare for, and a trip that he was always packed and ready to take.

Yibing came out of the bathroom wrapped in a towel. She saw him at the computer.

"You said you weren't going to check in until tomorrow."

"Sorry."

"Is everything okay?"

"Surprisingly."

"But you look worried," Yibing said.

"Not worried. Just wondering about some loose ends."

"Secretary Matthews?" she asked wrapping her arms around him from behind.

"Not her as much as the murder of her DSS chief."

"Murder? I thought it was a disappearance. An accident."

"You and the FBI, and her temp chief."

He explained his concern. The conversation took them to his living room couch where she asked if he had any tangible proof.

"No. But I kicked it over to my buddy at Langley to look into."

"Well then, let him do his job so we can enjoy our last days together before I fly out."

She was returning to Mexico City for a trade summit on nanotechnology.

"What worries you?" Reilly asked.

"Missing a meeting because of jet lag," she joked.

"No, really."

"I can't believe you want to talk about this with me in nothing more than a towel."

Reilly laughed. "A little. You've never told me about your worries."

"Well, in order, Taiwan, the southern border, whether we'll ever negotiate a two-state solution for Israel and the Palestinians, Gorshkov's next move, and, as a matter of fact, yours."

Reilly leaned in and kissed her. At the same time, he slipped his hand under her towel.

"Well," she whispered in his ear, "that's one worry off the list."

The time for talking was over. But Reilly knew his worry would return if and when Heath came up with anything on the woman in Miami.

35

SOUTH PACIFIC OCEAN

200 FEET BELOW THE SURFACE

Captain Song-Taek continued on course and on schedule. With each passing day and every mile closer to the American coast, he worked harder to disguise his concern for *the exercise.*

Exercise? Command had instructed him to use that term. He had a sinking feeling it was going to be more than that. But he wouldn't know until he could open a timed message on his computer.

Before leaving port he was told that he would be performing the greatest duty of his career in service of the Supreme Leader. They'd be testing the limits of the Democratic People's Republic of Korea's power and the capabilities of a new generation of weaponry. Neither Song-Taek nor the crew of the *Wonsan Yong-Ganhan* would know they were actually doing the bidding of Russian President Nicolai Gorshkov.

25,000 YARDS NORTH-NORTHWEST

SAME DEPTH

The USS *Annapolis* was a shadow, as invisible as the captain of the *Wonsan Yong-Ganhan* hoped his sub was.

"No change, Captain. No sign that she suspects us," Lt. Okim Katema reported.

"Thank you, Mr. Katema."

The identity of the North Korean submarine had been confirmed by its faint audio signals, exactly matching the sound of the screws with recordings in the *Annapolis* computer database. Onboard library files also contained a biography of its captain, a 53-year-old submariner who'd spent more than half his career undersea.

Zimmerman studied the file for the fifth time. The Navy had a psych-up on Jang Song-Taek. He was a hardliner, loyal to the core, a true believer in the right and might of North Korea, whoever led the country. This made him a dangerous foe, and considering how far his vessel was from North Korean waters, Captain Zimmerman had to view him as a deadly dangerous foe.

Ten minutes later, Zimmerman was back on the comm asking for another status update.

"Speed unchanged at four kilometers an hour. Signal comes in and out, but I'm still on him, sir."

"Don't lose him, Mr. Katema."

Okim Katema cupped both hands over his headphones and nodded. He needed rest, but he wasn't willing to go off-station yet.

36

MOSCOW APARTMENT

THE SAME TIME

Alina Ostrovsky pretended she was happy to see General Sergei Bortnik the same way she pretended other things. Hopefully, he would get what he wanted quickly and she would get something useful in return.

Bortnik came with chocolates that she could do without and a gold bracelet that she wouldn't mind wearing. She also was certain he had news to coax out. *No rush*, she thought; she knew the right nerves to touch.

"My darling, you look so stressed," she said in due time. "Why can't we take time together at a dacha at the Black Sea?"

"I wish, but I can't."

"Can't or won't, my sweet," she said. "We could have such fun. A few days away, who would care?"

Who would care? Bortnik thought. Surely not his wife who hadn't shown interest in him in years. He'd had her followed. He knew what she was doing. "Maybe Paris?"

"Paris? Really?" Ostrovsky said, her eyes lighting up.

"I'll have to come up with a reason. It's not easy with Nicolai—"

He stopped short. She began working the buttons on his shirt. Time to coax him.

"Sometimes I worry he's going too far, Alina."

Ostrovsky said nothing. Bortnik would keep talking especially while her hands kept doing what they were doing. They were now on his belt.

"He takes such risks. Beyond Ukraine and the Baltic."

"Shhh, you don't need to talk now."

She was at his zipper.

"Relax."

"Should anyone find out, it could lead to more sanctions or war."

Bortnik's pants slipped down.

"Too much work, not enough play," she said lowering his boxer shorts.

Ostrovsky wanted to know more. Everything. But slowly.

"Be here with me now," she whispered. "I'll make us dinner..."

Bortnik nodded. She backed him up into a cushioned chair.

"...After."

"My sweet you have quite the touch," Bortnik sighed.

"You took the words right out of my mouth," she said. "Speaking of—"

She began to give him what he loved and what ultimately led to his satisfaction, followed by confession. That's what she waited for. But today he had more stamina. Probably his Viagra. They moved to her bed.

An hour later she gasped, "Give a girl a break."

Sergei Bortnik laughed. "For a while."

He nestled up to her breasts, and she began to gently trace her fingers around his lips, eyes, and ears. She turned, looked at Bortnik, and caressed his forehead.

"Oh, there are those worry lines again. I guess I'm not doing a good enough job."

"It's not you."

She didn't say anything. The rules of the game and her training, meant only subtle prodding, no leading questions. Nothing beyond her sexual coaxing and her feigned interest.

Bortnik sighed deeply and asked, "What is it you like about me? I don't shower you with gifts."

"You did today, but you surely don't need to."

"You could have younger men."

"I have. They're not you," she said appealing to his ego. "I know I can't have you, but you care. They don't."

"I wish I could take you out in public," he said lifting up, "and show you off."

This was a question she deflected before. The last thing she wanted was to encourage him to leave his wife.

"Enjoy what we have," she said, "and sleep. I need my general to be strong."

Bortnik slipped back into her breasts. She was certain he was ready to talk.

"Unless you need to get something off your chest." She rolled over and laughed. "But I'd prefer you stay on mine."

He laughed as well. After a minute's silence, the confession began. "You're right, darling. I keep so much inside. At times I get so afraid for Mother Russia. The alliances that are made. Should the West ever find out—"

She was about to learn more. And when she did, so would her people.

37

HUMBERTO DELGADO AIRPORT
LISBON, PORTUGAL

Parisa Dhafari saw the old man sitting in the Terminal 1 passenger lounge. His fourth finger on his right hand pressed inward. She took him as her contact palming a small note. In a moment she'd know for certain. He slowly sauntered toward her. She extended her left hand down to her side. They casually swept past each other. Dhafari didn't acknowledge him as he slipped a small folded piece of paper into her palm. He had done his job and was out the door with a roller suitcase, blending in with people coming and going.

She waited to read the communique until she was in a restroom stall. It told her where to meet her next contact at the airport and how to identify her. Dhafari tore up the paper and flushed it down the toilet. Ten minutes later she stopped at a specific gate indicated on the note. She spotted her contact, a woman in her 30s wearing a business suit, hat, and veil. On the seat next to her, a black leather Ferragamo purse, a shopping bag from Chic Coração, and a copy of the day's *International New York Times*.

"Excuse me, is this seat taken?" Parisa Dhafari asked in English. "I've been on my feet for hours."

She wasn't just being polite. It was code.

"Yes. Walking on these hard floors can be tiring."

The woman provided the correct response. There were two more lines to exchange.

Dhafari said, "I should have worn better shoes."

The woman replied, "I swear, I'll never wear heels again when I travel."

With the script perfectly recited, the woman removed her purse and bag but left a newspaper on the seat. Dhafari picked it up and sat.

Two minutes later, and with no more words between them, the woman left. Dhafari nodded to her and nonchalantly read the paper's front page while deftly feeling for an envelope between the pages. It was there. Back in the ladies room she removed it and took out a ticket for her next flight, a Canadian passport with her photograph as a brunette and her new name, two credit cards, and $1,000 in U.S. cash.

Dhafari smiled inwardly. This was the ultimate assignment she had been trained for. She was more than ready. Eager, excited, thrilled.

It was well over a year ago when she first prepared for the mission. She and her team were presented with multiple scenarios, each with different operational requirements and details to master. They were prepared to operate in Brussels, London, Berlin, Taipei, Seoul, Mexico City, and Panama City, and five other international cities. Dhafari had visited each location, considered the best options for executing the plan, and mapped the safest routes for exfiltration. Now, the location was confirmed. She was satisfied with the selection. More than that. She was certain it offered the best opportunity for success.

Parisa Dhafari felt a stirring far greater than anything sexual. She was a masterful asset, a skilled assassin, and a loyal soldier. In her zeal, however, she failed to see that, like her sister, she was merely a tool.

Once on ground, Dhafari would meet her team, evaluate the final operational challenges, make appropriate adjustments, and retrieve equipment and weapons from rented storage facilities.

Her first class ticket earned her entrance to the TAP Premium

Lounge where Parisa Dhafari, now Thea Pappas, a Greek Canadian tourism blogger, enjoyed a glass of Porto Valdouro Rose Wine and appetizers, far better than she'd had on the submarine and the fishing craft. She laughed to herself thinking, *And far healthier than what she'd served Battaglio's Secret Service, by now fish food themselves.*

According to the schedule, she had four hours before departure, ample time to buy a suitcase and the clothes to go in it, and pick up a book for the three flights. The first leg, a nonstop to Rio de Janeiro. From there, she'd work her way up north to Mexico City, and then to her final destination.

As for the trip, she'd read, sleep, watch a movie or two, and think. Opportunity for it all on the long TAP Portugal flight, and the connecting Avianca and Copa Airlines legs to Panama City.

38

CIA HEADQUARTERS

LANGLEY, VIRGINIA

Bob Heath eased back in his office chair. The CIA operative, along with hundreds of others in America's intelligence and military services up, was trying to fill holes in their investigations. The trouble is they didn't have much to spoon, let alone, shovel in.

Heath had his computer open to the CCTV footage of Battaglio's flight crew leaving the terminal. Two men and one woman. Investigators had already determined that the woman, the lone flight attendant, was cleared as a last-minute substitution. Ordinarily, that wouldn't be a problem. But Battaglio's crash made it anything but ordinary.

According to preliminary interviews from the flight leasing company, the original flight attendant had come down with food poisoning. She'd called in on her way to the hospital and fortunately, as he was told, the copilot was able to find a replacement. That made the copilot a person of interest as well as the flight attendant, a woman named Shannon O'Connor.

Horst Mueller, the German pilot, didn't raise any immediate concern, but Peter Lee, the copilot, a South Korean national, was a red flag. North Korea had successfully infiltrated South Korean institutions and businesses for decades. Why not the aviation industry?

Heath played the video backward and forward. Mueller was seen in the open. So was Peter Lee. The woman walked to the left of the men and was mostly obscured from view.

Intentional? He wondered.

Heath called Katie Koehler at the FBI Criminal Justice and Information Division in the hills of West Virginia. She'd been scrutinizing Reilly's stills and videos along with the Puerto Rico footage. "Anything new on your end?" he asked Koehler.

"Not from me, but the bureau verified Battaglio's flight crew's IDs. Mueller, the German pilot, had twenty-one years with Lufthansa before going private. Married with four kids, impeccable record."

"The others?"

"Co-pilot, former South Korean Air Force captain before he went in for the money."

"Married, single?"

"Single. Thirty-seven."

"That's all you have?"

"Checking on more, but so far, nothing untoward."

"I want whatever you can find. His record, his routes, his parents. Everything. Now, what about the woman?"

"Her name comes up on scores of flights on private carriers."

"And facial rec matches?"

"Haven't run it yet."

"Please do."

"Roger, that. No one really knows much about the flight attendant except that she was recommended by the copilot. They flew her in from Miami."

"Thanks. If anything comes up—"

"Of course," Koehler said.

They hung up, and Heath played the video in slow motion. Forward, rewind. Forward, rewind. He looked for subtle signs or signals. There were none between Mueller and Lee, nor Mueller and O'Connor. But O'Connor and Lee appeared to connect. A smile from Lee. A flirtatious hair flip from the Irish woman in one of the final frames before they cleared view of the camera. Since Lee brought her in, Heath didn't consider that especially unusual. Then he did focus on something. He froze the video and stepped through frame by frame, settling on one moment.

He cupped his hand under his chin and stared at the footage, straining to see something he thought was there.

39

THE KREMLIN

Nicolai Gorshkov had survived economic squeezes from the West and coup attempts from within. He had spies everywhere, and people feared speaking out. As president, he was living in the shadows of Lenin and Stalin rather than their successors. He was the ultimate leader with ultimate power and little soul.

Gorshkov believed that the chaos he would create around the world would further weaken his enemies. However, he had learned that even a politically vulnerable American president could deal with an isolated threat. The same for the most feckless European leaders. But multiple challenges that simultaneously popped up around the world? No democratic government could keep its citizens together through oncoming and ongoing global crises.

The Chinese had a long view of how to exert ultimate authority worldwide. It was based on patience and strategic alliances, a one-hundred-year march toward overall economic domination. Gorshkov had a quicker route: destabilization, political wildfires breaking out across the globe, assassinations, kidnappings, rising oil prices, computer hacks, threats to electrical grids, and escalating regional conflicts.

For a time, Americans would try to hold onto their accumulated beliefs and fall in line with the notion that their democratic republic would forever prevail. It wouldn't. The difference in Russia, his Russia, was that under his rule, Russians would just fall in line.

He spun an antique globe in his office and knew he could stop it at any point. Right now he had created threats to America's dominance brewing in every continent and every ocean.

Machiavelli had nothing on Nicolai Gorshkov. He was writing his own story, and in his warped mind, no one would get in the way.

BEIJING, CHINA

ZHONGNANHAI, THE PRESIDENTIAL PALACE

China's President Yíchén Yáo had his generals and admirals to confer with. He had his diplomats evaluating discussions with their opposite numbers in Washington, his intelligence operatives intercepting phone transmissions, and his spies talking to their American assets. He also had a rather adept asset inside Moscow whose sexual favors had been producing very responsible intelligence.

Yáo also had another person whom he relied upon. A confidant and a fixer. A businessman and a spy. His name was Ey Wing Li. To his friends abroad and enemies at home, he was simply known as Sammy.

"Thank you for coming, my friend," the president warmly said when Wing Li arrived.

"Certainly, Mr. President. How may I serve you today?"

"By listening; by helping. As you have done time and time again."

Wing Li was one of the only people who was permitted to speak openly to the president.

"As I will always do for you."

The president poured a glass of Baijiu, a thirty-percent alcohol drink so similar to vodka it was called Chinese vodka. Wing Li sat in the president's spacious office with traditional fixings and souvenirs surrounding them: flags and photographs, historic tapestries, and paintings representing the dynasties. The carpet was, appropriately, red. Red for happiness, success, and good fortune. It was, of course, the national color of China. Red also worked for China as a Communist nation. The walls were blue symbolizing spring, immortality, and advancement.

Yichén Yáo saw himself as supreme, though not immortal, certainly president for the rest of his years. At 55, he expected that would be another three decades during which time he would see China's advancement in the world.

They toasted one another. Sammy didn't prompt President Yáo. The reason for the meeting would undoubtedly come first in the form of a parable. Yáo's parables always had meaning.

"A story, my friend," the president said true to form.

"Please," Wing Li replied.

"One cloudless evening with the full moon shining down," Yáo began, "a very clever man named Haojia went to his well to fetch water. To his great surprise, when he looked into his well, he saw the moon glistening below."

Wing Li recalled the Chinese fable, "Fish for the Moon in the Well," but he didn't interrupt the president.

"'Good heavens,' Haojia exclaimed. 'The beautiful moon has dropped and sunk in my well!' Driven by the desire to return order to the universe, he ran home and grabbed a hook he had for farming. He quickly returned and attached the hook to the rope on the well's bucket. Then he lowered it to fish for the moon.

"Over and over he dipped the line hoping to hook the moon. And over and over he missed. Finally, Haojia saw the moon in the bucket of water, though not understanding it was merely a reflection. He pulled the rope up, but suddenly it broke. The bucket plunged into the well, and Haojia fell flat on his back. Despondent and worried what this would mean for the nature of all things, he looked up and sighed. To his great surprise, he saw the moon back into the night sky. Thinking he had done it, he proclaimed, 'Ah, what a good job after all.'

"Haojia, dear Wing Li, felt very happy. He told everyone he met about his accomplishment, without recognizing the truth. He was a fool."

"Comrade," Yáo added, "if someone says that your idea is nothing more than fishing for the moon in the well, they mean that you aren't seeing things as they are. You are living a pipe dream. It may seem worthy, but it is not realistic.

"So here we are with the need to see things as they truly are, to be enlightened rather than play the fool."

Wing Li, Sammy, was certain the parable would lead to a political point. He didn't have to wait more than a moment.

"I am sending you to the United States…to talk with your friend who is close to the American Secretary of State, soon to be vice president. You must convey a warning I have learned from our most talented operative in Moscow. Information that could disrupt the balance of things. Our things."

The moon in the sky. Not in the well.

President Yáo explained what he had learned from Alina Ostrovsky through Chinese intermediaries. On one hand, it would appear that Yichén Yáo was doing America a favor. In reality, he was protecting his interests, maintaining the balance of things, a gesture of friendship that masked his true long-term goals.

"There is something else."

Yichén Yáo removed a limited edition $25,000 Mont Blanc pen from his desk. It was adorned with a dragon design that wrapped around the pen, representing the twists and turns of the Great Wall. Yáo used it for only the most official national proclamations and personal handwritten letters to world leaders. As Sammy stood and watched, Yáo composed a long missive. When he was finished, he addressed the salutation and envelope to President Nicolai Gorshkov.

"After Washington, you will go to Moscow. A meeting will be set. You will bring this letter to him, but first memorize it. Hand deliver it. Tell him I mean every word I wrote. Every word."

40

FBI CRIMINAL JUSTICE & INFORMATION SERVICES
CLARKSBURG, WEST VIRGINIA

Katie Koehler shook her head. "Son of a bitch."

She was good. She was exceptional, but Robert Heath had indeed spotted something she had missed. Now she wondered if it was anything worthy of consideration or just an example of a woman's prerogative to change her hair color.

Could three frames, one-tenth of a second tell a larger story? *Well,* she thought, *that's what I was trained to do: Watch, analyze, scrutinize, evaluate.* She was also paid to speculate because speculation often led to the discovery of facts.

Heath had given her several challenges: One, work with the best images she had and create something better. Two, give Heath her professional opinion on three specific frames. He didn't tell her what to specifically look for.

She enhanced the video quality. That was easy. But those three critical frames required more attention. Nothing jumped out immediately. She enlarged the image and enhanced the quality. *He spotted something. What was it?* Then she saw it. The back of the flight attendant's hair. A few strands were a lighter color.

What the hell? she thought. *So the flight attendant missed doing a better dye job. Maybe she was in a rush,* she told herself. Koehler had herself gone from brown-to-red-to dirty blonde in her crazy early 20s. And they probably weren't the best dye jobs either. But Robert Heath had a reputation for being especially dogged. This was what he wanted her opinion on.

Was she trying to change her look for any surveillance cameras? A good question.

"Bob," she began on the call, "I'm looking at those frames in question. I've blown them up, sharpened the picture, and I believe your question is about the flight attendant's hair. Am I right?"

"Absolutely," Heath said. "What's your thought?"

"Well, I do see some blonde peeking through under the red."

"Can you make any assumptions from that, Katie?"

"I can. The woman in the flight attendant suit is wearing a wig," she said. "It happens."

"And?"

"And what?" she asked.

"Is it your opinion that she's just going for a different look or trying to disguise herself?"

"Well, if she were changing her look for a while, she would have dyed her hair. I think this was a temporary change."

"Doesn't it make you suspicious?" he asked.

"Hey, you're talking to the queen of suspicious. They pay me to be suspicious."

"Then what do you think?"

"I'll start with the assumption that you had a good reason to send this to me. You didn't tell me what to look for, but I found it. You suspect the woman may be a person of interest, perhaps trying to hide her identity. That leads me to believe you have some other footage you want me to compare this against."

Heath said nothing.

"Wait!" she exclaimed. "It's the Miami boat rental footage and the still frames you sent me."

"Bingo. Run a comparison. Let me know what you come up with."

"Will do."

"While you're at it, give me the best high-rez version of her blonde or redhead that you can."

"Absolutely. Give me a few hours. I'll have glossies that look like they were done for *Vogue*."

If Heath's thinking was right, and the image led to a positive ID by a Miami boat rental clerk, the photo would land her somewhere far more appropriate than *Vogue*—the FBI's Most Wanted List.

41

Dan Reilly had done precisely what he'd needed to do. Nothing but relax and play with Yibing until she had to go to Mexico City for a conference in a few days. Tonight, however, he had plans to have happy hour cocktails with Howard Liberman, a good friend, DC attorney, and a well-known amateur historian on Georgetown lore.

Every time they got together Liberman regaled Reilly with another surprising story about their neighborhood. Liberman knew every nook and cranny where colonial patriots huddled and planned their attacks on the British, where scoundrels plotted against the republic, where cash payoffs passed across tables in sealed envelopes, and where trysts were sealed with a kiss. Liberman knew where history had been made and where political figures lived, both on the way up and on the way down.

Reilly first encountered him quite by accident. Liberman was giving a Saturday afternoon tour that Reilly heard while returning to his condo. He stopped, listened, and learned things he didn't know: Georgetown was, in fact, not named for George Washington or even town founders George Gordon or George Bell. The distinction went to England's King George II, who ruled the Colonies until he didn't. Georgetown was founded in 1751 and built on the backs of slaves. With the abolishment of slavery, Georgetown's population was equally split between former slaves and freemen. In 1871, Georgetown became an independent municipal government within the District of Columbia, overseen by the U.S. Congress.

Dan Reilly walked with the group, rolling suitcase in hand. After the tour ended, Reilly introduced himself. That was eight years ago. They've been friends ever since.

Tonight their walk took them to Martin's Tavern, Georgetown's oldest watering hole. Of course, Liberman had fascinating stories about the establishment. In Booth Three, John Kennedy proposed to Jackie. In Booth Two Senator Richard Nixon often dined on Martin's famous meatloaf. House Speaker Sam Rayburn mentored a young Lyndon B. Johnson in the 1940s in Booth Twenty-Four. Booth Six is where Harry and Bess Truman dined with their daughter Margaret while she attended George Washington University.

The dark wood and vintage sports photos contributed to the welcoming ambiance. The gin martinis, particularly the second, made the troubles of the world fade away.

Liberman had a deposition in the morning, so he passed on the third. Reilly was willing to stay but switched to an Irish coffee.

Enough play time, Reilly thought. *Back to work. But whose work? Kensington Royal's or Elizabeth Matthews?*

Matthews, America's, at least for now.

While sitting at the bar he scribbled notes on a napkin: names, places, events. Things on his mind.

Nothing or something? He cocked his head, underlined a few words, and circled others. *More than nothing, not quite something. Yet.*

He asked the bartender if he had any paper. He didn't. Reilly looked around Martin's. He shouldn't be able to throw a stick in any direction and not hit a lawyer, a legal aide, or a Congressional assistant without a yellow legal pad.

He saw one.

"Hold my seat and I'll take a black coffee."

He crossed to a table of four young men. By his calculation, they were well into their fourth bottle of On the Wings of Armageddon, the highly popular Imperial IPA by Washington's DC Brau Brewing Company. Their jackets were off, their ties were loosened, and their suspenders were pressed hard against their white shirts.

Definitely junior lawyers, Reilly thought. *If they came to talk about a case, the work stopped even though their notepads were out.*

"Hey buddy, mind if I borrow a few sheets?"

A late twenty-something with slick black hair combed back looked up at Dan Reilly and with a *why not* shrug, ripped off the top sheet he had stopped writing on and handed Reilly the whole pad.

"Take the whole thing," he laughed. "Not sure we're going to get anything more done tonight."

Reilly thanked him. Indeed he just might need more than a few sheets.

Back at his barstool, Reilly scanned his notes and began new lists. First on one page, then starting over on a second, and refining his thinking on the third, fourth, and fifth.

He studied his work. He ultimately settled on nine items that he grouped equally into three categories. Three. Three times three.

Reilly flashed on what he'd learned in his undergraduate college psychology class from Dr. Peter Corea and a history class from Tim Rupp.

The common theme from each: "Don't ignore the Rule of Threes."

We constantly lean into thinking in threes. Who hasn't said, "Bad things come in threes?" Celebrity deaths, catastrophes, accidents? It's basic human nature. We tend to look for patterns in random data. It's a natural way to explain disorder. But it is also a way to predict behavior.

Aristotle related threes to rhetoric, terming them ethos, logos, and pathos. Or character, reason, and emotion. It worked then. It works now, evident in messaging, marketing, religion, and politics. It's how we remember things.

Stop, look, and listen
Faith, hope, and charity
Reading, writing, arithmetic
Ready, aim, fire

From, the *Declaration of Independence*: "Life, Liberty, and the Pursuit of Happiness."

Lincoln's Gettysburg Address: "Government of the People, by the People, for the People."

Winston Churchill: "Now this is not the end. It is not even the beginning of the end. But it is, perhaps the end of the beginning."

Dan Reilly felt he was at the end of the beginning, but he didn't understand why yet. He flashed on his own personal threes:

His ex-wife Pam and the marriage he couldn't make work. Marnie Babbitt, the spy who deceived him, now dead, except in his nightmares. And the alluring, Dr. Yibing Cheng, who might be "the one."

Then he went to what he had written and organized on his last page: MURDERS, THREATS, ATTACKS.

Under MURDERS he listed Santiago, Battaglio, and the ghostwriter Robbins.

Next, THREATS: North Korea, Russia, and Iran. All with expanding explosive power.

For ATTACKS, the third category, he wrote The Suez Canal, The Strait of Hormuz, and the Panama Canal.

Nine items. Grouped equally into three categories. Three. Three times three.

All right, you've got fucking lists. Now what's the point? Anyone can group these. But what does it mean? He pushed himself to think beyond the mere events and places he had cataloged and ask himself the most important question.

His psychology professor in college stressed that in reasoning things out, everything that comes in three is perfect. "Three is the least number of items in a series that makes a pattern. That's how our lizard brains remember things."

Reilly's history teacher gave it a different spin. "It's like driving. We have three places to watch. Front, side, and back. Looking ahead is fairly easy but we don't see what's between the rear-view mirror and the side mirror. That's our blind spot. That's why history repeats itself. We don't strain our necks often enough to see what's actually racing toward us. Often it's too late when we do."

Where's my blind spot? Reilly asked himself. *What aren't I seeing?*

He came to a conclusion and drew another circle around MURDERS, THREATS, ATTACKS.

Instead of unrelated facts, what if they're not disconnected? What if they are one thing? The same thing?

Reilly took another sip of coffee, signed for the drinks, and before leaving, asked himself the hardest question of all. "What's next?"

The answer didn't come from his notes on the yellow pad. It would come from a man he'd meet later that night.

42

"Madame Secretary, one last time, please consider doing the Panama conferences remotely," pleaded Tom Hunter. "The forward team shares my nervousness."

Elizabeth Matthews laughed. "Nice try, Tom."

"It'd be a lot less worrisome for me, and you'd get to sleep in your bed."

"And let Billy Peyton broadcast all over the news that Elizabeth Matthews was too afraid to go? Not on your life. I've got my marching orders. You've got yours. Make me safe."

"Yes, ma'am." Hunter waited a moment and handed Matthews a file on his lap. "Here's the latest report. You'll see why I'm concerned." Hunter handed her a thick folder. It was full of bad news.

Matthews read the assessments from Panama. Local rebels were feeling their oats. Guns were coming in from Venezuela. Ships were in a queue offshore waiting for more fuel to make it around Cape Horn at the tip of South America. Some had already been boarded by insurgents. American engineers were working on the canal. No one had a firm date when it would fully reopen. People were on edge along Panama's main streets, and the backroads were ripe for thieves.

Adding to the uncertainty—China was sending troops to protect their interests in the facilities they owned.

To Matthews's thinking, this made her visit even more critical. "One misstep by any of the players could provoke the other into making the wrong move. That goes for us, too."

"I'll be by your side all the way, Madame Secretary. Just as Agent Santiago would have been."

Hunter now held the rank of DSS Interim Supervisor. He would be responsible for protecting the Secretary of State's life.

She looked up from her reading and nodded thoughtfully. "Thank you, Tom. Let's go through it."

Hunter produced another file and gave Matthews a copy of the itinerary and security procedures, starting from her flight out on Air Force Two, a Boeing C-32 primarily reserved for use by the vice president, the First Lady, and the secretary of state. She'd fly directly from Joint Base Andrews to Tocumen International Airport in Panama City. Five hours in the air not including helicopter time out of DC.

Her first day would be fairly quiet. Rest and staff meetings at the U.S. Embassy on Demetrio Basilio Lakas Avenue, followed by a cocktail reception with President Jacinto Espinoza and members of his cabinet at the *Palacio de las Garzas*, the president's residence in Panama's old town.

The following day's discussions would begin in earnest with Espinoza and his cabinet. That's when Matthews would formally present America's defense package and the decision to immediately recommission the U.S. base of operations at Fort Sherman. It had been turned over to Panama in 1999, but suddenly Panama had strategic importance again for America, not simply because of the attack on the Canal. China had ports on both ends, and its ships, commercial and military, now used them as refueling ports.

Espinoza would ask, "When?"

Matthews would tell him, "Within ten days."

There would be objection. Matthews would explain that it was not negotiable. The meeting would end however it was going to end: friendly or testy. Either way, American troops would be deployed.

Day three was to start with a breakfast with Marine Major General Constance Brooks and her senior staff, followed by a trip that started with a drive through Panama to the airport, then a short fifty-one-mile helicopter flight to Fort Sherman.

"I'm putting on extra personnel for your helicopter flights back and forth to the base," Hunter said. "The routes on the ground have you going through some narrow corridors. If you don't mind me saying, *you'd* make me much happier if you'd stick to the hotel."

"Can't."

Hunter smiled. "Didn't expect you would."

43

GEORGETOWN

Outside Martin's Tavern, Reilly was eager to connect with Bob Heath. In person would be best, but it was getting late. The phone would have to do. He'd be vague. Heath would gather enough to respond.

Reilly took out his phone, ready to dial. However, as he turned right onto Wisconsin he became aware of a low whir behind him. A whir, not a whine. He recognized the sound. It was the federally mandated passenger warning system in a Tesla, a computer-generated noise coming from under the passenger side of the bumper when it drove under 18 mph.

Reilly didn't look back. He didn't need to. He'd been followed before. He kept walking, made a left on Prospect, and picked up the pace. The vehicle stayed with him.

Reilly made another left on N Street NW. Busier. The follow-car would be held up by traffic.

Now he had time to think about options: Duck into another restaurant. Call for help. Run. Or stop and look back. He chose to stop, to get a look at his pursuer.

No Tesla.

Reilly assumed it drove around the block to cut him off ahead. Time for a countermove. He doubled back and made meandering turns away from his route home.

The subway station, he thought. The closest was back toward Martin's. A minute's walk from where he now was.

Reilly changed direction again and headed toward the Metrorail Station. On Prospect he saw that he had made a major miscalculation. A Tesla headed toward him, braked fast, did a U-turn, and picked up the chase, now making no effort to remain subtle.

Reilly darted in front of an oncoming Uber and cut across the street. The Tesla steered wide, sped up, and cut Reilly off at the intersection. Suddenly, the passenger side door flew open. A man riding shotgun jumped out and took up a position ten feet in front of Reilly. Reilly stopped in his tracks. The Tesla door opened and from inside came a hearty laugh.

Reilly peered in. It was dark. He couldn't see anything or anyone. But he recognized the laugh.

"Daniel, my friend. Come in," boomed Ey Wing Li, the Chinese fixer better known as Sammy.

44

WHATEVER SAMMY HAD TO DISCUSS waited until his driver pulled up along the National Mall in West Potomac Park.

"Let us walk, my friend," he told Reilly.

"It's late. Not a good idea," Reilly said. "Right here's fine."

"You worry too much."

"So I've been told."

Sammy laughed as he got out. "Trust me."

Reilly followed. It was apparent Sammy had already worked out the location. A team of six Chinese men was waiting for them. The handlers, likely all from the embassy, fanned out as they walked. Sammy steered them toward the Martin Luther King Memorial.

Minutes later they stood before a full-body likeness of Dr. King powerfully emerging from two large granite boulders to a height of thirty feet. King set a gaze that went forever, over the Tidal Basin, toward the horizon. Reilly had not visited the site before and was curious why Sammy had chosen it now.

"Staggering," Sammy offered as they came upon the work. "Magnificent. It's called Mountain of Despair, representing Dr. King's 'I Have a Dream' speech. It's as if it were lifted out of your Monument Valley with your four presidents."

Reilly admired the craftsmanship and artistry.

"Did you know this is the work of Chinese sculptor Lei Yixin from

Changsha, Hunan, China? He also sculpted Chairman Mao Zedong. I wanted to admire the accomplishment of a great artist from my country on display in yours."

Reilly thought Sammy might be missing the real impact of the sculpture. Dr. King's eyes were searching beyond the present for the justice and equality that he believed could be achieved for all people. He read the text carved into the rock. "Out of the mountain of despair, a stone of hope." He couldn't resist a slightly taunting comment. "A message worth taking home."

"It's you who will be taking a message away from our conversation."

"So I'm your go-between again?"

Instead of answering, Sammy asked, "Have we not known each other through good times and bad, Daniel?"

"Yes, we have."

"And we have not lied to one another."

"No, we haven't."

They had first met when Reilly was in the Army twelve years earlier. It was under difficult circumstances. Captain Reilly was tasked with locating two American congressmen who dropped off the radar in Macau. They were found, but not before one of the legislators had raped and killed a teenager. The girl was the niece of a Chinese businessman, who revealed himself to be the fixer for the government. That made him a spy and more recently, a diplomatic intermediary with Reilly in the middle. Only months earlier, Sammy had provided Dan Reilly with indisputable proof that the congressman who had murdered the girl was now the sitting President of the United States, Ryan Battaglio. That's what brought Battaglio down, though not revealed publicly.

"And now it is time to trust me again," Sammy said.

Reilly did not need to ask why. It was obvious. Sammy had traveled from Beijing to Washington for Reilly to convey a message undoubtedly for the secretary of state. Beyond her, the president of the United States.

Reilly nodded.

"My country has a friend, who you see as an enemy."

North Korea, reasoned Reilly.

"And this friend has another friend."

Reilly knew that was Russia. "Go on."

"One is the puppet, the other is the master. The master pulls the strings, the puppet moves as manipulated."

"A Georgetown poli-sci freshman could have put this together, Sammy. We're both out of school. The point?"

"The one acts without thought. The other is in full control."

"North Korea and Russia, Sammy. I can do without the metaphors."

"The new Supreme Leader has, what's your phrase, drunk the Kool-Aid. He is bolstered by Russian Federation gifts."

"What kind of gifts?"

"Big ones. Powerful ones. Fast ones. Dangerous ones. Even quiet ones." He stopped walking and rested his hand on Reilly's arm. "Long-range surface-to-air missiles, now capable of reaching your cities from their submarines."

Reilly took in a deep breath and replied, "Assuming my government doesn't know this, I'll need specifics. But if this is transactional and not just a tip, things get a lot more complicated."

Sammy tilted his head slightly. "Not everything has to be transactional. Though if your government is in a generous mood, we'll be happy to accept an easy solution on Taiwan."

Now Reilly laughed. "There are no easy solutions to Taiwan, and you and your president know that. Besides, it's not ours to negotiate."

Sammy continued, "Let's keep walking."

They took a few steps silently, and then the Chinese envoy/businessman/spy began again.

"A submarine from the Democratic People's Republic of Korea is crossing the Pacific. It represents a threat to the United States."

The conversation had suddenly turned more urgent.

"What kind of threat, Sammy?"

"I don't have specific details, but the intelligence is good."

"How do you know this?"

"We learned it in a time-honored manner."

To Reilly, this meant the bedroom, from a compromised insider.

"This could put your government on war footing. And yes, it could very well provide my country with a diversion that would allow us a window to move against Taiwan while you are dealing with your multiple, escalating crises."

"Isn't that what you want?" Reilly asked.

"Ultimately yes, but on a timetable we seek and terms that won't lead to nuclear war. We want you to locate the submarine and stop it. Convince your friend that whatever happens, we are not responsible."

"Why should I consider this?"

"Because the alternative is too terrible to consider."

Sammy had told him an incredible story. He liked Sammy. Sammy had been a reliable source for years. But he was also a high-level operative under Yáo. He could be conveying as much, if not more, disinformation as information. Reilly would have to sort this out with the Secretary of State in the morning.

Dan Reilly shook his head. "You know, just the other day I'd decided to focus on my day job. The one that actually pays me. But everyone seems to be conspiring against that." He sighed.

Sammy laughed. "Duty calls, but there's more, my friend. I cannot say whether it's related, but it also comes from our source."

"More pillow talk from the honey pot?"

"There's a plot that puts a certain lady in your president's cabinet in jeopardy."

Reilly grabbed Sammy's arms and shook him. "What kind of jeopardy!"

"Kidnapping."

"Where? When?"

"I don't know. But she's not safe."

"She has security."

"It won't be enough, especially if she's traveling."

Reilly left Sammy's comment hanging in the air. She was due to travel…to Panama, later in the week.

"All of this is from an obscure back channel conversation?" Reilly said. "Not good enough."

"We value the source."

"Jesus, Sammy. Whose plan?"

"I cannot share that."

"You can't or you won't? Please."

Sammy said nothing. Reilly filled in the answer. *Gorshkov.*

"Don't wait long," Sammy urged. "No longer than after your tête-à-tête tonight."

"My what?"

"Your rendezvous at your apartment. The beautiful Yibing Cheng."

"How the hell—?"

"Oh, I'm sorry. Have I made an intelligence blunder?" Sammy shyly offered.

"How—?" Reilly demanded.

"Why, it's on your calendar. For your own benefit, I suggest you remove a certain social media app on your phone designed and owned by a Chinese corporation."

Reilly slapped Sammy's back. "Well, you could have told me that earlier."

"The time seemed right now."

Sammy dropped off Reilly at his brownstone condo. They said goodbye. While still outside, Reilly deleted the social media app in question. Next, he pressed the speed dial connection to Matthews's cell phone. She didn't pick up, so instead he sent a simple four-word, all CAPS text:

MUST TALK: DON'T GO.

A MILE AWAY, and at an appointed time, more information was being passed. Inside a men's room at the Graham Hotel, named after former Georgetown resident Alexander Graham Bell, who was famous for his achievements in communication, one man passed a small envelope to a second. In spy terminology, this was a brush pass between quarterback and receiver. Casual, silent, and perfectly executed.

The item was small: a miniature USB drive small enough to fit in the palm of a hand. It had cost under five dollars but contained information so much more valuable.

Seth Sullivan, Billy Peyton's Chief of Staff, casually pocketed the drive. He was eager to see what was on it, but he couldn't appear too anxious to leave. First another scotch at the hotel bar.

The man who passed him the storage drive had left. He wouldn't see him again until the next arranged drop. Sullivan had no idea where the information came from, or that the man was a Russian operative, but it could help advance Billy Peyton's political career, and in the process, his.

Sullivan waited ten minutes, paid up, and hit the street. Fifteen minutes later, he was firing up his home PC waiting to open the file. The screen lit up with a warning:

The contents will be wiped two (2) minutes after first opening.

"Pretty *Mission Impossible*," Sullivan thought. But, with only 110 seconds left to absorb the information, he hurried. *Very good,* he thought.

Very, very good. Damaging good, even if it weren't true.

He withdrew the USB drive, smashed it, and flushed the pieces down the toilet.

Seth Sullivan would go to bed happy.

* * *

Four-point-two miles from where Sullivan had been handed the USB drive, a three-hour dinner cruise along the Potomac River was coming to an end.

Overhead, America's spy satellites were focused on the vessel. Onboard, there were nearly as many Capitol Police as there were members of House representatives and senators. A third contingent of security came with the Japanese delegation that had hosted the party boat.

The evening's topic was security and trade, with more emphasis on security—Japan's.

North Korea had launched more missiles over Japan. Alarms sounded every few days. The contrails were frightening the citizens. All it would take to escalate the situation would be for one missile to go off course, or remain on course and "accidentally" hit target.

The new Supreme Leader was acting bolder than his predecessor cousin. Japan wanted assurances that the United States would come to Japan's aid. So far the new American president had been relatively quiet on the subject. The Japanese ambassador, in polite but direct diplomatic-speak, explained that North Korea was filling the silence with the noise of missile launching. That was extremely troubling. He wanted his message to get to the leaders of Congress and the White House.

Senator Mikayla Colonnello, Chair of the Senate Intelligence Committee, was one of those people who had the president's ear. In a private conversation on the main deck, she told the ambassador that President Allphin was definitely watching the escalating situation and would soon visit Japan. Her responses did little to assuage the host's concerns.

The evening ended with polite bows. As everyone disembarked, Colonnello heard her name called with a sickly sweet Oklahoma drawl. "Mikayla, you have a minute?"

"Sure, Billy," she answered wishing she had departed earlier. Clearly this was no chance encounter. He was lying in wait for her.

Peyton steered Colonnello down the dock. Metro police had blanketed the area so they could talk free of civilians.

"What is it?"

"Just a little chat."

"About?"

"Oh, your friend, Elizabeth."

"You do know she takes phone calls," Colonnello replied.

Senator Peyton laughed. "Of course, but consider this more of a back channel conversation."

Colonnello stopped and faced Peyton. This wasn't going to be pleasant. Better to get this over with fast.

"Go ahead."

"She's vulnerable. If Allphin picks her for vice president, she'll probably get through the Senate. But she can't win the presidency. She shouldn't try. Shit will come out."

"Oh?"

"Don't give me that 'Oh.' It always comes out. If we don't have it yet, we will."

Peyton was counting on it. He'd been assured by his chief of staff he'd be getting some dirt soon. "Besides," he continued, "she should have been here tonight. I know it. You know it, and in a few minutes I'm going to tell the cameras, 'Elizabeth Mathews Secretary of State, skipped out on meeting the Japanese ambassador.'"

"She didn't skip out."

"That may be true, but the truth is so less interesting these days."

Colonnello scoffed. "Frankly I don't care what you do, Billy."

"You will. The administration is ignoring North Korea's ongoing threats against Japan. Quite simply, it shows Allphin's failure to protect one of America's staunchest allies. This was an important event. He blew it by not sending her. Matthews blew it."

"And if she had been here," Colonnello responded, "I have no doubt you'd come up with a different, but equally fallacious soundbite."

Peyton laughed. It wasn't a jovial laugh. He was mocking her.

"Face it, Mikayla, Allphin's asleep at the wheel, and he's heading for a crash. I suggest you advise your buddy Matthews to get off the Allphin bus."

"Thank you, Billy. I'm sure the Secretary of State will appreciate your concern. I'll pass it along."

"Political calculus, Mikayla. The country is ready for a change. Too much upheaval. Three presidents in eighteen months. You can't run a country this way."

Peyton stepped closer, right into her personal space.

"The people are ready for real leadership and a show of strength. Tell Elizabeth to get out of the way. Save the party a lot of pain and money."

Now she crept closer right into Billy Peyton's personal space.

"There's a basic fact you don't understand, Billy."

"Oh?"

"You're the one who's going to get hurt. And as far as I know, she hasn't made any announcement about running."

"Don't bullshit a bullshitter, Mikayla. She'll run. And she'll go down. Trust me."

"That's one thing I won't do, Billy. Not tonight. Not ever."

"Like I said, political calculus."

"Secretary Matthews is very good at math, and from what I've seen, you're not very good at counting votes. So bring it on, Mr. Minority."

That was Colonnello's intentional sleight.

"Make your announcement. Run. I have no doubt you'll mount a spirited, though debased campaign, littered with conspiracy lies and filled with personal attacks. But you will be met head-on. And you will lose."

"Senator, I take that as confirmation."

"For what?"

Peyton laughed. "Why, her candidacy for president."

He smiled his old country-boy smile and walked toward the TV cameras. Mikayla Colonnello wondered what Peyton had, if she'd been played, maybe even recorded.

On the last point, she had been.

46

IT HAD BEEN A BUSY NIGHT FOR REILLY. He didn't know whether Yibing would still be awake so he tiptoed in lightly and slipped into bed with Yibing Cheng. She stirred, rolled over, and kissed Reilly. She wanted to talk. He had another idea which seemed perfectly fine to her. Forty minutes later, when they should have been sleeping, Reilly was now needing to talk.

"Yibing, I told Elizabeth that I'm going to step back and focus on my company."

Matthews was also Cheng's boss.

"I thought—"

"I know, but it's too much."

"What did she say?"

"What do you think? She needs me."

"That's the thing, Dan. She'll always need you. That's who she is. That's who you are."

Yibing Cheng had his number. The Chinese national, now a U.S. citizen, had it from the moment they met in Beijing.

Reilly sat up. The covers slipped down, revealing Yibing's figure. The body that called to him. He smiled.

"What if we gave *us* a chance? What would it take?" he asked.

Yibing smiled but didn't answer.

"I've got marketable skills that could translate into some high-paying desk jobs here. Maybe that's what I should do. Say goodbye to both masters."

Yibing said nothing. She saw that he was trying to work things out. But this new thought was quite sudden.

"Hell, I could get a job at some Beltway think tank."

Now she leaned over and kissed him. "My mother used to say if she had wheels she'd be a wagon. Well, Mr. Daniel Reilly, she did not have wheels, and neither do you. Don't try to fool yourself, especially to me. You're not someone destined for a desk job. There's room for us in everything you do. And," she maneuvered on top of him, "there's room for you right here."

They eventually fell asleep in each other's arms. For a while, it was the best sleep Reilly had had in months. But Reilly awoke with three words swirling in his head, the words he had written on the lawyer's yellow pad: MURDERS, THREATS, ATTACKS. Considering his conversation they took on even more urgent meaning. He had to talk Matthews out of going on her trip.

47

"Con, Sonar. Update." Captian Dwight Zimmerman called out.

"Yes, sir." Okim Katema replied. "No change. Hope it doesn't slow anymore. We could lose her entirely."

"Roger that."

Zimmerman looked over the territorial chart spread across a table in the *Annapolis*'s comm. He asked himself the same question that had dogged him for weeks. *What's your game, Captain Taek? You didn't come all this way for nothing.*

* * *

Two kilometers away at a depth of 54 meters, or 177 feet, Captain Song-Taek also checked with his sonar operators.

"Hearing whales, schools of fish, sir. Probably tuna."

Probably was a word he didn't like. *Probably* had no business in the silent service.

"Listen harder, sonar." Two minutes later, Song-Taek gave a new order to the crew of the *Wonsan Yong-Ganhan*. "Take us to the bottom. We're going to sit tight."

The bottom this far off the coast ranged from 61 to 610 meters, roughly 200 to 2,000 feet deep. Where they were, the North Korea sub came to rest at 81 meters.

"All stop."

"All stop. Zero bubble, Captain."

Song-Taek looked at his watch. They were ninety minutes ahead of schedule, and so far, by all indications, they had evaded any American hunters. *Probably.* Now they would wait and listen even harder.

* * *

"Commander, the diesel's gone silent."

Sonar reported the bearing. "Dropped down ten feet and under five kilometers an hour."

"Best estimate, lieutenant?"

"She's playing possum, sir."

"Nav, get me close to where she should be. Within 100 meters. Two can play this game."

48

AN HOUR LATER

Billy Peyton's Capitol Police security detail called up to his apartment at the Watergate.

"I have a guest to send up if it's not too late, Senator. It's Mr. Sullivan."

"Fine, thank you. Send Sullivan up."

Peyton had a martini in hand when he opened the door. He offered Sullivan one. He declined.

They crossed to Peyton's living room. There, he put a Dave Koz smooth jazz album on his stereo, placed the needle on the vinyl, and turned up the volume.

The Senate minority leader sat in a contemporary black Roche Bobois armchair. Sullivan remained standing. He didn't intend to stay long. He gave his boss an oral report. Nothing in writing. When he was finished, Peyton was all smiles.

"Any photographs?" the congressman asked.

"None that I know of. Doesn't mean they can't be created."

"Any way she can disprove it?"

"Harder if it's true. But all we need to do is put it out there. America is not ready for a lesbian in the White House. Then we just let political momentum take over."

Peyton sipped his drink and continued. "I don't know. A denial from one boyfriend, let alone two, three, or four sinks it and I'm left holding my dick in my hand. Sex scandals aren't what they used to be." He took another sip. "No. We need more. We need better."

Seth Sullivan was disappointed, but he didn't fight Peyton over his answer. He'd communicate the disappointment in the morning and the fact that Peyton wanted better.

What he didn't know is that "they" already knew. The agent who'd delivered the USB drive in the bar bathroom had also deftly planted a bug under Seth Sullivan's jacket collar. A team was listening and recording inside an SUV parked a few spaces down the street from Peyton. Their report would be sent in an encrypted attachment to a Moscow email address as soon as Seth Sullivan, a very useful idiot, who worked for an even more useful idiot, left.

49

"Gentlemen," Parisa Dhafari began. "It's good to see you all again."

They were anything but gentlemen. The eight-man team was comprised of hardened combatants who had special training. There had been nine. One didn't like taking orders from a woman. Parisa Dhafari exerted her authority on her arrival. He was no longer part of the squad. He was no longer among the living.

They were meeting in a warehouse.

Dhafari had last seen them in Jakarta, Indonesia. They'd spent four months preparing for the mission.

Each of Dhafari's team members had distinct duties, all overlapped in the means and manner of eliminating any threats to come their way. They had no identity beyond animal code names: Fox, Dog, Tiger, Cat, Rat, Snake, Bull, and Wolf.

Dhafari chose for herself, a name from the arachnid world. Nothing complicated, but something that suited her well: Spider.

She knew everything about them. They knew nothing about her. Not her family story. Not her nationality or how many people she had killed in the line of duty. Nine just in the past ten days. They were paid to not question her authority, as Raccoon, the man no longer part of the team, had fully realized all too late. Least of all, they knew nothing of her association with Russian President Nicolai Gorshkov.

They had been in Panama for just a few days. They had worked out dozens of variables to the mission, training on Jakarta's streets and in the Java Sea.

Dhafari's menagerie of terrorists had arrived in Panama posing as an electronics salesman, graduate students, lawyers, and other positions. They each carried South Korean passports. They weren't from the South. As for Dhafari's cover story, beyond Spider, she traveled as Amir Taj, a French jeweler with money to burn for a Saudi prince she was hired to shop for.

"Have you stopped, been questioned, or suspected in any manner?" she asked everyone.

No one had a problem.

"Make sure it stays that way. If even one of you is compromised, we are all compromised. There is no room for failure."

They understood.

"Good, then let's go through the timetable."

THE KREMLIN
MOSCOW

"Thank you, Bortnik. There is nothing further you can do."

Nicolai Gorshkov beamed. "Your contributions will earn you the gratitude of the nation. My gratitude. If I ever made you feel ill at ease, accept my apologies. Mine is a job where I must take great care. Traitors are everywhere. But you, comrade, have proven your loyalty. Together we will watch how the news unfolds."

"Thank you," General Bortnik said. "But I do not understand."

"You don't because I have not given you all the pieces. Today you shall know more, so you can celebrate with me."

Bortnik had passed some recent tests of Gorshkov's. That was good, it would keep him close to power and maybe, just maybe, give him the opportunity to succeed where others had failed: removing Gorshkov.

He would still have to be careful and try to control his emotions.

In years past, he could have confided in his wife. No longer. She was a stranger to him. He had seen other highly ranked officers, some of them not even conspirators, who had misspoken or gossiped about how much better Russia would be without Gorshkov. Two had recently drunk from the wrong bottle, and another had slipped off the cable-stayed Zhivopisniy Bridge spanning the Moskva River. A fourth had been killed in a hit-and-run accident on Tsvetnoy Blvd. Add in protestors, journalists, and dissident teachers who had disappeared after criticizing the president, and the numbers jumped into the thousands. Gorshkov wasn't in Lenin and Stalin's category. Not yet. But he was getting there.

So, General Bortnik did everything he could to instill confidence in President Gorshkov. Thankfully, he believed he had one person who would listen as he vented, give him loving solace, and most of all some loud, wild pleasure.

WASHINGTON, DC

THE NEXT MORNING

On the fifth ring, Elizabeth Matthews answered her phone.

"Daniel, what's up?" she said.

He heard a low-frequency rumble. The ambient sound was immediately apparent.

"You're on a plane," he declared.

"I do that from time to time."

"Hope it's not where I think you're going this time?"

Matthews didn't respond. He read that as a confirmation.

"You did see my text," he said.

"Things have sped up a bit."

Damn! He was angry that he let his night with Yibing distract him.

"So why the call?"

"Actually, this isn't the best way to discuss this," Reilly replied.

"Can it hold?"

"No," Reilly said.

No one spoke as they both mulled over solutions. They broke the silence simultaneously.

Matthews: "I'll set you up with a SCIF." Reilly: "No, I'll catch a plane."

Matthews continued, "Dan, I'm going to be busy for the next few days."

"Better in person considering who came to me and what we have to discuss. It's urgent, and your flight has made it more so."

The Secretary of State thought for a moment. "Hang on."

Reilly walked to the bedroom while Matthews was offline. Yibing was up and in the shower. He silently watched her.

A minute later, Matthews was back.

"Tom's concerned," she said. "The schedule is tight. He doesn't want to throw off any timing. Lots of moving parts. The SCIF will be fine."

"Madame Secretary—"

Reilly rarely addressed her so formally. When he did, it was for good reason.

"Immediately."

"Unless you can get Scotty to beam you aboard," she joked.

"I'll get the next flight out."

"All right, Dan. You know where I'll be. I expect you won't need accommodations."

They hung up, and Reilly was ready to call Brenda to book him on a commercial flight. But he stopped. Given the connections he would need to make, there had to be a quicker alternative. There was. Heath.

Reilly phoned his friend at the CIA. He explained what he could and what he wanted.

"Impossible!" Heath replied.

"Make it possible."

Reilly was quickly cleared through security at Joint Base Andrews. An F/A-18F Super Hornet twin-engine tandem seat was fueled and waiting.

"Good morning, Mr. Reilly," announced the pilot standing next to the stairs alongside the plane. "I'm Weller. I'll be ferrying you today. Identification, please."

"Of course, Captain. Good morning." Reilly produced his ID.

"Thank you, Mr. Reilly. I'll be your pilot, your TSA, and customs agents," he said with a wink, "but I can't help much with services and amenities for our flight beyond a box lunch. Ever been in one of these babies?"

"No. Never thought I'd get the chance."

"Well, you must have a friend in high places to book you on such short notice."

Reilly laughed. "I suppose I do."

As they shared a hearty handshake Reilly studied the flier. Weller had a chiseled face and a flier's body. Not a pound of excess fat. He looked like he had stepped right out of an Air Force recruiting ad.

Reilly had packed to travel light. He left his suitcase at home. Everything was tucked into a small backpack that he would keep on his lap. Beyond the few toiletries, his passport, and one change of clothes he brought along, he figured he could pick up anything he needed in Panama.

"Well, you're in for an experience. It's got a real kick on take off. Once we're up I'll keep it smooth as possible. But I suggest you hit the head before we go. It's nonstop. We'll be meeting up with a KC-135 for topping off two hours out. That means no bathroom stop from here to there."

Reilly took the suggestion. The alternative would not be pleasant.

Fifteen minutes later Reilly, fitted in a flight suit and helmet felt every fiber in his body press against the seat as the plane accelerated to 175 mph within 1,800 feet of the runway. He'd never felt g-forces this intense. Nothing near it. At first, he couldn't talk, not that Weller would have answered as they climbed. He was busy getting them up to 40,000 feet, their cruising altitude. Hopefully, that's where Reilly's stomach would return to its proper place.

51

President Allphin was eager to hear what Admiral Nick Mirage, Chief of Naval Operations for the Joint Chiefs, had to say. He was told it was critical. But then everything seemed to rise to that level these days.

"We found the plane, sir," Admiral Mirage said even before sitting. "Or more accurately the wreckage."

Asking about survivors would have been ridiculous. Instead, Allphin asked where.

"The good news is the plane didn't go down in the Puerto Rico Trench. That's more than five miles deep. We have it only a little more than a mile down, some four hundred miles from the last recorded location. We picked up noise from IUSS sonobuoys."

"I-U-what?"

"Sorry sir. Our Undersea Surveillance System. Acoustic sensors recorded the crash and the breakup."

"Recoverable?"

"The pieces, yes. Or most of them. Remote salvage can retrieve 'vessels of opportunity.' But the victims? President Battaglio? Maybe if he remained strapped in his seat. God only knows what's left."

Mirage explained what likely happened. "Colliding with water from their altitude would be like hitting solid concrete. The jet would have cartwheeled on impact and torn apart. What didn't break up on the crash would have as it went down under the water pressure. No chance of survivors then or now."

"We're going to have to raise it," Allphin said. "If there are bodies to recover, we need to bring them back. Battaglio was president. A goddamned disgrace to the nation, but—"

Allphin stopped short.

"Sir?"

"Forget I said that. It's the old Speaker of the House talking."

"Yes, sir."

"What will it take to see this through?"

"Your order, time, and luck with the weather. The water's warm, and we're in the middle of hurricane season."

"You've got my verbal. Written authorization will be in your inbox by the time you get back to your office. But Admiral, don't take undue risks. If this stretches out, you won't hear any complaining from me. Ryan Battaglio can remain, quote–unquote, lost at sea. There are other things on my mind and yours that take priority right now."

"Roger that, Mr. President. I understand."

52

HEATH PICKED UP HIS OFFICE PHONE by the third ring. That was SOP. Generally, everything at the CIA had a degree of urgency. What he was waiting for now was of utmost importance. The name and number on the display told him this might move a simple inquiry into an active investigation.

It was Katie Koehler at the FBI labs.

"Yes, Katie. What do you have?"

"Ninety-eight percent confirmation," the FBI facial recognition expert replied. "Ninety-six percent from the computer analysis. I'll throw in the extra two percent based on my eye. The flight attendant and the woman who rented the Jet Ski are the same. What's more, I did a deep dive into her record with the airlines, and although the information is definitely in the system, no one has any memory of working with her. She had assignments in the log, but did she ever actually work the flights?" Koehler rhetorically asked.

"No," Heath quickly responded. History was filled in. Recent events connected. "What does that suggest to you?"

"I'm the computer geek, you're the spy," she said. "You tell me."

"She killed the DSS agent and she got to Battaglio. She's an assassin."

"Was. Battaglio's plane went down."

"Still is. The jet is gone, I'll stake my reputation that she's alive and well and responsible for at least one more death. The question is why the Secretary of State's DSS agent?"

Heath had a notion but he didn't share it with Koehler. Instead, he asked her to report her findings up the chain. He'd be doing the same thing on his end. Within minutes the directors of the FBI and the CIA would be up to speed. Whether or not they acted on the intelligence was unknown. But Heath knew someone who would. He called Dan Reilly.

Reilly's Super Hornet flew south at Mach 1.8, 1,380 mph. Now some ninety-five minutes out, they were lining up with a KC-10 tanker for refueling.

"You're in for a real treat," Captain Weller told Reilly over the plane's comm. "We'll pull up just behind the KC-10 and nudge right into the refueling basket they'll extend from the probe. Once we connect, we'll take on 3,350 gallons, then disengage and be off."

"No credit card needed?"

"Oh, you're paying for it. Your tax dollars at work, Mr. Reilly."

Reilly watched in awe. He'd seen videos of the procedure, but never expected he'd have an up-close view.

"Just give me a few minutes, we'll talk after we're hooked up."

"Yes, sir."

The refueling basket was released from an arm in the aft section of the tanker. The basket looked exactly like a huge badminton shuttlecock; probably designed that way for its aerodynamics. Reilly vowed to look that up on Google after he landed.

Now the Super Hornet drifted behind and below the KC-10. Reilly listened to the communication between Weller and the flying gas station. He found it fascinating and exciting, especially the moment when the basket perfectly aligned with the extended intake just to the right of the Super Hornet's cockpit. With the hose attached, refueling began.

"Gotta keep it nice and steady for the next eight minutes," Weller explained.

"Please do," Reilly replied.

Reilly watched as the KC-10 refueling crew deployed the tanker plane's extender.

"It's up to both of us to stay in formation," Weller said. "But we're good at it. And where else can you get service like this?"

"New Jersey?" Reilly joked.

Six minutes later, the captain announced, "We're good to go. Disconnect."

The KC-10 radioed, "Roger that."

Suddenly the jet took a sharp jolt accompanied by an ear-splitting bang. An alarm went off in the cockpit. Reilly's heart raced. Something was terribly wrong.

Without explaining anything, Weller broke right and put the Super Hornet into a dive away from the tanker. The g-forces immediately pinned Reilly to the back of his seat. Then they lessened as the plane slowed.

"Captain?" Reilly called out.

The alarms continued to blare.

"Not now."

Dan Reilly didn't need to be told twice. He heard fast radio communication back and forth. Much of it flight jargon. Calm and definitive.

Reilly checked that his safety belt was tight. It was. He looked up and around. That's when he spotted a crack in the cockpit canopy and focused on the refueling basket fluttering."

"Oh shit."

Weller heard the comment but ignored it. He was too busy at the controls. Finally, he spoke. "Mr. Reilly, we'll level at 8,000 feet. At that time I may need to blow the canopy. I'll try not to, but be prepared. We're going to make an emergency landing at Eglin."

"The crack?"

"Yes," Weller said. "The refueling basket became disconnected from the refueling probe. It smashed into our canopy, cracking it. We should be okay."

Should was vastly different than *would*. Reilly tried to get his breathing under control. There was nothing he could do beyond trusting the experience of his pilot and the airworthiness of the plane.

"How soon?"

"Twenty-two minutes, sir."

Reilly's pulse quickened hearing the way the pilot articulated, *"Sir,"* with authority and without inviting a reply. *Breathe in, breathe out*, he told himself. *Again, breathe in, breathe out.*

"Looks like we'll have to work out alternate transportation for you once we're on the ground," Weller added. "Right now, I'm just going to concentrate on putting us down safely."

Reilly had no problem with that. While the jet jostled, sometimes wildly, Reilly set his mind beyond the immediate problem to what would be waiting for him in Panama.

53

EGLIN AIR FORCE BASE

60 MILES EAST, PENSACOLA, FLORIDA

The last thing Reilly wanted to do was to get back on an F/A-18 Super Hornet. It was also the next thing he needed to do.

Based on what Reilly had told Heath, the Air Force had another plane ready to shuttle him to Panama. But before Reilly climbed into his second Super Hornet of the day, he made one more call to his friend.

"Has Watts reached Secretary Matthews?"

"Not directly. But her DSS detail head has been informed."

"Hunter?" Reilly asked.

"If he's the new guy, yes."

Reilly thought for a moment, then proposed, "They should change her schedule. Different locations, different times."

"That's a big request. On whose authority?" Heath asked.

"Why, yours Bob. You're very concerned. What's the phrase? Out of an abundance of caution."

Reilly heard Heath laugh.

"Take it upstairs."

"I'll do my best. In the meantime, get your ass back in that jet and take care of business."

* * *

Three hours later, flying at supersonic speed most of the way, Reilly landed at Panama International Airport. A car, arranged by the CIA, rolled up to the plane to take him to the American Embassy to see Matthews.

The trouble is she wasn't there. Elizabeth Matthews was on her way to the Presidential Palace.

PART THREE

"He who travels far knows much"
ORIGINAL UNKNOWN

54

PANAMA CITY, PANAMA

Three things happened within the same hour. Dan Reilly's jet touched down on Runway 03R/21L at Tocumen International Airport. Secretary of State Elizabeth Matthews's motorcade began to roll through the streets on a revised schedule. Parisa Dhafari's team—Fox, Dog, Tiger, Cat, Rat, Snake, Bull, and Wolf—took up specific points in the city.

Seconds after climbing down the ladder of the Air Force fighter jet Reilly called Matthews's cell phone. It rang three times, and a man answered.

"Hello."

"Who's this?" Reilly asked.

"Who are you?" the voice replied sharply.

Reilly identified himself.

"Mr. Reilly, this is Agent Hunter. And this is not a good time."

"I have to reach Secretary Matthews."

"Like I said—"

"And like *I* said," Reilly replied twice as strongly. "I have to reach her. Now!"

"She's on my phone on another call."

Reilly could hear her in the background.

"Get her off that and put her on! Do it, Agent Hunter."

"She's on with the president. Last I checked, he's more important than you. Call back later."

With that, the line went dead.

Inside the Lincoln Navigator, Matthews wrapped up her conversation and asked who she missed.

He shrugged. "Your friend Reilly."

"He had something for me. Get him back."

"As soon as we arrive. We have to pay attention. The route's not safe."

Matthews looked ahead. Directly in front and behind were identical Navigators, each with teams of four State Department Diplomatic Service agents. Rounding out the entourage were three police cars leading the way and another three in the rear. Inside her vehicle were two other agents under Hunter's command.

* * *

Dhafari's man Tiger hit the gas on a stolen Panama City dump truck after the first three police cars and the lead DSS Navigator passed. He crashed through the barrier smashing into the agent's vehicle and pinning it to the wall of an office building. From the top of the same structure, Bear fired a U.S. Army M79 single-shot grenade launcher, accurate in the right hands at 350 meters. Bear had the right hands and only needed one 50 mm grenade.

The Navigator burst into flames, which, on the narrow city street, effectively cut off three police cars, which Fox and Snake then eliminated from their high vantage points at the next block.

* * *

"Sharp right!" Hunter shouted from the rear. At the same time, he pushed Matthews's head down.

The driver sped up and turned the only place he could: where the dump truck had come from.

Matthews reached back for her cell phone. Hunter hadn't given it back.

"My phone!"

"Not now! Stay down!" he ordered.

He looked behind just in time to see the truck that had hit the Navigator back up directly into the first Navigator. The reverse of the action that had taken place in front of them now happened again.

Moments later, another grenade launched from above, followed by more that took out the remaining police vehicles.

"Straight! Go straight!" Hunter directed.

The agent in the front passenger seat keyed his radio.

"No!" Hunter ordered. "They could be monitoring our frequency. Keep your eyes open at the intersections for another choke point!"

Matthews pushed against Hunter as she tried to lift her head.

"Madame Secretary, head down."

The agent driving scanned ahead and above to the left. The agent riding shotgun did the same on the right for three blocks. So far it was clear and no one was following.

"Up ahead! Look, a parking lot on the right. Go in."

The Navigator steered in and crashed through the wooden barrier.

"Up or down?"

"Up! We'll call for a copter," Hunter exclaimed.

The Navigator tore around the bends, accelerating past the parked cars on the straightaways, slowing only on the turns. On each sharp turn, Matthews was violently tossed around.

"Tom!" she exclaimed.

"Not yet!"

Just as they pulled up to the rooftop level the driver stopped short. "Oh my God!"

"Keep going!" Hunter yelled.

"What?" Matthews asked, still with Hunter's hand on her head.

"There's a helicopter already here."

The Navigator pulled up as close as possible to the copter, a fire-engine-red Robinson R44 Raven II, which normally flew tours over the Panama Canal. Rentals went for $650 per hour. It was less if stolen.

The two lead agents unbuckled and jumped out with their SIG 229 pistols drawn. They were ready to commandeer the aircraft.

Instead two men they'd never learn were called Wolf and Rat stepped from behind two cars. The Diplomatic Security Service agents died without another thought.

"Tom!" Matthews demanded. "What's going on?"

"Not yet!"

The next thing the Secretary of State heard was shouting, the doors of her Navigator opening, Hunter whispering for her to keep down, and a woman's soft voice speaking with an accent. Then Elizabeth Matthews felt a sharp pin prick in her neck and something being slid over her head. She gave into the darkness. She had no choice.

55

DAN REILLY DIALED MATTHEWS AGAIN from his taxicab. This time it rang six times and went to an impersonal automated voicemail message.

"Name and number. Nothing else."

For anyone dialing the wrong number they'd never know they'd reached America's Secretary of State. Reilly hung up without leaving a message. Then, on second thought, he quickly dialed again. This time he did leave a message.

"Elizabeth. It's Dan. I'm here. We have to talk. No matter what you're doing!"

Matthews's phone was lying on the backseat of the Navigator with no one to pick it up. Reilly needed Hunter's cell phone number. He didn't have it, but Bob Heath would or could get it. It took ten minutes before Heath called back. Having it didn't make a difference. Reilly got Tom Hunter's generic message as well.

"Call me. Fucking call me, Hunter! It's Reilly!"

Reilly couldn't help but think that things were not good. He phoned Heath once more at the CIA.

"Bob, find out where Secretary Matthews is right now."

"Easy. Panama."

"I know that. I'm here, too. Exactly where?"

"It'll take a little time. Why?"

"Not over an open line."

"Okay. I'll—"

Heath stopped short. He received a flash alert on his computer. A definite ding that Reilly could also hear over the line.

"Oh God!"

"Bob, what?"

"Secretary of State Matthews. Dan," Heath said somberly, "her motorcade was ambushed. She's been kidnapped."

* * *

The Panama City traffic had come to a standstill. Police sirens blared. Uniformed members of Panama's National Police were checking every car. Reilly had more than a few miles to go.

"I'm sorry, mister. I don't know what's going on," Reilly's cabbie said.

Reilly did. He spotted five army helicopters overhead and people huddled in storefronts. A full search was on for the American Secretary of State.

Reilly called Heath again.

"Get off your fucking cell phone!" Heath demanded. "I cleared you through to the embassy to use a secure line."

"I'm on my way there, but the roads are impassable. I'm hoofing it. What do you have?"

"Eight down at intercept point. No tangos. Queen Bee unaccounted for."

Queen Bee was the code word for the Secretary of State.

"Now get off this line!"

Heath ended the call before Reilly. Reilly pulled two twenties from his wallet and handed it up to the 20-something Vitalpma Taxi Panamá driver. "Sorry, but I'm going to hoof it."

"Wait. I can get us there around traffic another way."

"You didn't know that before?" Reilly asked.

"It didn't sound as important when you got in."

"Will another forty help make traffic speed up?" Reilly said.

"I think it could, especially if you don't mind some bumpy going," the cabbie laughed.

"Hit it!" Reilly said.

The young man hadn't lied. He careened around corners, drove up onto sidewalks, turned down one-way alleys in the wrong direction, and raced through intersections as lights went from yellow to red. And then they ground to another halt. Police were holding up cars, examining trunks, questioning drivers.

"Any other solutions?" Reilly asked.

"Hold on!" He threw the car into reverse. As harrowing as the drive was so far, it got worse. Reilly searched for the safety belt. He hadn't put it on yet. The buckle was wedged between the seat and the seatback. He knew fumbling for it would make him nauseous. By comparison, the emergency maneuvers on the Hornet merely hours ago had felt smoother.

56

OFF THE COAST OF PANAMA

The Airbus H155 helicopter that had been ready at the parking lot flew low and fast, first due west. Seven miles offshore, Dog, a former North Korean Air Force fighter pilot, dropped below Panama's radar and skimmed just 50 feet above the waves at 180 mph, and on the prescribed course.

PANAMA CITY, PANAMA

Sirens cut through the air as Panamanian police cars, motorcycles, and military vehicles crisscrossed the city. No fewer than ten passed a white *SOS Ambulancia* screaming as fast as possible toward Gorgas Hospital on Calle 53 Este. It looked like a legitimate EMS. It had the right markings. But the driver ignored the hospital. He took a turn down Isla Flamenco and slowed toward Flamenco Marina.

In the back, attending to the patient, was a nurse. But not really a nurse. A doctor, lacking the same professional credentials, had hooked up an IV line to the woman in their care: Elizabeth Matthews.

The transport began from a floor below the rooftop level where the Secretary of State had been drugged and taken. The nurse looked over her unconscious patient, now bandaged and wearing a blonde wig to cover her short brown hair.

The nurse and doctor nodded to one another as they came to a stop. With the help of the driver, they off-loaded their patient and rolled her down the marina to a waiting Maritimo M60 three-decker yacht. The $2.5 million craft would cast off with no plans of returning. Their destination, a patch of jungle off the coast of Bohía Solano, Colombia, some 239 miles away. They'd make it under 10 hours.

Throughout the voyage, their passenger would sleep soundly while eyes focused skyward searching for the rogue helicopter that was spotted taking off from the parking lot, and then seen heading west over the Pacific.

The nurse changed into a bikini, suitable for a rich vacationer. The doctor emerged from a stateroom in Tommy Bahama head-to-toe. He'd done quite well with the IV line in the ambulance. He'd learned how to apply field medicine along with defensive driving and handling every imaginable firearm at FASTC, the Foreign Affairs Security Training Center at Fort Pickett, near Blackstone, Virginia. This was where agents of the Diplomatic Security Service went to train; where Tom Hunter went through the program with high marks. It was precisely why he had risen to Number Two under Carlos Santiago. Now, he was Number One. Tom Hunter was also a Russian sleeper cell agent, long ago embedded in American life and recently activated. He was key to the successful operation which Parisa Dhafari, now applying sunscreen, ran with deadly skill.

57

U.S. EMBASSY

PANAMA CITY, PANAMA

Dan Reilly rolled onto the semicircular driveway leading to the American Embassy located on a 43-acre plot of sloping land. He'd already passed through the exterior compound access control stations. Now at the foot of the white-stone four-story building, he paid his grateful cab driver $80 and another $20 tip. He got out and was stopped at step one by a Marine lieutenant.

"Sir, state the nature of your business?"

"I've been cleared by Langley," Reilly politely replied.

"Your identification."

There was no *please*. Reilly suspected this was not a day for *please*.

"Of course."

Reilly produced his passport and company ID. The officer examined them and compared the two photographs against the man facing him.

"You said you've been cleared by Langley."

"Yes, sir."

"I'll need to know more."

The Marine held onto Reilly's ID.

"I'm sorry," Reilly said. "I can't discuss that. If you check, you'll find that I'm expected."

The guard gave Reilly another once over without showing any expression.

"Stay here."

He stepped away and keyed a microphone on his lapel. Two other Marines came forward to block the entrance. Reilly knew he was being observed and recorded. If he smoked, this would have been the time for a cigarette.

Two minutes later, the officer returned.

"Mr. Reilly, you're good to go." He handed back the ID.

"Thank you."

Thank you was enough.

Inside, Reilly was again questioned and barred from passing through the metal detector until a DSS agent came down to lead him to the SCIF.

"This way, Mr. Reilly."

"Thank you."

That was the extent of the conversation. While his escort remained stone-faced, Reilly read the distress on others in the building.

Ten minutes later, he was sitting alone with the door closed in one of the embassy's Sensitive Compartmented Information Facilities. The room resembled a cargo container with a thick metal door. It was insulated to prevent any unintended radio or any data leakage from inside-out or outside electronic surveillance from penetrating inside.

Intellectually, Reilly understood that he probably couldn't have prevented Elizabeth Matthews's abduction. He was unaware that Matthews's trip had been moved up. However, he should have acted right after talking with Sammy. That was a mistake, and mistakes this grim would have serious consequences. He wanted to make up for it now.

He began his secure call with Heath.

"It was quick, Dan. Planned and executed expertly. What I don't get is how quickly it was put together. Details were under wraps. Matthews's trip was only announced, what? A week ago? And then pushed forward by the White House. How does anyone pull off so complex a maneuver so fast?"

Reilly had the answer. "Because it wasn't."

Heath wished they were on a video conference. Seeing Reilly's expression would have helped.

"What do you mean it wasn't? Of course it was."

"No. They were ready."

Reilly ran through his entire clandestine conversation with Sammy... the things he couldn't go over before: The warning. No, the warnings, plural.

"Bob," he said, "Sammy hinted there was much more."

The two men, 2,067 miles apart, each contemplated the ramifications. Reilly was the first to speak again. "What do you have on the abduction?"

Heath described how it came together. How the motorcade was strategically splintered. How there was only one clear route away. How Matthews's driver, now dead, drove up into a garage.

"Why the garage?"

"We're looking at CCTV cameras to see if her Navigator was cut off. It might have been the only way."

"And then?" Reilly asked.

"And then they were in the wind," Heath said. "Literally. A helicopter took off. According to first reports, the National Police logged sightings from people in the neighborhood and then sightings from tankers in the queue for the Canal offshore. Then it dropped off radar."

"Satellite imagery?"

"Coming in. So far limited to the city and the garage rooftop."

"Wait, they just happened to pull into a garage where a helicopter picked them up?"

"Yes."

"Any idea where the copter came from?"

"Just learning. The locals got a call from Pacifico Canal Tours. Seems that one of their helicopters disappeared during a rental around the same time."

"The pilot?"

"Longtime employee. But here's the thing. There was an unidentified body on the roof. We don't have confirmation yet, but—"

Reilly finished Heath's sentence. "The pilot was forced to land. Once on the roof, the passenger, also able to fly the copter, killed him. Any description of the passenger from the helicopter rental?"

"Not yet. So three dead on the roof," Heath continued. "The pilot and two DSS agents."

Reilly thought hard about his next question.

"And the backseat?"

"No one."

"There was another," Reilly said. "Matthews's new head of security, Tom Hunter."

"How do you know?"

"Because I talked to him on the phone while they were driving. He said he was right next to her."

"Then they took him, too."

Reilly said nothing. He was thinking again.

After ten seconds of silence, Heath asked, "Dan, are you still there?"

"I'm here."

"And?"

"Bob, why didn't they kill him, too?"

"I don't know. Another hostage?"

"I'm not so sure," Reilly said. "I'm really not sure at all."

58

THE PACIFIC OCEAN

"She's moving again, Captain."

"It would be a helluva lot easier if we could attach a GPS to the damned North Korean," Captain Zimmerman joked over sonar operator Okim Katema's shoulder.

Okim chuckled. "Yes, it would."

They both knew it wouldn't work. The device might make for a good submarine chase plot point in a thriller, but it wouldn't work in real life. It wasn't the pressure that would prevent it from working. It's the water. Water blocks radio waves. Submarines can't get GPS signals or transmit their location unless they surface.

But there are other means at the U.S.'s disposal. And every time the *Annapolis* pulled back and surfaced, even for mere seconds, they received the latest satellite imagery, audio from hydro-acoustic sensors, and SAR, synthetic aperture radar, which creates two-dimensional images and three-dimensional reconstructions of objects. The object of the past two weeks: *Wonsan Yong-Ganhan.*

"Ears on her, Okim."

"Roger that. Slow and steady goes the race."

"Still no indication she knows we're out here?"

Okim removed the cans from his ears and turned to face Zimmerman.

"No, sir. But they continue to be especially slow with timed rests and only minimal snorkeling."

"Okay, back to station. Report any change."

"Aye aye."

The further east *Wonsan Yong-Ganhan* sailed, Zimmerman had to conclude the North Korean was on a true course and possibly on a very bad mission. The Pentagon had ordered him to make firing solutions. He had done that days ago.

OFF THE PANAMA COAST

"Madame, look! Five o'clock." Dhafari's man shouted.

She turned her head and saw what alarmed Cat, the man who had driven the ambulance and killed the last of the DSS agents in the parking lot. Coming toward them fast were five swift Nighthawks.

"Police?" Cat asked.

"Binoculars," she demanded.

Cat found them on a shelf near the throttle. He handed them to her and saw the boats. She shook her head.

"Not police."

"Military?"

"I don't think so. But they've got guns."

She saw a man in a lead craft holding an automatic rifle. He was calling out instructions to the other boats. Dhafari couldn't hear him, but the intentions were clear: They were circling wide to surround her craft.

"Drop it down to an idle. Let's draw them in. I'll give them something to look at. Wait for my signal."

She opened a large plastic container the size of a hope chest. Inside, a selection of weapons. She removed two M79 shoulder-fired grenade launchers, similar to what they used in Panama City. She passed one low to Cat and the other to Tom Hunter. She slung an AK-47 behind her. Only the strap showed. That and a lot of skin.

"Wait for my order. No survivors."

Dhafari stood aft, offering a stunning target worth kidnapping.

The lead boat approached. The leader, clearly paramilitary, smiled broadly as he eyed the slim, barely clad, dark brunette on deck. Easy prey. Perhaps a rich South American. Maybe even a richer American from Miami. She'd surely bring a huge ransom. So would the yacht. *Not a bad day,* he thought. The others on board, whoever they were, might not make it any further.

The leader, Nasario Herrera, no older than twenty-seven or twenty-eight, signaled two of the Nighthawks to sweep ahead and cut off the yacht's forward route. The two other swift boats should come along either side. A classic box move. No escape for the pleasure craft. The yacht slowed but didn't stop.

Herrera pulled within 25 feet. Surprisingly, the woman simply stood and stared at him.

Odd, he thought.

He should have thought about it more. Herrera shouted in Spanish and English, "*¡Deténgase!* Stop! Heave to." For good measure, he raised his Belgian M249 light machine gun and aimed it at the woman on the yacht.

She smiled.

What the hell's her story?

Dhafari turned slightly to Cat and shouted over the engines, "Full stop." Cat understood it was to make their shots count.

"Do you need help?" Dhafari shouted in English.

Herrera laughed and in proper English from his boat replied, "Do I look like it?"

"You do, but it's already too late."

Herrera didn't know what to make of the comment. He yelled to the woman, "Prepare to be boarded. Should you refuse, you will die. I don't believe you want to die today."

Nasario Herrera had part of the statement right. Dying today was not on her list. As for boarding, that just wouldn't happen. She had her own prisoner, far more valuable than any this amateur would ever have.

"You shouldn't have approached," she called out. But by approaching the yacht, this crazy thief had sealed his fate and the fate of his crew.

"I am Nasario Herrera. I am the new Panama. You and your crew will be my political prisoners. You have no choice."

"Señor, you couldn't be more wrong."

With no warning, she raised her AK from behind her back. There might have been a fleeting thought that began to form in Herrera's cortex, the portion of the brain that governed thinking, learning, problem-solving, and reasoning. Obviously it didn't work well enough before to evaluate the threat and it was never going to work again. In four seconds, she swept his boat, cutting down Herrera and his five men.

Simultaneously, Cat fired ahead. The two boats were so close that the blast from his grenade launcher to one engulfed the second in a fireball. Hunter similarly eliminated the boat to starboard while Dhafari aimed portside. Two men had a split second to dive overboard. Dhafari riddled the others with her automatic and then spared the swimmers from death by drowning. They begged for mercy. Mercy was not on her list.

Dhafari told Tom Hunter to check on Matthews. For Cat, the command was simply, "Let's get back on our way."

Clear of the burning boats and the oil spill likely to engulf them all, Cat throttled the twin Volvo engines up to their maximum speed of 32 mph.

Dhafari allowed herself to relax. She opened a bottle of Panama Blue water and sat down taking in the rays. She felt they were far enough offshore that they would put ample time and distance from the carnage before any patrols got near. Even if they were spotted, there'd be no reason to consider a pleasure craft with a bikini-clad woman sunning herself a threat. After all, the stupid Panamanian rebels hadn't.

"How about some music, Cat?"

"Yes, ma'am."

"Something fun."

As the best of Tina Turner played on Spotify, Parisa Dhafari relaxed, having no idea that she had just eliminated a nuisance and saved the

Panamanian criminal justice system a good deal of time and money. Next stop, which they'd have to speed up to make: a planned rescue rendezvous with a low-flying helicopter that went even lower and stopped flying altogether.

What a productive busy day, Dhafari thought.

59

WHITE HOUSE SITUATION ROOM

They all looked grim…every member of the administration assembled in the White House basement Situation Room, particularly Admiral Rhett Grimm, the Chair of the Joint Chiefs. The CIA Director appeared remotely from Langley on a monitor. Also present was Senator Mikayla Colonnello, for reasons that were not immediately clear to the group.

"Gentlemen, ladies, let's start," President Allphin said entering and taking the seat at the head of the conference table. "I've invited Senator Colonnello because of her friendship with Secretary Matthews and in consideration that she's *Chair of the Senate Intelligence Committee.*"

The men nodded to Colonnello.

A map of metropolitan Panama was on one screen at the head of the room. A satellite photo of the area on a second. A third had no images.

"Gerald, you have the floor."

"Yes, Mr. President," the CIA Director said. "Our source in the Panamanian National Police reports they found the Secretary's Navigator. It was on the top level of a parking lot a mile from the attack. Two of the three DSS agents were killed."

"The third?"

"Agent Hunter, the Secretary's acting chief. It appears he and Secretary Matthews were abducted and flown out."

"Flown?"

"From a stolen helicopter on the roof. We're still collecting information. The pilot was killed."

"Then who's flying the damned thing?" the president asked.

"Likely one of the kidnappers."

"Jesus," Allphin said. "What about CCTV."

"They're checking."

"Thank you, Gerald. Okay, the floor is yours, Admiral."

"In addition to what Director Watts just reported, here's what went down."

National Security Advisor Dr. Hamza Ali, sitting to the right of the president, took notes. So did Secretary of Defense Vincent Collingsworth to his left, General Zarif Abdo, a member of the Joint Chiefs, next to him, and the other members of the National Security Council.

"Secretary Matthews was on her way to a cocktail reception at *Palacio de las Garzas* with President Jacinto Espinoza. *She was twelve minutes out when a well-planned attack separated Queen Bee—*"

"Secretary of State Matthews," chided the president.

"Yes, sir, Secretary of State Matthews, from her motorcade."

The CIA Director referred to a quick sketch he had made on a white grease board. He finished pointing to the location of the parking lot blocks away.

"Question for Director Watts," Colonnello said.

Watts was ready for her questions and more from everyone else.

"Director Watts, what about tracking devices? Any on the secretary's phone? Or," she paused, "don't you insert something in their butts?"

"A chip, no?" the CIA Director replied on the secure video line. "Her cell phone, yes. The car, yes. And each DSS member is wired. But no butt chip."

"For God's sake, my dog has one!" she declared. "Why not the president and the Cabinet."

Watts and President Allphin exchanged looks. Colonnello picked up on it.

"Oh my God," she declared. "So you do have them. Why not Elizabeth?"

"Senator, we'll table your question for another time. Do you have anything else?"

"Well, yes. Her phone and the agent who was also taken?"

"Left in the vehicle," Watts said.

"Then you have no idea where they are?"

"We're currently analyzing photos of air traffic from a geosynchronous satellite over the canal."

"How long will that take?"

"It's top priority. I should have an update soon."

Allphin wished he had a vice president across the table to consult. But his designee was somewhere in captivity. He turned to National Security Advisor Ali.

"How much longer can we keep a lid on this?"

"Not much, sir. CNN has already reported the attack. Since they know Secretary Matthews is in Panama, they've called for comment."

"All right then, here's what we'll say."

He outlined a message for the press.

WHITE HOUSE PRESS ROOM
THIRTY MINUTES LATER

Press Secretary Gluckin stepped up to the microphone. The room hushed as Gluckin gripped both sides of the podium, cleared her throat, and appeared deadly serious. The last time the press saw such a pose was when the White House announced that President Battaglio's charter had gone down.

"I will be brief, following which, I will take a few questions. I ask you not to shout out today. I'll call on raised hands."

The press secretary breathed in deeply, straightened, opened a folder, and began reading a bleak statement word-for-word.

"The State Department Diplomatic Service notified the White House that the delegation to Panama City, headed by Secretary of State

Elizabeth Matthews, was attacked at 1325 hours 1:35 p.m. local time, by masked insurgents. Six United States DSS officers were killed in the attack. Two have been taken to a hospital in Panama City. I have no information on their names. Another six Panamanian police were killed. In the attack, Secretary of State Elizabeth Matthews was kidnapped. It's presumed that her security head was also taken.

"President Allphin is currently meeting with the Joint Chiefs. He has spoken with President Jacinto Espinoza of Panama who has pledged his nation's complete support. We do not know who is responsible, whether they represent a country or are part of a terrorist organization. Panama, as you know, has seen a rise in insurgents since the Canal closure. So far, authorities in neither Panama nor the United States have received demands or communications from the kidnappers.

"The White House considers this an international criminal act without precedent. Assaulting, kidnapping, and assassinating United States government officials, their families, foreign dignitaries, and official guests is a crime under multiple U.S. codes. We will provide that information for you. Since 1982 the codes provide for extraterritorial jurisdiction over these offenses.

"No further information is available."

Hands shot up. Press members shouted out. Gluckin stood without calling on anyone. The reporters got the idea. Just hands.

The CNN White House Bureau Chief Marc Pitre was tapped first.

"Doreen, can you describe the actual kidnapping in any detail? Location? How it was carried out? And were there any witnesses?

"I can't. The delegation was staying at the United States Embassy and was on their way to a reception at President Espinoza's residence. Panama's National Police are questioning eyewitnesses. We have a team on the ground from our embassy. "

More rapid-fire questions followed. Word spread. Gluckin had a worldwide audience.

THE KREMLIN
MOSCOW

Nicolai Gorshkov's translator stood beside the monitor as the Russian president watched the live CNN International telecast. Gorshkov's English was good. He only missed a few words. When his translator tried to explain a nuance, Gorshkov wagged his index finger and said, "*Nyet!*" He wanted no interruptions. Gorshkov was intent on knowing his plan was proceeding well.

The attack and the extraction appeared to have gone perfectly.

U.S. EMBASSY
PANAMA CITY, PANAMA

Reilly was on his second cup of coffee with a half-eaten tuna sandwich when a young Marine walked up to him in the commissary.

"Mr. Reilly?"

"Yes."

"Come with me, please. There's a call coming through for you shortly in the SCIF."

Reilly nodded thanks and followed the Marine.

It was Heath again.

"Yes?" Reilly said.

"Got absolute confirmation. Hunter was with her in the car."

"I told you that." Reilly cleared his throat. "Okay, do me a favor. It may help all of us. Pull Hunter's file. His whole file. Whatever you can find. But do it yourself."

"Okay, but why?"

"Because he's not a hostage."

60

THE KREMLIN

MOSCOW

"Welcome, Mr. Ey Wing," Nicolai Gorshkov said through his Kremlin interpreter. "My sincere apologies for keeping such an illustrious envoy of President Yáo's government waiting."

Waiting would have been ten minutes, maybe twenty. Nicolai Gorshkov kept Sammy in a hallway for two hours.

The Russian President shook the Chinese envoy's hand at the center of his Kremlin office but did not invite him to sit. He wanted to keep the meeting short and be done with his business. Sammy sensed the maneuver and made a suggestion.

"This could take some time, Mr. President. We should sit. You may want to take some notes."

Gorshkov's mood instantly changed.

"I don't take notes, Mr. Ey Wing. I also don't take orders."

He crossed behind his austere, highly polished mahogany desk with elegantly designed gold inlay. Like many other objects in his office, it had been plundered by Vladimir Lenin's conquest of Lithuania.

"Nonetheless—" he gestured for the visitor to sit across from him.

Gorshkov's translator stood off to the side.

"Thank you," Sammy said. "I know you are watching world events closely and you and President Yáo share many of the same concerns."

Gorshkov heard the translation but said nothing. Sammy didn't expect any. Reactions would come later. This was just a tease.

"Accordingly, I have an urgent message from my president."

He removed an envelope from his suit breast pocket. Instead of handing it to the Russian president, he laid it on the desk with his hand over it.

"Thank you," Gorshkov said. "I'll read it at my earliest convenience."

Gorshkov reached for the envelope. Sammy did not remove his hand.

"First a preliminary request."

"A request?" Gorshkov replied.

"Yes," he said switching to Russian. "My Russian is exceptional. You may dismiss your able interpreter, who up to now has done a worthy job. But even you wouldn't want him to be party to—" Sammy tapped the envelope with his index finger.

Gorshkov's neck hairs prickled. No one in his country dared to speak to him with such directness. He measured his options: Dismiss the arrogance as the man's inexperience. After all, he had never heard of him. Excuse his visitor outright or read the damned note and be done with it.

Gorshkov smiled and decided he could afford five minutes. He excused the interpreter with a simple wave of his hand. Then he proposed a drink. A top-shelf vodka.

"Thank you, no," Sammy said.

Once they had the room to themselves, Gorshkov reached for the envelope again.

"In a moment, Mr. President."

Gorshkov opened his desk drawer and removed a silver letter opener with an intricately carved ivory handle. He waved it in the air and allowed the Chinese to take it as encouragement or a threat. Sammy was not deterred.

"Inside the envelope is a note written by President Yáo. Also in Russian. As you know, he studied at Moscow University in his twenties."

Gorshkov nodded once. He knew.

"I have memorized my president's letter. As President Yáo's emissary, I am prepared to discuss the contents, but not negotiate the terms."

"Terms?" Gorshkov asked.

"Yes, Mr. President. As you will soon see."

Gorshkov abruptly stood. "I will read the letter when I choose. If I choose." He brought the letter opener forward, over Sammy's hand. "This meeting is over, Mr. Ey Wing."

Sammy leaned back in his chair which closely matched the design of the desk. He ignored the order, lifted his hand from the envelope, and said:

> "The letter begins, With all due respect, to my dear friend, President Nicolai Gorshkov."

Sammy stopped and nodded toward the envelope. Gorshkov returned to his seat. The power base in the room had switched, at least for now. He took the envelope, slit it open, and pulled out a single, hand-written sheet of paper. Sammy continued reciting the contents as Gorshkov read along.

> "You have embarked on a dangerous journey that puts our relationship and mutual interests at risk. Your plans jeopardize those of the People's Republic of China. While you seek to destabilize the American government, you do so in dangerous ways. Your actions threaten my nation's foreign affairs and our entire economy as you draw the American president into a war with the Democratic People's Republic of Korea."

Sammy watched Gorshkov's entire body tighten. The Russian leader shot him a cold, cruel look. There would be more, far colder and far crueler.

> "What you do at your own front door is your business. Europe is your business. Ukraine and your nation's former republics are your business, up to the point that it affects us. But your back door is

Asia and the Pacific. Here you flirt with disaster. In response, I shall outline my ultimatum."

The Chinese let the last word hang in the air. Ultimatum, from the Latin *ultimatus*, a final demand. A condition, if rejected, would result in direct action. There was probably no stronger word in any political discourse than *ultimatum*.

"One: Return the woman Secretary of State alive. By now your operatives have taken her. There are other ways for you to manipulate the American election. Two: Recall the Democratic People's Republic of Korea submarine that threatens the United States; the submarine that you have armed with a nuclear missile. Three: Within the next three months, you will complete a negotiated settlement with Ukraine. Your misguided exploits have resulted in a global food shortage based on more than 40% reduction in exports from Ukraine. Exports we need. China will act as the arbitrator of the treaty. Four: You will cease any additional activities in the Middle East.

Gorshkov looked up, wondering how the Chinese knew about these plans. *A spy or a leak? A leak,* he decided. He would find the traitor and kill him.

Sammy continued from memory:

"Your actions threaten my country's relationships as well as my economic and strategic alliances around the world."

Now came the quid pro quo. The calculation for Gorshkov to consider from the ultimatum:

"If you do not agree to the first two terms, we will cancel our oil deal with you, Mr. President. We will seek new partnerships and buy directly from the Americans and Middle East producers. Considering the financial condition of the Russian Federation because of your failures in Ukraine, I'm sure we can agree that would not be a productive course to follow. We would prefer the status quo. The status quo serves us both. Patience, my dear President Gorshkov. Patience. As my people know, with time and patience, the mulberry leaf becomes a silk gown. You may give your compliance to my emissary."

The note was signed Yichén Yáo, President, The People's Republic of China.

Nicolai Gorshkov casually folded the paper and put it on his desk. His expression quickly hardened into the colder and crueler look Sammy expected from the autocrat.

"Mr. Ey Wing," Gorshkov glared, "You dare to insult me in my own office. You are a nobody! An envoy without portfolio. You have nothing to say to me!"

Sammy looked at his watch. "Mr. Gorshkov, President Yáo is at his telephone in his office for the next ten minutes. He would have had longer if you had not kept me waiting. You have his number. You can either call him or take what I have said, and what you've read, as his unequivocal position. If you call him, he will verify that I am his representative and the note is authentic. But," Sammy palmed a gold lighter from his pocket, "for all of our sake, neither of us would want a record of our conversation."

Sammy flicked the lighter open, took the letter, which had been written on flash paper, and lit it. It was gone in an instant.

Sammy kept his eyes on him. President Yáo would want to know exactly how Gorshkov reacted. Did his breathing quicken? Did he perspire? Did his hands twitch? Everything he did mattered. Everything he said mattered.

Sammy saw the tension in Gorshkov's face; the veins pulsating in his neck.

Gorshkov didn't reach for the phone. Instead, he opened his desk drawer.

A gun? Sammy thought. *He had shot people where I sat for less.*

The president removed an antique onyx chess piece. A king. He flipped it through his fingers.

"Mr. Ey Wing, I have heard your demands—"

"President Yáo's," Sammy corrected. He folded his arms.

"President Yáo's," Gorshkov acknowledged. "Now here is my list of counter demands. The People's Republic of China will construct five warships for the Russian Federation. Two world-class supercarriers. Cuba will be ours again. China will double our oil agreement for the next ten years at a fixed price. And we will come to a split on central African development. We both need the natural resources of the continent. There is enough to share."

With that, Gorshkov slammed the chess piece directly on the ashes of the letter, believing he reclaimed control of the meeting. The ashes scattered.

Sammy unfolded his arms, stood, and looked at his watch again. "Seven minutes, Mr. President. A call will confirm that I did not come to negotiate. You have heard the ultimatum. I'm also certain your devices have recorded our conversation for your review. You must accept all that President Yáo enumerated. He expects you to take these steps immediately, for our *mutual benefit*. Then, at a later date, we can talk about ways to strengthen our *mutual interests*."

Gorshkov said nothing.

"Thank you for your time, Mr. President. I'll let myself out."

* * *

Sammy had no doubt his route out of the Kremlin to his waiting limousine was being tracked by snipers who triangulated on him. His death would only exacerbate the situation. Gorshkov would pay, but that didn't make him feel any safer. He picked up his pace across the courtyard. The further he got, the more he believed he would survive the walk and return to Beijing.

Above the Kremlin, the snipers received orders to stand down. Sammy got into the backseat of the Russian *Aurus Senat* limo and left for the airport, certain that the Russian president was fuming. Under other circumstances, he wouldn't have minded killing Nicolai Gorshkov himself.

61

CIA

LANGLEY, VIRGINIA

Bob Heath, Associate Director for Military Affairs, could have called on any number of other officers in the building to do the research. He didn't. At least not yet. He and Reilly had known each other for nearly 15 years. From across the rugged Afghanistan landscape and the experiences they shared since, Heath and Reilly had learned to rely on each other. This was one of those times.

He started with Google, which proved to be a ridiculous start: 210 million hits on various Tom Hunters. Narrowing the field to the U.S. government brought it down, but nothing relevant and all old. As he expected, when he typed in State Department and Diplomatic Security Service he got nothing.

Next, he accessed Hunter's DSS application through an internal, but in no way, public portal. It came up and he made notes from the form. Place of birth, parents' names, siblings, high school, army service. Discounting the four minutes Heath spent on Google, it was a start.

Heath hopped onto his Pentagon link and moments later he was reading Hunter's record: Marine. Distinguished service. Germany with a stint at the American Embassy in Moscow. Total six years. Retired at captain rank.

He needed more. Back to his State Department app. He'd skipped over Hunter's written statement. Here he found more. In Hunter's own words, he stated that doors opened up to him after the service... doors to defense contractors, doors to lobbyists who represented defense contractors.

He was met with other opportunities as well. These were on Capitol Hill. Because of a stint in Russia. The House Intelligence Committee offered him a job. He turned it down citing the same reason he didn't accept the others.

"I'm really not political. More into serve and protect."

Hunter wrote in his statement that's what led him to apply at the State Department for a DSS position.

Heath dug further and read the reports on his application. At 32 he was accepted and sent to FASTC, the Department of State's Foreign Affairs Security Training Center at Fort Pickett. There he developed the skills necessary for a Diplomatic Security Service agent. What it takes to serve and protect America's diplomats and visiting foreign dignitaries. He excelled in every category: recognizing and deactivating explosive devices, high-speed defensive driving, detecting surveillance and threats, and providing emergency care in the field.

Tom Hunter was described by his instructors and reviewers as a rising star.

Now Heath wondered what the hell was driving Reilly. He appeared to be way off the reservation. But he looked further.

Going back to Hunter's application again he found the name of his high school in rural Kern County, California. Heath returned to Google. A picture of a modern school popped up. Under it a phone number, which he dialed. A recorded message gave him various choices. After listening to the menu he pressed 1 for the principal's office. A woman answered. The high school principal's secretary.

Heath's caller ID came up as unknown and in a pleasant, unde-manding voice he introduced himself in a general way that wouldn't cause concern. He said he was calling on a job promotion at the United

States State Department and wanted to reconfirm some information. Nothing critical. He gave the woman Tom Hunter's name as the applicant, and his high school years.

"I wish I could help you with Mr. Hunter's record. First of all, we don't give that information out on the phone. But I can save you the paperwork. The school was destroyed in a fire a year after his graduation. All school records leading up to that were destroyed. I'm sorry," she said.

"What about the cloud? Do you have backup?"

The secretary laughed. "I'm fairly new. But we have the same problem now that they had back then. Money. We have enough trouble stacking the shelves with books let alone having enough financial wherewithal for adequate cloud backup."

She punctuated her complaint with a question. "You work for the government. Maybe you can get us proper funding."

"You never know."

"Heard that before."

"But never from me," Heath replied. He wrote a note on a scratchpad. A reminder to make another call.

"One more question. What about anyone who might have known Tom Hunter when he was a student? Teachers, his coaches?"

"We've," she stammered. "We had a lot of turnover. Again before my time."

"I understand, but among those who were teaching then?"

"Look, Mr. Heath, we're a very small school. Like I said, we've had some real turnover, a horrible fire, and—"

"Yes," he offered hoping to encourage her.

"I can give you names, but they can't help you."

"Why?"

"They're gone."

"I don't understand."

"The same year as the fire, in fact just before, there was a terrible accident. The school basketball team was returning from an out-of-town game up Route 178." The secretary's voice dropped. "The bus ran off a mountain road into the river. I don't know the numbers. Twenty-nine, thirty, maybe more died. Students, teachers, the coaches, the cheerleaders."

Hunter typed keywords into the Google search window. The story was there. For the second time, he said he was sorry. But the words had the hollow ring of the expression *of hope and prayers* after horrible tragedies.

"Maybe someone set the school fire," she added. "Maybe it was God's will; a cleansing after the bus accident. It took years to rebuild. We're a regional school now. All new faculty."

Heath ended the call thanking the secretary, but feeling he came away with nothing more than a profound sense of sadness.

He tapped his fingernails on his desk in a rhythmic manner as he thought about where to look next or whether this was a Daniel Reilly goose chase. He came up with real estate tax rolls. *Maybe Hunter's parents are alive.* He phoned a poker game friend at the IRS with the hope he could collect on a favor. Unfortunately, fifteen minutes later he hit another dead end.

"Sorry, buddy. Out of luck. I found Chester and Sharon Hunter of Moreland Mill, California. But their last filing was years ago." Race gave him the date. He wrote it down on the same notepad as the Kern County school name.

"Really? Why?" Reilly asked.

"Don't know," Race replied. "Maybe no income."

"Including Social Security?"

"I suppose that's your next call."

Heath didn't have a personal contact, but his position at the CIA got him to the right desk and the right department.

"Shouldn't be a problem," Donna Griffin told Heath over the phone. "Give me a minute."

A minute was all the administrator needed.

"No filing for years. Because they both died."

She gave Heath the date of their last income tax statement.

He automatically added it to the pad and circled it. The date was the same as the bus tragedy and the high school fire.

"Any idea how they died?"

"Can't help you there," Griffin said. "Maybe county records."

Heath ended this latest call and returned to Hunter's State Department application. There, in his biography was the same date. He had overlooked it before.

Heath's fingers remained on the computer keyboard, confused and troubled. He leaned back in his chair and caught his vexing reflection on the computer screen. "Something's odd," he whispered.

He needed to dig further. Further got him to a one-paragraph story in the weekly *Tehachapi News*. It was short on details, but the names, dates, and places lined up.

> Chester and Sharon Hunter, lifetime residents of Moreland Mill, were reported killed December 20th, near Saas-Fee, Switzerland, when the small airplane they were flying in crashed. Authorities said the Hunters were on their way to see their son, Tom, age 19, who had won a skiing trip contest, only to suffer a devastating accident on the slopes himself. He is currently hospitalized.

Hunter had included the skiing accident in his biography. Heath next made a list of Saas-Fee, Switzerland hospitals to call. On his third inquiry, *Hôpital* Du Valais Site De Montana, Heath was told that the Hunter boy was flown to their facility via medevac helicopter. He was treated for facial injuries, broken teeth, and a broken arm, then moved to a rehab facility which was not in the *Hôpital* Du Valais records.

What a horrible time, Heath thought. *Hunter's heartbreaks and misfortune.*

But then another notion hit him. A notion that a CIA officer, a good CIA officer, was taught never to ignore: *Coincidences take a lot of planning.*

THE WHITE HOUSE SITUATION ROOM

THE SAME TIME

"For the next thirty minutes just give me options," the president said. "What we should do when we locate Secretary Matthews. When, not if," he stated. "I want workable proposals."

Twenty minutes in, the door opened. A man cleared his throat. It was an unmistakable sound from an unmistakable presence.

"If you'll indulge me for a moment."

Heads turned to former President Alexander Crowe. He wore a yellow sweater, white pants, and white shoes, no socks. He looked like he'd just come off the golf course. He had.

Everyone stood.

"Welcome, Mr. President," President Allphin said. "Glad you could make it."

"Thank you, Sean. Sorry I'm late. Traffic doesn't stop for me the way it used to."

The assembled members laughed.

Allphin explained that he had personally invited President Crowe.

"Thank you, Sean. On the way I spent time trying to work out exactly why you asked me here. After all, I have no position, no authority, and quite honestly, I'm rusty when it comes to strategy. So why? Then I realized what it was. I've known Elizabeth longer than anyone here. From the time I first met her at a Brookings seminar when she was an academic, to her Senate Intelligence Committee staff appointment, through her term as Under Secretary of State, and my elevation of Elizabeth to Secretary of State…fourth in the line of succession. Appointed to the office, unelected, but still in line. A valuable hostage."

Crowe circled the large oak conference room table. It was what he did.

"So you want to know how I think she will act? What she will do?"

He was answered with nods.

"I'll tell you. Elizabeth Matthews is the most capable, most resourceful person I have ever worked with. If there is any way to communicate with you, she will find it."

Crowe stopped behind the only empty chair but didn't sit.

"The kidnappers will try to break her. They won't succeed. If they torture her, she will die before she reveals America's secrets."

Crowe rounded the table again.

"What does this mean? The Elizabeth I know will buy you time. I suggest you use it wisely. Find her, and know that she will do everything in her power to delay and deny her captors before their patience runs out or—" He thought for a moment.

"Or?" Grimm asked.

"They will bargain for a trade."

"What kind of trade?" Dr. Hamza Ali asked.

"Something high stakes."

"What?" Ali demanded.

"Whatever's most valuable. Whatever's on the shortlist. If it's the Venezuelans, acceptance of the regime. The Chinese, more control of the Canal."

"Too dangerous for the Chinese," President Allphin noted.

"Cuba?" Grimm asked.

Crowe took his seat, paused a beat, and continued. "Guantanamo. They want us out. But it's not Cuba. Too little muscle, not enough willpower. Risk is too great for the reward."

"Then who and what?" Ali asked.

Crowe thought for a moment. "No, it's not a trade. It's a diversion. A distraction. What else is going on that we should be paying attention to?"

"The sub," Grimm declared.

Crowe raised an eyebrow.

"North Korean," the Admiral added without going further.

"Iran tying up Tajikistani oil routes across the Caspian Sea. With nothing we can do," Ali said, "except watch prices go up more."

President Allphin had another crisis. "And Turkey denouncing NATO this week and likely walking out and establishing exclusive trade talks with Iran."

"A diversion," Crowe said.

"And then they free her?"

"First of all, who's they? Second, no. Whoever *they* are changes the game board for the next election. Elizabeth is out. And without her running, Sean—"

President Allphin whispered one name and one name only. "Billy Peyton."

MOSCOW

Being a member of Nicolai Gorshkov's inner circle was all too often a lifetime or life-ending job. One of the reasons he often changed out members of his coterie was simply because he couldn't afford to trust anyone.

It was not inevitable, but it was possible that some, if not many, would ultimately conspire against him. For that reason, insiders constantly over emphasized their devotion to the president. Even if they were invited to openly criticize his decisions in meetings, they wouldn't because criticism was never forgotten.

The undeniable fact was that Gorshkov needed confidants but for only so long. He was most intent on his own well-being, expanding his empire, destabilizing the U.S. economy, and maintaining secrecy. That meant that his minions were constantly looking over their shoulders for tails and under their furniture for listening devices.

The paranoia extended well beyond all the president's men and the few women he entrusted with his secrets. One of them, Parisa Dhafari. So far she had done the work of ten. It was amazing how revenge could become such an effective psychological weapon.

Yes, while Dhafari had more than proven herself, the real test was to come. After that, if she survived, he would have her take care of critical problems back at home. Among them, a nagging feeling about General Sergei Bortnik.

Bortnik had not shown Gorshkov any outward worry, but he might have left sloppy clues to his attachment with the Canadian jet leasing company. Also, his wife was becoming an absolute embarrassment in the social scene. She was loud and brash. No wonder the general had his mistress on the side, an acceptable indiscretion for a man wielding power.

Perhaps, Gorshkov thought, *if the General comes to a sudden end, I will take the woman for my own.*

If and when were not *now*. That was his error in judgment or the FSB's inadequate snooping. General Bortnik was a very real problem, and what he had exposed under the covers was enough to put Gorshkov's grand plan into jeopardy. Had he known, Gorshkov would surely have acted. Because he didn't, no more than two kilometers away, the general was back in bed with the alluring Alina Ostrovsky.

* * *

"My darling," Bortnik said to his lover, "let us get away and enjoy the pleasure of being together without me having to look over my shoulder. Name the place and the time. But soon."

He was serious. He too had a nagging thought. It might only be a matter of time before Gorshkov turned on him. He had no reason to do so. But then again, the president never needed a reason.

"Where, my love?" she said from under the covers.

"Paris. And then—"

"Yes?"

"Anywhere."

Alina Ostrovsky lifted her head from the pleasure he had experienced and none that she had felt. She also had a definite sense this affair had gone on too long and her life might be in jeopardy.

"Yes," she said with feigned glee.

Yes, she thought. *Paris and then I'll be done with you.*

EMBASSY OF THE UNITED STATES, PANAMA CITY, PANAMA
THE SAME TIME, A WORLD AWAY

Reilly paced for the last hour. Pacing helped. Moving helped. Sitting and waiting did nothing except exhaust him. As he paced, he asked himself questions hoping to come to some answers: *What exactly happened on the roof? How far could the helicopter go? Why over the sea? Did it land on a yacht? Has anyone looked for yachts big enough to handle a copter landing? And what about Hunter? Hunter, Hunter, Hunter?"*

That's when a local police alert popped up on the computer at the desk he was sitting at. A tanker ship, idled off the coast, had radioed in about smoke on the horizon. Possibly a pleasure craft in distress. The U.S. Coast Guard had one of two medium 45' Response Boats nearby. It was redirected to the location where it found remnants of multiple small cigarette boats burning. Three, maybe more.

Odd, Reilly thought. *One would be an accident. Multiple? Especially today? How the hell does that happen?*

He continued reading. No survivors. Bodies floating.

The fact of the matter is, something like that doesn't just happen. It's made to happen. And that, in Reilly's judgment, meant it was not something to be ignored. Rather, it was a point to consider. *An attack, but by whom? Maybe people who blundered into a situation they hadn't counted on. People who got in the way of…a sea escape.*

A third update. Signs of a battle.

Shit!

Reilly texted Heath with an urgent need to talk. Thirty minutes later a Marine summoned him to the embassy SCIF. Bob Heath was on the line waiting.

"Sorry it took a while," Heath said, "It's all hands on deck here. Teams are focused on the helicopter that was last seen—"

"Forget the helicopter!' Reilly interrupted.

"What the hell?" Heath challenged. "The 363rd Intelligence, Surveillance, and Reconnaissance Group is all over it. So is everyone who's glued to the NSA's satellites."

"It was a diversion, Bob. Matthews was never on the helicopter."

Heath stuttered a reply. "How? Why? What?"

"Just hear me out."

"You better have something good."

"I've got a feeling."

"Oh, that's going to go over great."

"You want to hear it or not?" Reilly asked.

"Of course, I do."

"Then listen. Forget the copter. It was strictly a diversion," Reilly said. "A sleight of hand, perfectly executed. Keep your eye on the magician's pretty assistant, so you miss the trick."

"How so?"

Reilly read him the alerts. The news of the burning boats.

"I'm not getting it yet, buddy. Help me out."

"Multiple burning swift boats? The kind used by smugglers or piss ant rebels."

"So they had an accident. Who cares?"

"Wait." Reilly continued to read. When he finished, he asked Heath to put "an attack" at the top of the possibilities.

"Okay, why?" Heath asked.

"Their own stupidity. They were out to capture the boat or yacht. Snatch the rich foreigners for ransom. Trouble was they picked the wrong target. They picked the boat with United States Secretary of State Elizabeth Matthews aboard. The boat with people who had bigger guns and greater plans than theirs."

Reilly leaned into the speaker phone in the embassy SCIF. "Bob, check all yacht departures after the point of kidnapping plus, say twenty minutes. Boats big enough to carry serious weapons. That's what we need to be looking for. Not a helicopter flying off into the wild blue yonder. I bet that thing was scuttled."

"Dammit," Heath said, "I'll do you one better."

"Oh?"

"An EMS vehicle was seen heading down the street away from the garage. Away. Siren blaring. No one thought of stopping it."

Reilly replied, "Dollars to donuts you'll find that EMS near a dock empty."

"I'll take that bet!"

62

THE COLOMBIAN JUNGLE

NEAR BOHÍA SOLANO, COLOMBIA

THE NEXT DAY

Elizabeth Matthews opened her eyes, which were slow to focus. She saw netting above her and green above that. She rolled her head to the right and then to the left. Walls of green. She tried to make sense of her surroundings but she was too groggy to form a cohesive thought.

Her mouth was dry. She was aware of needing water. She tried to lift herself. It was hard. She tried harder. With her head slightly elevated she saw that she was bound with straps, the kind that are used to hold cargo down. She also saw an unconscious Tom Hunter similarly tied.

Nothing was making sense.

She heard people talking in low voices. They were too far away to pick out any words. Besides, they were drowned out by a cacophony of birdsong.

Matthews looked around her surroundings, taking inventory of what was there: cigarette packs, towels, toilet paper, and opened and unopened food cans. Most were American and Hispanic brands. American, including P&G, General Foods, and Goya. Latin foods from companies named Alimentex, Alimentos el Gordo, Panela, and Desmargo. They had Spanish labels she understood or could tell the foods by the photographs on the packaging: canned tamales, suckling pigs, sugar, and fruit in syrup. Some of the selections suggested she hadn't gone too far since…

Since what? What happened?

The ties that kept her down told her the obvious: *Kidnapped. But where? Still Panama. In the jungle? And for how long?*

She made that decision based on how desperately she needed to pee.

"Help!" she yelled. I need a bathroom.

She laughed to herself. *Like there's really a bathroom.*

While she asked for assistance, she continued surveying the space. She noticed especially colorful food cans labeled kimchi, spam, and sweet corn, some in English, others in Korean.

Hints, she thought. *No, it's all evidence.* In a matter of minutes, Elizabeth Matthews felt proud of herself that she had fairly well profiled her kidnappers' nationalities, though it puzzled her. Plus she determined, with her need for a bathroom, that a good deal of time had gone by since her abduction. She was further from Panama City than just the neighboring jungle. *Costa Rica to the north? Colombia to the south? Friendly or less friendly territory?*

For now, however, she had to figure out *who* had her. She was a hostage and a very valuable one at that.

She heard stirring over her shoulder. Hunter was awakening.

"Tom, are you okay?"

He was slow to respond.

"Tom, are you hurt?"

He groaned.

"Tom!"

"Yes." He spoke slowly and barely above a whisper. "Madame Secretary?"

"Just to the right of your feet."

He strained to see her. "I'm okay. How about you?"

"All right, no. Alive, yes. What do you know?" she asked.

"Nothing. What about you?"

Matthews decided not to volunteer any of her speculation in case someone was listening. She also wondered why Hunter was taken, too. After all, from what she remembered of the harrowing chase, the other DSS agents in the SUV were killed along with their escorts. *But why not Hunter? What value does he have, unless torturing him in front of me might make me break?*

"Don't worry, Madame Secretary. There are protocols for getting you out. The cavalry—"

"Shhh!" Matthews cut him off. She heard someone enter. She also didn't want to talk about rescue plans. Besides she probably had a better bead on where they were than any cavalry.

Matthews turned uncomfortably to the rustle of the canvas flap. She saw a woman outfitted in camo, t-shirt, pants, and a scarf covering her long blonde hair. With her, three equally clad men behind her, bald, hardened, and armed.

"Good morning, Secretary Matthews. Nice to see you rousing."

"Untie me. I need a bathroom."

The woman laughed.

"Really."

"In a few minutes. First I have some rules to run by you and your bodyguard, who didn't do such a good job yesterday guarding your body."

Elizabeth Matthews now had more information to process: First, they'd been on the run for a day, which generally supported her conclusion about possible locations. Second, the woman was in charge. She tuned her ear to her accent.

"Untie me first."

Not enough to make a judgment. Maybe with more conversation.

"I said—"

"I'm sorry. That's not how it works here. Rule number one, you listen to me. I make the rules. You follow them. When you don't," the woman crossed over to Hunter and pressed a pistol into his side, "he feels the pain. The more you ignore my rules, the more he suffers."

"Don't listen to her, Madame—"

The woman flipped her gun around and brought the grip down

hard on Hunter's ribs. He stifled a scream, but the lesson of rule one became apparent. She was in charge. No one else.

"Rule number two, you ask nicely for things you want."

"I want to be untied. The straps have been cutting into me. I also need water. So does he, and a bathroom."

The woman stepped between them and said nothing.

"Please," Elizabeth Matthews managed.

The captor smiled. "See how easy that is. However, you must realize we're short on first-class facilities, but these men will accompany you to a makeshift latrine. Don't expect any privacy. When you're finished, you'll have some restorative coffee and breakfast. Simple field provisions. You get what we get until the next stop."

Another bit of information. So, Matthews thought, *they're going to keep me alive. That means the cavalry better act fast.*

Matthews was shuffled into the jungle, and not politely. They watched and laughed as she took care of her needs. She used the time to get her strength back and listen, particularly to the birds. She wasn't an ornithologist of any note. However, before she was saddled with 24/7 security, she always loved photographing birds on her global trips, researching their behavior and distinguishing their birdsong. She was an amateur at best. But there were some she knew. When she was led to a disgusting dugout latrine she recognized a species. It was the Indigo-winged Parrot noted for its nasal "kraal" and its brilliant coloring: a blue cap atop a yellow head with a grayish bill and green body accented with splashes of red, teal, and purple. It was one of the rarest birds in the world and was native only to Colombia.

If given the opportunity to communicate the terms of her captivity, she would somehow signal where she was.

When Matthews returned and was retied, she asked a question she knew she wouldn't get an honest answer for, but she still might learn something. "Who are you?"

"I have so many names. You can use Victoria."

"You don't look like a Victoria."

"Then call me anything you'd like."

"Why did you kill my men and take us?"

"That should be obvious. We killed your men so we *could* take you."

Matthews was able to sit up now. She took in a deep, cleansing breath. She tuned her ear again to the voice like she did the birdsong. She considered the woman's accent a curious mix of proper cultured English with Middle Eastern origin. Looking at her, Matthews believed she might be Iranian, Saudi, or even Israeli. She needed to make a more critical determination.

Matthews noted how Victoria was armed. Definitely for the kill. She had her pistol, an AK of some caliber slung over her shoulder, a military knife, and God only knows what else in her web belt.

"What do you want?"

"Me? Some revenge. Your death could provide that, but I'm not authorized to do that."

She takes orders from someone else, Matthews concluded. *Possibly good.*

"On the other hand, your bodyguard is expendable, and fairly useless as you've seen. His well-being is entirely up to you."

"Then what do your *authorizers* want? A trade? You have to know my government won't trade."

Victoria—Parisa Dhafari—smiled again.

"Perhaps, but public opinion being what it is, seeing you on TV could change that. Particularly when the stakes increase. After all, you are Secretary of State of the United States, and if you live through this, maybe the next president. What's the old saying? What doesn't kill you makes you stronger."

Matthews said nothing.

"But we're getting ahead of ourselves," Dhafari said. "Now you will eat. Then we'll tidy you up for a quick hello to your president."

With that, Dhafari turned and left.

Matthews replayed all that had happened. One word the woman had said stuck out. *Revenge.* Was it solely personal toward her or directed at the United States as a nation? Learn that, and she'd be that much closer to understanding who was behind her abduction.

63

THE DAY STARTED FOR REILLY as the day before ended—full of anxiety.

He got little information from the embassy staff and closed lips from the Marines. His only source of news was his news feed and his conversations with Heath at Langley. It was time for another call with him.

"Any success overnight?"

"Some. Found the ENT. And you were right. A two-story ocean-worthy yacht left fifty minutes after the kidnapping. But—"

"Yes?"

"Not everyone's buying into the notion."

"Jesus, Bob. It's right in front of them. The helicopter is probably at the bottom of the ocean."

"They're wasting time. Not completely. Watts is working with Admiral Mirage in Joint Chiefs. Mirage. Lots can happen if he's all in."

"I want to talk to him."

"Unlikely. Explaining you to some of these folks could slow it down."

Reilly was frustrated. *Government*, he thought. *Can't live with it. Can't live without it.* "Okay then. Next topic," Reilly said.

Heath cut in. "Tom Hunter."

"As a matter of fact, yes."

"The information is not generally available."

"What do you have?"

"Holes. A surprising number of them go way back, starting with a disfiguring skiing accident in Sass-Fee, Switzerland. That was followed by a calculated tragedy: His parents were killed in a plane crash on the way to see him.

"Hunter recovered in a rehab facility. After that, he dropped out of college and joined the Marines where he worked his way up to captain serving with distinction. Another calculation. When he was discharged he shopped around for work and eventually settled on DSS. He took the DSS test and passed with flying colors, impressed everyone, and here we are."

"Go back to Hunter's Marine service." Reilly requested.

"Got it right here. Notable record. Mostly offshore. Germany and an assignment in Russia. He graduated from DLIFLC."

Heath used the acronym for The Defense Language Institute Foreign Language Center knowing Reilly had studied there as well.

"He mastered Russian, which earned him his two-year post in Moscow at the embassy. Again with high marks."

"The perfect candidate," Reilly observed.

"Except," Heath said, "for the holes. Well, for now, call them inconsistencies in the narrative: Hunter's high school record, destroyed in a fire the year after his skiing accident. The skiing accident itself that led to his parents traveling abroad and then dying in a plane crash. Former teachers, fellow basketball players and cheerleaders driving off a mountain road a month before. And something else, I'm still working on."

"Yes?" Reilly was totally engaged.

"The ski trip itself. I found a newspaper clipping that indicated he had won the Christmas trip to Switzerland."

"How?"

"I don't know. Some contest. No record."

"And from there?"

"Down a black hole where logic and reason go to die," Heath said.

"Or where theories are proven," Reilly asserted. "Tom Hunter wasn't killed during the kidnapping. He should have been. Everyone else was."

"Go on," Heath said.

Reilly replied, "He's with them. Whoever *he* is."

"And try this on for size," Heath added. "What if Hunter isn't Hunter."

"I think you better go through that slowly," Reilly replied, "because my mind is racing to a pretty scary scenario."

"In a sentence, Thomas Stanton Hunter is an enigma. His record, his family, and his friends have all been erased. Actual records that go back before his skiing trip are impossible to find. It's like he was in the witness protection plan for part of his life, except he wasn't."

The line went silent as Reilly took it all in. Then he whispered. "A sleeper spy, a replacement waiting to be awakened. And now fully awake, promoted with the sudden vacancy at DSS. The faithful Number Two, made Number One, just waiting for the time to be right. If it ever would be right. And then the vice presidency opened up."

"You thinking what I am, buddy?"

"I sure as hell am," Reilly said. "We have to find Elizabeth fast. Can you convince Director Watts?"

"We better hope so."

64

THE COLOMBIAN JUNGLE

After Matthews's first few hours awake, guards separated her from Tom Hunter.

"You're due a little privacy," Victoria/Dhafari told her. "We'll bring him back in as a reminder what of happens if you don't behave. And each time he's going to need more health care, which our plan doesn't provide for."

"I'm trying to figure out what drives you, Victoria," Matthews said while Hunter was taken away.

"A lot of things."

"Money?"

"Least of all money."

"I didn't think so. This isn't about any ransom."

The captor listened.

"I'm stuck on the word 'revenge.'"

Still no reply.

"Revenge is personal. That's for you. But not for your employer. I'd say that's political. He, am I correct to assume he?"

The woman who called herself Victoria blinked.

"Yes, political for him, and he's using your anger."

Victoria scoffed.

"Wow, there's a lot to unpack here," Matthews offered.

"And you're not my valet. So now your questions have earned Mr. Hunter his first punishment as a reminder that I ask the questions, not you."

She nodded to one of the Koreans who left to do her bidding. Dhafari smiled and said, "You're a smart woman. You'll learn." Then she followed her man.

Seconds later, Reilly heard Hunter's screams.

Dhafari returned an hour later with a bowl of soup, crackers, and a list of inane, random questions for the Secretary of State. Some on national security, which Matthews didn't answer. They earned Hunter more punishment. Others on her personal life, which Matthews found more interesting and suggestive of her line of thinking about the political nature of her kidnapping. *Things to use against me*, she judged. She didn't answer these either, and as a result, she heard Hunter suffering the consequences in his tent.

These sessions came every two hours. In between, Matthews was allowed to sleep, which she didn't do. Thinking time was more important. One of the things that first weighed on her was an increasing sense of guilt for the pain she was inflicting on Hunter because she refused to talk. Then a second thought: the timber in Hunter's voice sounded the same each time he was beaten. She heard no sense of exhaustion. *Is he that strong that he can withstand so much abuse?*

Matthews focused on a third notion. The level of questions she was being asked about intelligence and diplomatic initiatives would be more valuable to a major player, a nation, than rogue terrorists.

She thought about these things as she tried to rest on her grass mat with her arms tied to a stake, as she sat on the makeshift latrine, and as she was bound and dragged past Hunter's tent.

What the constant questioning and her sleep deprivation didn't do to break her will, the constant rain, the humidity, and the dampness that wouldn't dry were beginning to.

She went to a darker place. *A forced confession to some international crime? Hunter, then my execution, shot on video and seen around the world, a viral video of immense political proportions.*

Matthews tuned her ear to all the voices she heard at the encampment. There was a true variety. Of course, Spanish, but with so many accents, she couldn't identify anyone specifically. Asian, more specifically Korean. Logic would suggest North, not South. Then there was the woman, Victoria. The more she listened, the more convinced she was Victoria was possibly Iranian. *But this scheme seems too big for Iran and too dangerous. It has to be bigger.*

Her conjecturing was interrupted by Victoria's next visit.

"Elizabeth," Dhafari said, opening the flap to the tent.

"It's Secretary Matthews!"

"I think we've been together long enough. We can drop the formalities."

"How about you give me your real name, and I'll think about it."

Dhafari laughed.

"Then it's Secretary Matthews, and since your name isn't Victoria, there's no reason I should use it."

"You are everything I've read."

Matthews nodded just short of thanks.

"But now it's time to clean you up a little. You're going on TV."

"No videos! No recordings! I won't read anything."

Dhafari laughed. "...So says the woman tied and held hostage."

"That's right."

"Wolf," Dhafari said to one of her men, "see to it that Mr. Hunter is made more uncomfortable. Perhaps his fingernails this time."

Matthews shivered.

"Now!" Dhafari demanded.

The man smiled sickly and turned to leave.

"Wait," Matthews sighed. "What is it?"

Dhafari waved a paper.

"Let me read it first."

"No. I've seen you on TV. You're good with prompter cold reads."

Matthews shook her head.

"Change of mind," Dhafari noted. "Fine. Me too." She told Wolf to bring Hunter in. They'd torture him in front of Matthews.

Hunter was dragged by Wolf and Cat. He struggled. Cat pushed him to the ground and smashed his boot in Hunter's chest.

"Tom!" she said. At the same time, she thought, *That looked real.*

Hunter lifted his head. He had bruises, *But are they enough to warrant—?*

"Well," Dhafari said calmly and cruelly, "Mr. Hunter can either be your audience for a short recording, or you can be the audience for the removal of his fingernails."

THE PENTAGON

"With all due respect, Mr. Director. You want us to do *what* on the word of *who?*"

Admiral Rhett Grimm wore his name on his face and didn't hide his disbelief in his voice. CIA Director Gerald Watts figured it would be a hard sell. It was. He said, "We have an informal, quiet back-channel relationship with a Chinese operative."

"Who does?"

"An American businessman—"

"Oh, Jesus!" Grimm slammed his fist on the table. "An American businessman," he continued, "and a Chinese operative. Is this how we do things around here?"

"He also serves as a liaison to the Secretary of State," Allphin said. "We'd be wise to consider his report."

Grimm shrugged.

"I can vouch for him," Senator Colonnello said. "I've met him. I'm familiar with his record. He used to work at State and he was one of yours, General."

"One of mine?"

"Army, retired. He's the real deal."

"What the hell does that mean?" Grimm demanded.

"It means if Secretary Matthews trusts him, you should, too."

The room went silent until the president cleared his throat. Heads turned.

"General, it is not widely known, and it must remain that way, but this man is the reason Ryan Battaglio was exposed and why I now serve as president. If he's the source of Director Watts' intel, we should listen. Moreover, Admiral Mirage is already preparing plans based on the report."

"With all due respect, Mr. President, you mean opinion," Admiral Grimm stated, though he now figured out the source.

"Valued opinion," Watts interjected. "From our informant to my Senior Case Officer, Robert Heath. I think with that information, the Chair could determine through military records whom I'm talking about without stating names."

The Chair of the Joint Chiefs stretched his arms out on the table, clenched his fists, and then relaxed them. In those ten seconds, the temperature in the room lowered.

"Director Watts, you still have the floor," the president offered. "Let's get back on track."

"Yes, sir. We can only speculate where they took her, but the source is convinced the helicopter was a diversion. She was taken away by boat."

"Okay, speculate?" National Security Advisor Ali asked.

"North or south of Panama."

Grimm frowned. He was through arguing. Their source was an army man. That helped. Now to figure out the next steps.

COLOMBIAN JUNGLE

"The rain is coming down hard. Too noisy. We'll record when it's lighter. Take Hunter out."

Two men dragged the DSS agent back out.

"You do try my patience," Dhafari said. "How anyone works for you is beyond me."

"I'm not so bad when you get to know me. There's still time for you, Victoria."

"And you're tempting me to end yours."

With that, Parisa Dhafari left.

A few minutes passed, and Matthews decided to exert herself again and see where it might lead. After all, she was a negotiator. She decided to start negotiating on her own behalf.

"Get Victoria," she said to the captor hovering over her. "I want to talk to her."

"She decides when you talk. Not you."

This was the first time she heard from the man Victoria called Dog. *The accent is definitely Korean.*

"She doesn't know what I want to tell her. She won't be happy if that stops with you."

"Shut up!" Dog shouted.

Matthews shrugged her shoulders. "Then she'll hear about it from me when she comes back. That won't make Victoria happy."

Dog stormed across the tent. He slapped Matthews so hard she was knocked to the side as far as her ropes would allow.

"Not a good idea. She's wanted me to look good for the camera."

Dog swore under his breath. A mistake. Matthews recognized the expletive for *Fuck You* in Korean. *Confirmation.*

He pulled the tent flap aside and left, bracing himself against the driving rain and wind. The Secretary of State thought that round went in her favor.

At the same time, Parisa Dhafari was with Tom Hunter in another tent. He was no longer tied. He sat on a log with a bottle of Aguila, a Colombian beer. He gently rubbed his chest. They whispered.

"Jesus Christ, he fucking broke my ribs."

"You'll live," Dhafari said.

"Doesn't feel like it."

"She had to be convinced. You were the means. For everything to succeed, for you to return a hero, you have to act it."

Hunter winced at his pain.

"Take off your shirt," Dhafari said.

"You got something to bandage me up?"

"No," she replied.

"What then?"

"More," she smiled cruelly, "acting."

Cat approached holding a two-foot-long branch of a fallen Ceiba tree with sharp spiny protrusions.

"Why?" Hunter said, suddenly afraid.

"I had the sense that she noticed you hadn't been hurt enough. You need to hurt more."

"I do hurt."

"You need to hurt a lot more."

Twenty feet away Elizabeth Matthews heard blood-curdling screams.

65

PANAMA CITY

THE SAME TIME

It was the waiting that always got to Dan Reilly. Waiting to hear if his father would make it home from his deployment in Iraq. The waiting in traffic as rebels blocked the routes back to the Cairo Royal Star of the Nile; now this.

Reilly accepted a waitress's offer to top off his coffee. When she cleared earshot, he dialed Bob Heath on an open line.

"This is not a good way to talk," Heath said answering in his CIA office.

"And this is not a good way to deal with the problem," Reilly sharply responded.

"Give it time."

"What if time is not on the Secretary's side?"

"Dan, the director is in with the Joint Chief's committee now. Just wait a little longer."

Waiting—definitely what Dan Reilly hated the most.

* * *

Waiting was also something the Under Secretary of State couldn't afford to do. If Elizabeth Matthews wasn't coming back, Micky Rucireta had to be ready to assume responsibilities, at least on an interim basis. It started with two very different objectives. One, reviewing briefings with more scrutiny. Two, going through the paper that had accumulated on her boss's desk and the hundreds of emails in Matthews's inbox.

Rucireta was well into her third hour of organizing when she leaned back in Matthews's seat, sighed, and silently prayed. Taking in a deep breath and ready to continue she spotted something that was always on the corner of Matthews's desk and something she also always treated as a joke.

It was a simple four-inch square locked plastic box with a small metal hammer attached in a holder on top. The box was marked in Matthews's handwriting, BREAK IN CASE OF EMERGENCY.

It seemed like there were emergencies every day, some at the break-the-box level.

It looked like one of those souvenirs you could pick up at any novelty store. But now, Rucireta wondered. She remembered Secretary Matthews saying, "You know, if all else seems lost, just break the damned box, Micky."

They laughed about it time and time again. Rucireta wasn't laughing now. She reached for the box and put it front and center on the desk. Slipped the hammer out of the sleeve and said, "What the hell. If not now, then when?"

She brought the hammer down with a light tap. Nothing. Then again. The hammer, little more than a toy, wouldn't do it. So she put the box on the floor and went after it with the heel of her shoe.

The box splintered. She picked it up, looked inside, and saw a folded note. She opened it. It was handwritten by Secretary Matthews on State Department stationery. Rucireta recognized her hand. She read it slowly and shook her head in utter amazement. The note was abundantly clear: Matthews's specific wishes in an emergency, which this surely was.

Rucireta picked up the phone and called the White House, asking to be put through immediately to President Allphin.

COLOMBIAN JUNGLE

Hunter was returned to Matthews, now looking like the victim he was supposed to be. Cat and Wolf accompanied him. Hunter was bruised and bleeding. He looked at her through beaten, blurry eyes. He was in obvious pain.

"I understand you wanted me. Well, I want you to first see this," Dhafari said as she reentered.

Hunter was flung forward. He hit his head on a tent support.

"This is your doing, Madame Secretary," Dhafari said. "So, time to record or watch your DSS agent suffer. Oh, if you don't do as I ask, we'll send the video of you just watching. I don't think that will get you approval from Congress or the White House."

Elizabeth now understood. This was all about her. Her upcoming appointment. Her possible run for the White House. She'd live to be discredited. Either case, it was all clear to her now.

Matthews thought about her options. She believed there were always options. Maybe fewer this time, but there were options. Letting Hunter take a beating just provided one. The woman had talked and revealed her intentions. *No,* she realized. *Not her intentions. The country she worked for. But what country? More talk. More information.*

Dhafari's men set up a cell phone with a tripod grip mount. As they did, she asked Matthews again to read and nodded to Wolf, who immediately kicked Hunter on the kneecap.

"No, no, and no!" he pleaded.

"Look, I need my reading glasses for something this close. You're much too young to need any yourself, Victoria. If you live long enough, you'll know what I mean. But may I at least have mine?"

Dhafari laughed, then said, "I suppose a quick review wouldn't hurt."

She dug Matthews's glasses out of her purse.

"Thank you."

Next, the paper to read.

"Awfully small print."

She began to read. What Matthews was looking for was a word, a turn of phrase, or a grammatical error that might tip her off to the nation of origin. If she found something, she'd emphasize it, subtly, but it would be there for someone with a sharp ear.

There was nothing to work with. But she could try blinking, blinking or tapping out a Morse code message, which she'd learned in the Air Force. She rejected that. It worked in movies. She didn't think it would work here.

Matthews also knew rudimentary ASL, American Sign Language. But there was nothing subtle about it. And if the camera was tight on her then no one would see it.

But now with Hunter in the tent and placed behind her to be a prop in the shot, the angle might be wide enough to sign. Of course, any movements would have to be sly.

And then what should she communicate? She had an approximate idea how long the journey took them. The rest of the day, the night, and part of the morning. *That's something.* She didn't get a full count on the captors. She'd seen nine, including Victoria. *That's worth passing along. We're in the Colombian jungle. We're a little inland. But there's the scent of the ocean. That's worth passing along.*

But all that was too much. Location was most important. A reason to aim the satellite imagery.

"Are you reading or wasting my time?" Dhafari asked.

Time was another factor. *Waste it.*

"Look, this is stressful. Give me a moment to absorb this."

"Five minutes."

"Ten."

Dhafari nodded to Cat. He kicked Hunter in the side.

"Seven," she said.

"Seven. How will you get the message out? They'll be listening for cell transmissions."

"That's not your worry. Just read. It airs tomorrow."

Tomorrow? That means we're fairly close to a city where they can send the video file out via computer or cellular email. No, that can be tracked.

It'll be walked or sailed out.

"Read! I'll be back in six minutes."

* * *

During those same six minutes, Micky Rucireta was able to talk to the president.

"Yes, sir. That was her request. Contact him if anything happened."

"Read it to me again," Allphin said.

"Certainly." She did.

> If you've broken this little tchotchke we've joked about, then you now know it's not a joke. The situation is serious. No matter what danger I'm personally facing there's one person I want to have my back; someone who will know what to do or figure it out. Find Dan Reilly. Whatever's happened, I must need him.
>
> Elizabeth Matthews
>
> United States Secretary of State

"Well, I'll be damned," President Allphin said. "This guy does get around."

66

CNN WASHINGTON

THE NEXT DAY

A delivery man on foot handed a small brown envelope to a security officer at the CNN Washington headquarters at 20 First St NE, Washington, DC. The man's face was obscured by dark sunglasses, a baseball cap with no insignia, and a black hoodie. He wore thin leather gloves. He said nothing but pointed to the envelope. The officer saw that it was addressed to "Newsroom CNN."

"You'll have to sign in at the reception desk." The CNN security officer glanced over his shoulder and nodded to the front desk. When he turned back the delivery man was gone. The package was on the floor.

The officer felt the envelope. To his touch, he thought it was a small thumb drive. He walked it up to the desk.

"Something for upstairs," he said.

"Without a signature?" the seated officer replied.

"The guy took off."

Five minutes later the envelope was in the hands of the show producer, but Tina Ludwig was overwhelmed with format changes given the kidnapping and the ongoing search for Secretary of State Matthews. The White House still had no statement leading into showtime. She had guests for her anchor to interview, but the talking heads would be talking in generalities. Ludwig needed better. She insisted on better today. "Get me Carl Erwin!" she shouted to her senior producer, Charlie Jenkins.

"On it."

Erwin was the former CIA Director. He was also very close to someone much closer to the action, though she didn't know it. Erwin was a member of the Kensington Royal Hotels Crisis Committee.

"And," Ludwig added, "check this out." She tossed him the envelope.

Jenkins rifled through his computer for Erwin's cell. Because he was busy, he passed the envelope to a young segment producer. "See what's in here."

Marci Swift took the envelope. She was busy, too, finishing up a script for an upcoming anchor read. She waited ten minutes, then finally ripped it open, and read the note inside. It should have been read the instant the envelope arrived.

* * *

Ludwig, Jenkins, and Swift watched the footage. Then they brought in the DC Bureau Chief and put the new network president on the phone, the latest of a string of five who were still figuring out the job.

"How did it come into our hands?" the network president asked from Atlanta.

Ludwig explained the handoff from the lobby to upstairs.

"Oh, Jesus," he said soundly. "All right, here's what we're going to do. Make a copy and take it to the West Wing along with security. I'll call the White House and alert them. We'll put a hold on the video until 5 p.m. Between now and then, they can authenticate the footage and determine if it's real or a deepfake. You've got people to do that, too?"

Ludwig wasn't sure.

"Then find someone who can!" they heard over the speakerphone from Atlanta. "I'll get with legal and work out what we can say on the air."

"Do we even have until five?" Ludwig asked. "What if they sent the same thing to the other networks?"

"They may have, but we're going to do it the right way. Besides, *they*, whoever they are, have to expect that we'd try to authenticate it. But we won't have long. Use what time we have and alert our social media that we might have a breaking story for them. But keep the circle tight and guard the goddamned media. Also, have security check the surveillance cameras. If this thing is real, the FBI will want to see who dropped off the USB drive.

"Now, get moving!"

PACIFIC OCEAN

ABOARD THE *WONSAN YONG-GANHAN*

Captain Jang Song-Taek sat in his cabin holding a photograph of his wife, Ha-Eun. He was told she would be taken care of. She'd want for nothing if anything happened to him. His son and his family would be provided for as well.

If anything happened... he had thought but didn't vocalize. He couldn't vocalize. There was no room for individual thought in the Democratic People's Republic of Korea. He couldn't even question the meaning of the word "Democratic."

If anything happened...

He was approaching a window in which the new Russian missiles in his newly refurbished submarine could reach an American city. His orders were time-sealed in his computer, unreadable until a specified time. That time was quickly approaching.

But if this was merely a mission to probe, hadn't they probed long enough? They'd certainly sailed further than any sub in the fleet and presumably without being detected.

Then he revised his thinking. *What if we had been detected?* He recalled what the Admiral of the Navy told him when they met before sailing.

"Jang, I bring you the personal assurance of the Supreme Leader that your family will be taken care of if anything happens."

Comforting words. Personal words. Political words. But now "if anything happens" were troubling words.

He put the photograph of Ha-Eun back in his wallet with the photos of his grandchildren. They were the light of his life in the darkness of the underwater world he had spent far too many years away from them. He wanted to see them again. He feared he wouldn't.

If anything happens. If anything happens. If anything happens.

Jang Song-Taek, captain of the *Wonsan Yong-Ganhan,* knew the answer was in the unopened orders that were waiting to download at the appointed time.

He considered the possibilities. *It's a test of my loyalty. A test of my will and then home. Yes, I've had challenging orders before. Or, or, or....* And then he came back to the Admiral's nagging words: *If anything happened....*

He'd never been told that before. Not so precisely. Not with such sickly sweet insincerity from his country's naval commander.

He was now convinced there was more to the mission. With that realization came more questions. Harder questions.

Can I carry out an immoral order? An unprovoked attack? One that could kill hundreds of thousands, possibly more?

There was only one answer to each of the questions. If he failed to obey, then his wife, his son, and his grandchildren would face a very different, if not short, future at the angry end of anti-aircraft guns.

Time was running out, and the objective was getting closer.

THE WHITE HOUSE

"The clock is ticking, gentlemen." President Allphin corrected himself. "...And ladies." He addressed Senator Colonnello, Homeland Security Secretary Debra Sclar, and Under Secretary of State Micky Rucireta."

In addition to the Pentagon team, and the new cabinet members, FBI Director Reese McCafferty and Defense Secretary Vincent Collingsworth had rushed in with police escort sirens screaming.

"The Bureau is running another analysis of the video CNN sent, Mr. President," McCafferty said out of breath. "But even without it, we've got 97% facial recognition and 100% audio confirmation that we're looking at and hearing Secretary Matthews. She's clearly under strain, but her voice is clear. The footage is authentic."

"Mr. President, in the interest of National Security," Defense Secretary Collingsworth argued, "we should confiscate the CNN copy as well. More analysis might tell us her location."

The president looked at his watch. He turned to Attorney General Randy Kenton. "Rand, your opinion?"

"CNN has the footage. It's on their server and ready to run. If they don't run it, someone else will undoubtedly get it. Keep your deal with the network."

"Agreed."

Next, Allphin addressed his Chief of Staff.

"Tee up Doreen, Lou. She's going to have to face the press. The press will be at her door ten seconds after the video rolls. Maybe even before it's finished."

67

PANAMA CITY, PANAMA

Reilly finally moved out of the embassy and checked himself into the local Kensington on the Beach. He sat alone at the hotel bar completely frustrated, drinking an espresso, and taking a bite of a sandwich. No liquor. Not tonight. Not until Elizabeth Matthews was back safe and sound.

Over the shelves of liquor, four TVs, with the sound down, played different networks. One, a Spanish game show. Another, a telenovela. The third, a tight soccer game between Brazil and Argentina, held everyone's attention. The fourth TV, which Reilly had planted himself in front of, carried CNN. But no amount of wishing over the last two hours had brought him any update from the TV, let alone his phone.

He'd taken only a few bites of a *Cubana,* the hotel's signature bar sandwich loaded with a generous portion of roasted pork marinated in *mojo* sauce with orange and lime juices, oregano, garlic, and cumin. It was good, but he didn't have much of an appetite.

Reilly waved to the waiter that he was ready to settle up. The bill came, and as the hour flipped, Reilly stood. As he put down the cash, which included a more than adequate tip, he froze. A still frame of Elizabeth Matthews caught his eye but not just because it was her. It was a visibly weary Matthews, seated against a green background, and a man in stress behind her and off to the side.

A lower graphic slid across:

"Turn that up!" Reilly shouted.

The career bartender was in no rush, especially from the man who had ordered little and stayed so long. He raised a single finger for Reilly to wait. Reilly was through waiting. He pushed his food to the side, anchored his left elbow on the bar, and launched over. Reilly reached up to find the volume but the set was too high.

"The remote! ¡El mando a distancia!"

The bartender took one of four satellite TV remotes. First, the sound came up on the game.

"This one," Reilly pointed to the monitor with CNN. He added the necessary, "Por favor."

With the sound finally up and the anchor in mid-sentence, Reilly breathed a sigh of relief as he watched. *At least she's alive.*

"…and while CNN has been able to authenticate the audio and the video, we do not know who delivered it to our Washington, DC, studios. We'll show it now with a warning. It is a stark reminder of the danger Secretary of State Elizabeth Matthews faces and the challenges ahead for the administration of President Sean Allphin."

The anchor paused and nodded, a very human clue that he had already screened the footage and it had shaken him.

"My name is Elizabeth Matthews."

Matthews was holding a sheet of paper with her left hand. The other hand shook on her lap. She appeared weary.

"I am the United States Secretary of State. I am reading a statement provided by my captors. If I deviate from what has been written in any way this recording will stop, but not before you will see my security detail head punished for my indiscretion."

The camera panned over to a shirtless man, already roughed up. Reilly immediately recognized Tom Hunter. *Roughed up,* Reilly thought, *but not severely beaten.*

"He has already suffered because of my earlier refusal to cooperate."

The camera, Reilly concluded, was a cell phone shooting in a horizontal mode to include Matthews and Hunter.

She wiped away perspiration.

"Keep reading," yelled a male voice from off-camera.

Reilly recognized the accent.

But because Matthews hesitated, Hunter received a fast fist to his nose, enough to break it. He screamed.

"Continue!" the voice said.

Another word, another chance to compare. Damn, she knows exactly what she's doing.

At that moment, Reilly's phone rang. He pulled it from his breast pocket but missed the call. He stayed with the TV and ignored the number he missed.

Matthews raised the paper higher and closer. Her right hand remained on her lap, her fingers seemingly twitching nervously.

Reilly caught it. He'd never known Elizabeth to be outwardly nervous.

"This is a time for reckoning," she read. "For too long, the United States has maintained a military base and prison in Cuba against the will of the Cuban people. America's political and military support of the illegal Taiwanese government is in violation of the People's Republic of China's sovereignty."

She cleared her throat.

"Another," the unseen man yelled. Hunter pulled his arms and legs in tight against the blow that was about to come.

"No!" Matthews said. "I'm going on."

"Read!"

"America dares to bolster rogue regimes in Ukraine, violating promises made with the Russian Federation by expanding NATO. America isolates the Democratic People's Republic of Korea in support of the American puppet regime to the south. America threatens all those you do not govern."

This is going way off the rails, Reilly thought. *It's a litany of who's who and what's what of crazy totalitarian grievances. Almost absurd.*

Reilly's phone signaled an incoming text:

CALLED U. R U WATCHING? HEATH

Keeping his ear tuned to the TV, Reilly replied with a quick:

Y

"America is guilty of global interference, empire building, and crimes against humanity. If you value my life and are ready to make amends, then here is what must be done, Mr. President—"

Matthews paused. She slowly lowered her eyes, coughed, and shook her head. Reilly watched now not the way he knew most people were watching. He focused on her fingers which didn't stop moving.

"Read!" the voice shouted again.

Her left hand holding the paper shook.

Yes, Reilly noticed. *Clever.*

Hunter suffered a rifle butt slam to the groin.

Reilly now recognized what she was doing. He saw the subtle movements. It wasn't nervous twitching at all. His years in intelligence told Reilly exactly what Elizabeth Matthews was up to. She was sending a message in ASL, American Sign Language.

Whatever she was forced to read was now eclipsed by what she was surreptitiously signaling. Reilly ran through the bar and out of the restaurant while dialing a phone that he knew was waiting to be answered.

68

WORD SPREAD LIKE LIGHTNING. White House TV monitors had tuned to CNN to see how they'd present the video. Other sets had FOX News, MSNBC, and the business channels. Eight hours ahead, wide awake, Nicolai Gorshkov watched in the Kremlin. Within minutes, the broadcast networks broke into their regularly scheduled program with bulletins. In years past, wire service machines in newspapers and radio and TV stations would have been screaming five bells.

Sean Allphin paced. His senior advisors listened. They had seen the video already but watching it on TV made it all the more real.

Nicolai Gorshkov beamed in front of his bedroom TV. Parisa Dhafari had delivered better than any operative he'd entrusted. The next steps were even more critical.

President Yichén Yáo of China watched with his translator, senior generals, and Sammy Ey Wing. His country's name had been invoked. Gorshkov was pulling China further into his scheme and defiantly ignoring his ultimatum.

Ro Tu-Chol, the young, inexperienced, newly installed Supreme Ruler of North Korea, believed this was great news, with more to come. *What a lucky coincidence that America's attention is focused on the kidnapping of the woman cabinet member while my submarine pushes closer to its target. Soon the United States will recognize the awesome power of the Democratic People's Republic of Korea. My power.*

He had no idea it was no coincidence or how he was being used by his *friend* in Moscow.

* * *

Minutes earlier, only one pair of eyes had focused directly on Matthews's right hand. Now two people were aware.

"Play back the video. She's messaging us. And grab someone there who reads American Sign," Reilly breathlessly told Bob Heath. "I swear to God, she's telling us where she is or something key."

"Roger that."

"Also, get the sound analyzed. She took long pauses. Maybe there's something in the background that will help."

There was. The distinctive call of a bird native only to Colombia.

69

THE WHITE HOUSE

THE OVAL OFFICE

"Ludicrous!" National Security Advisor Dr. Ali declared. "We can't give in to demands. For that matter, any demands."

"Of course we can't," the President said, "and we won't."

"But we risk them killing Elizabeth," Ali solemnly added.

Sean Allphin nodded. The stark reality was Ali was right. The terms in Matthews's message were completely clear: her life for a disputed Naval Base on foreign land.

"If I may, Mr. President," Under Secretary of State Micky Rucireta said.

"Yes."

"What if Elizabeth's kidnapping was just to get our attention? What if the North Korean sub is the real thing to worry about?"

"Are you writing off your boss, Micky?" Allphin asked.

"Of course not. Just consider how vulnerable we are and the questions that will be asked. We couldn't prevent the kidnapping of an administration cabinet member and we can't defend our country? That's a pretty decisive message to our friends. To our enemies."

Allphin had the latest briefing on the North Korean sub and the danger it presented. Rucireta was right. And she was wrong. At least we can defend our shores.

The members of the National Security Council sat in silence until Admiral Rhett Grimm stood, straightened his uniform, and commanded everyone's attention. "All right, let's look at both issues as one. First, what do the kidnappers actually want? What's real?" He lowered his voice to a timber that reverberated inside everyone. "Second, what will happen if we eliminate the North Korean sub?"

No one answered, so Grimm did.

"The kidnappers want to embarrass us. They know we won't turn over Guantanamo or cave to any other demands. They'll string us out and then kill Secretary Matthews. The sub is on a mission that will either succeed or fail, but why? I'll tell you. Someone is trying to draw us into a war. North Koreans? They'd lose in a New York minute."

"Exactly," Ali said. "It's a setup."

"Whose?" Allphin demanded.

National Security Advisor Ali raised his hand. "I'll tell you."

THE COLOMBIAN JUNGLE

"Good evening. How are you feeling?" Parisa Dhafari asked as she opened the flap to Elizabeth Matthews's soggy tent.

"Go to hell."

"I've been there and back. They're pretty much the same."

"All things considered, I'd rather be home in my own bed," Matthews replied.

"As a matter of fact, I'd rather be in mine, but look at the positive side. By now you have the most famous face on earth. You'd be instantly electable."

"Except you have no plan of releasing me and no expectation that my country will negotiate."

Dhafari smiled cruelly.

"Besides, you haven't even made any attempt to hide your appearance. No mask."

"It's far too hot."

"It is hot," Matthews said. Then she switched to Farsi and added, *"But I can identify you."*

Dhafari tilted her head, a subtle enough confirmation.

"You apparently bring a great deal to your work: an Iranian with a British accent could be working for any number of countries. But I'll go back to something you said yesterday."

"What's that?"

"For you, it's personal. Or someone has made it personal for you. Manipulated you. If that's true, then Victoria, that makes you every bit like me."

"You know, Elizabeth, I admire you. I like strong personalities. Strong women. It says a great deal how far we've come." Then she laughed. "Yet, you're merely a pawn of your government."

"A pawn has value. I'm still alive at least long enough to get through your deadline and then maybe one more recording."

Dhafari circled her bound captive sitting on a straw mat in what appeared to be a most uncomfortable way.

"The clock is ticking, Elizabeth. This will all be over soon."

"Come on, Victoria. We both know your demands will never be met and I'm expendable. So between us girls, what's the real game?"

"That's above my pay grade."

"What if I pay you more? You must understand I have a credit card with no limit."

Dhafari said nothing.

"Life-changing money," Matthews added.

"With strings attached. I avoid strings. They always get tangled."

"I think you're already tangled up, Victoria. Like I said, I'm expendable, and I suspect you are, too. If not today, what about tomorrow? Do you trust everyone in your little army? Out here in the jungle. American satellites searching everywhere for us. They'll find me alive or dead. And they'll find you, possibly the same way."

Parisa Dhafari smiled. "Or they won't."

Matthews wondered what that meant and then she knew: *Victoria's leaving.* Time to push her further.

"The way I see it, you're lighting a spark expecting the U.S. to fan the flames. React. Jump into something bigger."

"I do what I'm told," Dhafari said.

"You mean ordered."

"Don't you?"

"I can resign at any moment. This is your moment, Victoria."

Parisa Dhafari had her own thoughts about the moment. *It's time to leave.*

THE WHITE HOUSE
THE OVAL OFFICE

"Your friend," Ali declared, "Nicolai Gorshkov. And like before, there will be no tracks to lead to him. But it's Gorshkov, somehow, someway."

"Make that *ways,*" the president corrected. "Now, let's play this out."

Allphin waited for his team to work through the possibilities. CIA Director Watts spoke next. "They, he, wants to bring you down. And with you, the republic."

"Tell me something I don't know."

"One by one," Admiral Grimm said. "We rescue Matthews or we don't. Her death or survival is meant to keep you occupied while the sub moves closer. We take out the sub without starting a world war. Quietly, no acknowledgment. If we need to do more, we attack Pyongyang's submarine ports. A little less quietly. If the Secretary of State becomes a casualty and we prevent a war, then we still come out ahead."

Grimm was living up to his name and reputation.

"Thank you, Admiral. But going too far is likely what Gorshkov is counting on. An attack on North Korea could give Yáo reason to move on Taiwan," Allphin noted.

CIA Director Gerald Watts cut in. "Yes, but we could advise him of the action and make it clear we know China's clean. After all, we received the tip through his emissary."

"Or we could redirect the 7th Fleet, Mr. President, and be prepared for

Beijing to use this as a reason to take Taiwan," Admiral Grimm replied.

"Mr. President," Under Secretary of State Rucireta interrupted, "I think, and I firmly believe, that Secretary Matthews would view any new deployment to Taiwanese and Chinese waters as a provocation that could lead to an immediate escalation. At this moment, neither we nor the Chinese should do anything to bring matters to the boiling point. We are agreed that Gorshkov is likely behind all that's going on. He wants to keep us busy on stupid shit. Create multiple fronts. Stretch us thin. Devalue you. So let's take Taiwan off the list."

There was overall, but not complete agreement.

"What about Cuba and Guantanamo? The demand Secretary Matthews read was for us to get out in forty-eight hours."

"And as you said, Mr. President, that's not going to happen."

"Then back to Elizabeth. I want her out and alive."

Collingsworth broke eye contact with the president. "I shouldn't be talking politics, but if we can't, the next election will be up for grabs. Your likely VP choice is gone. Without Matthews, Billy Peyton has a clear shot. And suddenly, Gorshkov has a bosom buddy in the White House. Everything changes."

Allphin puffed out a long, audible breath.

"And when we do get her back," President Allphin said like a true Commander in Chief, "Congressman Peyton stays on the outside looking in."

PACIFIC OCEAN

360 FEET BELOW THE SURFACE

Captain Zimmerman and his Executive Officer, Colin McQuinn, sat in Zimmerman's cabin. Both were onto their second cup of coffee. They'd talked through the rest of the season for their favorite NFL teams— Green Bay and Miami, respectfully, and their favorite Christmas movies—*It's a Wonderful Life* for the captain, *Die Hard* for the XO.

It was all small talk until Zimmerman ramped up to the reason he summoned McQuinn.

"Does the name Valentin Savitsky mean anything to you, XO?"

McQuinn frowned. "Familiar, but I'm not sure why."

"Not sure classes cover him that much these days. They should."

"Russian?"

"Yes, one of three Foxtrot commanders involved in a dangerous time in the world's history."

"The Cold War?" the XO surmised.

"The hottest part, 27 and 30, October, '62. The most dangerous days of the Cuban Missile Crisis."

McQuinn listened as Zimmerman's history lesson took shape.

"We'd been playing cat and mouse with the three subs that would endanger our enforcement of a blockade around Cuba. The Pentagon ordered U.S. Naval forces to track the subs. Track, but not attack. Then a more grave order came down from Secretary of Defense McNamara: induce the Soviet subs to surface. That could mean forcing them to exhaust their batteries or the release of grenades to signal the submarines up. If that failed, then depth charges.

"The fear in the White House was that our moves could lead the subs to arm and fire their torpedoes. What we didn't know at the time was that each Foxtrot carried not just conventional torpedoes but 15 kiloton nuclear torpedoes.

"Two of the subs, B-59 and B-130, surfaced when their batteries required recharging.

"But B-36 continued underwater and things got worse in the skies. Cuba shot down an American U-2 spy plane."

Colin McQuinn put his coffee cup down, mesmerized by the account. Captain Zimmerman stood. Without a great deal of space in his cabin he walked to his bed and back.

"The Russians were disciplined, but the greatest show of anger could come from an emotional response from the exhausted submarine captain onboard the B-36."

The XO filled in the name: "Captain Savitsky."

"Yes. And that was precisely the situation when Savitsky was unable to establish communications with Moscow. There were reports that he had become undone and ordered a nuclear torpedo to be readied to fire. Some accounts had him declaring, "We're going to blast them now! We will die, but we will sink them all."

"Oh my God," McQuinn said.

"Though the scenario is still up for debate, what occurred next was likely due to B-36's Deputy Brigade Commander, Second Captain Vasili Achipov. It's said he stepped in and calmed Savitsky. B-36 surfaced and a calamity of catastrophic proportions was averted in the Caribbean."

Zimmerman sat and allowed his Executive Officer to fully process the story.

McQuinn thought carefully and said, "The Korean captain may do what Savitsky didn't do, but with missiles."

"Correct. We must conclude that he's prepared to launch when he's in range. We must be prepared to stop him. I need to know that you're with me."

Just then, a seaman knocked on Zimmerman's cabin.

"Captain, sorry to interrupt."

Zimmerman opened the door.

"You're needed in the Control Room. We've lost the Kilo again."

* * *

"Status?" Zimmerman asked. XO McQuinn was by his side.

"We had her, sir. She's gone again." Okim reported.

"Gone or playing possum?"

"Possum again. It's been her routine. Every six hours on the nose. She's playing it cautious. We'll pick them up again. So far, they haven't acted as if they know we're on them."

"All stop," Zimmerman quickly ordered.

"Aye aye, all stop," command acknowledged.

Zimmerman continued. "They may not know, but if that captain is worth his salt, now's the time he'd want to lose anyone who's potentially on to him. And that's us."

"Yes, sir."

"Before we lost contact, any change from *Wonsan's* last bearing?"

"Holding steady to 91.72."

Zimmerman looked over the ocean chart presently up. "Our current position?"

The navigator pointed to the map. "Here, sir."

They were 1,745 nautical miles from the California coast. According to intel Zimmerman had on the ballistic missiles onboard, *Wonsan-Yong-Ganhan* was almost in range.

With the Russian story fresh in his mind, Colin McQuinn said, "I hope the Kilo captain has control of his sub and his senses."

Captain Zimmerman shook his head. "And if he is, that also means he's committed to following his orders, XO. We need to be ready to follow any we get or be prepared to act on our own the second *Wonsan-Yong-Ganhan* opens its launch tubes."

WHITE HOUSE

THE OVAL OFFICE LATER

Admiral Grimm received a text, which he reported to the National Security team.

"We've lost the North Korean sub again."

"Jesus, what's it going to take to find it?"

"Captain Zimmerman reports that the North Korean hasn't diverted from what's become its standard route and best routine."

"What about our satellites? Can't we track the thing from above?" President Allphin asked.

"Yes and no," Joint Chiefs Director, Operations Nick Mirage said. "In shallow depths, yes. When it's surfaced, yes. When it's running deep, no. And they're in deep waters now."

"You mean to say with all our technology we still can't pick out a goddamned Communist submarine on its way toward us with a fucking nuke onboard?"

"Sir, if I may," CIA Director Watts offered. "It's like trying to spot one person on the opposite side of a football stadium with 100,000 fans. You have binoculars. You can see everybody, but can you focus on anybody in particular? Possibly in time, if they're sitting, but if they're moving, it's much harder. The North Korean sub is moving in a very large ocean. Our best bet to reacquire the North Korean sub remains with the captain and crew of *Annapolis*."

"Then what?"

Admiral Grimm took the question. "We make some noise and let the captain of *Wonsan-Yong-Ganhan* know we're there."

"I suggest you make more than just *some* noise. How about a god-damned explosion onboard BEFORE it starts launching a missile. Isn't that what we were talking about earlier, Admiral?"

The president's statement was as close to a kill order as anyone had heard.

"Yes, it is, Mr. President. The time is near, or now, for you to make that order," Grimm stated.

Allphin pushed back away from the Resolute Desk. He stood and walked over to a credenza with busts of presidents he had on display—all of whom had, in Allphin's view, made the most momentous decisions in the republic's history: Lincoln, Roosevelt, Truman, Kennedy, Reagan, and Obama. The events: The Civil War, entering World War II, dropping the atomic bombs on Japan, the Cuban Missile Crisis, challenging Russia to strike down the Berlin Wall, and taking out Osama bin Laden.

As was the case on *Annapolis* a few minutes earlier and far away, the meeting was interrupted by a knock at the door. Allphin nodded to Chief of Staff Lou Simon to see who it was.

The president's secretary was at the threshold holding an envelope.

"I'm sorry to interrupt, sir. I've been told this is urgent," Lillian Westerman said. "This is for Director Watts."

Simon thanked Westerman. He returned and handed the CIA Director the note. Watts opened it and gasped. It was from Assistant Director Bob Heath holding fort at Langley.

"Excuse me, please," Watts said rising to his feet. "We know where Secretary Matthews is."

"Oh my God! Where?"

"In the Colombian jungle."

"How? Who told us?" the president demanded.

Watts smiled. "Elizabeth Matthews herself!"

70

THE PENTAGON

ONE HOUR LATER

Nick Mirage, Chief of Naval Operations made a call to San Diego, California. The man on the other end knew that when Mirage called it meant work—the specific type of work that U.S. Navy SEALs did.

"Commander," Mirage began.

"Admiral."

Kevin Kimball and Mirage had been close friends, a band of brothers from operations when Mirage himself had been a SEAL. They dropped the formalities right after the greetings.

"Chief," Kimball's SEAL designation, "get your ass to a SCIF. I have a live one for you."

"Roger that. My guys could use a little break from Old Town and get back to work. We're bored out of our gourd."

* * *

"People, gather round," Kimball said ninety minutes later. "Time to earn your keep. We have a genuine situation."

SEALs Team 3 lived for "genuine situations." That usually meant that someone else was likely to die.

Commander Kevin Kimball explained.

"We have a high-value hostage to rescue. Front-page stuff, but not with your pictures on it. We'll be going in blind and not under the best of circumstances."

Best of circumstances didn't exist in their line of work.

There would be sixteen on the mission, including Kimball, the Troop Commander. Under him in rank, though together they acted as a coordinated team, was his Troop Senior Enlisted E-8, Jimmy "Scope" Offerman. Most men had nicknames. Some of them obvious. Scope's wasn't to most, but it was appropriate, though people at the other end of his rifle never survived to brag about his aim. He was the hottest sniper in SEALs history.

Kimball had also tapped Morgan "Poker" Ellsworth, Winston "Knife" Bauman, Adam "Jet" Lopez, Nate "King" Weinreich, Jamil "Doc" Jefferson, and Kelvin "Woody" Gatson. Woody Gatson was named for his much-celebrated love life.

"Say your goodbyes, write your letters, and be ready. Wheels up in three hours."

"Where to, boss?" Knife, a thirty-six-year-old SEAL from Aiken, South Carolina, asked.

"The Disney Jungle Cruise," Kimball replied. "Dress appropriately."

* * *

Lieutenant Commander Kevin Kimball counted off his men as they loaded the Boeing C-40A Clipper, the Navy's version of the 737. The twin-engine jet idled outside a hangar at Marine Corps Air Station Miramar, north of San Diego. With a maximum cruising speed of 451 mph, Panama was well within its 3,400-mile range. No mid-air refueling would be necessary for the six-hour journey.

That would be the first leg. From Panama City's airport, the SEALs would transfer to two Sikorsky CH-53 Super Stallion Helicopters for the rocky flight to the USS *Cape St. George* off the coast of Colombia.

One Super Stallion would have been large enough for the 16-man SEALs team, back-up and equipment, but in the bad weather, which was coming, splitting the crew up was an insurance policy. At maximum speed and optimal conditions, they'd make it to the Ticonderoga-class Navy cruiser in under two hours. Today they'd have neither maximum speed nor optimal conditions. It was going to be a very bumpy ride.

Kimball needed to be ready when the "Warning Order" arrived from command. He was a career officer, twenty-two years in the service, and the hardest of the hard Navy SEALs. At forty-one, he was the GOAT, the Tom Brady of the service, the Greatest of All Time. Tops in swimming, tops in armed combat, and tops in successful extractions.

Over the past three years, when America needed to call on SEALs in the Pacific theater, Kimball got the nod. He'd parachuted from C-130 transports, crawled through swamps, and climbed cliffs in never-to-be-reported danger zones. But like other SEALs, his preferred manner of entry was underwater, one strong stroke, kick, and breath at a time.

* * *

SEALs, so-named for their missions in Sea, Air and Land, have President John F. Kennedy to thank for their transformation from a former Underwater Demolition Team. As SEALs, they came into existence on January 1, 1962, and soon earned respect and fear as the most versatile fighting force on the face of the earth, or fathoms below.

Three-star Admiral Nick Mirage, in the day known as Magician, had selected SEAL Team 3, one of eight platoons, for the rescue.

SEAL Team 3 deploys from Coronado, California, for objectives south in the Western Hemisphere, and west to Southwest Asia. They're attached to the Third, Fifth, and Seventh Fleet, mission-dependent. Most men and women who serve on those fleet ships don't know, don't need to know, or never know when SEALs are onboard.

Surprise is essential to SEALs' success. Surprise and secrecy. Secrecy is held close to the vest, and security is maintained from planning right through conduct of operations.

* * *

Kimball's team was packed and waiting for the Warning Order, the directive that triggers an operation. In this case, the rescue and exfiltration of America's Secretary of State.

A Warning Order generally gives SEALs as much as twelve hours to ready. Today, the clock was wound tighter.

BEIJING, CHINA

ZHONGNANHAI, THE PRESIDENTIAL PALACE

Yichén Yáo also issued an order. He gave it to his Director of China's Ministry of Security to pass along through a pre-established and circuitous clandestine route. It was a roundabout ticket home for Alina Ostrovsky after one intermediary stop with her Russian honey in the pot. The trip would sever her from her current entanglement. Permanently. What could be better than a romantic send-off in Paris?

71

THE WHITE HOUSE

OVAL OFFICE

"Where are we, Admiral?" President Allphin asked Admiral Grimm. "And how long?"

"Best estimate, twenty hours to get her out. Still within the original deadline. Everything is locked in, except—"

"Except for what?"

"The weather," Grimm replied. "We've got a fucking climate-changing hurricane with 20-to-30-foot swells and piercing rain."

"Impossible?"

"Not for SEALs. But it won't be a cakewalk."

"If I may." The interruption was from Admiral Mirage, who could speak from experience. "My guys will do our very best, Mr. President. And our very best does damn well in any weather."

It was a statement of true faith. If Mirage could have led the rescue himself, he would have. Instead, he chose the next best man as team commander.

OVER THE PACIFIC

Acting on the cleverly spelled out signs from Secretary Matthews, an Air Force AWACS was already in position circling an area ranging from

80–100 miles off the coast of Colombia, its ears listening for chatter on thousands of frequencies from cell phones, shortwave, VHF, ham radio bands, and more.

At the same time, an American U-2 mapped the Colombian coast from more than twice the height of the AWACS. But it was ultimately an MQ-9 Predator drone that located signs that suggested the encampment was below. First, it spotted plastic bottles and a cushion on the sand. The items could have come from anywhere, but the drone also picked up something 225 yards offshore. Eyes watching screens from the remote drone cockpit at Creech Air Force Base in Indian Springs, Nevada, outside of Las Vegas, saw what looked like the mast of a boat sticking occasionally visible over the waves. The evidence was mounting.

Of course, the basic notion behind such searches is that the subject *or* subjects want to be found. In this case, they didn't. So the analysts had to look *beyond the beyond* using the newest optical algorithms and thermal imaging.

Compounding the problem was the fluctuating temperatures brought on by heavy rain. And then there were the jungle's natural inhabitants. Warm-blooded four-legged predators could be easily eliminated by analysis, but the howler, spider, and gray-bellied night monkeys, though small, could be confused with humans. There were thousands.

ABOARD THE BOEING C-40A

The SEAL called Poker walked up the aisle to Commander Kimball's seat. "Now would be a good time."

Kimball pursed his lips and nodded. Now was exactly the time. He stood and gathered his fifteen men.

"You've seen the news. We've got ourselves an honest-to-goodness VIP to bring home, Elizabeth Matthews, the Secretary of State."

"That's not a bulletin," Doc joked. He was the team's physician. The team's, not the enemy's.

Kimball continued. "The spooks believe she's being held in Colombia, and I don't mean as in the 'Gem of the Ocean.' The country.

Not far off the coast. Between there and where we'll be staging will be some rough seas. Our first stop is Panama City. Then we'll copter onto the USS *Cape St. George*."

"What are we facing, boss?" Poker asked. Poker was Morgan Ellsworth from Chelsea, Massachusetts. He never showed anything but a blank face. Hence the name. But he wanted to know what cards the opposition held. "Any idea who? Level of sophistication?"

"TBD. Langley's working on more."

"Organized or disorganized?" Poker followed up.

"Organized enough to snatch the Secretary, kill most of her team, and get her out of Panama sight unseen."

"Estimate on the tangos?"

"Negative. The weather's too fucked up. We should be prepared for even or better numbers. Hopefully, we'll know before we launch."

"How do we go in?" King asked.

Kimball nodded to Scope to run through the plan.

"Hard and wet," he said.

"Then Woody's in the lead," the man named Knife joked.

Humor kept them sharp. Training made them ever-ready. They'd need it, maybe more than ever.

72

U.S. EMBASSY

PANAMA CITY, PANAMA

1840 HOURS THE NEXT DAY

Reilly decided to return to the embassy. It was a smart decision. He was easier to find, and it saved time.

He was given an empty office to camp out in. For four hours, he checked in on company business. At four hours and one minute a DSS agent entered.

"Mr. Reilly, come with me."

The please was implied, but unsaid.

"News?" Reilly asked enthusiastically.

"If a change of venue and moving to rations is news, then yes," Agent Thomas Claster said. "Wheels up for you, sir."

"To where?"

By now, he thought, *anywhere* would be fine. He'd been sitting around far too long. But the urgency suggested that *anywhere* was where Elizabeth Matthews had signed.

At that moment Reilly heard the unmistakable whooping of a helicopter. He knew the sound, a Sikorsky SH-60 Seahawk or something in the Sikorsky family.

"I take it this isn't for a tour of the Canal."

"No, sir. The USS *Cape St. George,* a Ticonderoga-class guided missile cruiser making a fast run to the staging area."

"Excuse me, staging area?"

"Don't know myself, but I'm buckling up with you. He said we should expect a rough touchdown."

"*He?*"

"The pilot, sir. And he said something else."

"What?" Reilly asked.

"We should take these."

Agent Claster held out a bottle of Dramamine.

While Reilly was swallowing, his cell rang. He laughed seeing the number. It was his ex-wife, Pat. She had an uncanny ability, maybe it was their lingering connection, to feel when trouble lay ahead. Probably their years together.

"Hi, Pat. Really can't talk now."

"Well, that's nothing new."

Reilly scoffed. "Yeah, right."

"It's just that I haven't heard from you in a while and—"

"Not all divorced couples talk to one another," he laughed.

"Suppose that makes us special. Anyway—"

Pat Reilly paused, hearing the background sound. "Helicopter?"

"Yup."

"Where to?"

"Parts unknown. Can't really say," Reilly replied.

"Can't?"

"Don't really know. That's the truth."

"Well, good luck. Be safe. If not for me, then for Yibing."

"Thanks, Pat. I appreciate that."

Dan Reilly hung up having no idea what he was flying into and whether his freelancing would be his death or the death of another relationship.

PACIFIC OCEAN
ABOARD THE USS *ANNAPOLIS*

"Okim," Commander Dwight Zimmerman said quietly to his chief sonar operator, "How's our bogie doing?" He rested his hands on the young man's shoulders.

"Still sitting pretty. Longer than before." Under his breath, he said trusting he hadn't lost the North Korean, "At least I hope so."

"Waiting?" Zimmerman asked.

"Permission to share only an opinion, sir," Okim Katema said softly.

Zimmerman was taken by the response. He raised an eyebrow. "Permission granted."

"Why come all this way and then just sit on your ass. What if it's where it wants to be?"

"Go on, sailor."

"She came all this way and now nothing. What if its mission is right here? She's in range."

ABOARD THE SIKORSKY
AN HOUR LATER

"Sorry, Mr. Reilly," the DSS said over the noise of the helicopter and the wind. "This kind of thing must be new to you."

Reilly smirked. "Not at all." Reilly gripped the seat as the Sikorsky was hit with ever-increasingly stronger gusts.

"Man, then you're booking the wrong airlines."

Reilly laughed. "You've got that right. More times than you can imagine"

"Really? I was told…"

Agent Claster stopped mid-sentence as the helicopter suddenly sank 100 feet in a matter of seconds. Reilly's stomach went on the same upsetting ride.

Once the Sikorsky righted, he continued, "…you're a hotel exec, waiting in the embassy for a meeting."

"That we're going to." Reilly paused, swallowed hard trying to quell his acid reflux and will the Dramamine to kick in more. "Except it's obviously not at the embassy."

"I guess there's a lot I don't understand about the hotel business."

Reilly laughed.

"You do know that where we're going the thread count will be a lot less than you're used to."

"Oh, I know all too well."

Another jolt. Stronger than the last. Reilly asked how much longer they'd be in the air.

Claster unbuckled and walked forward to check with the flight crew. He returned with an answer. "Captain says the winds are hurting us. Ninety minutes at least. Add more to set down easily."

With another sharp blast of wind, Reilly knew nothing was going to be easy about touching down on a moving ship on high seas during a storm. Even worse in a hurricane.

"We've run into this kind of trouble, sir." The agent added. "A few hours earlier it would have been different."

Two more sharp jolts.

Reilly tightened his safety belt and shoulder strap. "Trouble has a habit of catching up with me."

USS *CAPE ST. GEORGE*
OFF THE COAST OF COLOMBIA
LATER

The full moon, the high tide, and the winds now reaching hurricane level made Dan Reilly's approach to *Cape St. George* extremely perilous.

The crew was ready, but the pitch and roll of the ocean had to be strictly calculated for the Sikorsky pilot to achieve even the first step toward landing: lowering a wire line with an attached probe that would be hooked onto a device on *Cape St. George* called a Bear Trap.

The copter's wire flung wild above the ship. Rain-soaked and helmeted crew members, themselves attached to safety lines, attempted to grab the line.

The first pass failed. The wire swung violently as the helicopter hovered. On the second approach, the line nearly slashed one of the crew across the face. It missed by only two inches.

On the third attempt, one *Cape St. George* sailor hooked the wire but had to let go when the wind swept the helicopter wide.

It took two more tries before the crew snagged the line and passed the cable through an open trap on the deck. From there it was attached to a below deck ship-mounted winch. Next, a heavy-duty haul cable reeled in the helicopter. Once the Seahawk was on deck the Bear Trap clamped onto the Sikorsky's skids and pulled the aircraft across to the elevator. From there it was lowered below.

A young sailor opened the door. Dan Reilly got out, steadied himself, and swallowed hard, thankful he had taken the Dramamine.

An officer greeted him with an outstretched hand.

"Welcome aboard, Mr. Reilly. Pretty rough flight in," Lt. Jason Mayberry offered. "You need some time for yourself?"

"I'm okay, lieutenant," Reilly said noting the stripes. "Eager to find out what's happening."

What's happening was as specific as the conversation would get until Dan Reilly found out exactly what the plan was. He thought, *Not plan, mission. Presumably a rescue.*

From the moment the DSS agent summoned him in the embassy until this very second, Reilly considered the likely scenario: a stealth assault led by Navy SEALs.

Mayberry quickly led Reilly through a maze of hallways to the ship's CIC, the Combat Information Center. Reilly instantly knew its purpose. It was the ship's nerve center, home to radar operations, communications, and charts. But it wasn't his stop.

"Sir, this way," Mayberry said.

They moved past all the equipment and all the technicians.

"Here, sir."

He stopped at a door guarded on either side by two men in suits. Mayberry pressed a five-digit code into a keypad. An electronic lock unlatched, and a door to the War Room opened.

"Go right in, Mr. Reilly."

Reilly turned to thank the lieutenant who stepped back.

"They're waiting for you."

Inside, six uniformed flag officers.

"Mr. Reilly," *Cape St. George* Captain Andrew Policano boomed introducing himself. "So nice of you to drop in."

"Drop feels about right."

Policano laughed. "I know the feeling. The Navy, in its wisdom, lifted me out of the silent service and assigned me above the waterline. But it's nice to see some daylight, not that we have any today."

Until very recently, Captain Andrew Policano had commanded the USS *Hartford*, a Los Angeles-class submarine in the Atlantic. Though it hadn't made the news, and wouldn't, his quick thinking averted a secret attack on Boston harbor. Now, the Pentagon had their sites on him, with likely Admiral's stripes following his experience on the *Cape St. George*. He was that deserving.

"Well, Captain," Reilly continued, "I wouldn't miss this for the world. I just don't know what it is. What's the plan?"

Commander Kimball looked at Reilly suspiciously. *A civilian?*

"With all due respect, Mr. Reilly, I'm also not quite sure why you're here."

Reilly hesitated. This was not a resume question. "I guess you might consider me a friend of the family," he said cryptically. "An invited guest."

Kimball scoffed.

"Easy now," Policano said. He took a moment to identify all the players assembled for the mission. Men and women. Uniformed and not. Some appeared to be plotting courses on a map. Others were working on computers. Reilly took the civilians to be intelligence officers. He figured the toughest of the bunch were Navy SEALs.

Before he needed to explain more, Reilly heard a voice behind him.

"I can vouch for him."

Kimball looked at the second civilian entering. "And you're—?"

Bob Heath produced his CIA credentials. Kimball examined them. "Just here to listen and observe."

"Welcome to the party, Mr. Heath."

"Thank you." Heath greeted Reilly with a slap on the back. "Hey, Reilly, I thought you hated boats."

"This isn't a boat," Reilly said. "It's a ship."

"Whatever."

Reilly pulled Heath into a tight hug.

"All right, reunion's over. So, Mr. Friend of the Family and Mr. Spook, now that we're all here," the SEALs commander said, "we need to get to work."

Reilly took a seat. Heath sat next to him. After even a few seconds of rolling from the seas, both opted to stand. Better for their equilibrium.

One of the ship's intelligence officers clicked a remote. A video monitor switched from a round logo of the USS *Cape St. George* to a map.

"There. It's an encampment a little over a kilometer from shore. They're dug in under the jungle canopy. Some of it's shielded, but we've ID'd warm bodies. Nineteen so far. Maybe more."

"Secretary Matthews?" Reilly asked.

"We'll know for sure when we get there," Commander Kimball said.

"In these conditions?" Heath asked.

"We not big on sitting around."

73

U.S. SENATE OFFICE BUILDING

THAT NIGHT

Billy Peyton hustled into his office, slammed the door, and screamed, "Shit, shit, shit!" The only person with him was his Chief of Staff, Seth Sullivan. But that didn't keep his minions working in the suite of offices next to him from being within earshot.

"Goddamn her to holy hell! Matthews survives this, she'll smell like a fucking hero."

The president had just briefed Peyton and other Senate and House leaders and key members of the intelligence committees on the planned rescue. Allphin hadn't spelled out any details, but Peyton heard enough to make him silently steam while inside the Oval Office, and now in his own space, come to full boil.

"Fuck this! Fuck her!"

"If she's rescued," Sullivan said quietly. "And calm down. You don't want your staff leaking that their boss had a meltdown over Matthews."

Peyton took a deep breath. "You're right."

"Now tell me what's planned. Where is she?"

"Navy SEALs. They think they know where she is. Fucking Allphin wouldn't say. But it'll be just minutes before the end of the deadline Matthews gave."

Sullivan did a fast time calculation.

"Okay. There are ways to get out ahead of this," Sullivan said.

"How do you propose that? We were told to keep a tight lid on this."

"How many people were there?"

"Ten, twelve. I don't know. Why?"

"Then any of them could let slip. Blow up the plan."

"For Chrissakes! Allphin will know where it came from."

"Will he?" Sullivan smiled. "Figure there are more people who know than just those at your briefing. What about people up and down the line? The Pentagon? San Diego? Someone else in the White House?"

"How do you propose—"

Sullivan cut Peyton off. "Leave that up to me. Then, once word breaks, you go in full throttle and criticize the press for putting the Secretary of State's life in jeopardy. Suddenly you're the hero. And Matthews—"

Sullivan didn't finish the sentence.

Billy Peyton wanted to become president. Seth Sullivan wanted him to become president even more. Peyton didn't know the real reason. He never would.

"Who are you going to call?" Peyton asked.

"Not call. A text from a burner phone. Two if it takes more than one text."

"Who?"

"Someone always hungry for a good tip. Peter Loge at the *Post*. Loge is like a dog with a bone. He'll contact the White House. They won't confirm it, but they'll do it in such a way that he'll have what he needs. The job will be done."

"And if he doesn't go for it?"

"Deutsch at NPR. But Loge will bite."

"When?"

"Day after tomorrow. We still have time. The closer to the rescue attempt, the more urgent your complaint."

Billy Peyton smiled. This could play out very well whether Matthews lived or died.

74

COLOMBIA

THE SAME TIME

"I don't suppose you have a martini in there," Matthews asked her captor.

Parisa Dhafari was rummaging through a backpack, looking like she was arranging clothes for a trip.

"Afraid we're limited out here," Dhafari said.

"Too bad. I would love one right about now. How about you? Looks like you could use one, too."

"I rarely drink, it's . . . " She stopped short.

Matthews tipped her head. "Oh, right." The answer confirmed her assumption about Dhafari's heritage, but she still didn't know why Victoria would be leading a band of North Korean thugs.

Dhafari stopped packing. She looked ahead into nothingness, upset that she had given Matthews more information about herself. Now she shook her head, walked over to Matthews, and slapped her hard across the face. Hard enough to knock Matthews over. She fell on her arm. She felt a crack.

"You have nothing, Elizabeth," Parisa Dhafari said returning to her packing. "And it will do you no good."

More information. *They're going to kill me.* Matthews grimaced and willed the thought and the pain away. She decided to try another bargaining chip. *Negotiate with whatever time I have left.*

"I have a job. Apparently, you have yours."

"Finally something we can agree on."

"We could find more. I can help you, Victoria."

Dhafari scoffed. "That would make someone else very unhappy with me."

"I can protect you."

Dhafari ignored Matthews. She returned to her packing. Speaking over her shoulder she said, "Actually, it's you who needed better protection."

Dhafari had just revealed one more thing. Matthews went right to the meaning: Tom Hunter.

Throwing her backpack over her shoulder, Dhafari declared, "Shame you won't have a chance to make any new hires."

Then she left.

ABOARD USS *CAPE ST. GEORGE*

FOUR HOURS LATER

"We have a better window. Earlier than expected."

The assessment was delivered by Petty Officer First Class Suz Landay, *Cape St. George*'s Aerographer's Mate. The ship's meteorologist.

"How much earlier?" Kimball asked.

"Fourteen hours. The storm is speeding up."

"Fourteen. That's 0320." The SEALs commander looked at his watch. "That's six hours forty from now?"

"Yes, sir, 0320," Landay affirmed.

Kimball shot a look at his second in command, Jimmy "Scope" Offerman. "Can we be ready, Scope?"

"Can do."

"Then we go at 0320. Thank you, Aerographer's Mate."

"You're welcome but have to warn you. The seas are going to be a real mother."

WHITE HOUSE

TEN MINUTES LATER

"Mr. President, new schedule," Admiral Grimm said running into the Oval Office unannounced. "Word from *Cape St. George*. We're moving up the timetable."

"Is that good news or bad news, Admiral?"

"We'll know when we know, but the Pacific hurricane is intensifying, and we're looking at a tight window when we can get in and out as the eye passes over. Better than waiting," the Chair of the Joint Chiefs said. "We have to take advantage of it."

"That doesn't give me a good deal of confidence."

"We operate in every kind of weather, Mr. President. The SEALs know what they're doing."

"Time frame?"

"They go in less than six hours, 0320."

Allphin said a silent prayer after which he asked, "Will we have comms with the SEALs? And can we watch in the Situation Room?"

"If the uplinks work through the storm, yes."

"I'll get back to the House and Senate. The leaders were in a short time ago."

"I wouldn't do that," Admiral Grimm argued. "This is your first experience with a clandestine mission."

"Yes."

"In my estimation, less is best. And nothing is even better."

"But—"

"With all due respect, Mr. President, there's an expression that goes back to World War II. It was created by the War Advertising Council and plastered on propaganda posters."

"Which was?" President Allphin asked.

"Loose lips sink ships. Your friends across the street sail in a very leaky boat."

"You don't trust members of Congress, Admiral? Hell, I was the Speaker of the House."

"And when you were, Mr. President, you didn't know about everything. Let's keep it that way for now."

ONBOARD THE *CAPE ST. GEORGE*

There was an order to the next six hours. Most prescribed by training but some by ritual.

Since the launch was dramatically moved up, the SEALs did their best to get some shut-eye while *Cape St. George* cut the distance to shore to eleven miles. From there they'd have a grueling ride on two rubber rafts until they disembarked and swam the last 200 yards.

Given the likelihood of spotters on the beach even in the storm, the approach would be wide from the north where cliffs jutted up from the water's edge. Kidnappers would consider it too perilous a route for any rescuers. The SEALs were not just any rescuers. They were America's strongest fighters, swimming horizontally or climbing vertically. The hurricane, now named Pedro, would add to the challenge, but it wouldn't stop them.

WHITE HOUSE

THE OVAL OFFICE

"What's the chance they'll be seen?" President Allphin asked Admiral Mirage, Chief of Naval Operations. "Even given the fucked-up weather?"

"Our SEALs? Hell, no one would notice them in broad daylight walking up Main Street if they didn't want to be seen. And hell, that fucked-up weather will just make them stronger." Mirage took in a breath and thought, but didn't say, *At least I hope.* "And with the so low ceiling, they'll have all the cover they'll need."

"How low?"

ONBOARD *CAPE ST. GEORGE*

"...Ground level," Kimball explained to Dan Reilly covering the same points. "We'll use the eye of the storm for exfil. So every minute has to count."

"And we can count on the hurricane to cooperate?" Reilly asked without a hint of joking.

Cape St. George's meteorologist Suz Landay stepped back into the conversation. "If I may, it depends on several factors: The size of the eye. It can be just a few miles across to 100. How fast the storm is moving. How quickly it loses steam over land.

"In 2018 the eye of Hurricane Michael passed over Florida very quickly. Isaac in Louisiana took its sweet times. And then it comes down to what part of the eye you're in: The outer edge or close to the center. The center buys you more time."

"Thank you," Reilly replied, "but what are we looking at?"

The ship was suddenly hit by a huge wave. Reilly was thrown into a wall. Landay's map flew off the table. Captain Policano and Commander Kimball had grabbed onto a railing.

"You okay, Mr. Reilly?" Policano asked.

Reilly rubbed his elbow and flexed his arm. "Okay. Ready for the next one."

The next wave hit seconds later, but Reilly was ready. Holding on to a railing himself.

"It's going to be like this, but we're sea-worthy," the captain assured Reilly.

"Got it. Back to my question. How much time for exfil?"

"Sixty minutes. Maybe seventy from launching the bird to getting everyone the hell out of there before the ass end of the hurricane hits us," Landay said. "Based on latest reports from AWRON, the Navy's hurricane hunter that's aloft, Pedro is coming on at twelve miles an hour with an eye contracting to fourteen miles."

Landay showed Reilly her latest map. Reilly leaned in with one hand on the metal rail.

"Then what's the max time the helicopter will have at the landing zone?"

Kimball, who had been working on the calculations with Landay, answered. "Based on flying time—sixteen in, sixteen out—twenty-eight minutes, thirty-eight max. We can't have the copter in the air after the hurricane picks up again, and we certainly can't leave it on the floor. It'll get torn apart. We just have to get out on time."

"Put me on the Sikorsky," Reilly said.

Kimball looked at Policano, then the captain addressed Reilly. "Bad idea, Mr. Reilly. We'll have enough on our hands without—"

"With, commander. With," Reilly replied.

"On whose authority?"

"Secretary Matthews. She left standing orders."

Policano and Kimball talked to one another. Reilly returned both hands to the railing. After a minute's arguing, Captain Policano said, "You've bought yourself a ticket, Mr. Reilly. So right now you need to get some rest, too."

Policano turned to Lt. Rice who had been assigned to Reilly. "Escort our guest to sleeping quarters."

Reilly was shown to a hammock in the berthing compartment on the third deck. It swayed too much. He couldn't possibly sleep. After ten minutes of trying, he returned to the War Room. Andrew Policano laughed loudly. "My apologies. Lieutenant, show Mr. Reilly to my cabin."

He held two fingers up. "Wait. Give him a bucket. He may need it."

"I'd rather stay here," Reilly said.

"Really? When was the last sleep you had?"

When Reilly realized it was more than twenty-four hours, he said, "You're right. Thank you, sir."

Rice led Reilly to the captain's quarters. He stretched out on the bed, closed his eyes, and before falling asleep, measured what the next morning would bring. *People who are alive today will be dead tomorrow. He will be there, after. But after what? Elizabeth Matthews will come home, or she won't. And somehow the world will be different.*

75

CAPE ST. GEORGE WAS SLAMMED by a wave so hard the restraining belt holding Reilly in cut into his stomach. It didn't break the skin, but he felt the bruise.

Sleep was no longer possible. He got out of Policano's bed, at least happy that he didn't get sick. He slowly rose to his feet, and as he was getting his sea legs back, there was a knock at the door.

"Hey buddy."

It was Heath.

"When you're through losing your cookies you're wanted back on Broadway."

Broadway was the ship's name for the War Room.

"Be right out."

Reilly downed another Dramamine with water from the captain's cabin. He figured he'd need it.

* * *

Overhead, and above the storm flew a Boeing E-3 Sentry, a specially modified Boeing 707 better known as an Air Force AWACS, America's Airborne Warning and Control System. With its rotating radar affixed to the top of the fuselage, the plane's intelligence center scanned the sea, the shoreline, and inland. It flew a course 150 miles parallel to the Colombian coast at 29,500 feet, near the top of its flight profile. Closer to the coastline would have been better. Nonetheless, the E-3 Sentry was able to keep track of the mission with an overall surveillance area of more than 120,000 square miles.

The E-3 Sentry's focus was a corridor between the *Cape St. George* and the mainland target and outwards from the Navy cruiser to any surface craft that might appear as a threat. There were none, though submarines couldn't be ruled out. The AWACS eight-and-a-half-hour flying time could be extended by inflight refueling and additional cockpit crew members. The Sentry on duty today carried backups, and a KC-10 tanker was on the way.

* * *

Onboard *Cape St. George*, sight unseen by the ship's crew, Kevin Kimball prepared his SEALs. "We commit ninety minutes, ladies. Final checks." Next, he addressed Reilly. "And you, Mr. Reilly." He corrected himself. "Captain Reilly, U.S. Army retired, suit up and be ready to lift off when it's your turn."

* * *

Business was also very much at hand much further north and 350 feet below the surface. Patience suddenly paid off for *Annapolis*. The North Korean sub had been reacquired quite by accident. *Wonsan-Yong-Ganhan* scraped an uncharted coral ecosystem that formed on a sunken World War II Japanese battleship stuck on an elevated section of the Hawaiian trough, east of the islands.

Annapolis had heard the sound of metal against coral for twelve seconds. Amplified and carried by water, it was enough for sonar to get a lock.

Soon it would be time to make a decision.

Zimmerman gradually brought his sub up to a depth of 100 feet. Once level, he issued an order: "Deploy the antenna buoy."

The wired buoy silently slipped from *Annapolis* behind the nuclear submarine. The device allowed *Annapolis* to send and receive slow-speed encrypted data transmissions on a very low frequency that can penetrate salt water.

Captain Zimmerman reported their location and reacquisition of the enemy sub to USA Pacific Command. The coded response left no room for interpretation or debate. They were the orders of the president of the United States.

76

WHITE HOUSE SITUATION ROOM

90 MINUTES TO LAUNCH

The President's National Security Council members waited expectantly for what was about to happen. They sat around a long table facing a bank of live large screen monitors, two rows of four brought in for the mission. The images were coming into the White House via NSA fiber, relayed from the AWACS flying patterns off the coast of Colombia. A digital clock counted down the minutes until the SEALs' launch off the ship.

President Allphin entered. Everyone stood.

"At ease. Please sit. Admiral, are we on schedule?" Allphin asked Grimm.

"We've got a few more minutes if you need, Mr. President."

"The only place I need to be right now is here."

This was Sean Allphin's first time in the Situation Room during a live mission.

Grimm described what was on the bank of monitors. Three had six-way splits, labeled cameras representing the eighteen SEALs, but no video so far from their body cameras. Two monitors showed weather information from NOAA, including wind speed, with gusts hitting 85 mph at the landing zone.

"It'll get worse," Grimm said.

"And the SEALs?"

"Suiting up now. We'll see a test of the cameras, and then they'll launch."

Admiral Mirage walked through the timeline for the president.

"Seems like there's very little room for error, Nick."

"Zero room."

"And waiting out the storm?"

"According to the kidnappers' clock, not an option."

No one needed to say aloud what that meant. Senator Colonnello visibly shivered. She got up from her seat, walked around to the head of the table and whispered to the president, "May I speak with you in the hallway, sir?"

Allphin nodded to the Senator and announced to the room that he'd be right back.

Just beyond the door, Colonnello asked, "Do we even know if Elizabeth is alive? There's been no other communication."

Allphin looked upward. Colonnello took it as a sign that the situation was worse than she'd been told.

"Or has there?" she demanded. "Is she alive?"

"As far as we know, yes. This remains a rescue mission, Mikayla, not a recovery. But we'll know when we know, hopefully from Elizabeth herself when she's safely onboard *Cape St. George.*"

Senator Mikayla Colonnello understood and at the same time didn't. With all of America's eyes in the skies and boots that would eventually be on the ground, she wondered how this could have been pulled off. But she didn't share what she was thinking.

"There's no better team out there than our SEALs. You have to have faith, Mikayla, and faith in her. Elizabeth's a survivor."

"…Who's held hostage with demands we're not meeting," Colonnello starkly replied.

"And we're going to beat their time limit. What else would you have us do?"

With all the knowledge she had of America's military and intelligence capabilities, moments like this still came down to trust, trust in people who defended America for a living. The U.S. Navy SEALs.

"If anything happens to Elizabeth—"

"Mikayla, something already has! Now come back in because the Secretary will surely want to talk to a friend as soon as we get her out."

She didn't move.

"Senator, now!"

0240 COT (COLOMBIA TIME)

The communications technician and the computer display and airborne radar technicians concurred.

"They're good to go," the Mission Crew Commander reported to *Cape St. George.*

The message was also heard in the White House, where Admiral Grimm kept his eye on the live Doppler weather from the E-3. He hated hurricanes.

77

11 MILES OFF THE COAST OF COLOMBIA

Two Combat Rubber Raiding Craft (CRRC), by far the most portable inflatable boats in the Navy's service, were dropped into the sea and quickly manned by the SEALs. Each craft can fit up to twelve combatants with space for the SEALs equipment. For this mission, it was eight and eight.

The CRRCs were made with a single purpose: to be the most buoyant, most reliable, and strongest inflatable boat on the seas. They were about to be tested to the limit.

Considering the size of the swells, Kimball warned, "It's gonna be like riding the Tilt-a-Whirl from hell."

"Then hold the cotton candy until we get back," Poker said.

"Fuck the cotton candy. There better bottles of Hazy in the galley," Knife declared. He was referring to San Diego's favorite IPA.

And with that, the SEALs, wearing their combat wetsuits, specially made for amphibious missions, set off. Reilly, secured by a rope line so he wouldn't be blown or bolted off the deck, tried to watch. He automatically saluted below toward the men, though he couldn't see them or vice versa through the driving rain.

* * *

The SEALs laid across one another, seven on one side, eight on another, with one pilot forward on each CRRC. This gave them the lowest profile to the wind and a better chance of staying onboard.

Under normal circumstances, the CRRCs could push 17 mph. There was nothing normal about today's journey.

Vision was down to zero feet. They couldn't even see the incoming waves that rocketed them up and shot them down at twice the speed.

The men held onto the sides and reinforced one another. Tilt-A-Whirl didn't begin to describe it. All the rides in a carnival and all that SEALs training couldn't describe it. Time had no meaning. The only thing that mattered was surviving. Kimball constantly called out in CRRC One to make sure everyone was at the top of their game...and alive. Jimmy "Scope" Offerman did the same in CRRC Two.

Staying on course was up to the pilots reading their GPSs. And every push forward had to be met with adjustments. There was no straight line to where they were going.

Their best calculation was 1.3 hours to cover the distance. It took two. Even though they launched early, they needed to make up seven-tenths of an hour.

The GPS told them they were close. But before disembarking, they had to maneuver around rocks that jutted up 300 yards offshore. Hitting one could capsize a CRRC in seconds. Trying to swim past them in the dark and storm, might send them in the wrong direction long enough that they couldn't recover. But training got them beyond the present danger. At 200 yards, they cut the motors and slipped off. Two SEALs, Knife and Poker, slit the rubber hulls and scuttled the boats.

Kimball had picked the best men. The people who could take the most abuse.

* * *

Fourteen minutes later, they emerged from the sea in pairs a mile north of the easiest place to surface—the beach. But earlier satellite images had picked up a pair of sentries there, and though they were likely taking shelter now, it was too risky to challenge them. So they made their point of entry at the base of a cliff.

Climbing from the bottom to the top of something so battered for eons by the wind and waves was going to be work, exhausting work on top of the ordeal they'd just experienced. The rock face was smooth with no footholds. It offered nothing natural to work with.

Jet and King, the first to ascend, sized up the task.

"I'm getting to the point that maybe I'm too old for this shit," Jet said.

"You were born an old complaining man," King joked. "Let's go, you can retire later."

Jet attached the line to his harness. The other end, with twenty feet of slack, was extended to King. He ran the rope through a belay device attached to his harness. Jet drove in the first of his grappling anchor bolts into the rock wall and began the climb. He then connected the rope to a quick draw, a pair of carabiners attached by strong nylon webbing. If he lost his footing and fell, King would have the rope, preventing him from falling as long as the bolts held. If they did, the maximum distance he could fall was equal to twice the distance between the last bolt and his current position, plus the length of the slack in the line.

The SEALs mounted the rock face slowly, step-by-slippery-step. There was no fast at this job. Jet led one anchor bolt and one body length at a time. King followed. The slack was their lifeline.

The sound of the bolts driving into the cliff was barely audible below, but Kimball still heard, "Fuck!" followed by the sound of Jet's hammer hitting the ground. It had slipped out of Jet's hand in the rain. Fortunately, Jet had a backup. Two, in fact.

WHITE HOUSE
SITUATION ROOM

The SEALs cameras were on now. The president and the members of the National Security Council watched and listened, a reality show like commercial TV had never shown.

"Once above, the two SEALs will drop lines for the others," Mirage explained.

"How long?" the president asked.

"Been there done that. It takes as long as it takes."

Allphin thought this would be one for the books. He worried how the end would be written.

"There's no delay to what we're seeing?"

"Live. In the moment, sir."

The cameras attached to each SEAL needed constant wiping because of the rain. Soon they wouldn't have time to be concerned with the video they were sending back home.

78

1555 MILES WEST OF SAN FRANCISCO BAY

Wonsan Yong-Ganhan was at its appointed location. It stopped. Capt. Jang Song-Taek waited for his computer to release his time-triggered order. Considering the refitting his sub had gone through in Sinpo, the lethal armaments it carried, and the undersea fueling stations that had been used along the way, he had no reason to believe this was anything but a first strike. That would make *Wonsan Yong-Ganhan* a target and Song-Taek did not for a minute believe, as his sonar op did, that the Americans weren't close by.

USS *ANNAPOLIS*

Eight hundred yards, .454 of a mile, separated *Annapolis* from the North Korean sub. So far, there was no indication they had been discovered. But the longer the enemy sat, the more Capt. Dwight Zimmerman became concerned. No North Korean submarine had ever ventured so far from home and so close to mainland United States. This made for a very real and present danger, and his orders were absolutely clear.

COLOMBIA

THE SAME TIME

At the summit, Jet, then King, caught their breath but wasted no time before anchoring drop lines for the rest of the team to ascend. In fifteen minutes, possibly less, everyone would be up.

They did it in nine minutes. Now for the ground trek. First walking, then on hands and knees, and finally crawling. Still in pairs, they had their GPS to guide them. If that failed, they had good old-fashioned compasses.

They were aware of snakes. Knives were out, ready for coral, pit vipers, and even anaconda. The SEALs carried anti-venom. But possibly more dangerous were the crocodiles, native to the Colombian jungle.

The terrain resembled the best of the worst that their instructors had ever thrown their way. Gullies and swamp and mud. Everywhere mud. It ran deep in places and getting stuck would cost time.

They used their machetes to cut through thick brush. Then rain-filled streams flowed like raging rivers. For these crossings, they paired up with ropes tied around their waists...just in case.

Just in case happened. Woody was caught in the current. He was fine until his line, attached to Kimball, snagged and shredded against a rock. He was swept down toward the sea.

Poker dove in. He caught the current and swam hard. His partner Knife let out the slack on his rope. Poker grabbed Woody's heel and he worked his way up to his ankle and then Woody's leg. Still underwater, he raised his hand. A signal to pull. He got Woody seconds before he would have gone over a waterfall.

With everyone safely across, Kimball gave them a two-minute rest to take stock of their weaponry. Poker lost an M4 in the rescue. Woody's Sig Sauer handgun was also gone. They'd adjust. And the time for that would be coming soon if there were no more delays.

WHITE HOUSE

THE SITUATION ROOM

The incoming video was blurred. The audio from the field crackled.

"Can anyone enhance this?" Allphin asked. He was the Commander in Chief, but a technical neophyte.

"It's the best we can do under the circumstances," Admiral Grimm responded.

For the next five minutes, Grimm and Mirage provided the play-by-play.

"They're crawling now, and the sound you're hearing is a combination of wind, rain, and our SEALs breathing. As bad as it looks, the conditions are helping. No one's going to see or hear them coming."

"All right. So if all goes well—" Allphin acknowledged.

Mirage didn't like the President's "if," but he didn't comment.

"...How the hell do you get them out in the middle of the hurricane?"

"Precisely," Admiral Mirage responded.

"Precisely what?"

"Precisely in the middle of Hurricane Pedro. The eye. That's what we're backtiming toward, Mr. President." He reminded President Allphin of the window they'd have. "The calm after the storm we create. Once the enemy is neutralized, we'll get our bird in. You'll see that, as they used to say, 'In living color.' If the schedule holds, we'll be well off the island by sunrise."

Now Mirage realized he used the "if" as well.

The president looked at two clocks set in front of him to Eastern and COT, Colombia Time. COT was one hour behind.

"Anyone have any Tums?" Allphin asked.

* * *

Kimball panned his head from left to right. Everyone in the White House Situation Room followed his POV. It was slow and painful to watch. Harder to be there.

* * *

"Thank you," Allphin nodded taking the stomach acid relievers from National Security Advisor Ali. He focused on one of the televisions displaying a map of the island. On another, the latest live images from the satellite that had maneuvered over the territory.

CIA Director Gerald Watts took the remote from Grimm. He pressed the input calling up another computer source with satellite photos. He clicked through four slides and stopped on the fifth.

To the untrained naked eye, including the president's, they showed nothing beyond the mountainous terrain and the dense tropical forest. However, Watts said, "Interesting."

"What, Gerald? What do you see?"

Watts stood and walked up to the monitor and cycled through a series of enhanced images.

"What?" Allphin asked again.

"These are from the newest generation of our Capella Satellites, which we've just repositioned. They can normally view Earth regardless of cloud covering. Unlike earlier satellites, Capella-4 shoots radio signals that illuminate points of interest on the ground. These radar images are powerful enough to penetrate through building walls, or …"

He cycled forward.

"Dense jungle forests and tents."

COLOMBIA

"Hold up," Commander Kimball said. He was receiving the same images on his iPad. It gave him the best count yet on the enemy and their weaponry. All hand-carried. No heavy artillery.

The SEALs had the weather and surprise working for them. But when it came time, their aim had to be true. In the wind gusts even that wasn't guaranteed. So Kimball said they'd be moving closer. The shorter the distance, the better the chance that the speed of the bullet would win over the power of the wind.

"Okay, forward. Not a peep," Kimball ordered.

The next ten minutes were critical. No broken twigs. No heavy breathing. Weapons hot, with noise suppressors attached.

As he inched forward, Kimball weighed the enemy's mission and will. *They're not just everyday kidnappers. Mere kidnappers would have stayed in the city. Kidnappers wouldn't have been able to create such an elaborate exfil plan. Kidnappers couldn't have taken down four boats so easily. Simple kidnappers would have been simple. No, these are organized, well-trained, expertly led. They were serious about the demands, and they'd be expecting the U.S. to send a rescue force.*

That was textbook. That was Navy SEALs training. That was Kevin Kimball's intuition. *These aren't arrogant, self-deluded religious fanatics or a drug cartel. They're trained soldiers with strong command. And it's all about politics.*

Even though Kimball left the politics to others, he saw this as a play involving the next big election.

So Troop Commander Kevin Kimball had one objective. Locate and rescue the Secretary of State, code-named Queen Bee, and her DSS agent. To do that, people would die. If they did it right, most of the enemy wouldn't know it was coming.

79

USS *CAPE ST. GEORGE*

Reilly watched the same incoming live video that was piped into the White House. He leaned over to Heath and whispered, "Remember, we need Hunter alive."

Heath nodded. "Kimball knows."

"How much?"

"Just that," Heath said.

"Good. He's mine."

"He's more than yours, buddy. He's ours, and there's a lot we can learn from him."

COLOMBIAN JUNGLE

Kimball counted five tangos possibly returning from sentry duty to a supply tent. Scope had three in his field of view under a lean-to. Knife Bauman, now wearing infrared goggles like the others, had his eye on five heat signatures in a tent. One seemed sitting or kneeling weirdly. Lopez sighted another four in a second tent through his glass. Three more, weapons down, walked around the compound and smoked their wet cigarettes. Kimball figured at least four more were posted outside the perimeter to create a box. Five if they were standing on the outside of a star pattern which gave them greater protection. Doc Jefferson was there to administer medical care if necessary. None was planned for the bad guys.

In all, the head count was nineteen. It matched the satellite imagery.

Woody Gatson pulled his iPad out of a waterproof bag. He'd been sending nonstop data and receiving the intelligence relayed by the AWACS. Most of all, he wanted the storm status. The eye was due to pass over in twenty-two minutes and the winds were now gusting at 120.

The clock ticked. It was almost time to attack. Kimball held one hand, two fingers showing, and then two again. Four minutes.

THE WHITE HOUSE

Inside the Situation Room, Senator Colonnello watched intently. She suddenly bolted up and ran to the flat screen displaying the infrared video. She poked the monitor. There was an indistinguishable body digitizing in and out.

"That's her," she exclaimed. "That's Elizabeth."

"How the hell?" the president asked.

"No one else sits like that. One leg folded up under her butt, the other brought in at a 45-degree angle. I've tried it. We've laughed about it. I can't do it. But that's her style. That's Elizabeth!"

"I've only seen her sitting properly on a chair."

"You need to be drinking with her in her apartment," Colonnello said excitedly. "Trust me, that's Elizabeth Matthews!"

President Allphin smiled. Mikayla Colonnello had earned her seat in the Situation Room.

"Let the team know, Admiral."

"Yes, sir."

COLOMBIAN JUNGLE

Time. The five targets on the outer edge would be the first to go. Poker, crawling forward, then in a flash rising, took one out with his 6-inch blade. King another the same way. Doc nailed the third with his handgun, two other SEALs eliminated the remaining sentries with single suppressed sniper rifle taps to their skulls.

Kimball waved his index finger in the air. *Move forward.*

Each target had two SEALs attached. The sound, if any carried, would be no more than two quick pops.

Another finger point from Kimball. This one forward. One by one, without a moment to contemplate their fate, enemy combatants went down. The SEALs immediately pulled them off the rain-soaked battlefield and into the underbrush and sludge.

Now for the tents. Surprise was everything. One direction, no cross-shooting. No prisoners. Another team from the ship would land, examine, photograph, inventory, and bag up everything and, if time, everybody. Back on board *Cape St. George*, Navy forensics teams would begin the process of identification. Heath would be there to supervise.

But first, there were more targets to eliminate. King and Woody rushed Tent 1. Pop, pop. Pop, pop. On confirmation, a hard blow into their comms told Scope, Poker, Knife, and Jet they were clear to fire next. They took Tent 2 with eight silenced shots. Two double taps each. Four instant kills.

The rest of the deaths were not as pretty. Shots in the back as men ran. Three slit throats when the bullets didn't complete the job. In a matter of seconds, no one escaped the SEALs' stealth attack. No one.

Kimball called in the rescue. "Queen Bee secure. I repeat. Queen Bee secure!"

* * *

Cheers and applause broke out in the Situation Room.

"How is she?" President Allphin asked.

Admiral Mirage conveyed the question to the field.

Kimball replied, "See for yourself."

His camera showed Elizabeth Matthews bound on the floor, sitting with one leg under her butt.

Allphin smiled. "Well done, Commander. Well done." Then he gave a thumbs up to Senator Colonnello.

* * *

The reaction was the same in Broadway, *Cape St. George's* War Room.

"Captain Reilly, Mr. Heath," Capt. Policano said, "proceed to the copter and ready yourselves for takeoff. Don't be late."

"Yes, sir," Reilly said.

"Copy that," Heath confirmed.

* * *

"Madame Secretary," Kimball said over the noise of the storm, "I'm Commander Kevin Kimball. Are you all right?"

She pointed to her right arm. "Might be broken or fractured. Otherwise okay. But I'm afraid the worst is yet to come."

"We have a little break. The eye is moving over."

"I'm not talking about the storm."

"What threat?" Kimball urgently asked.

"The leader. A woman. Do you have her? Is she still alive?"

"She? Everyone's dead except you and your agent. No women."

"Just one. One woman."

Kimball repeated what he considered more important. "What threat?"

"I don't know, but it was clear there was a specific timetable."

Kimball helped Matthews up.

"Clear from who?" he asked.

"The woman. She called herself Victoria. That's definitely not her name. My best guess, she's Middle Eastern and she hinted at something dramatic ahead, probably thinking I'd never get out to warn anyone." Matthews switched back to her question. "You sure your team didn't find a woman?"

The SEALs' commander keyed his microphone broadcasting to his team. "Anyone find a woman tango?"

One after another the SEALs reported, "Negative."

He told her the count was nineteen dead. All men.

"Of course," Matthews said. "The backpack."

"What backpack?"

"She loaded up last night. She bolted before the storm hit hard!"

"You said she's from the Middle East."

"I think so."

"But everyone else looks Asian."

"Yes."

"Any clue where they're from or what brought them together?"

"Not directly. They kept quiet around me in the tent, but when they took me out to pee, I overheard them. Sounded to me like Korean, and I have no reason to believe it was from the South."

Kimball cut her free. Her wrists were raw from plastic ties cutting into her skin. She tried to raise her arm but winced.

"We'll get you treated. Doc is with your DSS agent now."

"Good. Now, what's the plan?"

"We're clearing an LZ now." He checked his watch. "Got to be honest with you. We're behind schedule. It took us longer to get in. And we're limited to the opening due to the storm and the winds on the other side."

"I know you're doing your best, Commander. Okay to see Agent Hunter?"

"Yes."

Kimball paused and remembered something else.

"Oh, and you've got a friend coming in. He was damned insistent."

"Who's that?"

"A guy named Reilly. He had some cockamamie story that you sent for him."

Elizabeth Matthews smiled. "As a matter of fact, I did."

80

THE CH-53 SUPER STALLION that had brought the SEALs in lifted off the deck for a second time into clearing skies and eerily calmer air. An easier flight than before. Along with Reilly and Heath, were combat-ready sailors from *Cape St. George* and a medical team of two, led by Lt. Commander Steve Hirsen. Altogether twelve, including pilot and copilot.

The mission was to get in and out before the weather turned. The race was on from the moment they took off. Mid-flight, the cabin got word from the ground.

"Problem. The LZ is not yet active. Repeat. LZ is not active yet."

Waiting was not an option. Hirsen walked back and gave the news to the passengers.

"A little change of plans. Not a problem for my team," Hirsen said. He knelt by Reilly and Heath. "But gentlemen, that'll mean you stay aboard."

"What?" Reilly exclaimed.

"There's a lot to clean up before putting the bird down. The SEALs are on it. But for now, we can't land. My guys will rappel down. When it's clear, we'll land and get you off just as soon as possible. But it'll be tight. Just a quick touch and go."

"No way."

"Sorry, sir. Lots of moving parts and parts that aren't moving so quickly. Downed trees and crap."

Hirsen stepped away. Reilly took in a deep breath. Heath patted his leg.

"We've got to get down there," Reilly said.

"You heard the lieutenant."

"I heard that he said they're rappelling."

"And?" Heath asked.

"Did you forget everything you learned?"

Reilly was referring to their time together in Afghanistan. Their combat experiences. Drops from rappel lines out of Black Hawks during air assault ops.

"That was more than a decade ago," Heath said. "These guys do it every week."

"Maybe so, but—" Reilly called to Lt. Commander Hirsen.

Hirsen returned. "Yes."

"We're jumping with you."

Hirsen looked at Reilly and over to Heath.

"That's not a very good idea. We'll be some 150 feet up. That'll give us 30 feet clearance above the trees. It's a high jump for a trained assault team. You're—"

"Combat vets," Reilly said.

"No disrespect, sir, but in what condition?"

"Strap us up. We'll worry about the condition," Heath replied for both of them.

* * *

Below and five miles away, the SEALs cut through the debris, one exhausting foot at a time. Considering the Super Stallion is 99 feet long, they needed additional room at the landing zone. At least another 25 feet. The SEALs knew they wouldn't have it in time. Scope gave Kimball the news.

"Plan B, boss."

"Already on it. They're dropping in. But don't stop."

Kimball checked his watch and calculated the time. He radioed *Cape St. George*. Word was relayed to the chopper and the White House. It would be tight.

81

"REILLY! HEATH! YOU'RE UP," Lt. Commander Hirsen yelled over the noise of the Super Stallion blades.

So far, six had gone down in pairs. Four more armed sailors would follow, then Reilly and Heath.

"You sure you got this?" Hirsen said as they were hooked up.

Reilly nodded convincingly. Heath less so. He was still hampered by a leg injury from Afghanistan.

They both wore a flight helmet with a visor and all-leather rappeller's gloves with double-leather palms and fingers to give them protection from the intense heat caused by their hands sliding down the rope during descent. They tethered to a harness from their safety belt and a rappel ring attached to the nylon rope.

At the copter's open door, the rappel master, a young corporal named Hernandez, pulled on the rope and double-checked the anchor point connections. They were good.

"You know, gentlemen," Hernandez said at the top of his lungs, "assault school is usually ten days long. You're cramming the course in minutes. Your boss must love you."

"Right now, the…boss…," Reilly said trying to relax his breathing, "is…the…woman down below…"

"Then get ready to serve the master. And remember from this height you might lose your depth perception. Make sure you take three

378

controlled brakes on your way to the ground."

The rappel master pivoted Reilly and Heath 180 degrees on the helicopter skid so they were facing him inside. Hernandez kicked their feet shoulder-width apart, pointed to their knees, and squeezed his fist. An order to lock their knees. Next, he pointed to their stomachs and yelled over the noise, "Bend down toward me and on my command, flex your knees and push away from the gear. Let the rope pass through your brake hand and your guide hand. That's how you'll manage your descent speed."

Hernandez showed them the proper placement: the guide hand above the brake hand, all the way down.

"Three jerky stops. Eight feet a second builds up damned fast if you don't give yourself nice and easy brakes."

Reilly remembered how hard those braking moves were on his back.

"Whatever you do," Hernandez said, "don't flip upside down."

"Roger that."

A moment later, with the end of the lines manned below, they get the word.

"Go!"

Heath and Reilly did. Fifteen seconds later they were safely on the jungle floor.

* * *

Reilly and Heath split up, each with their jobs. Reilly to check on Matthews; Heath to get a briefing from Kimball on the dead and whether the SEALs recovered any computers, sat phones, and evidence that could provide any hard intelligence. "I need to know what we have," Heath said, "since all nineteen are dead."

"Nineteen of twenty. There was another," Kimball replied.

"A woman?" Heath asked.

"How did you know?"

"I didn't until you just confirmed it. We've been on her for a couple of weeks. Since Battaglio's plane went down."

"Everyone was—"

"Maybe not," the CIA officer said.

Meanwhile, Scope pointed Reilly to Matthews's tent. He entered and saw three people—Matthews, Hunter, and one of the SEALs bandaging Tom Hunter.

"Oh my God!" Elizabeth Matthews exclaimed running to Reilly. Her right arm was already in a sling and she was feeling no pain thanks to a shot from Doc.

"I see you can still follow orders," she said.

"Every once in a while," he mused.

"I think this place could sure use better accommodations. Looking to build here?" she joked.

"Only thinking of getting you out of here as fast as possible!"

With Elizabeth doing okay, Reilly was now more interested in Hunter. He'd been beaten, but no worse for wear.

"Agent Hunter, you okay?" Reilly asked directly.

Hunter nodded. The SEALs' doctor agreed. "He'll be good to go in a few minutes."

Reilly nodded and addressed Matthews again, but now completely formally. "Madame Secretary, may I see you outside for a moment?"

She raised an eyebrow. "Absolutely, and I need to talk to you."

Reilly was acutely aware of the DSS agent's body tensing.

"Sit tight, Hunter."

Reilly opened the tent flap for Matthews. He followed her out. Ten steps away, with little more than light rain coming down, she stopped and faced him.

"Thank you for coming, Dan. Now I've got to get to the president right away."

"Okay. We'll set that up. In the meantime," he pulled her further away from the tent. "I have to talk to you about Hunter."

"Hunter?" she replied.

"Don't you think it's odd that he made it out with you when no one else did?"

"Yes. That's been nagging at me."

"Odd's not strong enough. Highly unlikely."

Matthews thought for only a second.

"Yes."

"And what does that tell you?"

"I wondered why."

"No time to get into it now. But his bio is pure fiction. Hunter is tied in with the woman. She did it, Elizabeth. She killed Santiago."

Matthews tried to reply. Reilly put his finger to his lips.

"Not now. After we're out."

"I need to know everything."

"You will. But believe me, there's a lot he can tell us."

Her facial muscles dropped.

"Then get me on that chopper."

The Super Stallion was hovering above, still unable to land.

* * *

Reilly returned to the tent. Doc was clutching his stomach, bleeding badly. Hunter was gone.

82

"THE FUCKER PULLED MY GUN AND SHOT ME," Doc weakly managed. "He went out that way." Doc cocked his head toward the back of the tent.

Reilly pressed his hand over the wound. It was bad.

"Took my Sig," he said fighting to stay conscious through labored groans and short breaths.

Reilly ignored the comment. "Got a medic on your team?"

"Yes, me."

"Right. Someone else?"

Doc nodded.

"Comms active?"

Doc nodded again, then he passed out.

Reilly figured the communications were voice-actuated.

He spoke into the microphone at the SEALs throat. "Man down. Man down. Doctor. South tent."

There was really no north, south, east, or west in the storm.

"Roger that," came a reply that Reilly didn't hear without the earpiece.

Seconds later SEALs Woody and Poker burst through the flap, quickly sizing up the sight. Woody stripped something off his web belt and demanded to know what happened.

"The DSS agent shot him."

"What the fuck?"

"I'm going after him. Take over."

"Yes, sir."

Woody pressed his hand hard on Doc's wound. Poker hit Doc's right thigh with a shot from a Morphine Sulfate Pen Injector he had on his belt.

"I need a gun."

"We'll get him," Woody replied.

"Give me a gun!"

Woody went on his comm. Reilly was not going to wait. He saw Doc had a second P226. He checked the load; 9mm Parabellum bullets. One in the chamber, eleven in the mag. Four had been used on the kidnappers.

"You know how to use that?" Woody asked.

"Yes!"

With that, Reilly was out the back of the tent. Thirty seconds had elapsed since Hunter shot Doc. Now he was in the wind, literally. And soon the winds and rain would hide his tracks.

Reilly spotted a path into the jungle. It was the best way in and it had fresh footprints.

Much of the jungle floor was ankle-deep in mud. Reilly sloshed through, fortunately wearing SEALs issue Danner Torrent waterproof boots.

Overhead trees swayed, cracked, and fell. Reilly wondered how he'd ever find Hunter in such chaos.

Hunter found him. He fired a round from the gun he used against Doc. The bullet whizzed wide past Reilly, splintering an already cracked low-hanging Ceiba tree branch. It crashed down, barely missing Reilly, but it provided coverage against the next two shots.

"Hunter there's no way out!"

Another gunshot.

"Oh, but there is," Hunter yelled. "It's been there for the taking. Mine."

"That's how the woman left?"

No answer.

"Come on. You can help instead of run. Who is she?"

Again, no response.

"You don't owe her anything."

Reilly's question was answered with another gunshot. Close to where Hunter expected Reilly to be. Too close.

But it also gave Reilly a sense of where Hunter was.

"She left you expecting we'd eventually figure it out. How you survived the kidnapping when no one else did. She left you to hang. She used you, Hunter."

Another shot. Closer. Reilly slowly moved forward through the mud.

"She used you and left you. She even had you beaten to make it look good. How's it feel to be her flunky?"

"And you're not, Reilly? Think about how Matthews used you."

Reilly said nothing. Keeping Hunter talking meant that he wasn't running.

"Not the same. I do what I want. You do what you're told. I'm surprised she didn't kill you earlier. You tell me that never occurred to you?"

"Reilly, your bullshit's not going to work on me. By tomorrow I'll be out of this fucking storm and country. And the world is going to be looking a lot different than it does today."

Jesus, Reilly thought. *Was this what Matthews needed to talk to the president about?*

"What's going to happen, Hunter?"

"You won't be around to see it!"

Hunter fired again. It went right below the fallen branch and through the leaves, a dead-on shot had Reilly not moved.

Reilly froze flat in the mud. The wind speed suddenly fell to zero. The rain stopped. *The eye,* Reilly thought. He cocked his ear to the sounds under the jungle canopy. He heard feet splattering through mud. Slow, heavy steps. Heavier with each foot forward.

Wrong shoes for an escape. And *the conversation was over.*

Reilly took up the chase. He cut down the distance between them by the minute. It only took three. Hunter whipped around, lost his balance, and then from his knees, aimed his stolen gun at the largest body mass facing him that was now no more than seven feet away: Reilly's chest.

Reilly hit the deck.

Click. Click. Click.

Hunter was out of ammunition. He hadn't calculated how many bullets had been used by the SEALs.

Reilly rose. The Sig Sauer was no longer in his hand. He'd dropped it when he went down. He dug through the mud. He didn't see the Sig Sauer. Hunter did and lunged for it. Reilly tackled him inches from the gun. They scrambled hand-over-hand, and Hunter crashed his foot into Reilly's abdomen. It knocked the air out of him. Reilly fell back into the foot-deep mud. Head up. Hunter leaped on top of him. He pushed Reilly's head into the soup.

Hunter, more fit because of his ongoing DSS training and whatever else he had wherever he had come from, brought his knee up to Reilly's throat.

Reilly choked. But his windpipe wasn't shattered. He kept his mouth closed in order not to take in any mud.

Hunter scrambled for the gun. Reilly got to his knees, then fully up. With a sharp kick to Hunter's left calf, he brought his enemy to his knees. But Reilly slipped just as Hunter rose. The DSS agent smiled devilishly.

"There's more to you than I thought, Reilly."

With that, Hunter raised his foot and thrust it to Reilly's chest, or where Reilly's chest had been. He'd rolled fast to his right nearly smashing into a sharp, broken mahogany tree branch that jutted out. He was alive by an inch.

Reilly's adrenaline gave him the energy to spring up. But Hunter, still having more balance than Reilly, managed a high roundhouse kick that knocked Reilly back down. He followed up with what would have been a smashing blow to Reilly's windpipe had Reilly not rolled again, this time to his left away from the branch.

Hunter, on his hands and knees, took the break to search once more for Reilly's gun. He put his fingers on it. But in that second, he lost his focus on Reilly because Reilly kept rolling and delivered an elbow into Hunter's right ear. He went down. Reilly locked his hands and brought them down on Hunter's head. A potential killing blow, but not quite. Hunter collapsed, face down in the mud.

Now Reilly combed through the slime. He quickly pulled his hand out and froze in place. A snake slid by him. A deep brown, spotted snake. He didn't know what kind it was, but right now he figured it was equally dangerous as Hunter.

Once the snake slithered past, Reilly moved slowly, grabbed Hunter by his hair, and pulled him up. He needed him alive.

A nice idea; the grip was not strong enough. The mud made everything slippery. Hunter regained his strength and with renewed fury, spun and lunged at Reilly, a madman going for the kill.

He grabbed Reilly by the waist, lifted him, and threw him to the ground. The ground, right near the snake. Reilly heard the rustling. He saw the snake and froze.

"Did you think this would be the day you would die?"

Reilly said nothing. *Snake, Hunter? Snake, Hunter?* Reilly chose to go after Hunter again. He backpedaled. Every muscle, every part of his body ached. Hunter came at him again. Reilly curled his knuckles tight. Then a loud hiss. Hunter made the mistake of looking. Reilly took the moment to pound an uppercut to Hunter's throat.

He gasped, staggered back, and fell. His had landed right on the fallen Sig Sauer. He raised the gun and coughed out a laugh.

"It's over, Reilly!"

At that moment Hunter felt something smooth and wet at his leg. Then a slight tickle. He automatically looked down. That's when he saw the head of the snake pop up. It wasn't a tickle, it was a bite. A fatal bite.

As he stared in disbelief, Reilly risking a bite himself, came at Hunter with all the power he could muster, head down directly into his foe's gut. This drove Hunter backwards. He staggered for more than fifteen feet, weakening with each step. Then he tripped and splashed into what had been a creek, but now in the hurricane, a river with no sympathy.

Hunter failed, but his strength was waning. Worse, he was not alone. Reilly saw it. Hunter didn't. A huge crocodile, at least 20 feet long and probably weighing a ton, was about to add another 210 pounds.

The first bite took Hunter's right leg off. He thrashed in the raging river. For a moment, his adrenaline competed with the snake venom. That moment ended with the crocodile's second chomp into Hunter's stomach. He screamed. A scream that could now be heard over the noise of the jungle. The scream brought SEALs Commander Kimball to where Reilly stood. A volley from Kimball's semi-automatic Barrett M82 immediately eliminated the threat at Reilly's feet that he had ignored—the deadly talla equis with venom to spare. Then he saw DSS Agent Tom Hunter struggling in the mouth of the huge Orinoco crocodile.

Hunter fought to get free. His weight versus the croc's thousand pounds. No real match, especially for a man bleeding out.

The beast pulled him under. Reilly heard a pop-pop. Even if Hunter was able to get a kill shot, he was as good as dead himself. Suddenly, Hunter's arm shot up above the water line; his hand still gripping his pistol. Then Reilly saw something he would never forget. Hunter's arm flopped into the current, separated from the rest of the DSS agent's body. It floated off on its own until it got wedged between two rocks. And there it flopped as if he was waving goodbye.

83

CLOUDS MOVED IN FAST OBSCURING THE SUN. The wind speed, which had gone from gale to nothing, picked up again. Soon the rain returned, heavy, pounding rain with more force than in the leading edge of the hurricane.

Reilly was given his options.

"We can hunker down here," Kimball said, "which is not a good idea. Or we make a run through the jungle to the extraction point. Which may be an even worse idea."

The forensic team, along with the rest of the SEALs, the Navy team, and the CIA's Bob Heath were with Matthews and already on their way to a new rendezvous point, the beach. Just ahead of them, Knife and Scope. Their duty: dispatch the remaining enemy sentries that would be looking in the wrong direction—to the sea.

"Your choice, sir," the SEALs commander said. "But if we're going to go, we have to go now. The bird can't wait for us and if we're stuck in the jungle—"

Kimball didn't need to complete the thought. Reilly knew. Surviving in the jungle with Cat 5 winds and all the other dangers he'd seen crawling and swimming just moments earlier would make for an unsurvivable experience.

"Let's blow this pop stand," Reilly said.

Kimball and Reilly double-timed through the path the SEALs had carved out.

* * *

Offshore, the Aerographer's Mate aboard the Ticonderoga-class ship watched the radar scope, read data coming in from NOAA weather satellites, and radio transmissions from the Super Hercules hurricane hunter. Suz Landay grew increasingly worried.

"The thing's still feeding," she told Capt. Policano. "The Super Hercules is clocking gusts up to 162 with sustained winds at 148."

"Any change in direction or rate of advance?"

Landay turned and faced Policano. Her expression said it all. Policano went to the comm station and radioed Kimball.

"Status, Chief?"

"We're hoofing it. Queen Bee has to be at exfil in fifteen. We're another fifteen behind."

"You're going to want to pick up the pace, Commander."

"Copy that."

Kimball didn't need to be told twice.

* * *

The bullet from Scope's MK 15 Mod 0 special applications sniper rifle tore out at 2,700 mph. In a fraction of a second, it splattered the head of the first exhausted North Korean sentry, instantly ending his thought of when he would get some sleep. He dropped where he was standing.

Twenty feet away and three seconds later, his partner, equally tired, was also put to rest.

Scope rose from his lair, folded the bipod which gave him a stable shot, and radioed, "All clear."

There were no other threats of the human sort at the landing zone. Word was relayed to send the rescue copter back in.

* * *

The CH-53 landed on the beach above the water line. Fortunately, the flooding rain was draining out rather than the heavy surge coming in. But that would change soon. Very soon.

Poker led Elizabeth Matthews and the second contingent of SEALs out of the jungle.

"Get in and buckle up, ma'am," he said.

She got a hand from a sailor onboard. Heath followed. King and Knife ran back into the jungle to meet up with Kimball and Reilly. The other SEALs stood guard around the chopper, its rotor blade turning and the pilot ready for a fast takeoff.

Matthews shouted over the noise of the Sikorsky. "What's the window?"

What she was really asking, was how much time they had before they'd have to leave *without* Dan Reilly.

Heath walked forward to Steve Hirsen. Hirsen took him to see the Sikorsky pilot, Lt. Charlie Huddle. Huddle simply pointed to the darkened skies rolling in from the west.

"We've got a few more minutes here. The problem will be fighting the winds on the ship and the heavy sea."

Huddle radioed for the latest update from *Cape St. George*. Hearing the report, he tapped his Casio G Shock watch and flashed ten fingers.

Heath returned to Matthews. "Ten minutes."

* * *

Reilly and Kimball slogged through the storm debris, ducking under branches, and jumping over pools of water. Hundreds, maybe thousands of birds and other creatures which had been quiet only minutes earlier, were screaming now in a frightening cacophony. They sensed the new danger coming.

Kimball led. Reilly followed. Suddenly Kimball stopped and raised his hand. Reilly froze. Kimball pointed three feet ahead. An olive and brown snake hung from a branch, its golden irises fixed on the SEALs its black tongue poking out. There was no question what would happen if they walked under it. The motion would trigger the instinctive reptile brain to do what it does. Strike to kill.

Kimball slowly pulled his Sig Sauer from his holster. The snake, a fer-de-lance, watched his move. At the same time, Reilly heard hissing sounds behind him. He had no weapon.

* * *

"Five minutes," the pilot shouted.

Matthews heard the warning. "Where are they?"

Heath hopped out of the Sikorsky to talk to Scope. Matthews couldn't hear anything over the blades but caught the nod. A no.

Heath returned. "We can't wait much longer." Except that wasn't everything the SEAL had told him. Kimball hadn't answered calls to his radio.

* * *

"Two more behind us," Reilly said.

Kimball nodded without turning back to Reilly. He was not ready to take his shot yet. His right hand wasn't fully up. With his left hand, he reached into his appendix-carry for his second handgun which he carefully withdrew and passed it back to Reilly.

Reilly reached forward. The hissing came closer from two angles, feet apart. Reilly knew a quick turn on his part would probably prompt the snake in front of Kimball to strike. The order of things should be Kimball shoots first, then Reilly.

He heard Kimball exhale. He did the same. The moment was coming.

Reilly held the gun with both hands. His right index finger on the trigger.

"On one," Kimball whispered. He began the countdown. A second between each number so Reilly would get the rhythm.

"One." Kimball fired. A kill.

Reilly spun around, found a target to his right, aimed and fired.

Kimball turned and saw a snake leaning over a branch, inches from Reilly's head. Pop, pop.

Three kills.

But there was a fourth threat. A crocodile ten feet away waiting for nature to take its course.

Reilly expertly delivered one bullet between the eyes. Kimball hit it with three others, quickly reloaded, and hit it with two more.

"Not too bad for twelve years out of the service," Kimball said, gratefully.

"I've been brushing up recently," Reilly replied. "At the FBI's Hogan's Alley."

"No snakes or crocs there to practice on," Kimball noted.

"I'll give them that recommendation just as soon as we get back."

Kimball smiled and called his position into his relieved second in command.

* * *

The CH-53 lifted off with everyone aboard. Elizabeth Matthews tapped Reilly's thigh three times and said a simple, "Thank you." They both knew there would be a great deal of debriefing later.

Before touching down on the ship, Commander Kimball approached Secretary Matthews. He held out his hand with his fingers closed over his palm. "I understand you like pins," he said loudly.

She nodded affirmatively.

Kimball opened his hand. He held a golden pin. She examined it.

"It's our Navy SEALs' Budweiser.

She raised an eyebrow.

"Our symbol." He pointed to the individual parts of the pin. "The anchor signifies the Navy. The eagle represents the air. The eagle's talons clutch a trident. That symbolizes Neptune and the sea. The cocked flintlock pistol represents our readiness on land and our constant state of awareness."

She smiled.

"I think you've earned all three, Madame Secretary. It's from us to you."

Elizabeth Matthews proudly put it on the ragged t-shirt she'd been wearing for days.

84

WHITE HOUSE PRESS ROOM

Press Secretary Doreen Gluckin entered the White House press room. She looked tired. No one would take issue with that. Not the press or the president. Like almost everyone in the White House press office, she'd been up for twenty-eight straight hours.

"I have an announcement to make," she said without revealing what was to come, "after which I will take a few, which means not a lot, of questions."

Her comment earned nods. The room remained uncharacteristically hushed.

She opened a small loose-leaf binder, her briefing book, and paged to a tab.

"Two hours and forty-three minutes ago," she gave the exact time, "American forces, members of the United States Navy SEALs, conducted an operation in the nation of Colombia. The mission was to rescue Secretary of State Elizabeth Matthews and capture or neutralize her kidnappers."

She paused. Pencils froze on pads. Reporters stopped typing on their laptops or cellphones. She looked up, directly at the exhausted press pool, many of whom had stayed close by.

"We have her. We have Secretary Matthews. She's now aboard the United States Navy Ticonderoga-class cruiser USS *Cape St. George*. She's being treated by doctors before coming home. I'll take your questions."

Hands shot up.

"Can you describe Secretary Matthews's condition?" asked Mark Hamilton, a veteran DC reporter, now MSNBC's White House correspondent.

"She's alive, Marc, and according to first reports, appeared very eager to be back in Washington. Emphasis on *very!*"

"Injuries?" he followed up.

"A broken arm. Beyond that, I have no other information."

Fox's Dick Taylor shot up his hand.

"Doreen, Colombia? Can you tell us where, what size force, and third, did we inform the Colombian government?"

She replied, "Yes on Colombia." She stopped there.

"The rest of my question?"

"It's 'I can't comment.'"

"Because—?"

"I don't have the details."

She did. At least some. But she was told to be brief, be good, and be gone. Gluckin did believe that the third question was one the White House would have to gingerly walk through: *Did we inform the Colombia government?* The answer was a definite no from White House Chief of Staff Lou Simon, who said, "Couldn't take the chance of a leak." With back channeling and negotiations, that would eventually be turned into, "We were in constant communications and had Bogotá's complete cooperation."

The deal might hinge on Colombia getting something in return: cash, military supplies, trade initiatives. Then on the other hand, maybe nothing. After all, Colombia was where the kidnappers went. The press secretary suspected it would be a call Secretary Matthews would be making herself.

The more she thought about it, the more she was certain the answer would be a simple, "Yes," to avoid any embarrassment or the suggestion of duplicity.

"Do we know the nationality of the kidnappers?" *The Hill's* Ross Bagley asked.

"No, Ross."

"Was everyone," Bagley reached for Gluckin's word, "neutralized?"

"I'm going to leave that to the Pentagon to comment."

With that, Gluckin closed her briefing book. She said, "Thank you," and left without stopping to answer any of the other questions yelled at her.

* * *

Watching CNN International 4,857 miles away, Nicolai Gorshkov slammed his hand down on his desk. He wanted the same answer. Parisa Dhafari had made it out. She was safely in Bahía Solano. But the others deserved to die. He hoped they had been and ID'd as North Koreans—as planned.

If however, Dhafari was to blame, then he'd see to it that she'd become just another jumper from a building in some exotic location.

But now he was focused on another objective. The time for it, which was supposed to be coordinated with Matthews's execution and reveal, was quickly approaching.

Of course, he'd have to deal with the fact that he ignored Yichén Yáo's unreasonable and unhinged demands. But China needed his oil far too much to blow the deal. Of course, they'd find their common ground again. Of course, they'd have to come to North Korea's defense and create an even stronger alliance against the West. That would mean more of Europe for Russia's taking, *with* the backing of Beijing.

Or so he convinced himself.

* * *

At his condo, Senator Billy Peyton screamed at his TV. "Jesus, can't you just die! It would make things so much easier."

Two people heard him. One was in the room. The other wasn't. Seth Sullivan sat in a brown leather chair in the corner of Peyton's living room with a cup of morning coffee. The other ears were listening through hidden microphones. The audio and transcript would be in Gorshkov's hands in minutes.

Peyton turned his rage toward Sullivan. "And we didn't even get to run your plan with that motherfucker Allphin moving up the rescue. Damn him."

"Settle down, Billy. You can still get out in front of this. We'll call a press conference."

"To say what? I wish she were dead!" Peyton blurted.

"You are going to say, with every bit of sincerity and to the core of your being, that the nation breathes easier tonight knowing that the Secretary of State is on her way home. You will thank the brave members of the military for their heroism. And you will thank the president for his resolve. You will talk about unity. You will put politics aside, and you will be on the news before Matthews. Then when we get some shit on her, you'll be able to feel betrayed. It'll work."

With that, Sullivan abruptly began writing on his cell phone memo app. "I'll have your talking points in ten minutes. Memorize them and be ready to meet the press."

85

ABOARD THE *WONSAN YONG-GANHAN*

2 HOURS 50 MINUTES LATER

An alert hit Captain Jang Song-Taek's computer. He placed his right hand on the wired mouse. He led the cursor over to the file pop-up and stopped. He removed his hand and reached for his wallet. Song-Taek slid his forefinger and thumb into the end of the card slot and withdrew the photographs he had looked at before. He placed them on the shelf facing him just above the monitor. With his hand shaking he brought the cursor back on the target and right-clicked to open the file.

Song-Taek read the timed order once, twice, three times. It was unequivocally clear. He glanced up at the photographs, closed his eyes, and silently wept.

ABOARD THE USS *ANNAPOLIS*

4 HOURS 57 MINUTES LATER

It takes about one-third of a submarine crew to drive the boat—officers and crew, from command to the power plant, and throughout the ship. But Zimmerman's order went to one person, the helmsman, Lt. Jordan Rich.

"Helmsman," Zimmerman said calmly, "back us out nice and slow. I want room to maneuver."

It was Zimmerman's experience coupled with his sixth sense that the enemy sub was too close to stateside and any closer would risk *Annapolis's* effective response time. Next, he ordered the Approach Officer to prepare the Firing Key Operator to ready the torpedo tubes. He followed it with an order he knew would create a sound heard onboard the North Korean sub. Maybe it would scare the captain.

"After room, open the outer doors. Flood one and two."

Within ten seconds *Annapolis* had the firing solution to sink *Wonsan Yong-Ganhan*. But in the blink of an eye, those seconds might not be enough.

"Captain, they're—" Okim on sonar cupped his ears. "I'm hearing…"

86

"LAUNCH, LAUNCH, LAUNCH!" Captain Jang Song-Taek ordered. He followed it proclaiming, "*Juche!*"

Juche. One word everyone on board knew. *Juche* defined the country's determination for political, economic, and military independence. *Juche* buttressed every personal sacrifice in the name of national sovereignty. *Juche* affirmed the single-minded North Korean mentality for unquestioned loyalty to the Supreme Leader.

"Sir! Enemy sub preparing to fire!" *Wonsan Yong-Ganhan's* sonar operator screamed. "Repeat. Enemy sub flooding tubes, ready to fire!"

Jang Song-Taek knew his orders were going to cost him his life and the lives of his crew. *How long have the American been out there? Probably the whole way.*

Now Jang Song-Taek at least prayed that his obedience to *Juche* would give his family a better life.

With the firing command, Song-Taek's missile launcher pressed a button at his station. A single hatch opened on the deck of *Wonsan Yong-Ganhan,* blowing a seal apart. Simultaneously, a valve opened at the bottom of the tube, shooting a burst of compressed air into it, preventing any water from flowing in. The blast forced the missile housed in the tube out at about 40 mph, giving it enough momentum to shoot through the last 40m of water.

Cutting across the waves, the engines ignited on the Pukguksong-3 missile, and it began its ascent.

* * *

Three hundred fifty yards away another sonar operator, listening equally attentively, called out. "Missile launch, missile launch!"

"Confirm!" Capt. Zimmerman demanded.

"Confirm missile launch, Captain," Okim Katema declared.

Zimmerman immediately issued two commands. First, "Launch Zapper!" It was the name he adopted for a top secret SLBM intercept, a highly advanced AIM-9X that had the firepower to bring down the North Korean missile...*if* he acted quickly enough. Then came his second order which could be carried out equally fast because *Annapolis's* torpedo tubes were already flooded.

"Prepare to fire tubes on enemy bearing."

In response three stations called out.

"Ship ready."

"Solution ready."

"Weapons ready."

Zimmerman gave the order. "Fire one! Fire two!"

A pair of MK-48 torpedoes were away, and the interceptor missile was aloft.

* * *

The *Wonsan Yong-Ganhan* sonar operator looked at Captain Song-Taek. There was no time for countermeasures. No time for evasive actions. The enemy was too close. Fatally close. No chance to get their own torpedoes away. No way to outrun the incoming death. They'd been fired on by a silent stalker. The North Korean commander accurately read the expression on Sonar's face. It was over. He held the photographs of his wife and children in his hand. At least their lives would be guaranteed.

And then a radical thought came to him milliseconds before the submarine exploded. North Korea was a hateful place.

87

THEY COULDN'T SEE THE DEATH of the North Korean sub, but the crew of *Annapolis* heard it.

The first torpedo penetrated the pressure hull near the seawater piping. It instantly created tremendous dynamic stress on the submarine's flanges and welds. Power went out. Without power, *Wonsan Yong-Ganhan* lost navigation and air. The second torpedo followed the course of the first and exploded within the ship. This brought a wave of pressure traveling hundreds of miles an hour, instantly flooding the compartments. Within milliseconds after that, the North Korean submarine, on a mission to kill upwards of five million people, went down to the bottom of the Pacific Ocean with fifty-two souls breathing their last breaths.

* * *

Annapolis surfaced. Zimmerman reported to USAPAC something he'd hoped he'd never have his name on but now was fully prepared to sign: confirmation of a kill.

Command would be spared hearing the crunching, cracking, and imploding sounds of the North Korean sub as it sank. But Zimmerman knew it would haunt him for the rest of his life.

He had another message to relay. Even more important: "Missile down. Missile down."

THE WHITE HOUSE

30 MINUTES LATER

Admiral Mirage cheered the loudest when the president announced that the North Korean ship had been sunk and its missile destroyed. Admiral Grimm applauded. Dr. Hamza Ali said a silent prayer. Senator Mikayla Colonnello and Under Secretary of State Micky Rucireta also caught up in the moment, nodded approvingly to one another.

"We were lucky today," the president said. "Two wins. There are a lot of people to thank, but there will be no ribbons. No celebration for the loss of the enemy's submarine. No mention of it to anyone. For now and forever. What you heard today never happened."

88

FOUR DAYS LATER

"Well, nice to see you all," press secretary Gluckin said taking the podium at 6 p.m. Eastern. She cleared her throat, scanned the assembled faces, and smiled. "I'm just here to make an introduction."

Reporters let out disappointed complaints, which Gluckin ignored. They wanted more details on Matthews's rescue. So far, none had come their way.

Raising her voice over the cross-talk, Gluckin declared, "Ladies and gentlemen, the president of the United States."

The door to her right opened. President Sean Allphin stepped in followed by two Secret Service agents. Others were already posted at the four corners of the press room.

"Thank you, Doreen," Allphin said.

He looked out, scanned for faces he knew, and saw more that he didn't. There had been some major upheaval within the ranks of the press corps because of more electronic and print consolidation. Fewer outlets, particularly when it came to local press.

"Hello everybody. As you know, we have been without a vice president since the assassination attempt against President Crowe. Nearly a year, which has been far too long. That is about to change. Today it is my honor to put before the Senate a candidate with incredible experience, someone extremely familiar with the inner workings of government. A worthy choice, a true patriot who has met, argued, and negotiated with many of the leaders who have shaped policy around the world. A candidate you have been covering over the last week for an entirely different reason."

The press stirred. This was real news.

"My choice, the nominee I proudly put forward today, could, if circumstances demanded, immediately step into the Oval Office with full authority and command. She comes a bit weathered after her ordeal, but no less enthusiastic and grateful to America's heroes who bravely came to her rescue under the worst of circumstances."

His statement was vetted by staff and completely calculated, though he spoke without the aid of a teleprompter.

Allphin continued. "Since I took office, there's only been one person I wanted, the most qualified person I have ever met. I'm honored to present for approval by the Senate, my choice for vice president of the United States…"

The door Allphin had walked through reopened. All eyes turned in anticipation to see Elizabeth Matthews in her first public appearance since her kidnapping. The only photo anyone had seen of her was a thumbs up with a smile taken onboard the USS *Cape St. George*.

"…Secretary of State Elizabeth Clarington Matthews."

Still cameras clicked, video cameras panned and zoomed, and reporters wrote their first impressions.

Matthews wore a blue skirt and matching jacket, a white blouse, and flats. No heels today. Not for a while.

On her left lapel, a notable pin—the Navy SEALs Trident given to her by Commander Kevin Kimball. She had a bruise over her left eye. Her right arm was in a sling.

"Madame Secretary, the floor is yours," the president said.

They shook left hands, a decision that had been made instead of on-camera hugs.

The president stepped to the side. Matthews smiled and addressed the press.

"Thank you, Mr. President. I am honored to have earned your respect and confidence. I promise I will do my best to serve the American people in these increasingly troublesome times, to work as your domestic partner and international emissary, and to faithfully execute the duties of the office of vice president."

The press pool camera zoomed in tighter, but not so tight as to exclude her pin.

She also spoke off the cuff.

"My years in the State Department have provided me with a great foundation for the challenges ahead, the relationships to build, and the hard conversations that are certain to follow."

Without naming names and places, she gave unmistakable hints to her immediate assignments. Finland, Panama, and Taiwan. Russia and China and their leaders. Presidents Nicolai Gorshkov and Yichén Yáo. Not hinted at, and never would be, was the fate of a North Korean submarine approaching the coast of California.

Then she pivoted to the questions the press wanted to ask but wouldn't get any answers to today.

"As for my recent experience," she flexed her right arm as far as the sling would allow, "I'm still healing and getting debriefed by our intelligence officers. So I really can't comment on any specifics other than to say I'm very happy to be back home and I share President Allphin's praise for all those who risked their lives to guarantee my safe return. Believe me, I'm at the head of the line wanting to know more. For now, the answers to most questions will have to stay with, 'No comment.'"

There were grumblings. "Madame Secretary—" *Washington Post* reporter Peter Loge shouted. "Do you have any idea who—"

"No...comment," Matthews said with deliberation. "When I can, I'll share what details are allowed within the limits of national security."

"Madame Secretary," NPR's Stan Deutsch called out. "You lost members of your security team. Can you give us specifics?"

"I can't. And before I comment, I intend to meet with the families they left behind."

She was learning that Tom Hunter's past was so muddled in lies that there was no family to contact. At least none in the United States.

"Will you be taking a break?" asked *Time* magazine's Christy Brooks.

"No break, Christy."

She followed up with, "What do the doctors say?"

Matthews raised her arm as far as she could. It wasn't far.

"No pickleball for a while and believe me, you would not have wanted to be in my shoes in the jungle. For the record, they were heels until even my captors thought it was stupid."

The answer lightened the room.

"All right, like you," she said, "I've got work to do. And I'm a little behind."

More good-natured laughs. Elizabeth Matthews was giving the press, and beyond the press, a preview of what an Allphin-Matthews administration would look like.

"I look forward to the confirmation process where certain members of the Senate across the aisle will relish asking me a wide variety of questions. I've been there before. I say, bring it on for the benefit of the entire country."

She turned to President Allphin and warmly offered, "Thank you, Mr. President."

They stood together and waved for the cameras. Allphin on the right, with his right hand. Matthews beside him, with her left arm raised.

Matthews was about to step off the podium but Joe Raco, AP's White House seasoned correspondent, stood and shouted a question that was surely on everyone's mind.

"Madame Secretary, do you see the vice presidency as a jumping off point? Will you eventually consider running for president?"

"Nice one, Joe. But, one job at a time," she replied.

"Are you getting pressure from the party? The buzz on Capitol Hill—"

Matthews looked at the president. Allphin gestured for her to take the question, whispering, "Get used to it."

"How about I clear the first hurdles first?"

It was as close to a confirmation as the press was going to get.

PYONGYANG, DEMOCRATIC PEOPLE'S REPUBLIC OF KOREA

FIVE DAYS LATER

"What do you mean?" the Supreme Leader demanded of his three senior admirals.

They answered in succession.

"It's gone. Perhaps the Russian missile exploded on launch."

"No, it had to be the Americans."

"Impossible, *Wonsan Yong-Ganhan* ran silent. It was the Russian's upgrades. Too rushed."

Ru Tu-Chol screamed. "Faulty Russian missiles! The Americans are to blame! Russia's fuck ups! Do you take me for an idiot? You assured me this was foolproof. Who's the fool? Not me."

"No, Supreme Leader," the three admirals said in unison. Each had been long-serving loyalists to the Democratic People's Republic of Korea, but not for much longer.

"And you've heard nothing from the captain?"

"No sir," stiffly replied Admiral Two. Jang Song-Taek is late reporting in."

"Late? Of course he's late!" Tu-Chol declared. "The captain you worshipped, that you entrusted, that you said was the best in the navy—that captain? It's an unmitigated failure. He's on the bottom of the ocean where he belongs. A failure."

He punctuated his comment with an unmistakable hint of what the admirals might also face. "Round up his family. They're an embarrassment to the nation."

PARIS, FRANCE

TWO WEEKS LATER

General Bortnik stood behind the doorman as he unlocked the suite at the Kensington Royal Parisian. He was quite pleased with the booking. He was going to be more pleased when Alina Ostrovsky, already checked in five floors below, joined him for a champagne breakfast and everything else he had planned for her. It included her putting on his gift, a revealing red silk negligee ordered and delivered by *Un amour de lingerie.* The lingerie was so revealing it put Victoria's Secret to shame.

When Ostrovsky arrived and saw the delicacies and Bortnik's present she cooed her perfected coo. She kissed him thinking of her first lover. And she changed into the negligee that left little to the imagination.

This was the morning, day, and night he had been waiting for. Away and with his lover. It was also the day that Ostrovsky would be free of the oaf. She didn't know how it would happen, but it would happen. She hoped quietly. She didn't like messes. The last one had been a mess.

A heart attack? Possibly, she thought. *A fall from his suite to the boulevard below? No, that had the earmarks of a Gorshkov assassination.*

Most of all she wanted it to be soon. Before she had to fuck him again.

The answer came with a knock at the door shortly after she emerged from the bedroom.

"Room service," a woman announced in French from the hall. "With compliments of the manager."

Bortnik smiled. He loved free things. He believed he deserved free things. *Perhaps oysters or some other sexual delicacy. And just in time.*

The woman was maybe French or Italian. She was 50, maybe 60. She smiled. Bortnik ignored her. He didn't have interest in lowly service people. He should have. She removed a hypodermic needle from under a lid in the cart she pushed.

Alina Ostrovsky and the maid exchanged knowing glances.

"Darling," Ostrovsky said drawing his complete attention, "I love what you gave me, but I still feel overdressed."

She stood and walked toward the bedroom. This was his last sight of her. His last thoughts ran from thoughts of pleasure to feeling tired. He never got to wondering why.

When the job was finished, the woman who was neither French nor Italian, 50 nor 60, spoke to Ostrovsky in Mandarin. They had gone through training together.

"He'll need more needle marks," Ostrovsky said. "Let me do it. One for every time I gave into him."

She stopped at 33. There would be few questions by the time General Sergei Bortnik was found naked in his bed. He would be taken to l'hôpital Laennec, nearby in the 7th arrondissement. A Chinese-educated doctor would examine the body and certify on the autopsy report that the general died of a drug overdose.

It was one execution that Nicolai Gorshkov wouldn't have to carry out himself. It was an assassination that would also bring Alina Ostrovsky home.

WASHINGTON, DC
THE SAME TIME

At the corner of his street, Seth Sullivan spotted an upside-down souvenir sticker of the Washington Monument on the side of the U.S. mailbox. It was a signal left for him to go to the established meeting point for another brush pass.

All right, he thought. *Things have not worked out as planned. But there are always new plans. New ways to win. New ways to elect Billy. We're still in it.*

Sullivan, happy with his ongoing deposits in his offshore bank account was encouraged that even though things had not gone right, they still needed him.

They?

They owned him. *They* controlled him. *They* got to him years ago the old-fashioned way: entrapment. Yet, he'd become filthy rich in the process, but politics is a filthy business.

Sullivan worked for them. He was going to find out what *they* wanted next.

* * *

There was always a *next* for Dan Reilly, and *next* was increasingly getting in the way of his limited time with Yibing. Like right now.

The phone rang. Reilly reached across the bed and saw the number. He sighed.

"You know, you can set office hours," Yibing Cheng said.

"It's Alan."

"And it's after 11. Whatever he has can't possibly be as much fun as what I have."

Yibing delivered the comment most seductively. She rolled over and found a way to emphasize the point.

"I'll make it quick."

"Then we'll make it slow." She rolled back over. "One minute. That's all you get."

One minute was all it took for Alan Cannon to brief Dan.

"Hey, sorry. I know it's late, but what's your schedule tomorrow?" Cannon asked.

"I have a late morning confab with a woman friend."

The Kensington International security chief correctly took that to be Elizabeth Matthews.

"Beyond that," Reilly looked at Cheng, "Yibing and I had planned some *downtime*."

She smiled back. She liked the suggestion.

"Sorry Dan, we've got good reason to pull the Crisis Committee together. At least as an advisory and guidance for you on our properties in Lebanon and Israel."

"What do you have?"

"Right now noise from my NSA contact. In a few days, it could be news. You should check with your Agency buddy."

"What kind of noise?"

"Intercepts from Iran. Some HVT targets just wrapped up a meeting in Tehran."

HVT—High-Value Targets—was a disconcerting term to hear, particularly if they were members of Hamas and Hezbollah, and particularly considering HVTs often aimed at soft targets. Hotels were soft targets.

"I'm just saying these guys rarely show up together. It's not good, pal. We have to be ready to evacuate. You were damned lucky in Cairo."

"Got it. I'll bring it up in my conversation tomorrow. Schedule the committee for 2 p.m. Central. I'll join in from here."

"Thanks," Cannon replied.

"And Alan—"

"Yes."

"No more calls tonight," Reilly said playfully.

"Promise."

EPILOGUE

ELIZABETH MATTHEWS had a lot on her mind and just ten minutes to share it. Dan Reilly had an agenda, too. He was crossing the loop adjacent to the Lincoln Memorial when he got another call from Alan Cannon.

"We're on with the Crisis Committee as planned, but it's heating up."

"Oh?" Reilly stopped walking and waved to Matthews and her contingent 50 yards away.

"Security spotted a team surveilling at Kensington Tel Aviv. Time to move to ORANGE."

"Skip ORANGE. Move up to RED. We'll talk about it this afternoon."

The call ended, and Dan finished crossing the distance to Elizabeth Matthews. U.S. Park Police were on patrol. She was also accompanied by her Diplomatic Security Service force with a new Director, Roger Cooper. After the Hunter debacle, still being thoroughly reviewed, Cooper, an eight-year veteran of the DSS, was nonetheless being double and triple checked.

Cooper had a day's warning on her intended walk, enough time to coordinate logistics, and a proper level of security with the U.S. Park Police. It was also enough time for another mole within the State Department to make a dead drop.

* * *

"This isn't good, Elizabeth," Reilly said upon meeting her and being patted down. All things considered, he took the search in stride. "You need to limit your public exposure until you're under full Secret Service protection."

"Don't worry."

Reilly scanned the mall and looked up. DSS agents and Park Police were covering at strategic points. A DSS twin-blade Bell 412EP helicopter flew wide circles overhead.

"I am worried. Situational awareness," Reilly said. "Just because we can see protection doesn't mean—"

"I know," Matthews interrupted. "Next time inside."

The warm fall day, maybe one of the last with temperatures in the low 80s, brought even more people out to the Mall Reflecting Pool and the historic memorials. Across the expanse were school children off-loaded from buses, young mothers pushing their strollers, foreign tourists, picnickers, bicyclists, and further off, politicos undoubtedly leaking tips to reporters.

While most of the Park Police held back at the perimeter 100 feet away, some did not. One of the "did nots," a sergeant, patrolled independently. Thirty minutes earlier, the officer had arrived on a motorcycle which, like five other Harley-Davidson FLHTP Electra Glides, was parked adjacent to the Lincoln Memorial.

The officer, decked from head to toe in Park Police blues and tactical gear, followed a visiting class of eighth graders up the fifty-eight steps from the plaza to the Lincoln Memorial Chamber. The students appeared more interested in the officer's M4 assault rifle than the statue of the 16th President of the United States.

"Here's something on the QT," Matthews said. "The party is already talking about me running for president after this term."

She and Dan Reilly stopped some 200 yards from the Lincoln Memorial.

"You're certain," Reilly replied.

"Far too early to contemplate. Maybe after I'm on the job as veep, and then some."

"Nothing like a kidnapping to up your stock," Reilly added dryly. "Indeed, President Elizabeth Matthews. It does have a nice ring to it."

"A lot has to happen between now and then," she said.

"You know Billy Peyton is going to squeeze you hard on Colombia and everything else he can dig up."

"And I'll look him straight in the eyes just like I have the reporters."

"And lie?"

Matthews corrected him. "And deflect. There was a lot that went down."

Reilly looked confused. "More than Colombia?"

Elizabeth Matthews shrugged. There were things even she didn't share with Dan Reilly. Like what happened to a North Korean submarine.

"Which brings me to the ongoing Daniel Reilly Question," she said changing the subject.

"Figured it was coming."

"Will you join me?"

Reilly looked out across the Mall.

"I've said it before, I'll say it again, Daniel. I need you."

Now he shrugged.

"I'll make it easier for you. I've talked to Shaw. Your boss and I have had ongoing discussions about you. He's given you the time to think about it. And I know you have."

Reilly nodded. He had.

"Now I'll tell you something you may not know. Shaw wants you as his successor. But he's willing to let you go—for a time—call it a leave of absence. The more experience you get, the more you'll bring back. Consider it a move from a hotel into a big white house."

"I bet you've been practicing that line."

"Maybe a little bit," she laughed.

Reilly sighed. With all the thinking he'd given the possibility and all the conversations with Matthews and Shaw, he still couldn't articulate an answer to "the Dan Reilly Question."

He glanced over to the Lincoln Memorial and thought. He'd never really considered if he'd have a place in history, in helping shape American foreign policy, in making real change. But it was seriously being offered to him.

"I don't know, Elizabeth."

"Of course you don't. You haven't heard what I'm about to propose."

* * *

The U.S. Park Police officer walked up to a discreet door at the Lincoln Memorial that was usually locked. This week it wasn't. Workers were back to make new rain repairs on the roof, applying a hot rubber membrane as a sealant. Posted at the door was a young Park Police Private First Class officer. He nodded to the Park Police sergeant, a woman he had not seen before.

"Hey," she looked at the private's nametag on his uniform, "Johnson—"

"Yes, ma'am."

"All quiet?"

"Yes, Sergeant."

"Does that include the workers up above?"

The young Park Police officer hesitated. "Well, I haven't—"

"Haven't what?"

"Checked them. Not since—"

"Jesus, Johnson, we've got a VIP on the lawn. Do you have any idea how exposed she is from an elevated vantage point?" The sergeant demanded. "No, of course you don't! We're going up."

"But I was told to stay and man the post," replied the officer wearing one chevron on his sleeve to her three.

"And I'm now ordering that we check them out!"

He hesitated.

"Now, Private!"

"Yes, ma'am," he said contritely. "But what about the door?"

"Closing it might be a good idea."

Johnson nodded.

They proceeded up a narrow staircase with the private in the lead. Three flights up, halfway to the roof, the Park Police sergeant, or the woman posing as a Park Police sergeant, reached from behind the young officer and silently slit his throat.

* * *

"What I want you to do and what I think you'll take are two different things," Matthews told Reilly.

Reilly listened.

"If elected—"

"*When* elected. If you can't take Billy Peyton down, then you shouldn't even be running," Reilly interjected.

"Okay, *when* that happens," she replied smiling, "I want you to be my National Security Advisor."

Reilly stifled a laugh.

"Hear me out. You're qualified. You're a decorated veteran. You've met, negotiated with, and stared down virtually every major world leader."

He nodded to that last fact.

"But," she continued. "There's probably no way you'll say yes to that. At least right away. So, I have two other options."

* * *

Parisa Dhafari opened the door to the roof of the Lincoln Memorial. She gave a friendly wave to the eight construction workers laying down the sealant. They took little notice of her. They should have.

As she nonchalantly walked toward the ledge, she brought up her M4 with an attached sniper scope and a Surefire Sound Suppressor to reduce the rifle's sound, flash, and dust signature. As the literature promised, it made for a more pleasant shooting experience.

She dropped the workers in eight seconds. A second for each man.

Only the last three had any awareness of what was to come.

* * *

"You're right, no to the first," Reilly said.

"Got it. And like I said, at least not right away. But second, I can hire you as an Under Secretary of State. That'll give you room to grow and in two years—"

This was answered with an even quicker and definitive, "No!" And for added measure, "No, thanks. No way. No how."

She laughed.

"But now we get to the third offer. This is the one that best matches your experience."

Reilly folded his arms ready to reject this one as well.

She told him, and Dan Reilly didn't say no.

* * *

Dhafari lay spread eagle across the section of the roof not yet laid with sealant. She propped her M4 on the ledge, careful not to expose anything other than the tip of the barrel to anyone below. She took in a succession of calming breaths, willed her heartbeat to slow, and then exhaled.

"Hello, Elizabeth," the assassin whispered as she adjusted her scope. "And Mr. Reilly, your reputation precedes you."

Parisa Dhafari steadied her aim, ready for her chambered five-five-six mm bullet to cast its vote in the next American Presidential election.

* * *

"Interesting," Reilly replied. "When did you come up with that title?"

"While I was tied up in the jungle. Lots of time to think about things."

Reilly smiled.

"You'd be under the radar but eye-to-eye with me."

"Direct access?" he asked.

"Yes."

"You'd listen to me?"

"Yes."

"Congressional confirmation?"

"Not required."

"Special Advisor to the Vice President of the United States," Reilly said. "I think I could live with that." He smiled and leaned in for a hug.

* * *

Parisa Dhafari pulled the trigger. Her target moved. She'd blown the kill with her first shot. The bullet hit the ground behind Matthews and kicked up grass and dirt. Dhafari let out an exasperated, *"Fuck!"* in Farsi. The translation was obvious, though no one around her was alive to hear her swear.

Reilly looked over Matthews's shoulder toward the sound of the thud. He spotted grass and dirt kicking up and instantly knew what was next. Another bullet.

"What?" she asked.

"Down!

There was no time to say anything else. Probably no time to act. He covered Elizabeth Matthews with his body and began to push her to the ground. Four DSS agents ran toward them not knowing what had happened and ready to take Reilly down. That's when Dhafari's second bullet was true. It hit Reilly's back.

Through her scope, Dhafari saw the man's legs begin to buckle. Elizabeth Matthews wobbled and fell first. Her white blouse was soaked in their blood. *Two for one,* Dhafari thought.

"Dan?" It was a gasp from Matthews followed by a gurgle. She looked into his eyes and struggled to say more but couldn't.

Reilly's breathing grew shallow. He clutched his chest at the exit point where the bullet had emerged and continued onto Matthews. He had a sorrowful look, but she didn't see it. She'd lost consciousness. Then Dan Reilly did.

THE RED HOTEL SERIES WILL RETURN

ACKNOWLEDGEMENTS

ED FULLER

RED ULTIMATUM is the fourth book in our *RED HOTEL* thriller series. The books, while fiction, are based in part on my life, with a focus on 51 years, including my time in the military, 40 years with Marriott International, and 15 years as a global consultant.

We faced numerous crises and resolved challenges together. These pioneers and the 80,000 associates who worked with me in 73 countries and evaluated situations in another 40 countries have my greatest admiration. Several of you might find yourselves as characters in the *Red Hotel* series. We will always be friends and more. YOU inspired me then and now.

There are simply no words to describe my enduring thanks to J.W. Marriott and Bill Shaw.

PIONEERS

Linda Bartlett, Yvonne Bean, Katie Bianchi, Harry Bosschaart, Stan Bruns, Nuala Cashman, Tony Capuano, Paul Cerula, Weili Cheng, Don Cleary, Mark Conklin, JoAnn Cordray, Henry Davies, Victoria Dolan, Roger Dow, Brenda Durham, Ron Eastman, Joel Eisemann, June Farrell, Fern Fitzgerald, Jim Fisher, Robert Gaymer-Jones, Jurgen Geisbert, Geoff Garside, Will Grimsley, Marc Gulliver, Debbie

Harrison, Ron Harrison, Tracy Halphide, Andrea Jones, Pam Jones, Simon Jongert, Nihad Kattan, Kevin Kearney, Chuck Kelley, Karl Kilberg, Brian King, Kevin Kimball, Tuni Kyi, Buck Laird, Henry Lee, Mike Mackie, Kathleen Matthews, Alastair McPhail, Scott Melby, Scott Neumayer, Anton Najjar, John Northern, Jim O'Hern, Alan Orlob, Manual Ovies, Jim Pilarski, Belinda Pote, Barbara Powell, Reiner Sachau, Mark Satterfield, Brenda Shelton, Craig Smith, Brad Snyder, Arne Sorenson, Jim Stamas, Peter Steger, Pat Stocker, Alex Stadlin, Susan Thronson, Myron Walker, Hank Weigle, Carl Wilson, and Glenn Wilson.

SPECIAL THANKS

I also want to thank the following friends and associates for their support and help in my times of success and need. The successes were spectacular! Gary Grossman has been a creative partner and friend in addition to being a talented co-author who makes the *Red Hotel* series special and our hours together fun.

Others who have inspired my work include an industry partner, Caroline Beteta, CEO of Visit California, who is creative, a dynamic leader, mentor, and master of managing relationships. My work as CEO of the Orange County Visitors Association and the 10 boards I served on helped me pass the 14 million mile mark on airlines as I continued to travel around the world. While I have had some ups and downs physically, I want to especially recognize and thank Michela, my wife, who is my best friend and has been with me every step of the way. My support and management team of Micky Rucireta, Brenda Shelton, and Dominique Williams.

ADDITIONAL ACKNOWLEDGMENTS

Naz Afshar, Tom Anderson, Dr. Ali, Steve Bemis, Dr. Brouwer, Jay Burress, Amy Chambers, Dr. Chen, Lynn Clark, Dr. Church, Steven Del Guercio, June Farrell, Bruce Feirstein, Dr. Han, Paul Hoffman, Tom Hunter, Dr. Jamal, Pam Jones, Paulette Lombardi-Fries, Paul

Merage, Doug Muldoon and fellow board members of the FBINAA Foundation, Christina Palmer, Andy Policano, Pam Policano, Sharon Sola, Chip Stuckmeyer, Dr. Tan and the staff at City of Hope, Nicky Tang, Christy Teague, and Brandon Young.

GARY GROSSMAN

Thank you to Ed Fuller for our truly creative collaboration. You are a true friend and a remarkable partner. Thank you for sharing your experiences and giving great life to our character Dan Reilly. Thanks to Beaufort Books President and Publisher Eric Kampmann, Senior Editors Megan Trank and Alexa Schmidt; our immensely talented Audible reader and editorial editor P.J. Ochlan; Also, Ed's fabulous team including Micky Rucireta, Pat Monick, and Holly Cliffe. Kudos again to Meryl Moss and her associates at Meryl Moss Media, and Adam Cushman, our cinematic book trailer producer, at Film 14.

Ongoing thanks to Bruce Coons, lifelong friend and technical advisor for all my thriller writing; Stan and Debbie Deutsch, Jim and Janna Harris, Chuck and Janis Barquist, Peter and Barbara Schwartz, Sandi Goldfarb, Nat Segaloff, Vin DiBona, Jeff Greenhawt, Jeffrey Davis, Linda Peek Schact, and Larry Mondragon. Also, ThrillerFest Executive Director and author Kimberley Howe; all my colleagues at the International Thriller Writers Association, attorney Ken Browning, and my manager Marc Pariser.

Special thanks to Dr. Gregory Payne, Emerson College Professor and Chair of the Department of Communication Studies, for hosting a dynamic weekly global Zoom forum that deep dives into the issues and crises of today and those we must consider as possible or highly likely tomorrow.

And finally with true loving thanks my entire family; Helene Seifer and our family Zach and Jake Grossman, Sasha Grossman, and Alex Crowe. You continue to inspire me with your love, creativity and dedication. I'm so very proud of you!

ABOUT THE AUTHORS

ED FULLER, is a hospitality industry leader, educator, and bestselling author. He is president of Irvine, California-based Laguna Strategic Advisors, a global consortium that provides business consulting services to corporations and governments. Fuller is also director of the FBI National Academy Associates (FBINAA).

Fuller's 40-year career in the industry was capped by his role as President and Managing Director of Marriott International for 22 years. As worldwide chief, he directed and administered corporate expansion by 551 hotels in 73 countries, and $8 billion in sales. During that time, he oversaw the creation of Marriott International's Global Security Strategy. His role put him in world hot spots at crucial times, from Tripoli to Cairo, Jakarta to Mumbai, with close contact with domestic and foreign intelligence operations. The plots for *Red Hotel, Red Deception*, and *Red Chaos* draw heavily on his experience and exploits.

Ed Fuller has served on numerous industry, educational, and charity boards. He was commissioner of the California Commission of Travel and Tourism. He served as a Boston University trustee, President of the Alumni Association, and now continues as an Overseer. He is a trustee of the University of California and director at California State University, San Marcos. Other boards include Mind Research, Concord Hotels, Mirage Investments, and Safe Kids. He is also President of the Orange County Visitors Association and chairman of the SAE Foundation.

Ed Fuller served as a captain in the U.S. Army and was decorated with a Bronze Star and Army Commendation medals. His colorful and real-world experiences are recounted in his top-twenty bestselling business book, You Can't Lead with Your Feet on the Desk, published globally in English, Chinese, and Japanese. Ed Fuller continues to consult on security issues around the world.

GARY GROSSMAN'S first novel, *Executive Actions*, propelled him into the world of geopolitical thrillers. *Executive Treason, Executive Command,* and *Executive Force* further tapped Grossman's experience as a journalist, newspaper columnist, documentary television producer, reporter, and media historian. In addition to the bestselling *Executive* series, Grossman wrote the international award-winning *Old Earth*, a geopolitical thriller that spans all time. With *Red Hotel, Red Deception, Red Chaos,* and *Red Ultimatum,* his collaborations with Ed Fuller, Grossman entered a new realm of globe-hopping thriller writing.

Grossman has contributed to the *New York Times* and the *Boston Globe*, and was a columnist for the *Boston Herald American.* He covered presidential campaigns for WBZ-TV in Boston. A multiple Emmy Award winner, Grossman has produced more than 10,000 television series and specials for networks including NBC, ABC, CBS, Fox, CNN, History Channel, Discovery, and National Geographic Channel. He served as chair of the Government Affairs Committee for the Caucus for Producers, Writers and Directors, and is a member of the International Thriller Writers Association. He was a 25-year Trustee at Emerson College and serves on the Boston University Metropolitan College Advisory Board. He has produced tributes for the prestigious Ford's Theater Lincoln Honors. Grossman has taught at Emerson College, Boston University, USC, and Loyola Marymount Universit

FOR MORE INFORMATION CONTACT:
WWW.REDHOTEL.COM